A HISTORY OF THE
CONIC SECTIONS AND
QUADRIC SURFACES

BY

JULIAN LOWELL COOLIDGE
Ph.D., D.Sc., LL.D.

DOVER PUBLICATIONS, INC.
NEW YORK

Published in Canada by General Publishing Company, Ltd., 30 Lesmill Road, Don Mills, Toronto, Ontario.

Published in the United Kingdom by Constable and Company, Ltd., 10 Orange Street, London WC 2.

This Dover edition, first published in 1968, is an unabridged and unaltered republication of the work originally published by Oxford University Press in 1945. It is reprinted by special arrangement with Oxford University Press.

Library of Congress Catalog Card Number: 68-11919

Manufactured in the United States of America
Dover Publications, Inc.
180 Varick Street
New York, N.Y. 10014

PREFACE

THE three familiar curves which we call the 'conic sections' have a long history. The reputed discoverer was Menaechmus, who flourished about 350 B.C. They attracted the attention of the best of the Greek geometers down to the time of Pappus of Alexandria. There followed a period of over a thousand years when they were almost completely forgotten, but a vivid new interest arose in the seventeenth century and continued until the end of the nineteenth. Even in our twentieth century new properties of systems of conics have been discovered. It seems certain that they will always hold a place in the mathematical curriculum. The beginner in analytic geometry will naturally take up these curves after he has studied the circle. Whoever looks at a circle will continue to see an ellipse, unless his eye is in the axis of the curve. The Earth will continue to follow a nearly elliptical orbit around the sun, projectiles will approximate parabolic orbits, a shaded light will illuminate a hyperbolic arch.

There are available a great number of treatises dealing with the conics in many different languages. I have not endeavoured to compete with them by writing a systematically ordered discussion. I am not aware, however, that anyone, with the exception of Dingeldey in the *Encyklopädie*, has written a history of the curves, and his treatment is too complete and condensed for easy reading. It seemed to me interesting to study the curves historically. We can trace the gradual development of the Greek interest in them. In the seventeenth century two new methods of approach sprang up almost simultaneously, the synthetic method of Desargues, the analytic one of Descartes. The two continued to compete down to our own time, a rivalry which has been of great value to geometry. A systematic account of this long development seemed to me worth preserving.

What has been said of the conics is largely true of the quadric surfaces. Naturally the amount of study that they have received is much less than that bestowed on the conics, but there is still much available material, as anyone will discover who looks at Staude's article in the *Encyklopädie*. A good part of what we know about the surfaces, and a good part of our technique in handling them, comes from an immediate extension of what we have done in the plane. But in some places the two theories diverge sharply. The conics have no properties akin to those of the rectilinear generators or the circular sections of the quadrics. On the other hand, the surfaces lack anything comparable to the great wealth of beautiful properties of the conics which spring from Pascal's theorem. In any case, it seemed to me that a history of the conics would be incomplete without a corresponding study of the surfaces.

A word about style and notation. At times I have followed the author's method of presentation fairly closely, in other cases I have tried to retain the general spirit of a proof, but have shortened the discussion by using some more modern considerations. The demonstrations of Apollonius, for instance, in their original form, are frequently very tedious. The same question arises in connexion with the notations used. A considerable variety are exhibited. The work of Newton or Euler is a good deal more vivid if one follows the original notation, but it is far easier to follow the reasoning of Fermat if we refuse to follow him in the use of the clumsy notation of Vieta. When it comes to explaining some of the more recent works dealing with the curves and surfaces I have adopted the rather curious practice of carrying two different notations side by side, the symbolic notation of Clebsch and Aronhold, and the subscript-superscript notation that came to us with the tensor calculus. No well-informed geometer can afford to be unfamiliar with either of these.

J. L. C.

CAMBRIDGE, MASS.
June 1945

CONTENTS

Chapter I. THE GREEKS

Chapter II. APOLLONIUS OF PERGA

Chapter III. RENEWED INTEREST IN THE CONICS

Chapter IV. THE GREAT PROJECTIVE SCHOOL

Chapter V. THE DEVELOPMENT OF THE ALGEBRAIC TREATMENT

Chapter VI. THE INTRODUCTION OF NEW ALGEBRAIC TECHNIQUES

Chapter VII. MISCELLANEOUS METRICAL THEOREMS

Chapter VIII. SYSTEMS OF CONICS

Chapter IX. CONICS IN SPACE

Chapter X. MECHANICAL CONSTRUCTION OF CONICS

Chapter XI. QUADRIC SURFACES, SYNTHETIC TREATMENT

CHAPTER XII.   QUADRIC SURFACES, ALGEBRAIC TREATMENT

CHAPTER XIII.   QUADRIC SURFACES, HIGHER ALGEBRAIC TREATMENT

CHAPTER XIV.   QUADRIC SURFACES, DIFFERENTIAL PROPERTIES

CHAPTER I

THE GREEKS

§ 1. Menaechmus.

THE curve most often seen in daily life, if we exclude the straight line from the category of things which we call curves, an unwise proceeding perhaps, the curve which we see most often, is the ellipse. I accent the word 'see'. The curve with which we have the most business is, of course, the circle. But when we look at a circle, unless the eye is exactly on the axis, what we actually see is an ellipse. It would be interesting to know whether early mathematicians, Sumerian, Egyptian, or Chinese, had the curiosity to speculate about the properties of this most often seen curve. If they did so, they have left absolutely no trace of the course which their speculations took. As far as our present knowledge goes, the ellipse, and for that matter the other conics, were first studied, and very extensively studied, by the Greeks.† We know what nation first studied these curves, we have a pretty clear tradition as to the man who first noticed them. This was Menaechmus, a writer about whom we have only very fragmentary information.‡ The reason why we give him the credit is that Eratosthenes, as quoted by Eutocius in his commentary on Archimedes' treatise on the Sphere and Cylinder, speaks of the way in which the Greek geometers were baffled by the problem of duplicating the cube: 'While for a long time everyone was at a loss, Hippocrates of Chios was the first to observe that if between two straight lines of which the greater is double the less it were discovered how to find two mean proportionals in continued proportion, the cube would be doubled, and thus he turned the difficulty of the original problem into another difficulty, no less than the former.' Eutocius goes on to say that Menaechmus found two solutions, one by finding the intersection of a rectangular hyperbola and a certain parabola, the other by finding the intersection of two parabolas.§ Proclus also speaks of Menaechmus as the discoverer of the conic sections.

And that is about all we know of the discovery of the conics by Menaechmus, a pupil of Plato and Eudoxus. If we grant that he discovered the conics in this way, it is easy enough to retrace the steps he probably took. Let us save trouble by using algebraic notation. If

---

† The best account I have seen of the early history of the conics is in the introductory part of Heath's Apollonius[1]. A still fuller study is found in Zeuthen[1]. I confess to finding this book too discursive, but there can be no doubt of the author's competence.

‡ Schmidt (q.v.).

§ Apollonius[1], pp. xviii, xix.

we have two lengths a and b and the mean proportionals are x and y, we have

$$\frac{a}{x} = \frac{x}{y} = \frac{y}{b}, \qquad \left(\frac{a}{x}\right)^3 = \frac{a}{b}. \tag{1}$$

If $a = 2b$, $$a^3 = 2x^3. \tag{2}$$

I note in passing that this solves the problem of halving the cube, not that of duplicating it. However, it is easy enough to pass from the one to the other. The algebraic formulae for Menaechmus' two solutions are

$$xy = ab, \qquad y^2 = bx; \tag{3}$$
$$x^2 = ay, \qquad y^2 = bx. \tag{4}$$

Let us consider these in reverse order. We have two parabolas with a common vertex, the axis of each is tangent to the other. How did Menaechmus come to these curves?

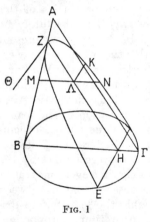

First of all it seems reasonable to assume that Menaechmus was familiar with Euclid III. 35 which states that 'If in a circle two straight lines cut one another, the rectangle contained by the segments of the one is equal to the rectangle contained by the segments of the other'. This amounts to saying that if an ordinate be erected at a point of a diameter of a circle, its square will be equal to the numerical product of the segments of the diameter. The idea then comes naturally that we might have a set of parallel circular sections of a cone, with the diameters in question all lying in one plane through the vertex. Then we cut by another plane so tilted that one segment on each diameter has a constant length. This appears in Figure 1.† We take what the Greeks called a 'right-angled cone', that is to say, a cone generated by rotating one arm of a $45°$ angle about the other, then cut by a plane perpendicular to one element. In the plane KMN, MN is the diameter of a circle,

Fig. 1

$$K\Lambda^2 = M\Lambda . \Lambda N = Z\Lambda . \frac{BH}{ZH} . H\Gamma = \frac{HE^2}{ZH} . Z\Lambda.$$

Now as this plane slides up and down parallel to itself HE^2/ZH has a constant value. Hence $K\Lambda^2$ is a constant multiple of $Z\Lambda$. This is

---

† This figure is taken from Apollonius², p. 22. Throughout this work I shall follow the figures of original writers as closely as possible, to give something of the original flavour. In consequence of this there will be a good deal of variety in the way that the figures are lettered.

Apollonius' derivation of the equation of the parabola. We may well doubt that it was original with him, for he says in the preface to his first book:† 'The first contains the methods of producing the three sections, and the opposite branches (of the hyperbola) and their fundamental properties worked out more fully than in the writings of the other authors.' It seems to me very safe to assume that, if Menaechmus really solved the problem of two mean proportionals by the intersection of two parabolas, he reached the curves in about this fashion. At the same time, he probably stated things in a much more complicated way and went through very much longer operations. He cannot have been much more concise than Apollonius. I will presently give an example of one of his statements.

Let us assume that Menaechmus reached his parabola in some such fashion as this, namely by cutting his cone by a plane perpendicular to one element of a right-angled cone; he might easily have had the curiosity to inquire what sort of a curve he might get by cutting a cone which is not right angled by a plane orthogonal to one element. Let us look for the ellipse. I take the figure from Apollonius, Book I. 13. The secant plane shall cut a curve with the diameter EP while it meets the base in the line HZ. BL is the diameter of the base perpendicular to this. Let a plane parallel to the base meet the cone in the circle $\Pi\Lambda R$ where ΠR is parallel to BL and $M\Lambda$ is parallel to ZH.

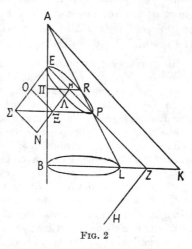

Fig. 2

$$M\Lambda^2 = \Pi M . MR.$$

$$\frac{\Pi M}{EM} = \frac{BK}{AK}; \quad \frac{MR}{MP} = \frac{LK}{AK}.$$

$$M\Lambda^2 = EM . MP . \frac{BK . LK}{AK^2}.$$

Now $\dfrac{BK . LK}{AK^2}$ is a constant.

Hence the square of the ordinate is proportional to the product of the segments on the diameter. This property of the ellipse was known to Archimedes, who also knew a similar property of the hyperbola. To

† Apollonius[1], p. lxx.

come more near to the form which Apollonius used, let us find such a length $E\Sigma$ that

$$\frac{E\Sigma}{EP} = \frac{BK.LK}{AK^2}.$$

$$\frac{E\Sigma}{EP} = \frac{M\Xi}{MP}.$$

$$M\Lambda^2 = EM.M\Xi.$$

The Greeks would say that the square on $M\Lambda$ is equivalent to a rectangle one of whose sides is EM, while the other $M\Xi = EO$ lies along the parameter $E\Sigma$ but forms with EM a rectangle which is short of the rectangle $E\Sigma NM$ by a rectangle $O\Sigma N\Xi$ which is similar to the rectangle $E\Sigma P$. This gives the meaning of Apollonius, Book I. 13, which I give *in extenso*:[†]

'Si un cône est coupé par un plan passant par l'axe, et s'il est coupé par un autre plan qui, rencontrant chacun des côtés du triangle passant par l'axe n'est pas mené parallèlement ni antiparallèlement à la base du cône, si, de plus, le plan de base du cône et le plan sécant se rencontrent suivant une droite perpendiculaire au prolongement de cette base, le carré de toute droite menée de la section du cône parallèlement à la section commune des plans, jusqu'au diamètre de la section, sera équivalent à une aire appliquée suivant une certaine droite, avec laquelle le rapport du carré de la section est le même que le rapport du carré de la droite menée du sommet du cône parallèlement au diamètre de la section jusqu'à la base du triangle, au rectangle sous les droites que découpe cette dernière droite sur les côtés du triangle, aire ayant comme largeur la droite découpée sur le diamètre par cette première droite, du côté du sommet de la section, et diminuée d'une figure semblable au rectangle délimité par le diamètre et par le paramètre, et semblablement placée. Nous apellerons cette figure une ellipse.'

It is simply astonishing that such an inconceivably long statement should lead to such a simple theorem. The word *ellipse* comes from the Greek ἐλλείπειν, to fall short.

Let us put this into modern notation, and suppose the lengths of the semi-axes, which are usually oblique, to be a' and b'; we will reserve a and b for the principal axes.

$$y^2 = kx(2a'-x), \qquad b'^2 = ka'^2,$$

$$y^2 = \frac{b'^2}{a'^2}x(2a'-x). \tag{5}$$

The corresponding parameter will be

$$2b'^2/a. \tag{6}$$

The equation of the hyperbola is easily found in similar form. I pass

† Apollonius[2], p. 28.

to a more difficult question, How did Menaechmus come to the equation of the hyperbola with the asymptotes as axes? We find a suggestion in Zeuthen[1], p. 463, which Heath follows in Apollonius[1], p. xxvi, and which comes to this. Suppose that we have a rectangular hyperbola

$$y^2 = x(2a-x).$$

If ξ be the abscissa from the centre

$$\xi = x-a, \qquad \xi^2-y^2 = a^2.$$

The distances to the bisectors of the angles will be

$$X = \frac{\xi}{\sqrt{2}}-\frac{y}{\sqrt{2}}, \qquad Y = \frac{\xi}{\sqrt{2}}+\frac{y}{\sqrt{2}};$$

$$XY = \tfrac{1}{2}a^2.$$

I confess to finding it a bit difficult to believe that Menaechmus could work out all this. But we are forced to accept something of the sort if we are to credit him with the discovery of the conic sections in connexion with the problem of duplicating the cube. However, he may have proceeded somewhat differently, perhaps as follows. In Apollonius[1], p. 53, we reach the asymptotes thus. Let PP' be a diameter of a hyperbola, and p the corresponding parameter. Lay off from P along the tangent two equal lengths PL, PL' such that

$$PL^2 = PL'^2 = \tfrac{1}{2}p.PP'.$$

Then if C be the centre, the lines CL, CL' will not meet the curve in any finite point. Apollonius calls them the asymptotes. Archimedes earlier was familiar with them, calling them the 'lines nearest to a section of an oblique cone'.[†] He also knew that, if from a point on a hyperbola lines be drawn in given directions to meet the asymptotes, the product of the lengths so determined is constant. We shall later see Apollonius' simple proof of this. Heath states (loc. cit.) his belief that this theorem was in Euclid's lost work on the conics. Might not Menaechmus also have been in possession of it?

§ 2. Aristaeus, Euclid, and Archimedes.

The next writer to deal with the conics was Aristaeus the Elder, whom we may place between Menaechmus and Euclid. His work was entitled 'Solid Loci'. All of our information about him comes from Pappus, whose account will be found in Pappus (q.v.), vol. ii, pp. 503 ff. An abridgement is found in Apollonius[1], pp. xxxi, xxxii. It runs as follows:

'The four books of Euclid's Conics were completed by Apollonius, who added four more, and produced eight books of conics. Aristaeus, who wrote

---

† Heiberg (q.v.), p. 56, and Archimedes (q.v.), p. liii.

the five extant books of Solid Loci, called one of the conic sections the section of the acute-angled cone, another the section of the right-angled cone, and the third the section of the obtuse-angled cone .... Now Euclid, regarding Aristaeus as deserving credit for the discoveries he had already made in the conics, and without anticipating him, or wishing to construct anew the same system, wrote as much about the loci as was possible by means of the conics of Aristaeus.'

The word 'loci' here refers to the locus with regard to three or four lines, an historically important question to which I shall return later. I do not think that we are to infer from this that Euclid's lost work was merely a copy of Aristaeus, nor yet that nothing was original with him. In his *Elements* there is much from Theaetetus, much from Eudoxus, yet certainly there is original matter. It seems to me that we run too great risks in saying just what was contributed by this author and what by that. Nor can we tell how much may have come down from Menaechmus. We may extrapolate back from the theorems which Archimedes says were known to the ancients, though we should not, for that reason, assume that Archimedes lists all the theorems about conics which were known before his time.

I think we are perfectly safe in assuming that Aristaeus and Euclid knew that in the case of a central conic the square of an ordinate is proportional to the product of the lengths of the segments it determines on the corresponding diameter. I cannot be sure that they knew of this in the oblique case, or only in the rectangular one. I next give certain theorems which appear at the beginning of Archimedes' quadrature of the parabola.

A diameter of a parabola, that is, a line parallel to the axis, bisects every chord parallel to the tangent at its extremity.

The intersection of a diameter of a parabola with the curve is midway between its intersections with the chord (conjugate to it) and with the tangent at the extremity of the chord.

All of these properties are proved in the elements of the conics.†

Newton's product theorem:

If through a point in a plane two lines be drawn in given directions to meet an algebraic curve in that plane, the ratio of the products of the distances along those two lines from the point to the curve is independent of the position of the point in the plane.

I do not suggest that the Greeks were familiar with this theorem in this general form. Here is the Greek statement:‡

† Archimedes (q.v.), pp. 234, 235.
‡ Apollonius[1], p. 95.

If OP and OQ be two tangents to any conic, and Rr, $R'r'$ two chords parallel to them meeting in J

$$\frac{OP^2}{OQ^2} = \frac{RJ.Jr}{R'J.Jr'}.$$

I think it is certain that there is some really simple way to prove this theorem by methods familiar to Archimedes' predecessors, though I have signally failed to find it. Ver Ecke gives Apollonius' proof with simplifications in Apollonius[2], pp. 211 f., but this is too long to reproduce here. It is too bad; the algebraic proof in Newton's general case is so easy.

The remaining theorems which Archimedes quotes as being found in the elements of the conics come to this. The square of the distance of a point on a parabola to a diameter is to the square of the corresponding ordinate as the principal parameter is to the parameter corresponding to that diameter.†

Let us pass to Archimedes himself. He does not put down all that he knew about the conics, either from study of the 'ancients' or by his own genius, but what he gives in his books on the measurement of the parabola, and on spheroids and conoids, shows a very good understanding of the curves. We find summaries in Heiberg (q.v.) and Apollonius[1], pp. xli to lxvii. Archimedes used the old terms 'sections of an acute-angled cone, etc.', but he seems to have been aware that all of the conics could be cut from any cone that had circular sections. At any rate we read (Archimedes (q.v.), p. 104): 'If a cone be cut by a plane meeting all sides of the cone, the section will either be a circle, or a section of an acute-angled cone.' This would seem to mean that through such a section we can pass an acute-angled cone of revolution, one element being perpendicular to the plane of section. In propositions 7 and 8 of his *Conoids and Spheroids* he shows how to fit cones to given ellipses. He knew that you could cut any type of conic from any cone with circular sections. In fact he knew that you could cut an ellipse from a circular cylinder. One wonders why this was not early used to give simple proofs of certain fundamental theorems. Probably the trouble was that the Greeks would consider it unsportsmanlike to use stereometric methods to find properties of conics, which were essentially plane curves.

Let us next try to find out what Archimedes knew about the individual conics besides the theorems which he assigned to the 'ancients'. He knew that corresponding ordinates of an ellipse and its major auxiliary circle have a fixed ratio which is the ratio of the areas. This he proved very neatly by the method of exhaustion. He knew very

† Apollonius[1], p. liii.

well that a diameter bisects all chords parallel to a tangent at its extremity, and doubtless he was familiar with the principal properties of conjugate diameters. He knew that the point of contact of a tangent to a hyperbola is midway between the intersections of the tangent and the asymptotes, and that a line parallel to an asymptote has but one finite intersection with the curve. His greatest interest was in the parabola, one of his books dealing with the quadrature of that curve. Of this he was justly proud: 'But I am not aware that any of my predecessors attempted to square the segment bounded by a straight line and a *segment* of a right cone, of which problem I have discovered the solution.'[†]

He had the pretty theorem that, if V be the middle point of the ordinate through P and if the tangent at P meet the diameter through V in T while this diameter meets the curve in Q, then $TQ = QV$. This enabled him to draw a tangent to a parabola through a given external point. Perhaps his most original work in connexion with the parabola dealt with parabolic segments and floating bodies, for here questions of centre of mass appear prominently. They are summarized in Heiberg (q.v.), Apollonius[1], p. liv, and Zeuthen[1], pp. 432 ff. The methods show remarkable power, but their repetition would lead us too far afield.

§ 3. Pappus of Alexandria.

The last writer whom I shall mention in the present chapter lived many centuries later, in the third century of our era to be exact. He lived after Apollonius, whom we shall study in the next chapter. But Apollonius is important enough to have a chapter to himself; Pappus' work was less original and calls for less attention.

The work of Pappus which concerns us was his *Mathematical Collection*. This is a commentary on all of the Greek mathematics known in his time. It is impossible to decide what is straight copy from previous writers and what is original with Pappus. Of the eight books of the collection only the seventh, the longest, concerns us. This opens with a discussion of analysis and synthesis, which amounts to a distinction between necessary and sufficient conditions. Then we have the so-called 'Treasury of Analysis', an enumeration of the following works:[‡]

Euclid's 'Data', one book.
Apollonius' 'Cutting of a ratio', two books.
Apollonius' 'Cutting of an area', two books.
Apollonius' 'Determinate section', two books.
Euclid's 'Porisms', three books.

[†] Apollonius[1], p. lviii; Archimedes (q.v.), p. 233.
[‡] Pappus (q.v.), vol. ii, p. 479.

Apollonius' 'Inclinations', two books.
Apollonius' 'Plane loci', two books.
Apollonius' 'Conics', eight books.
Aristaeus' 'Solid loci', five books.
Euclid's 'Surface loci', two books.
Eratosthenes' 'Means', two books.

The most important contribution which Pappus made to our knowledge of the conics was his publication of the focus, directrix, eccentricity theorem. We must consider this in some detail. He begins with
an easy geometrical demonstration which we abbreviate by putting in
modern analytic form.[†] If a curve have a Cartesian equation of the
type
$$x^2 = r^2[y^2 + (a - x)^2],$$
it is a conic. Then comes, in Ver Ecke's translation:

'Soit la droite AB donneé de position. Soit un point Γ donné dans le même
plan; menons la droite $P\Gamma$ et la perpendiculaire PE et que le rapport soit
celui de la droite $P\Gamma$ à la droite PE. Je dis
que le point P est lié à une section de cône, et
que celle-ci est une parabole lorsque le rapport
est celui de grandeur égale à grandeur égale, une
ellipse lorsque il est de grandeur plus petite
à grandeur plus grande, et une hyperbole
lorsqu'il est de grandeur plus grande à grandeur
plus petite.'[‡]

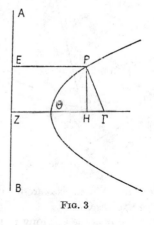

Fig. 3

The proof, when the ratio is unity, goes as
follows (Fig. 3). Draw the perpendicular ΓZ
and the line PH parallel to AB. Since the
square of the line PE equals the square of
the line $P\Gamma$, it follows that the square on
PE is the sum of the squares on PH and
$H\Gamma$. Moreover, the line ΓZ is given in position and the two points Γ, Z are given.
Consequently, the point P is attached to a parabola, for that has been
previously shown. This amounts to saying
$$(Z\Theta + \Theta H)^2 = PH^2 + (\Theta\Gamma - \Theta H)^2,$$
$$PH^2 = \Theta H(2\Theta\Gamma),$$
which is the characteristic form for the equation of a parabola.

Pappus goes on to prove the converse, and there the matter ends. We
have no manuscript of his giving the proof when the ratio is not unity.
It is not difficult to supply such a proof as Pappus might have given,

† Pappus (q.v.), vol. ii, pp. 794 ff.   ‡ Ibid., p. 801.

but this seems beside the point. Is the theorem original with him?
Zeuthen has a very definite view:

Wenn Pappus dort nämlich einen vollständigen Beweis dafür aufgestellt
und durchführt, dass der geometrische Ort für Punkte deren Abstände von
einem gegebenen Punkte und einer gegebenen Geraden in einem gegebenen
Verhältniss stehen, eine Ellipse, Parabel oder Hyperbel ist, jenachdem das
Verhältniss $\lessgtr 1$; so muss Euklid diesen Satz in der angeführten Schrift benutzt
haben, und das Bedürfniss nach einem Hülfsatze muss dadurch entstanden
sein, dass er ihn nicht bewiesen habe.'†

I confess that I do not find this reasoning absolutely convincing.
On the other hand, if the theorem were original with Pappus, he might
well have laid claim to it, or
given it the prominence which it
deserves.

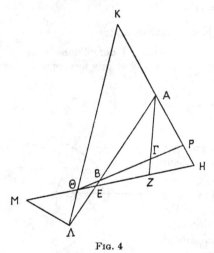

FIG. 4

I mention next another vital
theorem containing the germ of
what blossomed centuries later
in the theory of conics, and of
which we have no earlier proof.
This is the invariance of the
cross-ratio of four collinear points
under a projective transformation. Here is Pappus' statement:‡
'Menons transversalement sur
trois droites AB, ΓA, PA les
droites ΘE, ΘP. Je dis que le
rectangle compris sur les droites
ΘB, ΓP est au rectangle compris
sur les droites ΘP, $B\Gamma$ comme le
rectangle compris sur les droites ΘE, ZH est au rectangle compris sur
les droites ΘH, ZE.'

The proof is too long to reproduce here. Moreover, although we have
no earlier mention of the theorem, we may well doubt whether it was
really his discovery. The corresponding theorem for great circles on a
sphere was known a hundred years earlier.§ Is it conceivable that the
more complicated theorem was discovered a hundred years before
the simpler one?

Another interesting theorem that occupied Pappus was that of
determining an ellipse through five given points. He does not give a
necessary and sufficient condition that a conic through five given points
should be an ellipse. He considers that the curve is completely known

† Zeuthen¹, p, 213.   ‡ Pappus (q.v.), vol. ii, p. 672.
§ Björnbo (q.v.), pp. 99 ff.

if he has found the centre and one diameter, for then we can easily find the conjugate diameter and parameter.

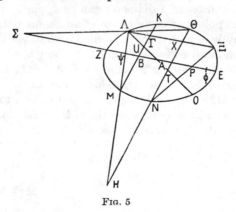

Fɪɢ. 5

We first find two pairs of points connected by parallel lines. Let the five points be Θ, K, Λ, M, O. We draw through Θ a line parallel to KM and find where ΛO meets these parallels in U and T. We then apply Newton's product theorem to the pairs of lines through U and T. This will give us N where $\Theta\Gamma$ meets the curve. If we bisect the parallel chords KM and ΘN in B and A, we find a diameter. We wish to find its extremities. Through Λ draw a parallel to this diameter, its intersection Ξ with the curve is found by Newton's product

$$\frac{AE.AZ}{A\Theta.AN} = \frac{X\Xi.X\Lambda}{X\Theta.XN}.$$

Hence $AE.AZ$ is known, as is $BE.BZ$.

Now find Φ and Ψ on the diameter so that

$$AE.AZ = AB.A\Phi; \qquad BE.BZ = BA.B\Psi.$$

Then Φ and Ψ are known.

$$\frac{AE}{AB} = \frac{A\Phi}{AZ}, \qquad \frac{BE}{BA} = \frac{B\Psi}{BZ},$$

$$\frac{BE}{BA} = \frac{\Phi Z}{AZ}$$

$$\frac{B\Psi}{BZ} - 1 = \frac{BE}{BA} - 1 = \frac{\Phi Z}{AZ} - 1,$$

$$\frac{\Psi Z}{BZ} = \frac{A\Phi}{AZ}.$$

In this way Z is found, and E by a similar device. From these we can find the centre. The length of the conjugate diameter is found similarly. Heath remarks: 'It is noteworthy that Pappus' method of finding the extremities of a diameter can be applied to the direct construction of the points of intersection of any conic determined by five points with any line, and there is no doubt whatever the construction could have been followed by Apollonius.'[†] There is a long discussion of the problem of determining a conic by five points in Zeuthen[1], pp. 184–284, in connexion with Aristaeus' Solid Loci, i.e. conics. The whole question is tied up with the four-line problem, to which we shall return. Little could the Greeks dream of the vast simplification that would come with the discovery of Pascal's theorem.

† Apollonius, p. clv.

CHAPTER II

APOLLONIUS OF PERGA

THROUGH many centuries the words 'Apollonius' and 'conic sections' were wellnigh synonymous. Much has been written about this man, sometimes called 'The great geometer'. The best brief summary of what he tried to do is found in his own words. I give Heath's translation, somewhat abridged:

'Now of the eight books, the first four form an elementary introduction, the first containing the modes of producing the three sections and the oppposite branches (of the hyperbola) and their fundamental properties worked out more fully and generally than in the works of other authors; the second treats of the properties of the diameters and axes of the sections as well as the asymptotes and other things of general information, and necessary for determining limits of possibility, and what I mean by diameters and axes you shall learn in this book. The third book contains many remarkable theorems useful for the synthesis of solid loci and determination of limits; the most and prettiest of these are new, and when I discovered them I observed that Euclid had not worked out the synthesis of the locus with respect to three or four lines, but only a chance portion of it, and that not successfully. The fourth book shows us in how many ways the sections of cones meet one another, and the circumference of a circle; it contains other matters in addition, none of which have been discussed by previous writers .... The rest are more or less by way of surplusage, one of them deals somewhat fully with minima and maxima, one with equal and similar sections of cones, and with theorems involving the determination of limits, and the last with determinate conic problems.'

It is clear from all this that it is wellnigh impossible to say just which theorems are old and in original form, which old but revamped, and which completely new. Probably most of what comes after Book IV is original; the long discussion of normals, in which he took particular pride, is doubtless original with him. On the other hand, we can by no means feel sure that Apollonius inserted in his writings all that he knew about the conics; few intelligent writers do this. He makes no mention of the focus of the parabola, though he was probably aware of the existence of this interesting point, nor do we find anything about the directrix. If Zeuthen[1] (see reference, p. 10) is right in the assumption that Euclid was familiar with the focus-directrix-eccentricity theorem it is most surprising that Apollonius should not mention it.

Apollonius begins with the study of the cone, i.e. the cone with circular sections. He then proceeds to find the three types of sections as

† Apollonius[1], pp. lxx, lxxi; also Apollonius, pp. 2 ff.

we showed above (pp. 2, 3) calling them by the familiar names. For the parabola we have

$$E\Gamma^2 = BA \cdot AE, \tag{1}$$

where AB is the latus rectum or parameter. For the ellipse, since

$$\frac{EH^2}{AH \cdot HB} = \frac{\Gamma P^2}{\Gamma B^2}, \tag{2}$$

where Γ is the centre,

$$EH^2 = AH \cdot \frac{\Gamma P^2}{\Gamma B^2} \cdot HB. \tag{3}$$

In modern notation,

$$y^2 = 2m'x, \qquad y^2 = \frac{b'^2}{a'^2}x(2a' - x), \tag{4}$$

the parameters being m' and $2b'^2/a'$.

The hyperbola has a similar equation. The characteristic properties

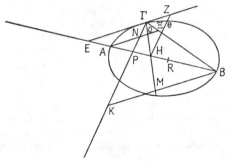

FIG. 6

of conjugate diameters appear at once, and we quickly learn that any chord through the centre is bisected there.

Next we come to the tangents. The natural way to reach the tangents to a conic is by projecting tangents to the circle, and later writers did this, but the Greeks preferred to treat the conics as plane curves, and avoid the use of a third dimension. Apollonius begins by drawing a line through the extremity of a diameter parallel to the chords which that diameter bisects. He then shows that this line never meets the curve again. But he goes further: he shows that any other line through the point of contact will have another intersection. A construction for the tangent comes in Book I, proposition XXXIV. Let the ordinate through Γ (Fig. 6) meet the corresponding diameter AB in P. Let us find E beyond A so that $\dfrac{EA}{EB} = \dfrac{AP}{PB}$. I shall show that $E\Gamma$ is tangent to the curve by showing that Z, any other point of it, is outside the curve. We draw $ANO\Xi$ and $Z\Theta H$ parallel to $E\Gamma$ and ΓP respectively.

$$\frac{AN}{KB} = \frac{AP}{PB} = \frac{EA}{EB} = \frac{\Gamma\Xi}{\Gamma B},$$

$$\frac{N\Xi}{KB} = \frac{\Gamma\Xi}{\Gamma B}$$

$$AN = N\Xi.$$

$$AN.N\Xi = N\Xi^2; \qquad AO.O\Xi = (N\Xi+\Xi O)(N\Xi-\Xi O) = N\Xi^2-O\Xi^2;$$

$$AN.N\Xi > AO.O\Xi.$$

$$\frac{KB}{MB} = \frac{N\Xi}{O\Xi} > \frac{AO}{AN},$$

$$KB.AN > MB.AO,$$

$$\frac{KB.AN}{E\Gamma^2} > \frac{MB.AO}{E\Gamma^2}.$$

$$\frac{KB}{E\Gamma} = \frac{PB}{EP}, \quad \frac{AN}{E\Gamma} = \frac{AP}{EP}, \quad \frac{MB}{E\Gamma} = \frac{HB}{EH}, \quad \frac{AO}{E\Gamma} = \frac{AH}{EH}.$$

$$\frac{PB.AP}{HB.AH} > \frac{EP^2}{EH^2}, \qquad \frac{P\Gamma^2}{HO^2} > \frac{EP^2}{EH^2} = \frac{P\Gamma^2}{HZ^2}.$$

$$HZ > H\Theta.$$

Had Apollonius realized that harmonic separation is a projectively invariant property, he might have deduced this from the harmonic property of the polar, which is proved, at great length, in Book III. 37. We see, incidentally, that the tangents at the extremities of a chord meet on the corresponding diameter. I now pass to a rather long theorem. Let R (Fig. 7) be the middle point of the diameter.

$$\frac{EB}{EA} = \frac{PB}{AP}, \quad 2ER = EA+EB; \quad 2PR = PB-AP.$$

$$\frac{EB+EA}{EB-EA} = \frac{PB+AP}{PB-PA}.$$

$$\frac{2ER}{AB} = \frac{AB}{2PR}.$$

$$ER.PR = \frac{AB^2}{4} = AR^2.$$

$$PR.EP = PR(ER-PR)$$

$$= PR\left(\frac{AR^2}{PR}-PR\right)$$

$$= AR^2-PR^2 = AP.PB.$$

Now draw RL meeting the tangent at A in Z. Let Λ be any other point of the curve; a line through it parallel to the tangent at L meets

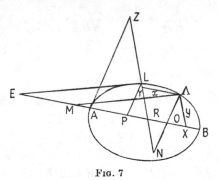

FIG. 7

AB in M, while the line through Λ parallel to the ordinate LP meets AB in O and LR in N.

$$\frac{\triangle\Lambda OM}{\triangle LPE} = \frac{\Lambda O^2}{LP^2}; \qquad \frac{\triangle RNO}{\triangle RZA} = \frac{RO^2}{RA^2}.$$

$$\frac{\triangle RZA - \triangle RNO}{\triangle RZA} = \frac{AO.OB}{RA^2} = \frac{a'^2\Lambda O^2}{b'^2RA^2}.$$

$$\frac{\triangle RZA - \triangle RNO}{\triangle\Lambda OM} = \frac{\triangle RZA}{\triangle LPE} \cdot \frac{a'^2LP^2}{b'^2RA^2}$$

$$= \frac{\triangle RZA}{\triangle LPE} \cdot \frac{AP.PB}{RA^2}$$

$$= \frac{\triangle RLP}{\triangle LPE} \cdot \frac{AP.PB}{RP^2}$$

$$= \frac{PR}{EP} \cdot \frac{AP.PB}{PR^2}$$

$$= 1.$$

$$\triangle RNO + \triangle\Lambda OM = \triangle RZA.$$

This is Apollonius, Book I. 43. It is to be noted that the right-hand side is independent of the position of the variable point Λ. From this Heath[†] draws a very interesting conclusion. Let us take any two diameters of an ellipse as oblique Cartesian axes. The coordinates of Λ shall be (x, y). The $\triangle\Lambda MO$ is unaltered in form as Λ moves around the curve, so that its area is proportional to y^2.

$$\triangle RNO = \triangle YN\Lambda - YRX\Lambda + \triangle\Lambda OX.$$

† Apollonius[1], p. 34.

Each of the areas on the right is unaltered in form as Λ moves; their areas are proportional respectively to x^2, xy, y^2. It appears then that the equation of a central conic referred to any two diameters RA, RL as axes will be of the form

$$\alpha x^2 + \beta xy + \gamma y^2 = F.$$

Apollonius follows with theorems dealing with the passage from one diameter to another, and with problems of construction.

His second book begins with a study of the asymptotes. Doubtless he first reached these as lines parallel to the generators of the cone in

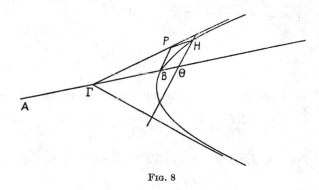

FIG. 8

a plane through the vertex parallel to the secant plane, but he was not willing to leave them there. Suppose (Fig. 8) that AB is a diameter of a hyperbola. At one extremity we draw a tangent, and take thereon a point such that

$$BP^2 = \tfrac{1}{4}p \cdot AB = b'^2.$$

$$H\Theta^2 = \frac{b'^2}{\Gamma B^2}(\Gamma \Theta^2 - \Gamma B^2),$$

where $H\Theta$ is any ordinate.

$$\frac{H\Theta^2}{\Gamma \Theta^2} < \frac{BP^2}{\Gamma B^2}.$$

This shows that every point on this half of the curve above the diameter ΓB is below the asymptote ΓP. On the other hand, it is easy to show that any line through Γ in the angular opening $B\Gamma P$ will meet the curve. We see by the symmetry of the definition that B is the middle point of the segment of the tangent between the asymptotes, and hence Θ, which is the middle point of a chord parallel to the tangent, is also the middle point of the segment cut on that chord by these same asymptotes.

Suppose, next (Fig. 9), that the asymptotes meet the chord HP in A, Γ. Θ is again the common middle point, B the centre. Through H

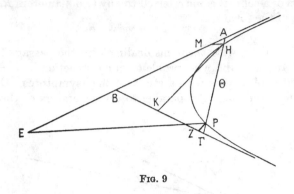

FIG. 9

and P draw lines in given directions meeting the asymptotes in M, K, E, Z.

$$\frac{EP}{MH} = \frac{PA}{HA}; \qquad \frac{ZP}{KH} = \frac{\Gamma P}{\Gamma H}.$$

$$P\Theta = \Theta H; \quad \Gamma\Theta = \Theta A; \quad \Gamma P = HA; \quad \Gamma H = PA.$$

$$\frac{ZP}{KH} = \frac{HA}{PA}.$$

$$EP.ZP = KH.MH.$$

We see in this way that the product of the distances from all points of a hyperbola to the asymptotes, measured in given directions, is the same, a theorem known to Archimedes, and at least under special circumstances, to Menaechmus.

The remainder of Book II is given to tangents and conjugate diameters and, lastly, the axes. These latter are found, in the case of the central conics, by the very natural method of constructing a circle concentric with the conic and intersecting it. A good problem is No. 50 —to draw a tangent to a central conic through a given point. When the point is on the curve we drop a perpendicular on an axis and find its harmonic conjugate with regard to the ends of the axis. When the point is not on the curve we connect it with the centre, then construct its polar, which is the line through its harmonic conjugate with regard to the ends of the diameter through it parallel to the tangent at an end of this diameter. It is to be noted that this method may fail in the case of the hyperbola. The Greeks were not able to handle harmonic questions very well for lack of algebraic skill.

In Book III. 41–4 we have some theorems which deal with conics as envelopes of their tangents. For instance, let a tangent at the variable point E of an ellipse meet the tangents at the extremities of the diameter BA in P and Γ (Fig. 10). It shall meet the conjugate

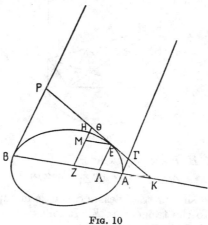

Fig. 10

diameter in Θ while it meets BA in K. The diameter $Z\Theta$ shall meet the curve in H and a line through E parallel to BA in M. The polar of K shall be $E\Lambda$.

$$ZK.Z\Lambda = ZA^2; \quad ZK/ZA = ZA/Z\Lambda = AK/\Lambda A.$$

$$BK/ZK = \Lambda K/AK; \quad BP/Z\Theta = \Lambda K/AK = \Lambda E/A\Gamma.$$

$$BP.A\Gamma = Z\Theta.\Lambda E = Z\Theta.ZM = ZH^2.$$

Hence the product of the lengths which a moving tangent cuts on two parallel tangents, measured from their points of contact, is constant. Next we find some theorems about the foci of a central conic, introduced in rather a blind fashion.

At this point we run into the method of 'application of areas', which was essentially the Greek method of solving mixed quadratic equations. I will not go into this, merely referring to any book dealing with Greek mathematics. Apollonius finds the points of the major axis of a hyperbola whose distances from the centre are $\sqrt{(a^2-b^2)}$. These are the foci. We have just seen (Fig. 11)

$$A\Gamma.BP = b^2 = AZ.ZB,$$

$$\frac{A\Gamma}{AZ} = \frac{ZB}{BP}.$$

Hence triangles ΓAZ, PZB are similar.

$$\angle PZB + \angle ZPB = \angle PZB + \angle \Gamma ZA = \tfrac{1}{2}\pi; \quad \angle \Gamma ZP = \tfrac{1}{2}\pi.$$

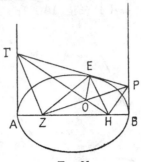

FIG. 11

The points Γ, Z, H, P are concyclic:

$$\angle H\Gamma P = \angle HZP = \angle A\Gamma Z; \quad \angle ZP\Gamma = \angle BPH.$$

He next proves by similar triangles, and a little manipulation, that OE is perpendicular to the tangent at E. It follows that E, O, H, P are concyclic, as are E, O, Z, Γ; hence

$$\angle HEP = \angle HOP = \angle ZO\Gamma = \angle ZE\Gamma.$$

This gives the important theorem that a tangent to a central conic makes equal angles with the focal radii to the point of contact.

If we draw a line through Z parallel to HE to a point on the tangent, the distance will be equal to ZE, and this distance plus HE will be twice the distance in this direction from the centre to the tangent. But this latter is found to be equal to AB. We thus get the fundamental theorem that the sum of the focal distances of points of an ellipse is constant. One wonders whether Apollonius, or some earlier writer. did not reach this by simpler methods, which are certainly available.

The remainder of Book III and the beginning of Book IV is given to the three-line and four-line locus. The latter is the locus of a point which moves in such a way that the product of its distances from two given lines, measured in given directions, bears a fixed ratio to the product of its distances from two other lines, measured also in given directions. When two lines fall together, we have the three-line problem.

This dreary problem, whose algebraic solution gives a conic immediately, seems to have haunted the Greek mind. We noted at the beginning of the present chapter Apollonius' statement that others had unsuccessfully tried to solve it. But Apollonius himself does not appear able to carry it through.† Certain modern mathematicians have put

† Pappus (q.v.), vol. ii, p. 507.

not a little time and strength into the attempt to complete such proofs by what we might call strictly Greek methods. I mention especially Zeuthen[1], pp. 126–63, and Heath in Apollonius[1], pp. cxxxviii to cl. Most surprising is Zeuthen's statement in this connexion (p. 163) that the Greeks were familiar with the Chasles-Steiner theorem that the locus of the intersection of corresponding rays of two projective pencils is a point conic. I confess that it seems to me that there is very little basis for such a general statement. We shall meet the four-line locus again.

The remainder of Apollonius Book IV deals with the intersections of two conics. Let us take IV. 25, which tells us that two conics cannot intersect in five points. Suppose that we have two conics, neither of

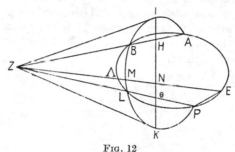

FIG. 12

which is a hyperbola, which intersect in five consecutive points A, B, L, P, E. I mention in passing that it never occurred to Apollonius that the five points might be arranged in different orders on the two curves. If AB and PL are not parallel, let them intersect in Z. This will have the harmonic conjugates H and Θ with regard to AB and PL. We draw $H\Theta$ and suppose it to meet one conic in I, K. Then ZI, ZK are two tangents to that conic. As there is no intersection between B and L, ZE must meet the two conics in different points, yet as $H\Theta$ is the polar of Z with regard to each conic, ZE would have to meet each in the harmonic conjugate of E with regard to Z and K.

In his fifth book Apollonius takes up his favourite study, the normals to conics. He realizes that a normal has two essential characteristics, it is an extremal among the segments from a point to a curve, and it is perpendicular to a tangent at its point of contact. First he finds his extremal, then he proves the intuitively evident perpendicularity. Let him speak for himself:[†]

'In the fifth book I have laid down propositions relating to maximum and minimum straight lines. You must know that our predecessors and contemporaries have only superficially touched upon this investigation of the

† Apollonius[1], p. lxxiv.

shortest lines, and have only proved what straight lines touch the sections, and conversely, what properties they have in virtue of which they are tangents. For my part I have proved these properties in the first book (without, however, making use in the proof of the doctrine of the shortest lines), inasmuch as I wished to place them in connexion with that part of the subject in which I treated the properties of the three conic sections in order to show at the same time in each of the three sections numberless properties, and necessary results appear as they do with reference to the original transverse diameter. The propositions in which I discuss the shortest lines I have separated into two classes, and dealt with each case by careful demonstration; I have also connected the investigation of them with the investigation of the greatest lines above mentioned.'

Apollonius gets down to business in V. 5 and 6. If Γ be a point of the major axis whose distance from A the nearest end of that axis less than one-half the parameter, then A is the nearest point of the curve, and B the other end of that axis is the furthest point. I shorten his proof slightly.

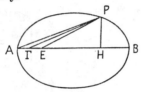

FIG. 13

Let $AE = \dfrac{b^2}{a}$; $PE^2 = EH^2 + HP^2$

$$= \left(AH - \frac{b^2}{a}\right)^2 + \frac{b^2}{a^2} AH(AB - AH)$$

$$= AE^2 + e^2 AH^2,$$

where e is the eccentricity.

$$A\Gamma^2 < AE^2 < EP^2 < \Gamma P^2.$$

Suppose next (Fig. 14) that Γ is between E and B. Through A draw

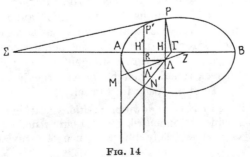

FIG. 14

a tangent, and take AM thereon so that $AM = \dfrac{b^2}{a}$. Let Z be the centre, and P such a point on the curve that when H is the foot of the ordinate $\dfrac{\Gamma H}{ZH} = \dfrac{b^2}{a^2}$. Let P' be any other point of the curve, H' the foot of the ordinate. Let ZM meet PH in Λ and $P'H'$ in Λ'.

$$\frac{\Gamma H}{ZH} = \frac{b^2}{a^2}, \qquad \frac{H\Lambda}{ZH} = \frac{b^2/a}{a} = \frac{b^2}{a^2}.$$

$$\Gamma H = H\Lambda, \qquad H'N' = \Gamma H'.$$

$$PH^2 = \frac{b^2}{a^2}(AZ + ZH)(AZ - ZH)$$

$$= b^2 - \frac{b^2}{a^2}ZH^2 = 2\,\text{quad.}\,AM\Lambda H.$$

$$\Gamma H^2 = 2\Delta\Lambda H\Gamma,$$

$$\Gamma P^2 = 2\,\text{quad.}\,AM\Lambda\Gamma,$$

$$\Gamma P^2 = P'H'^2 + \Gamma H'^2.$$

$$P'H'^2 = b^2 - \frac{b^2}{a^2}ZH'^2 = b^2 - \frac{b^2}{a^2}ZH^2 \cdot \frac{H'\Lambda'^2}{H\Lambda^2}$$

$$= b^2 - ZH \cdot \Gamma H \cdot \frac{H'\Lambda'^2}{H\Lambda^2}$$

$$= b^2 - \frac{ZH}{H\Lambda} \cdot H'\Lambda'^2$$

$$- b^2 - ZH' \cdot H'\Lambda'$$

$$= 2\Delta AMZ - 2\Delta H'\Lambda'Z$$

$$= 2\,\text{quad.}\,AM\Lambda'H'$$

$$= 2\,\text{quad.}\,AM\Lambda\Gamma - 2\,\text{quad.}\,H'\Lambda'\Lambda\Gamma.$$

$$\Gamma P'^2 = 2\,\text{quad.}\,AM\Lambda\Gamma - 2\,\text{quad.}\,H'\Lambda'\Lambda\Gamma + 2\Delta\Gamma H'N'$$

$$= 2\,\text{quad.}\,AM\Lambda\Gamma + 2\Lambda\Lambda'N'\Lambda.$$

$$\Gamma\Gamma'^2 - \Gamma P^2 = 2\Delta\Lambda\Lambda'N'$$

$$= HH'(RN' - R\Lambda')$$

$$= HH'(HH' - R\Lambda').$$

But $\qquad \dfrac{HH'}{AZ} = \dfrac{R\Lambda}{AZ} = \dfrac{R\Lambda'}{AM}.$

$$\Gamma P'^2 - \Gamma P^2 = HH'^2\left[\frac{AZ - AM}{AZ}\right]$$

$$= HH'^2 e^2.$$

This shows that P is the nearest point on the curve. Apollonius' discussion is a bit longer, but amounts to this. The most distant point is found similarly, and there are like but longer calculations when the point chosen is on the other axis, and when the curve is a parabola. It follows immediately that if P be the nearest point of the curve to a general point U it is also the nearest point to the intersection of PU with either axis. Suppose further (Fig. 14) that the tangent at P meets the axis in Σ

$$ZH.Z\Sigma = a^2,$$

$$ZH.H\Sigma = a^2 - ZH^2,$$

$$\frac{a^2}{b^2}[\Gamma H.H\Sigma] = \frac{a^2}{b^2}PH^2,$$

$$\Gamma H.H\Sigma = PH^2.$$

This ensures that ΓP is perpendicular to $P\Sigma$, so that the shortest line is a normal. It seems safe to assume that what Apollonius did was this. He started with the intuitively evident fact that the shortest distance was normal and wrote this last equation. That leads back to $\frac{\Gamma H}{ZH} = \frac{b^2}{a^2}$, which was the equation we used to determine P. I mention in this connexion that many subsequent writers, such as Newton, were more preoccupied to find ΣH the so-called 'subtangent' and ΓH the subnormal, than to write the equation of tangent or normal. It was these 'subs' that enabled them to construct tangents and normals. The subnormal of a parabola is constant.

Following these developments Apollonius puts forth a large number of theorems dealing with normals and their intersections, and some properties of the evolute, although, of course, he had little conception of an envelope in general. The evolute was essentially the locus of points where two of the normals fall together. We have seen that ΓH is proportional to ZH which decreases as H approaches the centre, while PH increases and the normal becomes steeper. Hence normals at two points of the same quadrant of an ellipse intersect across the major axis. Then comes a long investigation (V. 45, 46, 47, 48) to show that normals at three points of the same quadrant cannot be concurrent. Finally we have rules showing how many normals pass through each point in the plane. This is a remarkable piece of geometry, but depressingly long. It covers sixteen large pages in Apollonius[2]. A point where two normals fall together is on the evolute, whose equation is determined in this way by Heath.† The remainder of Book V deals also with normals.

† Apollonius[1], p. 177.

Book VI is given to similar and equal conics. Two conics are defined as *similar* if the ratio of two ordinates of corresponding sets is equal to the ratio of the distances of their feet from the corresponding centres. Apollonius defines as the 'figure' of a central conic, corresponding to a given diameter, a rectangle whose dimensions are the length of the diameter and the corresponding parameter, that is $2a$ and $2b^2/a$, a clumsy enough contrivance. We have then Theorem XII, which tells us that two ellipses or hyperbolas are similar when we have such a correspondence between two diameters that the angles with the tangents at their ends are equal, while their 'figures' are similar rectangles. This involves

$$\frac{b_1'^2}{a_1'^2} = \frac{b_2'^2}{a_2'^2};$$

$$\frac{P_1H_1^2}{A_1H_1.H_1B_1} = \frac{P_2H_2^2}{A_2H_2.H_2B_2}; \qquad \frac{A_1H_1}{A_2H_2} = \frac{A_1B_1}{A_2B_2} = \frac{H_1B_1}{H_2B_2};$$

$$\frac{P_1H_1}{A_2H_2} = \frac{P_2H_2}{A_2H_2}.$$

He then shows that parallel sections of a cone are similar conics. The culminating theorem is that which shows that we can cut from a given cone of revolution a conic equal to a given conic.

The last book, VII, returns, curiously enough, to conjugate diameters. Take the ellipse. Apollonius calls two points of the major axis 'homologues' if the ratio of their distances from the centre is b^2/a^2. By their aid he is able to show that the sum of the squares of the lengths of two conjugate semi-diameters is constant; in the case of a hyperbola the corresponding difference is constant. Zeuthen truly remarks[†] that the proof is by no means as simple as one would expect in the case of such a simple theorem.

† Zeuthen[1], p. 394.

CHAPTER III

THE RENEWED INTEREST IN THE CONICS

§ 1. The first awakening.

PERHAPS the most striking fact in the whole history of the conic sections is the complete loss of interest in them during a very long period. It is less than twenty-three centuries since Menaechmus first encountered the curves that may be cut from a quadric cone. During twelve of these centuries, that is to say, from the time of Pappus to the beginning of the sixteenth century, there was no progress at all, and very little for a century more. But when things did finally start, they started with a rush. Here is Cantor's judgement: 'Auch die Lehre von den Kegel-schnitten konnte nach Apollonius eine wesentliche Ergänzung nicht finden.'† Perhaps this judgement is pessimistic, but if I had excluded Pappus I might have added five centuries to the period of quiescence, as we have no direct trace of the writings of Theon and his brilliant daughter Hypatia.

The first glimmering of the new interest is to be found in Valla (q.v.). This book is a sort of encyclopaedia dealing with the seven liberal arts. In Book XIII, Ch. III, we find the title 'De conica sectione'. Here is an historic account mentioning Euclid, Apollonius, and Pappus, and stressing the problem of the two mean proportionals. I confess to finding it pretty obscure, and cannot see any real progress in it. I note in passing that Cantor (vol. ii, p. 345) wrongly assigns this section to Book IV. Something more important appeared two decades later in Werner (q.v.). This writer also was exercised over the problem of the two mean proportionals and duplica-

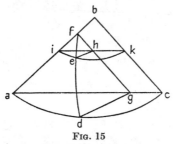

FIG. 15

ting the cube, as we see from the title of the essay immediately following which tells of eleven methods for attaining this much-sought end. He gives methods derived from various Greek authors, and in the section beginning 'Ut Menaechmus' the solution through the intersection of two conics.

Werner begins by considering only the cone of revolution, and reaches the parabola in Theorem V. Our Fig. 15 is a reproduction of his. Let *abc* be a meridian section of a right-angled cone. The plane of the parabola *fed* cuts the meridian

† Cantor[2], p. 350.

plane to which it is perpendicular in *fhg*, the axis of the parabola. This is parallel to the generator *bc*. The plane *iek* is so chosen that $fh = eh$.

$$dg^2 = ag.gc = \frac{fg.ih}{fh}.hk = \frac{fg.eh^2}{fh} = fh.fg.$$

This is in no way original, except in so far as it introduces *fg*, the latus rectum. An ingenious method for plotting the parabola by points appears in XI. Let us take (Fig. 16) a pencil of semicircles mutually tangent at *a*. Let *ab* be the desired parameter. We erect successive perpendiculars, then

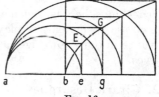

$$eE^2 = ab.be,$$

$$gG^2 = ab.bg.$$

FIG. 16

The points *E*, *G*,... lie on the desired parabola. I do not remember having seen this in any previous writer. He presupposes the properties of the tangent plane to the generating cone and gets the tangents to the conics as intersections of those planes with the plane of the curve, a method universally used after his time. Why the Greeks did not use it I do not know. Presumably they objected to using a third dimension. Werner proves at great length that the vertex of a parabola is midway between the foot of an ordinate on the axis, and the intersection of the axis with the tangent at the top of the ordinate—a familiar enough theorem.

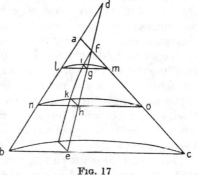

FIG. 17

Werner reaches the hyperbola in the following fashion. A cone (Fig. 17) of which *abc* is a meridian section is cut by a plane in *f*, *i*, *k*, *h*, *g*. This is perpendicular to *abc* and to the parallel sections *ilm*, *kno*; it meets *ba* extended in *d*.

$$ig^2 = lg.mg, \qquad kh^2 = nh.ho;$$

$$\frac{gm}{ho} = \frac{fg}{fh}, \qquad \frac{lg}{nh} = \frac{dg}{dh};$$

$$\frac{ig^2}{kh^2} = \frac{lg.gm}{nh.ho} = \frac{fg.dg}{fh.dh};$$

$$\frac{ig^2}{fg.dg} = \frac{kh^2}{fh.dh}.$$

This is the Archimedean form for the equation of a hyperbola. In XX he draws a line through the centre of the curve such that the curve approaches it indefinitely. In XXII he shows that if two sides of a parallelogram lie on the asymptotes of a parabola, and one vertex is on the curve, the area is constant; a less sweeping theorem than one proved by Apollonius.

The most curious feature of Werner's work is that he makes no mention of the ellipse. The explanation would seem to be that, like Menaechmus, he was principally interested in duplicating the cube, and the ellipse has no part to play in that matter. His work marks no real advance in our knowledge, but certainly shows a new interest in these curves.

§ 2. Girard Desargues.

I said at the beginning of the present chapter that the real advance in our knowledge did not come till the seventeenth century, so that at most we can only credit Werner with recalling to men the existence of these interesting curves. The real forward steps began in 1639; they were taken by a strange, contentious, and very original writer, Girard Desargues, in his 'Brouillon projecte d'une atteinte aux evennemens des rencontres d'un cone avec un plan'. This book is written in a strange obscure language with numerous curious and ill-chosen terms, invented by the writer to denote simple configurations. Thus 'nœuds' are points on a line through which pass other lines. 'Branches couplées' are two segments of a line the product of whose lengths is constant. 'Souche' is the mate in an involution of the infinite point. He has a marked fondness for botanical terms. Fortunately we have an explanation of what Desargues is trying to say and a glossary prepared by Poudra in Desargues (q.v.).

The work begins with a long study of pairs of points of an involution, that is to say, pairs of points on a line, the product of whose distance from a fixed point is a given positive or negative number. All of this is studied in great detail. Then he introduces Menelaus' theorem, attributing it to Ptolemy. This tells us that if a straight line meet in B_1, B_2, B_3, the sides of a triangle whose vertices are A_1, A_2, A_3

$$A_1 B_2 . A_2 B_3 . A_3 B_1 = A_1 B_3 . A_2 B_1 . A_3 B_2.$$

He shows by means of this theorem that an involution of collinear points is projected into another such involution, a fact of capital importance to him as he wishes to base the theory of the conics largely on involutions. He calls four harmonic points a 'four-point involution' and shows that this also is a projectively invariant configuration. I mention especially that he has very clearly in mind the concept of an

infinite point on a line, and speaks of parallel lines as those which share
an infinite point. He stresses the fact that if one member of a harmonic
set be at infinity, its mate is midway between the members of the
other pair. He also shows that, if we have four harmonic lines, that
is, four concurrent lines which project harmonic points, and if the
members of one pair cut at right angles, they bisect the angles of the
other pair.

Desargues next introduces the conics under the bizarre title of

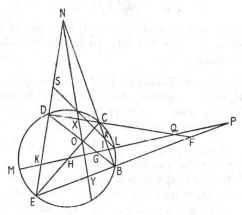

Fig. 18

'Coupes de rouleau'. His order of presentation becomes confused at
this point. He gives a construction of the polar of a point outside a
conic, calling it a 'transversale', before giving any proof of the uniqueness of the construction. I will simplify matters by rearranging the
order and modernizing the notation without departing from his
essential method. Our Fig. 18 is copied from his Fig. 14.

Suppose, then, that B, C, D, E are four points of a circle. I take them
as the vertices of a complete quadrangle. A transversal meets the circle
and the pairs of sides in the point pairs LM, ΓQ, IK, GH. Let us
prove that these are pairs of an involution.

We have, from the power property of a circle,

$$PL.PM = PB.PE; \quad QL.QM = QC.QD; \quad FB.FE = FC.FD$$

$$\frac{QL.QM}{PL.PM} = \frac{QC.QD}{PB.PE} = \frac{QC}{FC}.\frac{QD}{FD}.\frac{FB}{PB}.\frac{FE}{PE}.$$

$$\frac{QI.QK}{PI.PK} = \frac{IQ}{IP}.\frac{KQ}{KP}.$$

Applying Menelaus' theorem twice to the triangle QFP with the transversals CIB, DKE

$$\frac{QI.QK}{PI.PK} = \frac{CQ}{CF}\cdot\frac{BF}{BP}\cdot\frac{DQ}{DF}\cdot\frac{EF}{EP}$$

$$= \frac{QL.QM}{PL.PM};$$

$$\frac{QI}{PI}\cdot\frac{PL}{QL} = \frac{PK}{QK}\cdot\frac{QM}{PM}.$$

This establishes the fact that ML, IK, PQ are pairs of an involution. Since an involution is projected into an involution when a circle is projected into a conic, we have

Desargues's Involution Theorem 1] *If a system of conics, degenerate or not degenerate, be given passing through four points, no three of which are collinear, they will meet any transversal not passing through one of their common points in the pairs of an involution.*

This theorem is equally true in the limiting cases where the intersections fall together in various ways. We may state the matter algebraically by saying that a system of point conics linearly dependent on two of their number will meet a line not through one of their common points in the pairs of an involution. The special case where only the three pairs of sides of the quadrangle were involved was known to Pappus.†

Let us now see how Desargues obtains the polar theory. We begin again with the circle (Fig. 18) and consider the triangle XYF and the transversals BD, CE.

$$\frac{OX}{OY} = \frac{DX}{DF}\cdot\frac{BF}{BY}; \qquad \frac{OX}{OY} = \frac{CX}{CF}\cdot\frac{EF}{EY}.$$

Similarly,

$$\frac{NX}{NY} = \frac{DX}{DF}\cdot\frac{EF}{EY}; \qquad \frac{NX}{NY} = \frac{CX}{CF}\cdot\frac{BF}{BY}.$$

$$\left(\frac{OX}{OY}\right)^2 = \left(\frac{NX}{NY}\right)^2; \qquad \frac{OX}{OY} = -\frac{NX}{NY}.$$

The line FO will thus meet NBC and NDE in two points harmonically separated from N by pairs of points of the conic. Since harmonic separation is projectively invariant, we have

Theorem 2] *The locus of points harmonically separated from a given point by pairs of points of a conic is a straight line which connects the*

† Pappus (q.v.), vol. ii, p. 675.

*points of contact of the tangents from the point, when the latter is outside.
It connects, also, the remaining diagonal points of every complete quadrangle, whose vertices are on the conic, and one of whose diagonal points
is the given point.*

Desargues treats a diameter as the polar
of an infinite point, an excellent way. He
connects his theory of the conics with the
classical Greek theory by showing, p. 202,
how to work over from his involution
theorem to the Greek equation of the
curve. The work is a bit long and blind.

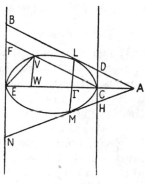

Desargues introduces the asymptotes
rather sketchily, as self-conjugate diameters, showing that they meet the curve
at no finite points. He gives a straight-
forward proof that if tangents be drawn
at the extremities of a diameter the
product of the lengths cut on them by a
variable tangent is constant. We have (Fig. 19)

Fig. 19

$$CD \cdot EB = CH \cdot EN = b^2.$$

If, then, EF is the parameter $= 2b^2/a$,

$$CD \cdot EB = \frac{EC \cdot EF}{4}.$$

He constructs the parameter ingeniously like this. Bisect the angle
BEC by a line meeting the curve in V. CV meets the tangent at
E in F for $\dfrac{FV}{VC} = \dfrac{FE}{EC} = \dfrac{VW}{WC}$. If a circle be constructed on BD as a
diameter, which meets the major axis EC in Q and P,

$$DC \cdot EP = CD \cdot EB = QC \cdot EQ.$$

He adds 'et la pièce EC est égale à la somme ou la différence des deux
droites menées du point d'attouchement comme L a chacun des points
P et Q, scavoir, à la somme ou la différence de deux droites menées
comme LP, LQ, et la touchante mi-partit un des angles que ces droites
menées comme PL, QL font entre elles'. This theorem is true, but
I agree with Poudra†: 'Je ne vois de quelle proposition précédente il
tire ces deux autres'.

Let me try to pass a judgement on this strange man. He was the
first writer upon the conic sections, after Apollonius, who showed
marked originality. He was familiar with the writings of Apollonius,

† Ibid., p. 288.

but tried to get as far away from them as he could. He was the first
to stress purely projective methods. To him we owe the involution theorem for a pencil of conics, the quadrangle construction of the polar, and
the adjunction of the infinite domain. He started the school of geometers
who confined themselves to purely projective properties. We shall see
in the next chapter what a great development this school attained.

§ 3. Blaise Pascal.

The most famous follower of Desargues, one of the few men who early
appreciated the importance of his work, and understood it, was the
famous theologian whose name appears above. He had great mathematical precocity. At the age of sixteen he had completed an extensive
treatise on the conics which, unfortunately, is now lost. Leibniz saw it,
and stated that the basis was largely the method of perspective, that
is to say, central projection, but it contained also the 'hexagramma
mysticum' which we shall take up in a moment, Whoever has heard
of this not very mystic figure, will acknowledge its great fruitfulness as
a source of theorems, even though he may hesitate to accept the dictum
of Mersenne, quoted by Chasles:† 'et qu'en les déduisant de son hexa-
gramme mystique il est tiré de ce seul principe quatre cent corollaires,
comme le dit le Père Mersenne dans sa traité De mensuris ponderibus
etc.'

Most fortunately there survives an eight-page document where the
mystic hexagon is found. It is reproduced on pp. 252–60 of Pascal
(q.v.), vol. i. The title is 'Essay pour les coniques'; it appeared in
1640 and was sent by Mersenne to Descartes, but remained unknown
to the general mathematical public for nigh on a century and a half.
Here is the exact enunciation of the hexagon theorem (Fig. 20):

Si dans le plan MSQ du point M partent les deux droites MK, MV et du
point S partent les deux droites SK, SV; que K soit le concours des
droites MK et SK, V le concours de MV, SV, A le concours des droites MA,
SA, et U le concours des droites MV, SK et que par deux des quatre points
A, K, M, V, qui ne soient pas en mesme droite avec les points M, S comme
par les points K, V passe la circonférence d'un cercle coupant les droites
MV, MP, SV, SK es points O, P, Q, N; je dis que les droites MS, NU, PQ
sont de mesme ordre.'

I note first the statement that three lines are of the same order, which
does not at first seem to make much sense. But herein he reveals his
connexion with Desargues, who says:‡ 'Pour donner à entendre de
plusieurs lignes droites qu'elles sont toutes entre elles ou bien parallèles,
ou bien inclinées à mesme point, il est icy dit, que toutes ces droites
sont d'une mesme ordonnance entre elles'. Also Pascal:§ 'Quand

† Chasles, p. 73.   ‡ Desargues (q.v.), vol. ii, p. 104.   § Pascal (q.v.), p. 252.

plusieurs droites concourrent ou sont parallèles entre elles, ces lignes
sont dites de mesme ordre ou de mesme ordonnance.'

The lines *MS, NO, PQ* are said to be concurrent or parallel. The
theorem is, then, that if the vertices of a hexagon lie on a circle, the
intersections of the opposite sides are on a line, or the line at infinity.

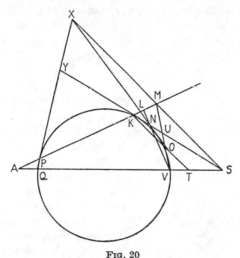

Fig. 20

How did Pascal prove it? We have no faintest clue. He points out
that as it is a projective theorem, if true of a circle, it is also true of a
general conic. This suggests that he first proved it for the circle, though
I know of no proof for this special case that is as easy as the best proofs
for the general case. He makes no mention also of the converse of the
theorem which is equally true. The number of proofs which have been
devised since his time is almost fantastic. Perhaps the simplest is
that based on the fact that if three curves of the third order in a plane
have eight common points, they are linearly dependent, and so have a
ninth point in common.

Pascal follows these remarks with some unproved theorems concerning the segments which a conic cuts on the sides of a triangle or quadrilateral. He finally announces that he will treat

'Cette propriété dont le premier inventeur est M. Desargues Lyonnois, un des
grands esprits de ce temps, des plus versez aux Mathématiques et entre autres
aux coniques, dont les escripts sur cette matière quoy qu'en petit nombre, en
ont donné un ample témoignage à tous ceux qui en auront voulu recevoir
l'intelligence. Je veux bien advouer que je doibs le peu que j'ai trouvé sur cette
matière à ses escripts et que j'ai tasché d'imiter autant qu'il est possible'.†

† Pascal (q.v.), p. 257.

§ 4. Claude Mydorge.

I said at the beginning of the present chapter that when interest in conics returned in the seventeenth century it came back hard. A proof of this is found in the fact that almost contemporary with Desargues and Pascal we find another Frenchman who gave much attention to these curves. This was Claude Mydorge, whose work (q.v.) appeared in 1641. He follows the classical tradition more closely, and his work is far less original. He makes no more attempt than they to cover all the known facts about the conics, but stresses certain topics which interest him especially. There are 308 folio pages, and the work is divided into four books.

Mydorge's cone is any cone with circular sections, and the secant plane need not be perpendicular to any element. A diameter is a line bisecting parallel chords, and tangents are treated by the method which became universal after Pappus, namely, by intersection with tangent planes. On p. 53 he finds the asymptotes very prettily. Connect the centre of a hyperbola with the vertex of the cone from which it is cut. This line will be outside the cone. The tangent planes through it will cut the plane of the hyperbola in the asymptotes. The foci are found by means of the parameter.

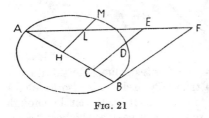

Fig. 21

Mydorge's second book is given to plotting conics given by certain data. Here is an example. To construct as many points as desired of an ellipse, when a diameter and one corresponding ordinate are given (p. 86). Let the diameter (Fig. 21) be AB and the ordinate CD. Find E on CD so that

$$CD^2 = BC \cdot CE = \frac{b'^2}{a'^2} \cdot AC \cdot CB.$$

Let F be the intersection of AE and the tangent at B,

$$BF = CE \cdot \frac{2a'}{AC} = \frac{2b'^2}{a'},$$

so that this is the parameter. If, thus, we draw a general line through H an arbitrary point on AB, parallel to CD and if it meet AF in L we must find M on HL such that

$$HM^2 = BH \cdot HL = BH \cdot BF \cdot \frac{AH}{2a'}$$

$$= AH \cdot BH \cdot \frac{b'^2}{a'^2}.$$

Sometimes, as on p. 103, the statement of a problem is inadequate. Here we are asked to circumscribe a parabola to a given triangle. The book is largely devoted to equal conics. I find on Chasles's p. 89 the statement that Mydorge proved that if the ends of a line-segment of given length move on two mutually perpendicular lines, a point which divides the segment in parts having a fixed ratio will generate an ellipse. I have not found this in Mydorge's work, nor is it very important to do so, as the theorem appeared many centuries before in the work of Proclus, as we shall see in the chapter devoted to instruments for drawing the conics.

It is safe to say in general that Mydorge's work abounds in particular theorems, but offers little in the way of general methods. Therein it differs *toto caelo* from that of Desargues and Pascal, each of whom endeavours to derive a maximum number of results for a single theorem. His proofs are frequently neater than those of Apollonius. It was a common aim of writers at this time to try to beat Apollonius. They often did so in the sense that they found something simpler, but seldom indeed did they produce a *tour de force* comparable to Apollonius' best, as, for instance, his theory of normals.

§ 5. St. Vincent.

No more than six years elapsed after the publication of Mydorge's work before another large volume appeared dealing with the same subject. In 1647 there came off the press the great work of St. Vincent of Bruges, *Opus quadraturae circuli et sectionum coni*. This I have not seen, but there is an easily accessible digest by Bopp in St. Vincent (q.v.). This commentator uses algebraic formulae freely, so that it is not possible to reconstruct the original from what he gives.

I must say at the outset that St. Vincent does not seem to have been familiar with the writings of any of the geometers whom I have mentioned in this present chapter. He makes no attempt to find the properties of the conics by projection. He follows the classical tradition by deriving the properties of the curves from their equations. He tries to improve on Apollonius, but not through making a complete break. Each conic has its own book, the ellipse producing 204 theorems, the parabola 364, and the hyperbola 249. He takes the ellipse in what one might call the Archimedean form

$$\frac{y^2}{y'^2} = \frac{x(2a'-x)}{x'(2a'-x')}.$$

He also uses the Apollonian form with a parameter. I cannot see that he had any interest in harmonic properties, but he had a lively interest in tangents, which appeared as lines at the extremities of diameters parallel to conjugate chords. But his most original and characteristic method consists in reaching the conics by geometrical transformations, not only central projections, but others. He even transforms a straight line into a conic. Bopp too easily associates these with the methods of Newton and MacLaurin which we shall take up in the next chapter. The construction of an ellipse from its auxiliary circle is essentially a parallel projection. Here is something more

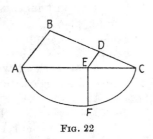

FIG. 22

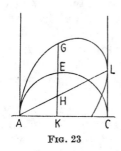

FIG. 23

original.† Let ABC be the vertices of a triangle (Fig. 22); D a variable point on BC and DE parallel to AB. Construct EF perpendicular to AC so that

$$BD.DC = EF^2.$$

The locus of F is an ellipse. We see, in fact,

$$\frac{BC^2}{AC^2} = \frac{BD.DC}{AE.EC} = \frac{EF^2}{AE.EC}.$$

This is a birational transformation of line to conic, though not a Cremona transformation of the plane. We find a more interesting transformation from line to conic in his CXLIX which appears three pages later (Fig. 23). Construct a circle on AC as diameter, let AL make an angle of 45° with AC. A perpendicular at the variable point K on AC meets AL in H and the circle in E. Take

$$HG = KE,$$

$$HG^2 = AK.KC = \tfrac{1}{2}AH.HL.$$

He recognizes the striking fact that the conic touches the circle but also crosses it.‡ This is the earliest mention I have seen of the osculating circle. There is another transformation, called 'Transformatio sub tensa' by Bopp, who draws special attention to it.§ It is essentially the 2 to 2 transformation

$$x' = x; \quad y'^2 = x^2 + y^2.$$

† St. Vincent (q.v.), p. 145.   ‡ Ibid., p. 148.   § Ibid., p. 295.

As an example (Fig. 24), let Q be a variable point on a fixed line through B. Let $QK = HD$,

$$\frac{HD}{HE} = \frac{QK}{LK} = \frac{BD}{LD}.$$

Then the locus of H is a conic with D as focus and LE as directrix. I am not sure that St. Vincent proves his transformation in this way, Bopp gives no clue. The author used it to prove rather a dull theorem about a tangent and the foci.

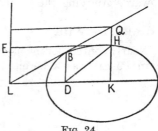

St. Vincent had a neat construction for the parabola which amounts to this. Through the point $(-2p, 0)$ a line is drawn meeting the Y-axis in B. A perpendicular thereto at B meets the

FIG. 24

X-axis in A. If A and B have the coordinates $(x, 0)$, $(0, y)$ we can say of the point (x, y)

$$\frac{y}{x} = \frac{2p}{y},$$
$$y^2 = 2px,$$

so that we have a parabola. Bopp describes this, inaccurately, as[†] 'Einer der frühen Fälle der MacLaurinschen Erzeugungsweise oder eine Anwendung des Pascalschen Satzes'.

St. Vincent was particularly interested in computation. Here is an example. We find in Cantor[1], vol. ii, p. 715 the following curious statement: 'Gregorius hatte dort nachgewiesen dass Flächenräume welche durch eine Hyperbel deren eine Asymptote und Parallelen zur andere Asymptote begrenzt sind, in einem Verhältniss stehen welche gleich sei dem exponenten der Potenzen als Welche die abschliessenden Ordinaten kundgeben.' Now let us see what St. Vincent himself says:[‡] 'Dico superficiem $DEPQ$ toties continere superficiem $HICK$ quoties ratio lineae DE ad PQ multiplicet rationem HC ad CK.' This is true. We verify it analytically. Let the hyperbola be

$$xy = k.$$

Let
$$\frac{x_2'}{x_1'} = \left(\frac{x_2}{x_1}\right)^r,$$

$$\int_{x_1}^{x_2} y \, dx = k \log \left(\frac{x_2'}{x_1'}\right) = kr \log \left(\frac{x_2}{x_1}\right) = r \int_{x_1}^{x_2} y \, dx.$$

This, of course, is simple enough. How St. Vincent worked it out we do

† St. Vincent (q.v.), p. 226.   ‡ Ibid., p. 264.

not know. Bopp suggests† that he began with the commensurable case. Perhaps he only considered this, perhaps he introduced the method of exhaustion. It is probable that he replaced small elements of area by trapezoids nearly equal to them. It seems to me rather futile to speculate too far. But it is interesting that he went so far towards studying the logarithmic function.

§ 6. Jan De Witt.

Nearly contemporaneous with Desargues and his great fellow country-man Pascal was a heroic Dutchman who attained high celebrity in statecraft, but whose heart was also in mathematics, the Grand Pensionary Jan De Witt. In the first part of his work, which was printed in 1658 and is included in Descartes[2], the conics are approached in a manner which was then unusual, even though it has since become familiar, as the loci of moving points. We have just seen that St. Vincent did something analogous in his transformation from line to conic, and Descartes himself had kinematic ideas of generation, but De Witt's method was not identical with either of these.

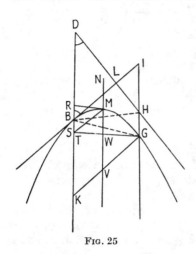

FIG. 25

Suppose (Fig. 25) that in the fixed triangle DBL the angles at D and B are equal. Let H move along DL. Draw a line through it parallel to DB. We find the variable point G on this line as the intersection with BG where $\angle DBH = \angle IBG$. We draw GK parallel to IB. It appears then that the triangles DBH, IBG are equiangular.

$$\frac{BD}{DH} = \frac{KG}{KB}; \qquad DH = BI = KG;$$

$$KG^2 = DB \cdot BK.$$

Constat itaque curvam intersectionis, uti praedictum est, descriptam eam ipsam esse, quae Veteribus Parabola.'‡ He recognizes the general equation for the parabola. It appears, however, that the point B plays a very essential role in the construction. The next thing to do is to show that any other point would do as well. We remember that BI is the tangent at B and DB is the parameter. Let M be any other

---

† St. Vincent (q.v.), p. 265.   ‡ De Witt (q.v.), p. 164.

point on the curve. Through it draw the tangent MR and MS so that
$RB = BS$; also the line MWV parallel to the diameter. Draw GWT
parallel to MR and GVK parallel to MS (Fig. 25). Take $MN = \dfrac{MR^2}{BS}$.

$$MS^2 = VK^2 = DB.BS$$

$$\frac{GK}{TK} = \frac{MS}{RS} = \frac{DB}{2MS} = \frac{DB}{2VK}$$

$$2GK.VK = TK.DB.$$

$$GK^2 = DB.BK.$$

$$
\begin{aligned}
GV^2 &= (GK-VK)^2 \\
     &= DB(BK-TK+BS) \\
     &= DB.RT \\
     &= DB.MW.
\end{aligned}
$$

$$GW^2 - GV^2 \cdot \frac{MR^2}{MS^2}$$

$$GW^2 = NM.MW.$$

It appears in this way that we might use M as well as B to determine
the curve. De Witt then proceeds to determine the hyperbola. This
goes quite easily. A line AB rotates
about a fixed point A while B, E, and
D trace a fixed line, and BE is a fixed
length (Fig. 26). Through E draw a
variable line parallel to a fixed line AI,
and let this meet AB in C. We seek the
locus of C. Whoever has heard of
the Chasles-Steiner method of reaching
the conics sees at once that B and E
trace projective ranges; hence the
pencil of lines through A and the pencil
of parallels EC are projective; hence
C traces a conic with one asymptote
parallel to BE and the other parallel
to AI. But De Witt never heard of
all this. How does he proceed? When B reaches D on AI, E reaches
F. Through here draw a line parallel to AI. We see that the curve
will never cross this, nor yet BD, but will come infinitely close to each
of these.

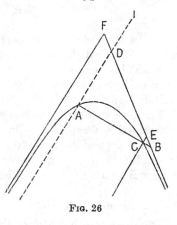

Fig. 26

$$\frac{CE}{EB} = \frac{AD}{DB} = \frac{AD}{EF};$$

$$CE.EF = EB.AD = \text{const.}$$

But CE and EF give the distances from C to each asymptote measured parallel to the other 'Manifestum est curvam . . . eam ipsam esse quae Veteres Hyperbolam vocarunt.'[†] He finds several of the properties of the curve in this way.

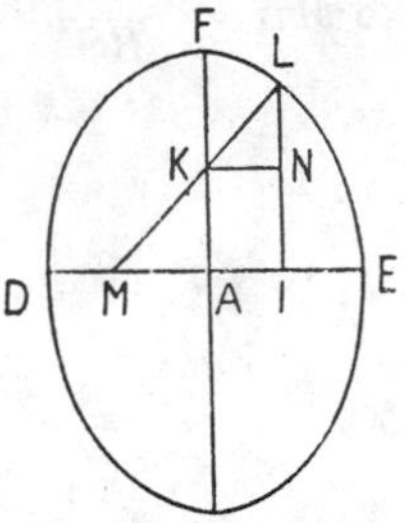

De Witt's method for finding the ellipse is more complicated, and is based on the theorem that if a line segment of fixed length move with its ends on two fixed lines, a point fixed on the segment or segment produced will trace an ellipse. The proof where the two lines are not mutually perpendicular is rather complicated. Here is De Witt's proof for the simple case where they are perpendicular (Fig. 27). Let MK be the moving segment, L the tracing point. We shall have

$$DA = AE = KL; \qquad AF = ML;$$
$$KL^2 = DA^2; \qquad KN^2 = AI^2.$$

Subtracting, $\qquad\qquad LN^2 = DI \,.\, IE$

$$\frac{LN^2}{LI^2} = \frac{KL^2}{ML^2} = \frac{AE^2}{AF^2},$$

$$LI^2 = \frac{AF^2}{AE^2} \,.\, DI \,.\, IE.$$

This is a form of the equation of the ellipse familiar to the Greeks. The merit of De Witt is not that he discovered a number of new theorems, but that his method of approach through moving points is really novel, even though subsequently Newton, MacLaurin, and nineteenth-century writers improved upon it.

Three years before this work of De Witt appeared the *De sectionibus conicis* of Wallis (q.v.). The spirit of this is entirely classical; the author's avowed object is to show how much more quickly the results found by the Greeks may be expressed in algebraic symbolism. He also flirts with Cavalieri's indivisibles.

§ 7. Philippe de la Hire.

The seventeenth century, which was so rich in scientists interested in the conic sections, produced one more synthetic geometer who contributed mightily to our knowledge of these curves, the voluminous writer whose name appears in the heading of this section. He was a pupil of Desargues. He was familiar with the algebraic work of Descartes, and we are indebted to him for two cardinal principles of algebraic geometry.

FIG. 27

---

† De Witt (q.v.), p. 182.

His first is the original statement of the technique for Cartesian geometry in three dimensions: 'Je considère d'abord que pour déterminer un point hors d'un plan à l'égard d'une ligne droite donnée sur ce plan, il faut trois conditions; la première est la grandeur de la perpendiculaire LA menée du point L au plan; la seconde la perpendiculaire AB menée du point A à la ligne donnée OB, et la troisiéme la partie OB de cette ligne comprise entre un de ses points O et le rencontre B. C'est pourquoy je fais†

$$OB = x, \qquad AB = y, \qquad LA = z.'$$

Our other debt of a fundamental nature to La Hire is for being the first to recognize that in Cartesian geometry the two coordinates play essentially the same role: 'On peut changer les parties de la Tige en Rameaux et les Rameaux en parties de la Tige.'‡

La Hire was surely interested in Cartesian geometry, but his best contributions to our knowledge of the conics came through synthetic methods, of which he was a master. His first work on the subject appeared in 1673: *Nouvelle méthode en géometrie pour les sections et les superficies coniques*. This is extremely rare; I have not been able to see a copy. Apparently it was highly original, containing among other novelties a method of deducing the properties of a general conic from those of a circle, not by a central projection, but by the transformation of homology that afterwards became so dear to Poncelet.

Apparently this work of La Hire did not meet with the success which the author thought it deserved, a cross which many authors have had to bear. In any case he looked out for a powerful patron, and dedicated his next work La Hire[1] to Colbert with many expressions of gratitude and devotion, ending with: 'Mais quelque soin que j'aye pris de perfectioner ces Ouvrages et quelque succez qu'ils puissent avoir, je croirois toujours avoir inutilement travaillé, s'ils ne me servoient principalement à vous témoigner le profond respect avec lequel je seray toute ma vie, Monseigneur, de votre Grandeur le très-humble et trés-obéissant serviteur.'§ Truly has it been said: 'Gratitude is a lively sense of benefits to come.'

It would be hard to find a book offering an easier introduction to the conics. Each type of curve is considered separately, starting with some characteristic property. The ellipse appears as the curve where the sum of the distances from the two foci is constant. This leads immediately to the properties of the tangent, the conjugate diameters, and the equation in Greek form. The book would be as usable to-day as it was the day it was written. He follows with La Hire[2], which is a continuation published the same year, and gives a simple Cartesian

---

† La Hire[1], p. 210.   ‡ Ibid, p. 232.   § Ibid, dedication.

discussion of the conics. We find something arresting on p. 440 of his *Méthode de la construction des equations analytiques*, which is essentially a continuation of La Hire[1] and La Hire[2]: 'Un point estant donné dedans ou dehors une Section Conique et sur un mesme plan; il faut méner une ligne perpendiculaire à la Section; . . . en ne se servant que du cercle et de la Section donnée.' A construction of a normal depending on the intersection of a conic with a rectangular hyperbola had already been found by Apollonius, but was not in the Greek tradition of ruler and compass. Obviously a problem leading to an irreducible equation of the fourth order is not a ruler and compass problem. La Hire comes nearer to the Greek tradition, but his proof is essentially analytic. He eliminates y between the equations of the circle and the normal through a given point, thus getting an equation of the fourth order in x. He then devises a circle which will lead to the same equation through elimination.

La Hire's greatest work is his *Sectiones Conicae* of 1685, La Hire[3]. Those who read Latin with difficulty will find a pretty complete account

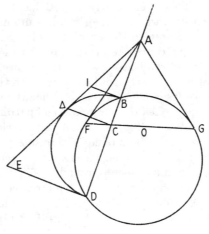

Fig. 28

by Lehmann in La Hire[4]. There are nine books, the first beginning with a long account of harmonic separation on a straight line, stressing its projective invariance, and pointing to the special case when one point is at an infinite distance. We find the harmonic properties of the complete quadrilateral and complete quadrangle slightly disguised. The harmonic property of the polar of a point with regard to a circle is proved in the following simple fashion. Let AF, AG be tangents to a circle (Fig. 28) from an exterior point A through which passes the arbitrary secant $ABCD$. A semicircle is described on BD as diameter. A line through C perpendicular to AC meets this semicircle in Δ. Lines through B and D parallel to $C\Delta$ meet $A\Delta$ in I and E.

$$AB.AD = AF^2 = OF^2 + OA^2$$
$$= FC.CG + CO^2 + OA^2$$
$$= FC.CG + AC^2$$
$$= BC.CD + AC^2$$
$$= A\Delta^2.$$

When $A\Delta$ is tangent to the semicircle

$$\frac{CD}{CB} = \frac{\Delta E}{\Delta I} = \frac{DE}{BI} = -\frac{AD}{BD}.$$

We have here Apollonius' theorem for the harmonic property of the polar proved for the circle. There follows the construction of the polar of a point by means of a complete quadrangle. The polar of an interior point is found as the line perpendicular to the diameter through the point passing through that point whose polar goes through the given point. The harmonic property of the polar of an inside point is then easily shown, and then La Hire makes his first important advance over Desargues by showing that if a point trace a straight line, its polar will rotate around the pole of that line.

In Book II La Hire takes up the cone of Apollonius, the general cone with circular sections. He introduces new definitions, as that which gives the name 'directrix' to the line which is projected to infinity when a conic is projected into a circle. The polar properties of conics are deduced at once from those of circles. In Book III he finds the Archimedean equation for a conic in the following simple fashion. Let AB (Fig. 29) be a diameter of an

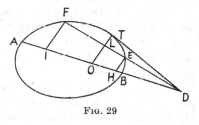

Fig. 29

ellipse, HE, IF two ordinates conjugate thereto. FE shall meet the diameter in D; the case where this point is at an infinite distance is handled separately. TO is the polar of D and is parallel to the ordinates; it meets FE in L. Clearly D and O are harmonically separated by A and B as well as by H and I. AB, IH, DD are pairs of an involution.

$$\frac{AH.BH}{AI.BI} = \frac{DH^2}{DI^2} = \frac{EH^2}{FI^2};$$

$$\frac{AH.BH}{EH^2} = \frac{AI.BI}{FI^2}.$$

From this Archimedean form we easily find the parameter and so the Apollonian form. The remainder of the book follows Apollonius more or less closely.

La Hire's fourth book deals with the asymptotes. The fifth gives metrical theorems about diameters and parameters, the sixth treats Apollonius' old subject of similar conics. We find something more interesting in the seventh, where he definitely pits himself against the 'Great Geometer' in treating normals, following his predecessor by first finding points of the curve nearest to points of the axis. He also constructs the general normal by the intersection with a rectangular hyperbola. The foci which figured prominently in La Hire[1] do not appear here till Book VIII and are sketchily treated. In Theorems XXVI and XXVIII he gives clumsy proofs of a pretty, and, I think, original theorem, namely, the locus of the vertex of a right triangle whose sides touch a central conic is the director circle, or the directrix when we have a parabola. The student of invariant theory will find here the simplest simultaneous covariant of the conic and the circular points at infinity. We shall meet this curve again when we take up the algebraic discussion of invariants. In XXIII he proves the pretty and useful theorem that conjugate lines through a focus are mutually perpendicular. The ninth book is given to problems in construction, and is followed by an appendix in which he shows how completely he has covered the results of Apollonius.

What shall be our final judgement of Philippe de La Hire? He certainly was in possession of about all existing knowledge of the conics. He wrote a very readable book. His exposition is far in advance of that of Apollonius. His skilful use of projection, harmonic section, poles, and polars marks a real advance. His omissions are few, but very striking. We find no mention of Desargues's involution theorem, not a word of Pascal. The four-line problem which exercised Apollonius and Pappus, not to mention Descartes, finds no place. As an expositor he was thoroughly admirable, as an original mathematician he is not to be mentioned in the same breath with Apollonius, whom he strove so hard to surpass, perhaps not even with Desargues.

CHAPTER IV

THE GREAT PROJECTIVE SCHOOL

§ 1. Newton, MacLaurin, and Brianchon.

WE saw in the last chapter how there gradually emerged in the study of the conic sections certain theorems of a non-metrical, projective character. I mean by this that they deal with properties which are not altered by a linear transformation. The first and foremost of these is the invariance of the cross ratio, a fact announced by Pappus, but perhaps discovered before his time. We have the two theorems which bear the name of Desargues. The first is his two-triangle theorem which tells us that if two triangles, either in the same plane or in different planes, are so situated that the lines connecting corresponding vertices are concurrent, then the intersections of corresponding sides are collinear, and conversely. The second is his involution theorem which says that if the vertices of a complete quadrilateral lie on a conic, a transversal not through a vertex will meet the pairs of sides of the quadrilateral and the conic in pairs of an involution. As the involution is completely determined by the quadrilateral, this will be true for every conic through the vertices. There is a theorem dual to this for circumscribed quadrilaterals, but this was not seen at that time. Then we have Desargues's construction of the polar of a point, and Pascal's theorem. Geometers came gradually to the idea that properties of conics which grew out of these were not only more general, but frequently more interesting than the widely scattered metrical theorems. So it came about that in the next two hundred years after the time of La Hire, the greatest advances, whether by synthetic or algebraic methods, were in the projective theory of the curves.

Newton shows much interest in conic sections in his *Principia*, calling them 'trajectories'. He wishes to determine a conic from various sets of data. First come some constructions when one focus is known, a natural assumption for an astronomer. Then when no focus is known he begins with certain lemmas, of which the most interesting is Lemma XXI. I quote:† 'If two movable and indefinite right lines BM, CM drawn through B, C as poles do by their point of concourse M describe a right line MN given by position; and two other indefinite right lines BD, CD making with the former at these given points B, C given angles MBD, MCD, I say that the two right lines BD, CD at their point of concourse D describe a conic section passing through B, C and vice versa.'

† Newton[1], p. 77.

This is known as Newton's 'organic construction' of a conic. I do not quite know what he means by his vice versa: usually if D describe a conic through B and C, M will do the same thing. His proof is rather long, depending on some lemmas invented, apparently,· *ad hoc*. The modern proof comes from the fact that as the pencils $B(M \ldots)$, $C(M \ldots)$ are projective, so are the pencils $B(D \ldots)$, $C(D \ldots)$, and then applying the Chasles-Steiner theorem which we shall come to later in the chapter. Newton needs this theorem to determine a trajectory through five given points. Let the points be A, B, C, D, E. We take $\angle ABC$ and $\angle ACB$ as the fixed angles, B and C as the 'poles'. Transform DE into DE', draw $B'E'$. Then transform this line back. It will be easy to find the tangents at B and C, also to find where a line through either point meets the curve again.

The construction of a conic through four given points, tangent to a given line, depends on finding the point of contact, which, by Desargues's involution theorem, is a double point of the involution on the line determined by the pairs of lines through the four points. But Newton does not seem to have heard of this: I doubt whether he had ever heard of Desargues anyway. His own ingenious construction is like this. Find where the line connecting two of the points meets the assumed tangent, and draw through there a line parallel to that which connects the other two. This we do twice. Now in speaking of Archimedes, p. 6, we mentioned Newton's product theorem. In the case of a conic the ratio of the product of the distance from a point to two pairs of points of the curve lying in given direction therefrom is independent of the point chosen. By using this theorem three times we find the point of contact. The same device works when we have three points and two tangents.

The next problem clearly is to determine a conic, given two points and three tangents. Here Newton gives us something new and very interesting, his Lemma XXII:

'To transform a figure into other figures of the same kind. Suppose the first figure (Fig. 30) HGI to be transformed. Draw at pleasure two parallel lines AO, BL cutting any third line given by position in A and B, and from any point G of the figure draw out any right line GD parallel to OA till it meet the line AB. Then from any given point O in the line OA draw to a point D the right line OD meeting BL in d and from the point of concurrence draw the right line dg containing any

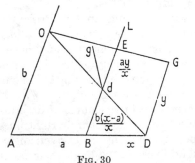

Fig. 30

given angle with the right line BL and having such a ratio to Od as DG has to OD. And g will be the point of the new figure corresponding to G.'

Newton proves that if G trace a straight line, so will g, and if one point trace a conic, so will the other. His proof is a bit long, but the transformation is simplicity itself if we set up the equations. The coordinates of G shall be (x, y), while those of g are (x', y'). Then, by definition,

$$dg = dE = \frac{ay}{x};$$

$$x' = \frac{ax+py}{x}, \qquad y' = \frac{bx+qy-ab}{x},$$

where p, q are functions of the angles which the axes make with one another and with dg. Here we have a linear transformation of the plane, the earliest discovered, as far as I can see, which was not a simple central projection or a member of the conformal group. Newton sees clearly that the Y-axis goes to infinity. As to the problem of passing a conic through two points tangent to three lines, he throws to infinity the line connecting the intersection of two tangents with the point where the third tangent meets the line connecting the two points. So we have the problem of constructing a conic tangent to two parallel lines, which passes through two points, and touches a line parallel to that connecting the points; the problem is solved by the product theorem. When one point and four tangents are given, we use the linear transformation to pass over to the case where we seek a conic through a point touching four lines, parallel in pairs. The centre of their parallelogram is the centre of the conic, and the conic will pass through the reflection of the given point in this. We are thus thrown back on the last case. There remains the case of five tangents. Newton's method here is very long. The reader familiar with projective geometry will see how easy all of these are when we use the theorems of Pascal, Brianchon, and Desargues. But Brianchon was not yet born, and Newton does not seem to have heard of either of the other two. His invention of this linear transformation was a real contribution to geometry, seldom mentioned in appreciations of his work.

Newton's organic description was generalized in various ways, especially noteworthy being that associated with the name of Colin MacLaurin. This able writer in MacLaurin[1] and MacLaurin[2] carried Newton's construction further, applying it to curves of any order. In 1733 there appeared Braikenridge (q.v.) with an important theorem which I phrase as follows:

Theorem 1] *If the sides of a moving triangle pass through three fixed points, and two vertices trace straight lines, the third vertex will trace a conic through two of the given points.*

Braikenridge states in the preface of his work that he was familiar with this in 1726. MacLaurin came right back at him in MacLaurin[3], claiming that in 1722 he was in possession of material which he meant to publish, but unfortunately had postponed publication. He had communicated some of his theorems, including this one, to Braikenridge. I cannot make out just when this communication was made, but he certainly claimed that Braikenridge had published another man's discovery as his own. I refuse to go any further into this unpleasant question, but must point out that Braikenridge stated the theorem clearly, which MacLaurin never did. As a method of construction it is better and more general than Newton's organic one, for it is purely projective with no metrical element such as a fixed angle.

I close the present section with brief mention of another writer on projective geometry, somewhat subsequent to those just mentioned, Charles Julien Brianchon. This enterprising young man, while still a student at the École Polytechnique, discovered the theorem which has borne his name ever since. I will return to it in a moment. He later became an artillery officer interested in the applications of geometry to artillery problems. Brianchon[1] includes a study of transversals, a branch of geometry recently brought into prominence by Lazare Carnot. Two or three theorems lie at the base:

Menelaus' Theorem 2] *If the points B_1, B_2, B_3 lie on the corresponding sides of the triangle whose vertices are A_1, A_2, A_3, the necessary and sufficient condition that the three points B_i should be collinear is that algebraically*

$$A_1 B_2 . A_2 B_3 . A_3 B_1 = A_1 B_3 . A_2 B_1 . A_3 B_2.$$

I have noted this theorem before in connexion with Desargues. Here is a dual theorem:

Ceva's Theorem 3] *The necessary and sufficient condition that the three lines $A_i B_i$ should be concurrent is that algebraically*

$$A_1 B_2 . A_2 B_3 . A_3 B_1 = -A_1 B_3 . A_2 B_1 . A_3 B_2.$$

Brianchon starts off with the following which is very simple:

Theorem 4] *If three coplanar lines, concurrent in S meet a transversal in A, B, C, the fraction $\dfrac{AB}{AC} \cdot \dfrac{SC}{SB}$ is independent of the choice of transversal.*

The projective invariance of the cross ratio comes at once out of this. He gives a proof of Pascal's theorem which would have been quite accessible to Pascal. He paid much attention to limiting cases. Presently he gives a theorem, previously given in Brianchon[2].

Brianchon's Theorem 5] *If a hexagon be circumscribed to a conic, the lines connecting opposite vertices are concurrent.*

Let us pause at this point to note that Pascal had proved his theorem nearly a hundred and fifty years earlier, and fully a hundred years earlier still La Hire had proved that, if a point trace a straight line, its polar will rotate about the pole of that line. If then you have a Pascal hexagon, and polarize in that conic, you have a Brianchon hexagon. It is truly astonishing that no one before Brianchon made this obvious remark. This writer studies various limiting cases of his theorem; he is also interested in Newton's problem of determining a conic from five linear conditions. I give his treatment to compare with Newton's.

Given five points of a conic, to determine others. Draw an arbitrary line through one of the points. This shall contain a side of a Pascal hexagon which uses the given points as vertices. We have enough data to construct the Pascal line, and so a sixth vertex.

Given five points of a conic, to construct a tangent at one of them. An inscribed pentagon and the tangent at one vertex form a limiting case of a Pascal hexagon. Hence, in the present case, we can construct the Pascal line, and so the tangent at one point.

Given five tangents, to find other tangents we follow the first of these constructions, step by step, replacing points by lines, lines by points, and Pascal by Brianchon. We can similarly find the points of contact of the five given points.

Given four points and a tangent. We find the double points of the involution determined on the given tangent by conics through the four points, and apply Desargues's involution theorem. The dual case of four tangents and one point can be handled by corresponding methods, but apparently Brianchon was not familiar with the dual to Desargues's theorem. He shows, however, that, if we have a set of conics tangent to four lines, they have a common self-conjugate triangle, that formed by the diagonal triangle of the quadrilateral. This enables us to find three other points, then throw back on the last case.

Given three points and two tangents. This is a good deal more difficult. Consider (Fig. 31), a conic through A, B, C touching RT at R and ST at S. There are three conics through the point pairs RR, SS, namely, the given conic, the lines RT, ST, and the line RS counted twice. They cut any transversal in three pairs of an involution. The intersection of AB with RS gives a double point, AB as one pair, and the intersections with RT, ST as another, or the point L is determined by these two pairs. M is found in the same way. The line LM gives

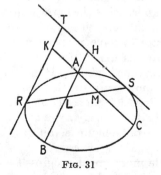

FIG. 31

us the points R, S. The dual case where we have two points and three tangents may be handled by a dual method, but Brianchon did not know this, and developed a complicated procedure which I will not repeat. We are very safe in saying that Brianchon is well ahead of Newton in solving these particular problems.

§ 2. Jean Victor Poncelet.

Few mathematical treatises were ever composed under as depressing conditions as the *Traité des propriétés projectives des figures*, Poncelet (q.v.), which was commenced while the writer was a prisoner in the Russian military prison at Saratow in the year 1813. Perhaps it would be an exaggeration to say that this was the one good thing that came out of Napoleon's Russian campaign, but the world will always be in debt to the writer for beginning such an important work under such unfavourable circumstances. His first writing, expanded and revised, was published in 1822, and the second edition saw the light some forty years later, but the general spirit remained unchanged throughout.

It has been said that Newton was the first writer to draw a sharp distinction between algebraic and transcendental curves. Poncelet was the first to separate sharply the projective properties of loci, those which are unaltered by a projection from plane to plane, from non-projective ones. The former cluster about the concurrence of lines, the collinearity of points, and cross ratios, though Poncelet stressed the latter less than one would expect. It is truly extraordinary what a great and beautiful edifice can be erected on such simple foundations. Poncelet, like Desargues, recognized parallel lines as meeting on a line at infinity, which amounts to saying that they are the projections of lines meeting on a so-called vanishing line.

He begins with a chapter dealing with central projection. Then he approaches the hardest question of all, What shall we do about complex points and lines? We cannot neglect them altogether if our theorems are to have proper generality; the algebraist has complex quantities at his disposition, even though it was not until decades later that anyone, namely Hamilton, gave a satisfactory definition of what complex quantities really are. What shall the pure geometer do? Poncelet proceeds as follows: 'En général, on pourrait désigner par l'adjectif *imaginaire* tout objet qui d'absolu ou réel qu'il était dans une certaine figure, serait devenu entièrement impossible ou inconstructible dans la figure *corrélative*, celle qui est censée parvenir de la première par le mouvement progressif et *continu* de quelques parties, sans violer les primitifs du système.'†

This sounds really learned, but on closer examination we note that

† Poncelet (q.v.), p. 28.

this does not tell us what an imaginary object really is, only what it once was. Let a line cut an ellipse twice. If it move parallel to itself until it becomes tangent, the two intersections fall together; after that they disappear: Poncelet would have us say that they become imaginary. They are almost real in the sense that the intersection of their line with a diameter in the conjugate direction may be taken as the point midway between them, and the square of their distance is a real negative number. We may easily find a representation of such a complex pair in two real points of the line with the same middle point and the same positive number for the fourth power of their distance. Analytically, if we take a pair of axes, one in the direction of the line, the other in the conjugate direction, and write

$$\frac{x^2}{a'^2}+\frac{y^2}{b'^2} = 1, \qquad \frac{x^2}{a'^2}-\frac{y^2}{b'^2} = 1,$$

the intersection of one curve with lines parallel to the Y-axis may be taken to represent the intersections of the other curve with these same lines. The actual chords of one curve are called 'ideal chords' of the other, and the two curves are called 'supplementaries'. An elaborate account of this method of representation will be found in Ch. III of Coolidge[1]. Poncelet proves that two conics with no common chord have two common ideal chords, usually distinct. A pretty application appears in the case of circles. All circles orthogonal to the circles through two real points have a common ideal chord. His exposition would have been even more satisfactory had he been in possession of Steiner's concept of the 'power' of a point with regard to a circle. He does, however, develop the pretty quadratic transformation which consists in replacing each point by the point conjugate to it with regard to all circles through two given points. He shows soon after how any conic and a point inside it can be projected into a circle and its centre, and how two conics with two distinct intersections can be projected into two circles. The projection will be real when they have a common ideal chord, and then he remarks: 'Deux cercles, plantés arbitrairement sur un plan ne sont pas tout à fait indépendants entre eux, comme on pourrait le croire au premier abord, ils ont idéalement deux points imaginaires communs à l'infini.'† I do not know of a more important remark more casually made in all geometry. Unfortunately, Poncelet did not himself appreciate its full importance, nor begin to deduce the great number of important consequences.

In Section II he takes up projective properties in earnest: poles and polars are fundamental, some of Carnot's transversals appear. Pascal's theorem is proved by throwing a conic into a circle while two pairs of

† Poncelet (q.v.), p. 48.

opposite sides of the hexagon become parallel. Brianchon comes from Pascal by polarizing in the conic itself, and then we have the converses of the two.

At this point Poncelet makes a curious switch to the study of centres of similitude, and the transformation of central similitude, known to the Greeks. This is not projective, and seems rather out of place.†

In Section III he returns to projective questions, systems of conics, and the transformation which he calls 'homology'. Suppose that we project a plane figure from two points V_1, V_2 on another plane. The relation between the two coplanar figures thus produced is called 'homology'. Corresponding points are collinear with the intersection of the plane and the line $V_1 V_2$, corresponding lines meet on the intersection of the two planes. A point goes to a point, a line to a line, a conic to a conic, pole and polar to pole and polar. Let us show that two coplanar conics c_1^2, c_2^2 which do not have four-point contact can be transformed into one another by homology. Let V_1 be an arbitrary point outside the plane. c_1^2 shall be projected from V_1 into c^2 in another plane. Let V be the intersection of two common tangents of c_1^2 and c_2^2, its polars meeting the respective conics in $A_1 B_1$ and $A_2 B_2$. The planes $V_1 V A_1 A_2, V_1 V B_1 B_2$ shall touch c^2 in A and B. Let Q_2 be an arbitrary point of c_2^2. The plane $Q_2 V V_1$ shall meet c^2 in Q. $Q_2 Q$ shall meet $V V_1$ in V_2. If, then, we project c_2^2 from V_2 on the plane of c^2, we shall have a conic touching c^2 in A and B and passing through Q, and this is clearly c^2 itself. The great advantage of this transformation compared with a projection from plane to plane is that it can easily be stepped up into three dimensions, and Poncelet does just this later in the book. I note in passing that the linear transformation used by Newton, and described on p. 46, is not of this simple type.

At this point Poncelet gives a good deal of attention to problems of construction. Two conics which do not have four-point contact can be carried simultaneously into two circles. To these we apply a simple quadratic transformation. It will carry a straight line into a conic, as he shows, by methods which can easily be improved on. This conic goes through a number of easily recognized points, and so we are led to the beautiful

Theorem 6] *Given a pencil of conics through four points. If a point trace a straight line, not through a vertex of the common self-conjugate triangle, its conjugate with regard to all of the conics will be a conic through the double points of the involution which the conics cut in the line, the six points harmonically separated by pairs of the original four points from points of the given line, and the vertices of the common self-conjugate triangle.*

† Coolidge[2], pp. 65 ff.

This is called the 'eleven-point conic'. The prettiest special case is where the conics pass through the vertices and orthocentre of a triangle. By Desargues's theorem all such conics must be rectangular hyperbolas, for their involution on the line at infinity has three pairs of mutually perpendicular directions, so that all pairs are mutually perpendicular. The eleven-point conic is easily seen to be the locus of the poles of the given line with regard to the given conics. We thus get, finally,

Feuerbach's Theorem 7] *The locus of the centres of the rectangular hyperbolas through the vertices and orthocentre of a triangle is a circle through the feet of the altitudes, the mid-points of the sides, and the points half-way from the orthocentre to the vertices.*

This is the famous nine-point circle of Feuerbach. It is tangent to the inscribed and three escribed circles.†

Poncelet is particularly fond of conics with double contact. These can be carried by homology into concentric circles, whose properties are easily found. Suppose that we have two conics which have double contact with a third. We transform the two into conics having double contact with a circle, the line connecting the poles of the chords of contact going to infinity. We have two conics having double contact with a circle, the chords of contact being diameters of the circle. Clearly the whole figure is transformed into itself by a reflection in the centre of the circle.

Theorem 8] *If two conics have double contact with a third, the chords of contact and a pair of common chords of the two are concurrent.*

We can find an even easier algebraic proof by abridged notation.

In the fourth section of Chapter I Poncelet takes up metrical questions involving the foci. These would have been much easier had he realized that a focus is the intersection of tangents to the conic from one of those circular points at infinity which he himself discovered; still more so had he anticipated Laguerre by showing that the circular measure of the angle of two lines is $1/2i$ multiplied by the natural logarithm of the cross ratio which they, as a pair, form with the two lines from their intersection to the circular points. But Poncelet did not know this. He was, however, able to prove the pretty theorem that mutually conjugate lines through a focus are mutually perpendicular, and the equally pretty one that if a variable tangent to a conic meet two fixed tangents, the points of intersection subtend a fixed angle at a focus. On p. 271 we have another beauty. If two moving points of a conic always subtend a right angle at a fixed point of the curve, the line connecting them passes through a fixed point of the normal at the fixed point. There follows an interesting determination of the normals through a general point of the plane, Apollonius' old favourite. The feet of these normals are the points where this conic meets that curve which is the locus of the intersections of perpendiculars from the given point on moving tangents with the corresponding diameters. Now this locus is a conic, for it is the eleven-point conic of the line at infinity with regard to the given conic, and a circle whose centre is the given point. It is interesting to compare this simple determination with those of Apollonius and La Hire. The remainder of the first volume is devoted to polygons inscribed in one conic and circumscribed to another, a subject to which we shall return in a later chapter.

Poncelet starts his second volume with a study of 'centres of mean distance' of points of a line with regard to groups of m points thereon. This is a projective generalization of the relation of the infinite point to the centre of gravity of the group. There follows a long exposition of the method of polar reciprocation in two dimensions and three. This, unfortunately, is not free from error. Thus we find in Poncelet (q.v.), vol. ii, p. 78, the erroneous statement that the developable formed by the tangents to a space curve of order m is of order $m(m-1)$. This is grossly wrong. He reasons as follows. The order of the developable is the number of tangents which meet an arbitrary line l which we may assume to be vertical. This is the same as the number of tangents from the intersection of l with a horizontal to the projection of the given curve on that plane. The order of this curve is m, and there would be $m(m-1)$ tangents from a general point if the plane curve had no singular point. But Poncelet failed to note that the projection of a space curve will usually have a number of double points. There follow sections dealing with transversals and general algebraic curve theory, and a long supplement largely devoted to saying unpleasant things about contemporary French geometers. It was written by an embittered old man, not by an enthusiastic young officer.

Poncelet had a disagreeable controversy with Gergonne. This mathematician made the brilliant observation that in plane projective geometry points and lines play essentially the same role, two of one kind always determine one of the other. In three dimensions points and planes correspond similarly, three of one kind determine one of the other, unless they belong to the same line. Lines correspond to themselves. This is the great principle of duality of projective geometry, but Poncelet said it was nothing by his method of polar reciprocation, in a conic or quadric. Gergonne replied that the conic or quadric of reciprocation was an entirely needless element in the situation, duality

was intrinsic in the system. Poncelet gives a long and biased account
of the whole controversy (Poncelet (q.v.), vol. ii, pp. 386–97, or, more
briefly, Coolidge[2], p. 95). What a pity that such a beautiful and important work should be marred by such lamentable exhibition of
disappointment.

§ 3. Michel Chasles.

The last writer belonging to the two-century-old school of French
synthetic geometers was Michel Chasles, an enthusiastic, fruitful, and
uncritical writer. Geometry owes him much, and his was a name to
conjure with. I once read somewhere that a young man was asked
what theorem was associated with the name of Chasles; he replied
'Aucun, il-y-en a trop'. But, as I said, he was eminently uncritical, as
one can see by turning the pages of the influential Chasles[1], and he had
a fixed idea that everything worth while in mathematics that had been
discovered since classical times was of French origin.

Chasles's best contributions to projective geometry are found in the
notes to Chasles[1]. In fact, the notes cover more pages than the main
text. The first of these which touches our subject is Note IV, dealing
with the method of finding the foci of a conic directly from the cone
whence it was cut. We have seen that the Greeks did not bother with
the foci until the conic and its equation were well established. On p. 285
Chasles gives, without demonstration, a method of his own for finding
the foci; on p. 286 comes a theorem ascribed to Quetelet and
Dandelin, which he says is recent.

Theorem 9] *If a central conic be cut from a cone of revolution, its foci
are points of contact of the two spheres inscribed in the cone, which touch
the plane of the conic.*

This theorem is, of course, very familiar nowadays; the proof comes
at once from the constant sum or difference property of the two foci.
Chasles's most important work appears in Note IX, which is given to
the study of cross ratios. In this he was anticipated by eight years in
the work of Möbius, but as Chasles could not read German,† we need
not accuse him of larceny. If we define as a cross ratio of four lines of a
pencil the same function of the sines of their angles as gives a cross
ratio of four collinear points in terms of their distances, it appears at
once that a cross ratio of four points is that of lines connecting them
with any fifth point not on their line. Here we have, in simplest
form, the proof of Pappus' theorem that cross ratios are unaltered by
projection. We may define cross ratios of sets of coaxal planes in like

† Chasles[1], p. 215 note.

fashion. Chasles recognizes that four collinear points have, in general, several ratios,

$$\frac{ac}{ad} : \frac{bc}{bd} = \lambda, \qquad \frac{ac}{ab} : \frac{dc}{db} = \frac{\lambda}{\lambda-1}, \qquad \frac{ab}{ad} : \frac{cb}{cd} = 1-\lambda.$$

He notes the relation between the first and third, but not that between the first and second, and quite overlooks the fact that there are three more cross ratios, the reciprocals of these. He then passes to the study of involutions of collinear points or concurrent lines, pointing out how in a hyperbolic involution the members of each pair are harmonically separated by the self-corresponding members. If we say that two points are conjugate with regard to a conic when each is on the polar of the other, a form of words we have used already, with a similar definition for conjugate lines, we have

Theorem 10] *Pairs of points on a line which are conjugate with regard to a conic form an involution.*

Theorem 11] *Pairs of coplanar lines through a point which are conjugate with regard to a conic will form an involution.*

Chasles[1] notes, p. 326, that if a conic be cut in pairs of points by radiating lines, the lines connecting these points with any point of the conic will form an involution, with a dual theorem for pairs of tangents. And then we get the most important theorem of all:

Theorem 12] *Given two pencils of coplanar lines in one-to-one correspondence in such a way that corresponding cross ratios are equal, the intersections of corresponding lines will generate a conic through the centres of the two pencils.*†

Chasles calls this the converse of Desargues's involution theorem. I don't exactly see why. What right have we to attribute it to Chasles? Chasles[1] appeared in 1837, but Steiner published the same theorem in 1832. I do not see how to settle the question as to which man deserves the credit for discovery, and prefer to call it the Chasles-Steiner theorem, for in 1828 appeared Chasles[2], with the exact dual:

Theorem 13] *Given two sets of collinear coplanar points in one-to-one correspondence, in such a way that corresponding cross ratios are equal, the lines connecting corresponding points are tangent to a conic which touches the two given lines.*

The proof of this is quite different, but I find it impossible to believe

† Chasles[1], Note XV, p. 335.

that Chasles, knowing this, did not at least surmise the dual. Here is his proof of 12 (Fig. 32):

$$\frac{AB}{AC}\cdot\frac{A'C}{A'B}=\frac{A'B'}{A'C'}\cdot\frac{AC'}{AB'}$$

$$\frac{\sin\angle AHL}{\sin\angle AHM}\cdot\frac{\sin\angle A'HM}{\sin\angle A'HL}=\frac{\sin\angle A'KM}{\sin\angle A'KL}\cdot\frac{\sin\angle AKL}{\sin\angle AKM}.$$

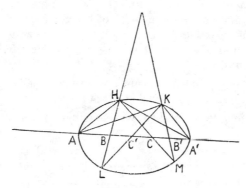

FIG. 32

The discovery of the possibility of generating a conic by projective pencils of lines opened a very wide door. We get a better statement in Chasles[1], p. 340:

Theorem 14] *Given two homographic pencils in the plane, the lines of one will meet the corresponding lines of the other in the points of a conic through the centres of the two pencils.*

I cannot find exactly where he defines the word 'homographic'. It is curious also that he does not point out that, when the line common to the two pencils is self-corresponding, the conic consists of this line and another one. This theorem certainly gives the most important projective property of the conics, and has as much importance for the synthetic geometer as the equation has for the algebraist. On p. 338 he draws immediately from Desargues's involution theorem the pretty result that, if the vertices of a complete quadrilateral lie on a conic, the product of the distances of a point on the curve to a pair of opposite sides bears a fixed ratio to the product of the distances to another pair of sides. And what is this but an absolutely simple solution of that problem of four lines which worried the Greeks so sorely? It is worth noting also that these projective properties of conics suggest at once similarly obtained properties of ruled surfaces of the second order, and space curves of order three.

Chasles takes up the theory of conics in other works, especially in Chasles[3], but it is the notes to Chasles[1] that give his freshest and most important contributions to the subject.

§ 4. Jacob Steiner.

Chasles was the last important member of the great French school of projective geometers. After his time primacy in this subject passed across the Rhine, never to return. The first, and most acclaimed, if not really the most notable, member of the German school was Jacob Steiner. The most outstanding character of his famous work, Steiner[1] (q.v.), is that it is absolutely 'systematisch'. The whole is based on three fundamental principles:

I. Points, lines, and planes are the raw material of geometry. All other figures are constructed out of these.

II. The principle of duality, whether in two dimensions or three, is basic.

III. The connecting relation is that expressed by the word 'projective' as applied to ranges of collinear points, pencils of concurrent coplanar lines, and axial pencils of planes through one line. These last are the three 'fundamental one-dimensional forms'.

But here I must remark that he does not seem to say exactly what he means by the word 'projective'. Presumably it is what Chasles calls 'homographic', i.e. one-to-one correspondence with equality of corresponding cross ratios, but he never states this in so many words. Moreover, he treats all distances as positive, and says that four points are harmonic when their cross ratio is unity. He avoids the ambiguity involved in treating cross ratios in this way by adding a definite order of sequence. His great Steiner[1] begins with about a hundred pages of discussion of the projective relation. Especial stress is rightly laid on the theorem that this relation is completely determined by the fate of three elements, and from this follows the equally fundamental principle that two fundamental one-dimensional forms are projective when, and only when, they are connected by a string of projections and intersections.

Steiner is now ready to tackle the conics. A conic is defined as a non-circular section of a cone which has circular sections. As all angles inscribed in the same circular arc are equal, the cross ratios of the lines connecting four points of a circle with any fifth point are the same. It is also easy to show that four tangents to a circle meet any other two tangents in tetrads of points with the same cross ratios. But cross ratios are unaltered by projection. Hence if four points of a conic be connected by lines with any fifth point of the curve, the cross ratios are the same. A moving point on a conic will then determine projective pencils at any two fixed points of the curve. The converse of this, as Steiner notes, is our Theorem 14, and this with its dual is the basis of his whole treatment of conics. I cannot see, however, that he anywhere actually proves that every such curve can be cut from a cone with circular sections. Passing over this slip we are able to prove many important properties of conics in the easiest possible fashion. Pascal and Brianchon come easily, as does the whole theory of poles and polars. Incidentally, he turns up (p. 356) this theorem which we shall need later:

Theorem 15] *If the vertices of two triangles lie on a conic, their sides touch a conic, and conversely.*

Steiner after this is able to step into three dimensions, and treat the quadric surfaces as ruled surfaces generated by projective pencils of planes or projective ranges of points on two skew lines. The space cubic curve and developable are found by taking three pencils or ranges. And here (pp. 409 ff.) he brings in something really novel.

Suppose that we have two planes ϵ, ϵ_1 and two skew lines r, s, neither of which lies in either of the planes. If P be a point of ϵ, not on the common line of the planes, nor on either of the given lines, it shall correspond to the point P_1 in ϵ_1 where that plane meets the line through P coplanar with r and s. Now this transformation from ϵ to ϵ_1 is not a linear one, for a line in one plane will determine the generators of a quadric through r and s; this will cut the other plane in a conic. This, as far as I know, is the first reference to a quadratic transformation in all geometry, except for Poncelet's eleven-point conic, and a brief reference in Pappus (q.v.).[†]

The first part of Steiner ends with 'Aufgaben und Lehrsätze'. These are in the nature of problems and puzzles. I am not perfectly sure that Steiner himself, ingenious as he certainly was, could solve them all, at least by orthodox methods such as he developed. On p. 448 we have this problem: 'Three conics have two common points, what is the locus of points whose polars with regard to them are concurrent?' If we follow the French school, we project these two into the circular points at infinity, and ask, 'What is the locus of points whose polars with regard to three circles are concurrent?' This is the common orthogonal circle. I confess I do not see the geometric proof, though I doubt not it is easy. Hence in the general case we have a conic through the two given points such that at each intersection with one of the given conics the tangents to the two curves are harmonically separated by lines to the given points. On the next page we have the same problem

† Vol. ii, p. 496.

set for three conics in general position. If we give this up in despair as a problem in synthetic geometry, and try it algebraically, we see that the locus is the Jacobian cubic of the three curves, which is not reachable by pure geometrical methods. Steiner seeks also the envelope of the line connecting a point and its mate in this relation. It is the so-called 'Cayleyan' envelope of class 6.

In the second part of the present work Steiner takes up the problem of finding what constructions are possible with a ruler and one fully drawn circle whose centre is marked. This idea was first broached by Poncelet. Steiner gives a number of metrical constructions, which do not concern us here, but there is also some projective material, where the data are a ruler and a fully drawn conic, whose centre, however, is not known. For instance, given two projective ranges of points $ABC, A'B'C'$ on the same line, where are the self-corresponding points? I introduce here von Staudt's convenient symbol for 'projective'

$$ABC \ldots \barwedge A'B'C' \ldots .$$

We take a fixed point V (Fig. 33) on the given conic, and project into $A_1 B_1 C_1, A_1' B_1' C_1'$. We have then the projective pencils

$$A_1(A_1' B_1' C_1' \ldots) \barwedge A_1'(A_1 B_1 C_1 \ldots).$$

But as $A_1 A_1'$ is self-corresponding, the locus of the intersections is the line $H_1 K_1$. These are projected back into the desired points HK.

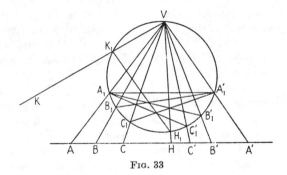

FIG. 33

The solution of this problem enables Steiner to proceed to other interesting problems, as this, on p. 512. Given five points of a conic A, B, C, D, E, to find where it meets a line l. We determine two projective ranges on l by projecting B, C, D from A and E, then find the self-corresponding point. Or take the problem already studied by Newton and Brianchon: Given four points of a conic and one tangent, where are the possible points of contact? The conics through four points cut a transversal in the pairs of an involution, and this will be determined by the intersections with the pairs of lines joining the given points. The double points of the involution are self-corresponding in a projective transformation, so the problem is thrown back on the last one.

It does not seem to me, on the whole, that Steiner can be counted as a geometer of the first rank. He did, however, set the subject of the projective geometry of the conics on a very systematic basis, and he settled once for all the Poncelet-Gergonne controversy by showing how absolutely fundamental is the principle of duality. But he was ingenious rather than profound, and his originality showed more in matters of detail than in striking new departures.

§ 5. von Staudt.

The most original and profound of the projective geometers of the German school was Georg Karl Christian von Staudt, long professor at Erlangen. His great passion, like Steiner's, was for unity of method, but he saw far deeper into the questions involved than did his acclaimed predecessor. He pointed out that there was an inherent contradiction in the traditional treatment of projective geometry. The superstructure is projectively invariant, cross ratios are projectively invariant, but they are originally defined in terms of distances and angles, which are not invariant projectively. The first task that he set himself was to eliminate this extraneous metrical element.

His first work, von Staudt[1], begins with a long discussion of points, lines, and planes. He postulates a Euclidean space, with a plane at infinity. I now define two figures which I have mentioned before, and which are fundamental with von Staudt.

Definition] Four coplanar lines, no three of which are concurrent, are said to form a complete quadrilateral, of which they are the sides. Their six intersections are called the vertices. Two vertices, not on the same side, are defined as opposite. A line connecting two opposite vertices is called a diagonal. The three diagonals form the diagonal triangle.

Definition] Four coplanar points, no three of which are collinear, are said to form a complete quadrangle, of which they are the vertices. The six lines connecting them are the sides. Two sides, not through the same vertex, are said to be opposite. The three intersections of pairs of opposite sides are called diagonal points, forming the diagonal triangle.

At this point I must point out a difficulty which never occurred to von Staudt. How do we know that these figures exist anyway? How do we know that the three diagonals of a complete quadrilateral are not concurrent? or that the diagonal points of a complete quadrangle are not collinear? As soon as one draws the figure, the suggestion of either of these possible disasters appears preposterous, but that is not mathematics. The difficulty was first cleared up, as far as I know, in Enriques (q.v.), p. 360. Here are two other definitions of von Staudt's.

Definition] Four collinear points, of which two are a pair of opposite vertices of a complete quadrilateral and the other two are the intersections of their diagonal with the other two diagonals, are called a harmonic set.

Definition] Four concurrent coplanar lines, of which two are a pair of opposite sides of a complete quadrangle, and the other two are the lines joining their diagonal point with the other two diagonal points, are said to form a harmonic set.

These definitions need elaborate justification. First we have Desargues's two-triangle theorem (p. 45).

Desargues's Two-triangle Theorem 16] *If two triangles be so situated that the lines connecting corresponding vertices are concurrent, the intersections of corresponding sides are collinear, and conversely.*

It is to be noted that this theorem is equally true whether the two are in the same plane or in different planes. As a matter of fact, it is not possible to prove the theorem for the plane without either making some non-projective assumptions or else presupposing a third dimension. Thus, it is possible to construct a plane geometry where the theorem is not true. From this theorem comes one which tells us that if two complete quadrangles are so placed that five sides of the one meet five sides of the other in collinear points, the sixth pair meet in a point of the same line. From these two theorems we may deduce the uniqueness of the construction for a fourth member of a harmonic set when three are known, the symmetry in the roles of the two pairs in a harmonic set, and the fact that four harmonic lines will always meet a transversal in four harmonic points. And now von Staudt makes a most original definition. Recalling Steiner's definition of the range of collinear points, the pencil of concurrent coplanar lines, and the axial pencil of coaxal planes, as fundamental one-dimensional forms, we have:

Definition] Two fundamental one-dimensional forms are said to be projective if they are in one-to-one correspondence, and if harmonic separation in the one corresponds to harmonic separation in the other.

It is clear from this remarkable definition that figures which are homographic in the sense of Chasles, or projective in the sense of Steiner, are also projective in the sense of von Staudt; but how about the converse? It was beyond the strength of von Staudt to prove this,†

† Von Staudt[1], p. 50.

for he had no real way to handle continuity. The theorem that a one-to-one correspondence with correspondence of harmonic separation is a Steiner projective correspondence is, however, true, that is, in the real domain. The following proof is from Darboux[1]. Let us assume that we have a projective correspondence in the von Staudt sense which leaves invariant three points of a line. We wish to show that every point of the line is invariant. We assume

$$x' = f(x), \qquad 0 = f(0), \qquad 1 = f(1), \qquad \infty = f(\infty).$$

Now we assume as an axiom that separating pairs of points are carried by projection into separating pairs of points, and two pairs of points of a line are non-separating when, and only when, they are harmonically separated by a third pair. On our line a point is between two others if it is separated from infinity by them, and this relation of betweenness will be maintained by the present transformation, and so finally our transformation is a continuous one, and f is a continuous function. Since $0, x, 2x, \infty$ are a harmonic set

$$f(2x) = 2f(x), \qquad f(\tfrac{1}{2}x) = \tfrac{1}{2}f(x)$$

since $a, b, \tfrac{1}{2}(a+b), \infty$ are harmonic

$$f(a+b) = f(a)+f(b),$$
$$f(rx) = rf(x),$$

when r is rational. But since the function is continuous, this relation is always true. Hence

$$f(x) = f(1x) = f(x1) = xf(1) = x.$$

Our transformation is the identical one, which is what we wanted to show. It is interesting to speculate as to what happens in the complex domain. It is not hard to show that as a result of our original definition

$$f(xy) = f(x)f(y).$$

The question then arises as to whether, in the complex domain, the equations

$$f(x+y) = f(x)+f(y); \qquad f(xy) = f(x)f(y); \qquad f(0) = 0;$$
$$f(1) = 1; \qquad f(\infty) = \infty$$

require the transformation to be either the identity or the exchange of conjugate imaginaries. I have been told that such is not the case, but have seen no proof. It is, however, true that a point-to-point transformation of the real projective plane, which carries collinear points into collinear points, is a linear transformation, in terms of homogeneous Cartesian coordinates. This comes from the fact that it is projective under von Staudt's definition.

It is high time to return to von Staudt. Provided with this definition, he shows that a projective transformation is uniquely determined by the fate of three points, though his proof is faulty, for the reason given above. If in such a transformation of a one-dimensional form into itself one pair correspond interchangeably, the same is true of every pair, and we have an involution of Desargues. It appears that there are two types of involutions. In the hyperbolic type each pair are harmonically separated by the two self-corresponding members; each element and its mate trace the form in opposite senses. In the elliptic form there are no self-corresponding elements; each element and its mate trace the form in the same sense.

And so, at long last, he is in a position to move into two dimensions. He gives in detail the theory of projective transformations of the plane, point to point and line to line. Corresponding to these so-called *collineations,* there are *correlations,* one-to-one transformations of point to line, collinear points to concurrent lines. A complete quadrilateral goes into a complete quadrangle; harmonic separation is invariant. A transformation of this sort is called a polarity if the result of performing it twice is the identity. Such a transformation will be completely determined by a self-conjugate triangle, as well as one pole and polar. And now for the conics. Suppose that we have a plane polarity, where a single point A lies on the corresponding line. Take any other line through A. The polar system in the plane sets up an involution on this line, and as it has a self-corresponding element, there is another such, and so one other point of the line lies on the corresponding line in the polarity. We have, thus, a curve, the locus of points which lie on the corresponding lines in the polarity, and this curve is defined as a conic. von Staudt is unable to show that it is a continuous curve, but it is evident that a line which passes through the corresponding point does not meet the curve again.

Let us now pause to note that we have swung through a complete circle, from Desargues and Poncelet who started with a conic and defined a polar system, to von Staudt, who starts with a polar system and reaches a conic. His method has the advantage that it is based on a minimum of assumptions, and can be extended at once to three dimensions, as we shall see in a subsequent chapter.

von Staudt is not able to say much about his conics until he has developed one or two fundamental theorems. Let A, B, C be three points of a conic, the tangents at A and B meeting in H. We take a range of points on AC and the range, projective therewith, where their polars meet BC. C will be a self-corresponding point in this projectivity; hence the lines connecting corresponding points will pass through a fixed point, which we find to be H by taking two special cases. Now turn things about, taking a line k through H. If we take pairs of conjugate points thereon, and connect them with A and B these lines will meet in a variable point C of the conic. If, therefore, a point move on a conic, it will determine projective pencils at any two points of the conic. Now suppose, conversely, that we have

$$A(X \ldots) \barwedge B(X \ldots),$$

where AB does not correspond to itself. Let AB correspond to b through B and BA correspond to a through A. Let a, b meet in H, while G, K are a pair of points harmonically separated by A and B. Finally, let HG meet AC in P and BC in Q, where AC, BC are a corresponding pair. We may set up a polar system where GHK is a self conjugate triangle, and P corresponds to QK. This will give a conic touching a at A and b at B and passing through C and this will determine a projective relation between the pencils at A and B identical with the given one. Here we have the Chasles-Steiner Theorem 14, which enables us to do all that Steiner did with regard to conics. Here are five of von Staudt's theorems dealing with conics. I am not sure whether he was the original discoverer.

Theorem 17] *Given two conics lying in different planes but with two common points, two quadric cones pass through them.*

I cannot believe that this was von Staudt's invention. His proof may be condensed to this. Let the two conics be c_1^2, c_2^2, the two points H, K. The tangent planes to the two curves at these points shall meet in a line m, which cuts the plane of c_1^2 in P_1 and that of c_2^2 in P_2. Let an arbitrary plane through m meet c_1^2 in $A_1 B_1$ and c_2^2 in $A_2 B_2$, while it meets HK in E. The lines $P_1 P_2, A_1 A_2, B_1 B_2$ are concurrent in a point V, whence the conic c_1^2 is projected on the plane of c_2^2 in a conic which passes through A_2 and touches c_2^2 at H and K, i.e. into the conic c_2^2 itself. A second projection comes from the intersection of $A_1 B_2, A_2 B_1$.

Theorem 18] *If two complete quadrangles have the same diagonal points, they either have a pair of common sides, or their eight vertices lie on a conic.*

If a vertex of one quadrangle lie on a side of the other, another vertex must lie on that side, and the two other vertices on the opposite side, otherwise the two could not have the same diagonal triangle. If no vertex of one lie on a side of the other, a conic through all four vertices of the one, and one vertex of the other, will pass through all four vertices of the other.

Theorem 19] *If two complete quadrilaterals have the same diagonal triangle, they either share two sides or their eight sides touch a conic.*

Suppose, now, we have two conics which share four common points.

We easily find by a limiting case of Brianchon's theorem that the diagonal triangle of the quadrangle of the points is that of the quadrilateral of tangents to either conic at these points.

Theorem 20] *If two conics intersect in four points, the eight tangents at these points touch a conic.*

This is called Salmon's conic. We shall meet it in a subsequent chapter.

Theorem 21] *If two conics have four common tangents, the eight points of contact lie on a conic.*

von Staudt made two other really notable contributions to projective geometry in von Staudt[2] which I shall merely sketch. I said that he noted the inconsistency arising from the fact that, whereas cross ratios are projectively invariant, they are based upon distances which are not invariant projectively. He set about remedying this by devising a projective basis for cross ratios. The distance of two points is a cross ratio which they, as a pair, make with a point at a unit's distance from one and the infinite point as another pair. We measure distances by laying off successive unit lengths, and this is a process of finding successive harmonic conjugates. Harmonic separation is defined by means of the complete quadrilateral. Hence we may define a rational cross ratio by a finite succession of harmonic constructions, just as we define a rational distance by a finite succession of laying down a unit. Irrational cross ratios are defined by a limiting process analogous to that involved in defining irrational distances.

Again, we saw how Poncelet, with his supplementaries and ideal chords endeavoured, not too successfully, to find something purely geometrical to replace the algebraist's use of complex numbers. von Staudt is very bold here. He defines an elliptic point involution, with a specified sense of description, as a complex point; the same involution, with the opposite sense, is defined as the conjugate point. There are corresponding definitions for complex lines and planes, and then he proves at great length how all the theorems of projection and intersection which hold in the real domain hold in the imaginary one also.

A strikingly original and profound geometer.

§ 6. Linear systems.

The Greeks, as we have seen, discovered a multitude of theorems concerning individual conics. They seldom considered more than one conic at a time, except to show that there could not be more than four intersections, or when it was a question of similar conics. Desargues's involution theorem leads to the study of conics through four points, or the limits of such systems. Now a system of this sort, algebraically considered, has the property that if we know the equations of two members, those of all the others are linearly dependent on them. These considerations lead us naturally, as we shall see in a subsequent chapter, to the study of systems of conics whose equations are linearly dependent on two or more than two. This amounts to saying that the coefficients are subjected to a certain number of homogeneous linear conditions. The algebraic approach is certainly the natural one here, but there is a certain amount of synthetic theory which fits naturally in with what we have given in the present chapter. I do not know what geometer first had the idea of studying such linear systems synthetically; I suspect Steiner. The earliest published article seems to be Steiner[4]. What follows is more or less a condensation of Reye[1], Part I, pp. 220–48.

Suppose that we have two triangles ABC, $A'B'C'$ which are self-conjugate with regard to a conic:

$$A(BCB'C') \barwedge A'(BCB'C').$$

We have, then, by Theorems 12 and 15:

Theorem 22] *If two triangles be self-conjugate with regard to a conic, their vertices lie on a conic, and their sides touch a conic.*

Suppose, on the other hand, that the sides of the triangle $A'B'C'$ are the polars of the vertices of the triangle ABC, and vice versa. The two triangles are conjugate with regard to a conic.

Let BC meet $B'C'$ in $\bar{A}$:

$$A(BC\bar{A}A') \barwedge A'(C'B'A\bar{A}) \barwedge A'(B'C'\bar{A}A).$$

This gives us, by Desargues's Two-triangle Theorem 16:

Theorem 23] *If two triangles be mutually conjugate with regard to a conic, they are Desargues triangles.*

Suppose, next, that we have a point conic c_1^2 and a line conic γ_2^2 so related that there is a triangle circumscribed to γ_2^2 which is self-conjugate with regard to c_1^2. Let c_2^2 be the polar reciprocal of γ_2^2 with regard to c_1^2, so that there is a triangle inscribed in c_2^2 which is self-conjugate with regard to c_1^2. Let A be any point of c_2^2, B an intersection of c_2^2 with the polar of A with regard to c_1^2, and C the pole of AB. Then by Theorem 22 the triangle ABC and the original triangle have their vertices on a conic, that is to say, C is a point of c_2^2. We have thus an infinite number of triangles inscribed in c_2^2 which are self-conjugate with regard to c_1^2 and so an infinite number of triangles circumscribed to γ_2^2 which are self-conjugate with regard to c_1^2.

But we may go farther. Let t be a common tangent to c_1^2 and γ_2^2, P_1, P_2 its points of contact. Then P_2 is the pole with regard to c_1^2 of the other tangent to γ_2^2 from P_1. Let P_3 be the point of contact of this last tangent with γ_2^2. P_2P_3 shall meet c_1^2 in R and S. These points are harmonically separated by P_2 and P_3 so that $P_1\,RS$ is a triangle, inscribed in c_1^2 which is self-conjugate with regard to γ_2^2. By reasoning like that in the last paragraph there will be an infinite number of such triangles.

Theorem 24] *If a point conic and a line conic be so situated that there is a triangle circumscribed to the line conic which is self-conjugate with regard to the point conic, then there are an infinite number of such triangles, one side being an arbitrary tangent to the line conic. At the same time, there are an infinite number of triangles inscribed in the point conic, which are self-conjugate with regard to the line conic, one vertex being arbitrary on the point conic.*

Two conics having this relation are said to be 'apolar'. The reader can easily find what happens when one or the other is degenerate.

Suppose that two pairs of opposite sides of a complete quadrangle are conjugate with regard to a conic. The polar of a vertex will be cut in the same involution by the pairs of opposite sides, according to Desargues's involution theorem, and by pairs of points conjugate with regard to the conic.

Theorem 25] *If two pairs of sides of a complete quadrangle be conjugate with regard to a conic, the third pair are conjugate also.*

Hesse's Theorem 26] *If two pairs of vertices of a complete quadrilateral be conjugate with regard to a conic, the third pair are conjugate also.*

In such a case we shall say that the quadrangle or quadrilateral and conic are 'polar'. The reader can easily see what happens in limiting cases.

Let A, B, C be vertices of a triangle which is not self-conjugate with regard to a conic, D the point of concurrence of the lines AA', BB', CC' where $A'B'C'$ is the conjugate triangle (Theorem 23). Then the quadrangles $ABCD$, $A'B'C'D$ are polar. The vertices of a self-conjugate triangle and any point not on one side will form a polar quadrangle. Conversely, every polar quadrangle can be formed in one of these two ways. If we have $ABCD$, a polar quadrangle where ABC is not self-conjugate, the polar of A will meet any conic through $ABCD$ in two points of the involution given by the quadrangle. These two points and A will be the vertices of a triangle which is self-conjugate with regard to the original conic.

Theorem 27] *If a complete quadrangle be polar with regard to a line conic, every point conic through its vertices is apolar to the given line conic.*

Suppose that we have two point conics, meeting in $ABCD$, which are apolar to the same line conic. If any three of the four points give a self-conjugate triangle, the quadrangle is polar. If not, the polar of *A* with regard to the line conic will meet each point conic in a pair of points conjugate with regard to the line conic. Hence, by Desargues it will meet each pair of opposite sides of the quadrangle in conjugate points, or the quadrangle is polar.

Theorem 28] *If two conics intersecting in four points be apolar to a line conic, the quadrangle of the points is polar.*

Suppose that *ABCD*, *ABC'D'* are the vertices of two polar quadrangles. If the triangle *ABC* be not self-conjugate, the conics *ABCDD'*, *ABCC'D'* when distinct are apolar to the line conic, so that *ABCD'* is a polar quadrangle, but *D* is the only point that completes a polar quadrangle with *ABC*.

Theorem 29] *If two quadrangles polar to the same line conic have two common vertices, and these two do not join one of the others to make a self-conjugate triangle, the six points lie on a conic.*

We have now sketched three linear systems of point conics: the four-parameter system of all conics apolar to one line conic, the three-parameter system of conics apolar to two (these are usually the conics with a common polar quadrilateral), and the one-parameter system of conics through four points, or the limit of such a system. There remains the difficult but interesting two-parameter linear net of conics apolar to three independent conics, say $\gamma_1^2, \gamma_2^2, \gamma_3^2$. We assume that these are not tangent to four lines, nor the limit of such conics; they are linearly independent in line coordinates. If a line rotate about a point *P*, its poles with regard to these three trace three projective linear ranges. The lines connecting corresponding points on two of the ranges will envelop a conic tangent to the bases of the ranges, as we see by Theorem 13. We have three such conics, and they have three common tangents, each containing the three poles of a line through *P*. There are, thus, three lines through *P* whose poles with regard to the three conics are collinear. Let l_1, l_2 be two of these lines and m_1, m_2 meeting in *Q* be the two lines conjugate to them with regard to all three conics. Consider the quadrangle whose vertices are *P*, *Q*, $l_1 m_1$, $l_2 m_2$. Two pairs of opposite sides are conjugate with regard to all three conics; hence by Theorem 25 the third pair are also. It appears thus that *PQ* is the third line through *P* with three collinear poles, that is to say, the three lines through *P* and the three containing their triads of poles are sides of a quadrangle which is polar with regard to all three given conics. Hence there are a pencil of conics through them apolar to the three.

Theorem 30] *The point conics apolar to three linearly independent line conics form a two-parameter system. A pencil of these will pass through an arbitrary point in the plane.*

The lines whose poles with regard to γ_1^2, γ_2^2, γ_3^2 are collinear, envelop a curve of the third class. Its line equation is obtained by equating to zero the Jacobian of the three polynomials in line coordinates which give the original three-line conics. In the same way the points whose polars with regard to three linearly independent point conics are concurrent generate a curve of the third order; it will be the locus of the intersections of line-pairs in the system linearly dependent on the original three. An infinite number of conics apolar to all three will touch an arbitrary line in the plane, and three other lines.

A two-parameter system such as is described in Theorem 29 is called a two-parameter net. We shall see in a later chapter that it consists in the first polars of all points in the plane with regard to a given cubic curve. Clearly we must postpone this till we take up the algebraic treatment of apolarity.

CHAPTER V

THE DEVELOPMENT OF THE ALGEBRAIC TREATMENT

§ 1. Fermat, Descartes, and Newton.

It is commonly believed that algebraic geometry was invented by René Descartes—'Proles sine matre creata' was Chasles's picturesque statement. Other writers have given Fermat credit for earlier discovery. I see no reason to acknowledge this priority, but T think we are safe in conceding him independence.† Moreover, as I have insisted throughout, the Greek method of handling the conics is essentially algebraic, disguised in geometrical form. Consequently, I will not say that either Fermat or Descartes absolutely originated the algebraic method of handling geometrical questions, great as was the importance of the work of both.

Fermat's contribution is found mostly in his treatise *Ad locos planos et solidos isagoge*, which is contained in vol. i of Fermat (q.v.). I shall follow Tannery's translation in the third volume of the same work. The advantage here lies not only in the greater facility which many of us have in reading French as compared with Latin, but also in the greater ease of interpreting equations when they are put in modern symbolism. Thus Fermat writes

$$A \text{ quad. aequabitur } E \text{ in } D.\mathrm{b}+D \text{ pl.}$$

Tannery interprets this $\quad a^2 = 2ed+d^2.$

I do not understand the distinction between quad. and pl. The b. after D stands for bis, the coefficient 2.

Fermat's own statement of the fundamental method of analytic geometry is found on p. 91 of the first volume:

'Quoties in ultima aequalitate duae quantitates ignotae reperiuntur, fit locus loco et terminus alterius ex illis describit lineam rectam aut curvam. Linea recta unica et simplex est, curvae infinitae, circulus, parabola, hyperbole, ellipsis, etc. Quoties quantitatis ignotae terminus describit lineam rectam aut circulum, fit locus planus; at quando describit parabolen hyperbolen aut ellipsin, fit locus solidus; si alias curvas dicitur locus linearis'.

This is essentially a definition of the terms planar, solid, or linear (that is, curvilinear) locus. This idea is developed by showing how a simple equation leads to a familiar curve. The coordinates are not allowed to take negative values, they are looked upon as essentially the

† Coolidge², p. 122.

lengths of certain lines. The abscissa is measured from the origin along a fixed line, the ordinate from the end of the abscissa in a given direction, which need not by any means be perpendicular to the axis of abscissae. The main problem is to find what sort of a locus is determined by an equation of the first or second order, the essential device being to change coordinates till something familiar appears. Let us take some examples:

$$z^{II} - da = be.$$

The exponent II indicates that we have an area. Vowels always indicate unknown quantities, consonants known ones—not a bad plan. He is obsessed with the idea, which Descartes discarded, that equations must be homogeneous. Equations of the first degree are supposed to involve lengths, quadratic ones involve areas, cubic ones volumes, etc. To solve the equation above, find r so that

$$z^{II} = dr, \qquad \frac{b}{d} = \frac{r-a}{e}.$$

The left-hand side is known, the locus is a line through the point $(r, 0)$ in a known direction. Suppose next that we have

$$d^{II} + ae = ra + se.$$

We transform this to

$$(a-s)(r-e) = d^{II} - rs.$$

This is equivalent to $a'e' = d^{II} - rs,$

and this is a hyperbola with the asymptotes as axes. The most difficult case which he handles is

$$b^2 - 2a^2 = 2ae + e^2,$$
$$b^2 = a^2 + (a+e)^2.$$

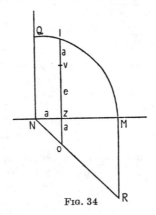

Fig. 34

Now take $NM = b$, $NZ = a$.

Draw a circle with N as centre, NM as radius.

$$ZI^2 = b^2 - a^2,$$

$$ZV = e; \quad VI = OZ = a, \quad VO = a+e; \quad \angle RNM = 45°.$$

$$VO^2 = (a+e)^2 = b^2 - a^2$$
$$= MN^2 - NZ^2$$
$$= \frac{MN^2}{NR^2}(NR^2 - NO^2).$$

This shows that V traces an ellipse, of which NQ and NR are conjugate semi-diameters. Fermat rightly remarks that any equation of the second degree may be attacked by similar methods; or we may say, broadly speaking, that he shows that any quadratic equation represents a conic, a pair of lines or a line counted twice—no mean achievement. He also studied the solution of the cubic and quartic equation, by reducing it to the search for the intersection of two conics. He recognized that an equation involving three variables could be interpreted to represent a surface, but did not bother to follow up this fruitful idea.

The other reputed inventor of analytic geometry was René Descartes, but he was only incidentally interested in the conic sections. His technique is far superior to Fermat's, for several reasons. To begin with, he introduces exponents, although, strangely enough, he and his successors down to the end of the eighteenth century continued to write square terms in the form xx. He banishes once for all the idea that there are different kinds of quantities, linear, square, solid, etc., and the resulting superstition that equations must be homogeneous. What he is interested in is numbers. The number x^2 or xx as he write it, is simply the fourth term in the continued proportion

$$1 : x : : x : xx,$$

while $\sqrt{x}$ is the mean proportional between 1 and x.

Descartes also takes the very radical step of attacking the Greek tradition that the only permissible instruments for geometrical constructions are the compass and ungraded ruler. He advocates the use of various kinds of link works, and other instruments. He even goes so far as to allow the use of moving curves, although it is not clear to me whether he would allow us to use curved disks which roll upon one another. He did not assume that his axes were rectangular. His closest contact with the conics comes in his solution of the famous four-line problem. His work, somewhat abbreviated, is about like this. If a point have the coordinates (x, y), its distance, in a given direction from a given line, is a constant multiple of the difference between its ordinate and that of the point on the line having the same abscissa, so that we can express this distance in the form

$$px+qy+r.$$

In the four-line problem he takes the intersection of two of the given lines as the origin, and one of the four distances as y. This gives the equation of the locus in the form†

$$y^2 = 2my - \frac{2n}{z}xy + \frac{bcfg(lx-x^2)}{ez^3-cgz^2}.$$

By introducing new constants this can be changed to

$$y = m - \frac{n}{z}x + \sqrt{\left(m^2+ox+\frac{p}{m}x^2\right)}.$$

The small o does not mean zero. The point (x, y) shall be C,

$$(x, m) = K \qquad (0, m) = I, \qquad \left(x, m-\frac{n}{z}x\right) = L, \qquad \frac{LK}{IK} = \frac{n}{z}.$$

L traces a fixed line through I,

$$LC = \sqrt{\left(m^2+ox+\frac{p}{m}x^2\right)}.$$

LI bears a fixed ratio to x,

$$LC^2 = n+sLI+tLI^2.$$

This shows that C traces a conic. Descartes discusses in great detail the various cases which can arise.

Descartes was also interested in a question which was occupying the attention of mathematicians more and more in his time, and for some decades afterwards, that of drawing tangents to given curves. His idea is that a tangent is perpendicular to a normal, and a normal is the

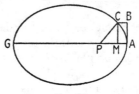

FIG. 35

radius of a circle, two of whose intersections with the given curve fall together. Let us try this out in the case of an ellipse. In Fig. 35 let

$$CB = MA = y; \qquad CM = AB = x; \qquad PC = s = \text{normal},$$
$$PA = v, \qquad PM = v-y.$$

† Descartes[1], p. 22.

Let the ellipse be
$$x^2 - ry + \frac{r}{q}y^2 = 0.$$
$$x^2 + (v-y)^2 = s^2,$$
$$y^2 + \frac{q}{q-r}[(r-2v)y + (v^2 - s^2)] = 0.$$

This equation has equal roots and so must be equivalent to
$$y^2 - 2ey + e^2.$$

Eliminating e we have v in terms of y, q, r, clumsy enough.

Another writer whom I should mention in this connexion is John Wallis, whose *Sectiones conicae* in Wallis (q.v.) apparently was an important book. For this I can see no obvious reason. The first half is devoted to the method of indivisibles, published some twenty years earlier by Cavalieri, and a study of the conics as sections of a cone. In the second part, which is occupied by what he calls the direct study of the curves 'absolute consideratae', he sets out the Greek form of the equations in more modern algebraic terms. I cannot see in this any great advance on his predecessors.

I pointed out in the last chapter, p. 43, that Newton was deeply interested in the conic sections, and showed some results he obtained by synthetic methods. But his contributions to the algebraic theory of the surfaces were equally important. He was the first writer to allow the coordinates to take negative values. He laid the lines for further progress in the rectification and quadrature of curves. A very significant advance appeared in his use of the method of undetermined coefficients. It is true that Descartes also describes this in general terms, for he writes: 'Mais je veux bien en passant vous avertir que l'invention de supposer deux équations de même forme pour comparer tous les termes de l'une à ceux de l'autre, et aussi faire naître plusieurs d'une seule dont vous avez ici un exemple, peut servir à une infinité d'autres problèmes.' But Descartes made no particular use of this method, while Newton did. For instance, we have in Newton[2], p. 210, the problem of passing a parabola through four given points. He says that every parabola has an equation of the form
$$y = e + fx \pm \sqrt{(gg + hx)},$$
and then finds the coefficients to fit. But of course his greatest contribution is in the application of the differential calculus to problems of involving tangents. He even uses partial differentiation for this purpose. The equation of the curve being
$$F(x, y) = 0,$$
the slope of the tangent is $\quad \dfrac{\dot{y}}{\dot{x}} = -\dfrac{F_x}{F_y}.$

§ 2. The immediate successors.

It was natural that the work of Descartes should call to life a certain number of expositors. Frequently their writings tended to muddy the waters rather than to clear them. In Descartes[2] we find quite a series of commentators, including Schooten, De Beaune, and De Witt (q.v.). The second part of this last work seems to me decidedly inferior to the first, which we described in the last chapter, pp. 38 ff. He gives a good deal of attention to the general equation of the second order, seeking to determine the meaning of the various coefficients. His notation is at times baffling. He writes

$$yy \infty dx.ff$$

where we should write

$$y^2 = dx \pm f^2.$$

He finds the equation of the ellipse from the two-focus definition, squaring twice. Like the Greeks, he writes the equation with the origin at the end of the major axis. He gives the usual geometrical proof that the tangent bisects the exterior angle between the focal radii, a much easier proof than that of Apollonius iii. 48. I wish I knew whether this was original with him. A very real advance in elegance comes with La Hire[2]. I have already mentioned that we are indebted to him for pointing out that the two coordinates play essentially the same role; he also clarified Fermat's idea that an equation in three variables represents a surface. The first writer who put the algebraic study of the conics on anything which we could call a modern basis was the Marquis de l'Hospital, to whom we must pay a good deal of attention. We find in Ball (q.v.), p. 380: 'He wrote a treatise on analytical conics which was published in 1707, and for nearly a century was deemed a standard work on the subject.' He combined synthetic and analytic methods most happily.

L'Hospital (q.v.) begins with the parabola defined by the focus-directrix property, and early establishes the standard equation

$$y^2 = px.$$

It is easy to see that any line through the origin, except the Y-axis, will meet the curve again. If we take a point (x, y) on the curve and connect it with $(-x, 0)$ by a line, taking this as a Y'-axis, while the line through (x, y) parallel to the X-axis is taken as a X'-axis, we quickly find the new equation

$$y'^2 = qx'.$$

As this is identical in form with the last, we see that the line through (x, y), $(-x, 0)$ is tangent to the curve. We have also immediately the fact that a tangent bisects the exterior angle between a focal radius and a parallel to the axis.

The ellipse is defined by the two-focus property. Instead of introducing two radicals, l'Hospital (pp. 19 ff.) proceeds in the following ingenious fashion. Let the length of the major axis, that is to say, the sum of the two focal radii, be $2t$. The foci shall be $f = (m, 0)$, $F = (-m, 0)$.

$$Mf^2 = (x-m)^2+y^2, \qquad MF^2 = (x+m)^2+y^2.$$

$$MF^2-Mf^2 = (MF+Mf)(MF-Mf) = 2t \cdot \frac{2mx}{t}.$$

$$\left(t+\frac{mx}{t}\right)^2 = (m+x)^2+y^2.$$

He reduces this to the standard form

$$y^2 = c^2 - \frac{c^2x^2}{t^2}.$$

L'Hospital next passes to the study of conjugate diameters. Through (x, y) draw a line to $(t^2/x, 0)$ which is the harmonic conjugate, with regard to the ends of the axis, of the foot of the ordinate. The diameter parallel to this is defined as conjugate to that through (x, y), although he has not shown that the relation between the two is symmetrical. He then shows that the equation of the curve when any pair of conjugate diameters are taken as axes has the same general form, involving only the squared terms and the constant. This is done by straight algebraic manipulation. This shows that the line whose description I have just given is a tangent—rather a clumsy way to reach this result. L'Hospital was a pupil of Johann Bernoulli, and was active in introducing the methods of the infinitesimal calculus, but he kept all that in another part of his brain and made no application to the conics. On p. 35 we find the pretty theorem that if through a point A on an ellipse we draw a tangent meeting a pair of conjugate diameters in D and E, $DA.AE = OB^2$ where B is the end of the diameter conjugate to that through A. His proof is clumsy, but he makes use of it to determine the axes of an ellipse, when we know a pair of conjugate diameters in position and length.

The hyperbola is taken up first, much as is the ellipse; the standard equation, except for the exponents, is written

$$y^2 = \frac{c^2x^2}{t^2} - c^2.$$

He is a little vague as to whether the two branches should be counted as part of the same curve or not. The lines

$$y = \frac{cx}{t}, \qquad y = -\frac{cx}{t}$$

are defined as asymptotes, and their properties easily found.

The chapter specially devoted to the hyperbola is followed by one where the three conics are treated together. We find some pretty problems. For instance, p. 95, to draw two tangents to a central conic from an exterior point. Draw a diameter through the point, and find the harmonic conjugate of the point with regard to the ends of the diameter. Through here draw a line parallel to the conjugate diameter: this will give the points of contact. Or again, given a central conic, to find a pair of conjugate diameters making a given angle. We draw any diameter, and construct thereon two circular arcs in which the given angle is inscribed. The construction then is easy, because the lines connecting any point of a central conic with the ends of a diameter are parallel to conjugate diameters. On p. 103 we find an interesting method for describing an ellipse. Let us connect the point $(-r, -2b/r)$ with the origin, and the point $(0, r)$ with $(2a, 0)$. Eliminating the variable r from the equations of these lines we have

$$y^2 = \frac{b^2}{a^2} x(2a-x),$$

the equation of an ellipse in Greek form. What we have here are two lines, one rotating around the origin and the other around $(2a, 0)$, and they trace projective pencils, so that we have a special case of the Chasles-Steiner theorem of which we said so much in the last chapter.

We find a most interesting theorem on p. 137. Let AA' and BB' be two parallel chords of a conic. The segments of the curve outside the chords AB and $A'B'$ have the same area. For the line connecting M the middle point of AA' with N the middle point of BB' will be the conjugate diameter, and it goes through the intersection of AB' and $A'B$. Now let a line parallel to the chords meet AB in H, $A'B'$ in H', and MN on O, while it meets the curve in K, K'.

$$HO = OH'; \qquad KO = OK'; \qquad KH = H'K'.$$

Hence, by the principles of the calculus the two segments are equal. Another interesting idea appears on p. 147, where he explains the idea of logarithms by studying the area between a hyperbola and its asymptotes.

I am not surprised that L'Hospital set the standard for many years to come in exposition of the theory, although certain writers made improvements in detail. Among these I should cite Guisnée (q.v.), about whom all I can discover is that he died in 1718 after being Professeur Royal de Mathématiques et Ingénieur Ordinaire du Roy. He wrote an excellent book which I think, with slight alterations, would be perfectly acceptable to-day.

§ 3. Leonhard Euler.

I cannot say that this universal genius in mathematics seems to have contributed greatly to our knowledge of the conics, but his approach was different from that of his predecessors, and for that reason we should pay him some attention. He was not, like L'Hospital, intent on writing a good book about particular curves; he was writing about the applications of the calculus in general, and applications to curves in particular. A conic was a curve whose Cartesian equation was quadratic. Yet strangely enough, when he comes to these particular curves, he leaves the calculus aside. His general equation is[†]

$$0 = \alpha + \beta x + \gamma y + \delta xx + \epsilon xy + \zeta yy,$$

$$yy + \frac{\epsilon x + \gamma}{\zeta} y + \frac{\delta xx + \beta x + \alpha}{\zeta} = 0.$$

If half the sum of the roots of this equation in y be $\bar{y}$

$$2\zeta\bar{y} + \epsilon x + \gamma - 0.$$

This equation represents a straight line, and is the locus of the middle points of chords parallel to the Y-axis. As the form of the equation is unaltered by any change of Cartesian axes, this shows that every such locus is a straight line. He eventually reduces his equation to the Greek form

$$yy = \frac{h}{k}(ax - xx).$$

Assuming the axes to be rectangular, he shows how to find the lengths of the diameters of a central conic. A clumsy calculation shows that, when

$$\epsilon\epsilon - 4\delta\zeta \neq 0,$$

every diameter goes through the point $\left(\dfrac{2\beta\zeta - \gamma\epsilon}{\epsilon\epsilon - 4\delta\zeta}, \dfrac{2\gamma\delta - \beta\epsilon}{\epsilon\epsilon - 4\delta\zeta}\right)$. The properties of diameters come next, and the canonical equations.

In the sixth chapter of Euler (q.v.), vol. ii, the three conics are treated in detail. The general equation is

$$yy = \alpha \mid \beta x \mid \gamma xx;$$

$\gamma = 0$ gives a parabola; $\gamma > 0$ a hyperbola; $\gamma < 0$ an ellipse. The ellipse

$$yy = \alpha x + \beta\gamma - \gamma xx$$

becomes

$$y^2 = \frac{b^2}{a^2}(a^2 - x^2);$$

$$\alpha = b^2, \qquad \gamma = \frac{b^2}{a^2}.$$

† Euler[1], vol. ii, p. 65; Euler[2], vol. ii, p. 40.

Focal radii $\qquad\qquad a \pm \dfrac{x\sqrt{(a^2-b^2)}}{a}.$

The tangent is found by harmonic separation on the axis.

In Euler[1], p. 70, we find what seems to be the erroneous statement that the foot of a perpendicular from a focus of a conic on a tangent lies on the tangent at the vertex; this is only true of the parabola. The fact that a tangent bisects the internal or external angle between focal radii is proved in a clumsy fashion. Conjugate diameters appear on p. 71 with the proof that the sum of the squares of the lengths of two conjugate semi-diameters of an ellipse is constant. We have also the pretty theorem that the line connecting a point of an ellipse with the end of the major axis is parallel to the line connecting an end of the minor axis with the end of the diameter conjugate to that through the given point.

The passage from the ellipse to the parabola is made in a process like this. I modernize the notation. We write the equation in Greek form

$$y^2 = \frac{b^2}{a^2} x(2a-x).$$

This may be written

$$y^2 = 2(1+e)dx - (1-e^2)x^2,$$

where e is the eccentricity and d the distance from focus to vertex. Now keep d constant and pass to the limiting case where $e = 1$,

$$y^2 = 4dx.$$

Reaching the parabola in this way we find that the tangent bisects the angle between a focal radius and a parallel to the axis, and the vertex is midway between the foot of an ordinate and the intersection of the tangent with the axis. We also find that the subnormal has a constant length.

The treatment of the hyperbola follows the same lines as that of the ellipse. We have the neat theorem that if the foci be F and G, and the tangent T meets the tangents at the vertices in V and v

$$TV . Tv = TF . TG.$$

As the distance from the centre to the intersection of the transverse axis with the tangent at (x, y) is a^2/x becomes infinite, this point becomes the centre

$$y^2 = \frac{b^2}{a^2}(x^2-a^2), \qquad \frac{y}{x} = \frac{b}{a}\sqrt{\left(1-\frac{a^2}{x^2}\right)}.$$

When x becomes infinite we find the limiting form of the tangent, that is to say, the asymptote $\qquad bx \pm ay = 0.$

If (x, y) is a point of a hyperbola, the line through it parallel to the asymptote meets the other asymptote in

$$x' = \frac{bx + ay}{2b}, \qquad y' = \frac{bx + ay}{2a}.$$

The distance of this latter point from the centre is

$$\frac{bx + ay}{2} \sqrt{\left(\frac{1}{a^2} + \frac{1}{b^2}\right)}.$$

The distance between the two points is

$$\frac{bx - ay}{2} \sqrt{\left(\frac{1}{a^2} + \frac{1}{b^2}\right)}.$$

The product of these two distances is

$$\frac{a^2 + b^2}{4}.$$

This is also the product of the distances to each asymptote, measured parallel to the other asymptote, 'Quae est proprietas primeria hyperbolae ad asymptotas relatae.'[†]

Clearly the product of the distances to these lines in any two given directions is constant. Thus if a line through M on the curve meet the asymptotes in Q and R

$$MQ \cdot MR = q^2,$$

where q is the distance parallel to QR to the point of contact from an asymptote.

The last theorem in the present chapter is this. If r be a point of an asymptote, and if a line through it in a given direction meet the curve in m and M,

$$rm \cdot rM = \text{const.}$$

Euler's proof is long and clumsy; a very easy one can be based on Newton's product theorem. I note in conclusion that Euler makes no mention of the directrix. In fact Pappus' focus-directrix theorem pretty much disappears from notice for centuries.

† Euler[1] (q.v.), p. 80.

CHAPTER VI

THE INTRODUCTION OF NEW ALGEBRAIC TECHNIQUES

§ 1. Abridged notation and linear dependence.

ANYONE who to-day reads the work of L'Hospital and Euler receives the impression that the algebraic study of the conics has been pushed about as far as it can go without the introduction of some new method of attack. Of course, there is no limit to the amount of complication which a malevolent person might introduce, but what would be the use? Theoretically the methods of these writers are sufficient to find, let us say, the Cartesian equation of a conic tangent to five given lines, but the details would be burdensome in the extreme. And while the algebraists seemed to be completely bogged down, the projective geometers Desargues, Pascal, Poncelet, Chasles, and Steiner were discovering a perfect wealth of beautiful theorems with astonishing ease. Clearly something drastic had to be done.

The first step in the new advance was taken by a 23-year-old 'élève ingénieur', Gabriel Lamé. He gives us his general idea in the introduction:†

'Cet ouvrage était projeté depuis longtemps, et devait être plus considérable . . . . Quant aux réflexions qu'il contient, j'avoue qu'elles m'ont été suggérées pour la plupart, par les problèmes que j'y ai fait entrer, tandis qu'au contraire, des réflexions générales auraient dû me conduire au choix des exemples. Il aurait fallu du temps, et beaucoup de talent pour faire disparaître l'apparence de cette inversion, je ne possédai ni l'un ni l'autre.'

One is naturally drawn to such a modest young geometer. It is also interesting to note, in passing, the characteristic Gallic turn of mind, which tries to deduce particular cases from accepted general principles, rather than to build general principles on observed particular facts. He gives on p. 12 a very profound piece of advice for every aspiring geometer:

'C'est presque toujours en faisant dépendre la solution d'un problème de celle d'un autre plus simple, et cette seconde d'une troisième et ainsi de suite, que l'on parvient à une question dont la réponse est évidente . . . . Il arrive souvent que le problème auquel on descend n'est qu'un cas particulier du problème à résoudre.'

Lamé's first idea is that often one does not care about the make-up

---

† Lamé[1], pp. v, vi.

of a polynomial; one needs it as a whole, and may replace it by a single letter. We find a good example on p. 28:

'J'essayerai de lever cette difficulté en m'appuyant sur ce principe évident: que si on combine les équations de deux lieux géométriques d'une manière quelconque, l'équation résultante exprime un troisième lieu géométrique sur lequel se trouve l'intersection des deux premiers.'

We have here a very loose statement of a very important principle, for the phrase to combine 'd'une manière quelconque' can mean almost anything. What Lamé means is to take a linear combination. If two loci be given by equating two polynomials to zero, a linear combination of them equated to zero will give a locus through all of their common points. So far very good. Unfortunately at this point he makes a statement which is also true, but for which he gives no sufficient reason, his logic is faulty:

'De ce que cette combinaison peut se faire d'une infinité de manières, je concluerai que si l'intersection de deux courbes, de deux surfaces, doit se trouver sur une troisième courbe, une troisième surface donnée, il doit exister une équation combinée de celles des deux premières courbes, des deux premières surfaces qui exprimera la troisième courbe, la troisième surface donnée.'†

Here he mixes necessary and sufficient conditions for fair. He assumes that as each of an infinite number of linear combinations of two polynomials when equated to zero gives a third locus through all points common to the loci obtained by equating the given polynomials to zero, then every locus through all of these points may be obtained in this way. The true answer is a good deal more complicated than this, when singular points and tangency appear.‡

Let us look at Lamé more closely. When will three lines

$$ax+by+c = 0, \qquad a'x+b'y+c' = 0, \qquad a''x+b''y+c'' = 0$$

be concurrent? Lamé assumes

$$a'' = am+a'm'; \qquad b'' = bm+b'm'; \qquad c'' = cm+c'm'.$$

Here is something more substantial.§ Through a fixed point pairs of lines are drawn meeting a conic. The four intersections are taken as vertices of a complete quadrangle, of which the given point is one diagonal point. What is the locus of the other diagonal points? Lamé writes the conic

$$y^2+px^2 = 2qx.$$

The given point shall be (α, β), a variable diagonal point (α', β'). Two lines through the first point shall be

$$(y-\beta)^2+2A(x-\alpha)(y-\beta)+B(x-\alpha)^2 = 0,$$

† Lamé[1], p. 28.
‡ See Nöther (q.v.) and Coolidge[3], pp. 29 and 244.   § Lamé[1], p. 45.

the corresponding pair of sides through the other point

$$(y-\beta')^2+2A'(x-\alpha')(y-\beta')+B'(x-\alpha')^2 = 0.$$

The equation of the given conic must be a linear combination of these two. This will require, as we learn after a long calculation (unless we assume that we know the answer),

$$\beta\beta'+p\alpha\alpha' = q(\alpha+\alpha'),$$

as this is linear in α' and β', the locus is a straight line. We note, also, that (α,β), (α',β') appear symmetrically. This is, of course, Desargues's construction of the polar which we saw on pp. 29, 30, the earliest analytic treatment I have seen.

A direct descendant of Lamé, in the order of ideas, is Bobillier, who unfortunately died at the early age of 35. We find some hint of abridged notation in Bobillier[1]. He jumps into the middle of things with no preliminary discussion. Let the sides of a triangle have the equations

$$A = 0, \qquad B = 0, \qquad C = 0.$$

A general circumscribed conic can be written

$$aBC+bCA+cAB = 0.$$

The straight line $\qquad bA+aB = 0$

meets the curve only at $A = B = 0$ and so is the tangent there. Take two such tangents

$$bA+aB = 0, \qquad cA+aC = 0.$$

Here is a linear combination of them which goes through the other vertex

$$\frac{B}{b}-\frac{C}{c} = 0.$$

The three such lines are linearly dependent. Hence the lines connecting the vertices of a triangle with the points of contact of an inscribed conic are concurrent. This is a limiting case of Brianchon's theorem. Dual to it we have the fact that the lines connecting the pairs of points of contact meet the opposite sides in three collinear points.

The writer returns to the conics in Bobillier[2]. Suppose that a circle and a conic intersect in four points which are vertices of a complete quadrilateral, the equations of whose sides are

$$A = 0, \qquad B = 0, \qquad A' = 0, \qquad B' = 0.$$

The conic will have an equation of the type

$$aAA'+bBB' = 0.$$

If we choose as rectangular axes the bisectors of the angles between

$$A = 0, \qquad A' = 0$$

the equation $AA' = 0$ will have no term in xy. Neither will the equation of the circle, which will be of the form

$$\alpha AA' + \beta BB' = 0.$$

Hence $BB' = 0$ lacks a term in xy so that all conics through the four points lack this term for their equations, or all have the same directions for their principal axes. This gives us:

Theorem 1] *All conics through four concyclic points have the same directions for their principal axes. These will be the directions of the bisectors of the angle between each pair of opposite sides of a complete quadrilateral, four of whose vertices are the given points.*

This result may be obtained with equal case from Desargues's involution theorem, applied to the infinite line. We get immediately:

Theorem 2] *The circles through two points of a central conic meet it in pairs of points whose joining line has a fixed direction.*

Bobillier points out that this theorem is really due to Plücker[1] and used there to give a very easy construction for the osculating circle at a point A. First pass a circle tangent at A and find B, C where it meets the conic again. Through A draw a line parallel to BC and let it meet the conic at D. The circle tangent at A passing through D is the desired circle.

I return to the conic

$$aAA' + bBB' = 0$$

and consider the pair of lines

$$cA - bB = 0, \qquad cB' + aA' = 0$$

and the pair $\qquad c'A - bB' = 0, \qquad c'B + aA = 0.$

If we eliminate c or c' we see that the lines of each pair meet in a point of the conic. We have, thus, six points of the conic, the line†

$$cc'A + abA' = 0$$

is a linear combination of each of the pairs

$$A = 0, \quad A' = 0; \qquad cA - bB = 0, \quad c'B + aA = 0;$$
$$cB' + aA' = 0, \quad c'A - bB' = 0.$$

It is the Pascal line of the hexagon.

While I am on Pascal, I will give two other proofs, also based on linear dependence. The first is from Salmon (q.v.), p. 245. Let the equations of the six sides of the hexagon, taken in order, be

$$a = 0, \quad b = 0, \quad c = 0, \quad a' = 0, \quad b' = 0, \quad c' = 0.$$

† Bobillier gives these wrongly, putting b for $-b$.

Let $d = 0$ pass from the intersection of $a = 0$, $c' = 0$ to that of $a' = 0$, $c = 0$. The equation of the conic can be put into each of the forms

$$ac - bd = 0, \qquad a'c' - b'd = 0.$$

Hence
$$ac - a'c' \equiv (b - b')d.$$

The curve on the left goes through the intersection of the two lines, $a = 0$, $c = 0$ with the two lines $a' = 0$, $c' = 0$. Two of these are on the conic. Hence $b - b' = 0$ goes through the intersection of a with a', and of c with c' as it evidently goes through the intersection of $b = 0$, $b' = 0$. Hence it is the Pascal line.

The following seems to me even simpler, in fact it is the simplest proof I know. I do not know where I first saw it, and so like to imagine it is my own. I keep the previous notation for the equations of the sides, and write
$$abc + \lambda a'b'c' = 0.$$

This is a curve of the third order, and, regardless of the value of λ, it goes through the six vertices of the hexagon, and the intersections of the opposite sides. If we choose λ so that it shall meet the conic in a seventh point, it must include the conic as a part of itself. The remainder is a straight line connecting the intersections of the opposite sides, the Pascal line. This proof is immediately reversible, giving the converse of Pascal's theorem. Proofs like these and the ones of Bobillier immediately preceding them are peculiarly elegant: one does not have the impression, however, that the method is capable of very great extension.

Shortly before the appearance of Bobillier's work there appeared G. C. F. Sturm (q.v.). This work is so much less fresh and original that I find it hard to believe that Bobillier may have copied from him. He starts with a statement of the general principle of linear dependence, then gives at great length Desargues's construction for the polar, his work not being essentially different from Lamé[1]. He follows with a demonstration of the harmonic property of polars, which was, of course, known to the Greeks. In the second part we find Desargues's involution theorem; his editor Gergonne cannot refrain from explaining in footnotes how much better some of Sturm's work might have been done.

The greatest impetus to the study of linear dependence and abridged notation was presently given by Julius Plücker, a close student of French geometry, and a contributor to Gergonne's *Annales de Mathématiques*. In Plücker[3], which is largely occupied with the sixty hexagons determined by six conconic points, we find an extension of the principle of abridged notation which we can explain as follows. Suppose that we have proved a projective theorem by allowing certain symbols to stand for polynomials, and have set up equations involving linear dependence. By manipulating these we prove the linear dependence of certain other polynomials, and so show that certain loci have common points. By changing the definitions of the original polynomials we change the concurrence theorems which emerge at the end. Here is a further account of the progress of his ideas:[†]

'Als ich damals absichtlos einige Kreise auf das Papier bezeichnete kam mir aus dem Anblick der Figur die Vermuthung dass die drei gemeinschaftliche Chorden, je zeier von drei gegebenen Kreisen, in demselben Punkte sich schneiden. Bei der Verification dieses Satzes auf analytischen Wege erwartete ich auf Eliminationen zu stossen, ich suchte Weitlaufigkeiten und fand keine; ich kam zur Beweise dieses Satzes durch die einfächste Verbindung dreier Symbole'.

His proof, presumably, is this. In the three equations of the circles let the coefficient of x^2+y^2 be the same

$$A = 0, \qquad B = 0, \qquad C = 0.$$

The common secants are

$$A-B = 0, \qquad B-C = 0, \qquad C-A = 0,$$

and these are linearly dependent.

Plücker's statement that he learnt in this way a theorem of which he had never heard before surprised me not a little, for I learnt the fact with its demonstration in school. The concurrence of these lines is an immediate result of Euclid III. 35 and 36. In Poncelet (q.v.), vol. i, pp. 40–1, we have what is essentially the same, the concurrence of the radical axes of three circles whose centres are not collinear. Poncelet states that Monge was the first to prove the concurrence of the chords; I regret that I have not been able to find this in Monge's work.

The general task which Plücker set before himself in writing the two volumes of Plücker[2] was to devise algebraic methods which would lead swiftly and easily to the beautiful results which the synthetic projective geometer had been developing in recent decades. He felt there must be simple algebraic manipulations corresponding to the operations of the geometers. He saw that the algebraists possessed an enormous advantage when it came to dealing with complex elements. He was surprised to note the curious resemblance of his technique to that of the synthetic geometers. 'Die Beziehung der Ponceletschen Methoden zu den meinigen hat mich mehrmals überrascht, und zwar so mehr als die Art der Beweisführung eine so ganz verschieden ist.[‡]

The work begins with a long discussion of the straight line, especially concurrence and collinearity theorems. His general equation for a line is

$$y = ax+b.$$

† Plücker[2], vol. ii, p. iii.   ‡ Ibid., vol. i, p. v.

The formula for the distance from a point to a line appears often. The circle also is treated at length. The conics do not appear till p. 127, the definition of a curve of the second order being one with an equation of the type $$Ay^2+Bxy+Cx^2+Dy+Ex+F = 0.$$

The first problem is to change axes, to find the canonical forms, and to classify. He finds not too satisfactory meanings for the various coordinates, the conception of invariants had not yet emerged. On p. 156 he seeks the condition that a straight line should touch a conic. He does not dare use the calculus for this purpose, but adopts a concealed calculus form. To find the slope of the tangent he assumes that (x'', y''), $(x''+k, y''+k)$ are both on the conic, then finds the limit of k/l as the two points approach. He defines as the 'polar' the line whose equation is that of the tangent when the given point is on the curve. The tangency condition is obtained by assuming that a line contains its pole. He points out that the same condition could be obtained by eliminating one variable between the equations of the line and the conic, and then assuming that the resulting quadratic had equal roots. He then attacks the difficult problem of finding the equations of the tangents to a conic from a given point, say (x', y'). He writes first $$(y-y') = a(x-x').$$

If we introduce the tangency condition we have a quadratic expression in a. Let the roots be a and a'. The equation of the two tangents is $$(y-y')^2-(a+a')(y-y')(x-x')+aa'(x-x')^2 = 0.$$

We then substitute the values, from the quadratic, for the symmetric functions $(a+a')$, (aa')—good mathematics that.

On p. 177 we begin a long chapter on the relations of a conic to a pair of lines. We should expect to find great stress laid on Desargues's polar theory and the Pascal theorem, but I do not find either. Osculation comes in the next chapter, and then a last section called 'Allgemeine Schemata' which contains general projective theorems, solved by linear dependence.

The second volume of Plücker[2] is more interesting and original. It is almost entirely devoted to the study of conics expressed in line coordinates. Plücker was perfectly familiar with the dispute between Poncelet and Gergonne which we mentioned on p. 54. He explains his own relation to the controversy in the introduction. The essential thing is what seems to be the first systematic attempt ever made to study curves from their tangential equations.

The first chapter is devoted to the point. If we write a line $$Ay+Bx+C = 0,$$ its intercepts are $-C/A$, $-C/B$, and these are called the 'coordinates' of the line. The equation becomes illusory when the line is parallel to an axis, and inadequate when it goes through the origin. Changing notation, if we replace A, B, C by u, v, w, then a linear equation

$$au+bv+cw = 0$$

tells us that the line passes through the point a/b, b/c, or, when $c = 0$ that it has a given direction. We call this the equation of the finite or infinite point. The first section closes with a study of the centres of similitude of two circles. We define as a curve of the second class any envelope corresponding to an equation of the form

$$Aw^2+2Bvw+Cv^2+2Duw+2Euv+Fu^2 = 0.$$

The first thing to do is to find a canonical form. This is done by shifting to parallel axes. We then get the not too satisfactory equation

$$A^2w^2+(AC-B^2)v^2+2(AE-BD)uv+(AF-D^2)u^2 = 0.$$

This is studied at considerable length. A focus is defined as a point where the two tangents have the slopes $\pm i$. The foci receive considerable attention, as does the director circle, the locus of points where the two tangents are mutually perpendicular. We saw on p. 44 that La Hire was familiar with this curve. We reach something really better on p. 113 in a section entitled 'Neue Tangententheorie'. He confesses that the underlying idea comes from Lacroix, *Calcul différentiel et intégral*. Let the tangential equation of a curve be

$$U(u, v, w) = 0.$$

If (x, y) be the point of contact of a tangent, we have

$$ux+vy+w = 0.$$

Now this point lies on an infinitely near tangent; hence

$$du\,x+dv\,y+dw = 0.$$

The differentials are not completely independent, they are connected by the equation

$$\frac{\partial U}{\partial u}\,du + \frac{\partial U}{\partial v}\,dv + \frac{\partial U}{\partial w}\,dw = 0.$$

These two equations must mean the same thing; hence the equation of the point of contact must be

$$\frac{\partial U}{\partial u}\,u + \frac{\partial U}{\partial v}\,v + \frac{\partial U}{\partial w}\,w = 0.$$

If the equation of the given curve be quadratic, the point defined by this last equation is called the pole of the line. When the line is not a tangent, the pole is the intersection of the two tangents at the points where the line meets the curve, so that we are back at our previous pole and polar theory. Also, the coordinates of the point of contact are linear and homogeneous in terms of the line coordinates, and vice versa. The point equation of the conic is found by writing the condition that a pole lies in its polar.

At this point Plücker, being interested in certain metrical questions, changes to non-homogeneous coordinates. His new canonical form is

$$(u-u')^2+(v-v')^2 = k^2.$$

The line $u'v'$ is called the 'directrix'. The origin is its pole and is a focus. The ratio of the distances of a point on the curve from focus and directrix is found to be $\dfrac{k}{\sqrt{(u^2+v^2)}}$. He does not study more than one focus at a time nor take up confocal conics, which would have entered easily here. On p. 183 we have linear dependence in line coordinates, especially the dual Desargues's involution theorem which tells us that the pairs of tangents from a point to a set of conics, linearly dependent on two, in line coordinates, will be pairs of an involution. If two pairs of lines of such an involution be mutually perpendicular, the same is true of every pair; the double lines are the isotropic lines through that point. Consider now the system of conics tangent to four lines, no three of which are concurrent and no two parallel. They are linearly dependent in this sense. Hence if we go to the intersection of the director circles of two, we reach a point where, in Plücker's phrase, all are seen at right angles. Three of the conics degenerate into the pairs of opposite vertices of the quadrilateral formed by the four lines. We thus get Plücker's proof of the

Gauss-Bodenmiller Theorem 3] *The circles whose diameters are the diagonals of a complete quadrilateral pass through two common points.*†

The work of Plücker marks a very decided advance over that of any previous writer about the conic sections. He was out 'to beat the synthetic geometers' and he succeeded to no small degree. One may perhaps question the wisdom of writing at such length, two volumes of nearly three hundred pages each. We can also see now that further advance came soon after, which made his work outmoded. His notation is capable of improvement. But there can be no doubt as to the extent of our debt to him. After his time the concepts of linear dependence, line coordinates, and abridged notation, became standard practice in every work on analytic geometry that undertook to go beyond the elementary portions.

§ 2. Linear coordinates.

The striking lesson that one learns from the method of abridged notation is that in many cases the meaning of the individual letters

---

† Gauss only proved that the middle points of the three diagonals are collinear. I have not been able to find out anything about Bodenmiller. The earliest proof I have seen of the whole theorem is Gudermann (q.v.), p. 138.

is a matter of quite secondary importance. This suggests that we might use the same operations when some other form of coordinates were used, and this leads to the idea of introducing a greater flexibility into the coordinate system. As a matter of fact, we have noticed how the earlier writers on analytic geometry by no means required the axes to be rectangular. When metrical considerations are involved, rectangular Cartesian coordinates are the best for practically all purposes, except when we are dealing with spirals, or a few transcendental curves, and curves related to the circle. When we wish to retain parallelism, but do not care about the circular points at infinity, when we are doing geometry under the group of affine transformations, oblique cartesian coordinates will sometimes fit better. But the idea comes very naturally that, when we are interested in purely projective questions, when the line at infinity is no more interesting than any other line, and the only essential thing about the equation of a straight line is that it is of the first degree, is there not a distinct advantage in loosening up the coordinate system still farther?

It is hard to say who first thought of the idea of using more general linear coordinates. The two earliest writers on the subject first published in the same year. Let us be generous and give the credit to the less famous of the two, Carl Wilhelm Feuerbach. His little brochure Feuerbach[2] first saw the light in 1827. Now he was not at all interested in plane geometry at this point, still less in introducing a new algebraic technique. He had published a previous booklet, Feuerbach[1], dealing with the relations of various points to a triangle. He wanted to do something similar for the tetrahedron. But the synthetic methods which worked so well *in plano* broke down in three-space. He sought to develop a helpful algebraic apparatus. I will simplify his work by introducing determinants, and confine myself to two dimensions.

Suppose that we have four points, no three collinear,

$$P = (x,y), \quad P_1 = (x_1, y_1), \quad P_2 = (x_2, y_2), \quad P_3 = (x_3, y_3). \tag{1}$$

I write the obvious identity

$$\frac{1}{2} \begin{vmatrix} x & y & 1 & \dfrac{ux+vy+w}{\sqrt{(u^2+v^2)}} \\[2ex] x_1 & y_1 & 1 & \dfrac{ux_1+vy_1+w}{\sqrt{(u^2+v^2)}} \\[2ex] x_2 & y_2 & 1 & \dfrac{ux_2+vy_2+w}{\sqrt{(u^2+v^2)}} \\[2ex] x_3 & y_3 & 1 & \dfrac{ux_3+vy_3+w}{\sqrt{(u^2+v^2)}} \end{vmatrix} = 0. \tag{2}$$

If we expand this in terms of the last column, each term will be the algebraic distance from one of our points to a given line, multiplied by the area of the triangle formed by the other three points. Here is Feuerbach's statement of the corresponding identity in three dimensions:† 'If five points are given of which no four are coplanar, and if we multiply the algebraic distance of each of these from a given plane by the volume of the tetrahedron whose vertices are the other four points, the algebraic sum is 0.'

Since our rows are linearly dependent we may find three such multipliers p_1, p_2, p_3 that

$$x = p_1 x_1 + p_2 x_2 + p_3 x_3,$$
$$y = p_1 y_1 + p_2 y_2 + p_3 y_3,$$
$$1 = p_1 + p_2 + p_3.$$

Note that $$p_i = \triangle PP_j P_k \div \triangle P_i P_j P_k.$$

We may call p_1, p_2, p_3 the Feuerbach coordinates of the point (x, y). They are the algebraic distances of (x, y) from the sides of the triangle divided by the corresponding altitudes. If P lie on the line given by the last column, and if d_i be the distance of P_i therefrom,

$$d_1 p_1 + d_2 p_2 + d_3 p_3 = 0,$$
$$p_1 + p_2 + p_3 = 1.$$

Note that for a finite line we could not have $d_1 = d_2 = d_3$, for three points which were at the same algebraic distance from a given line would be collinear, but P_1, P_2, P_3 are supposed not to be so. We may take
$$p_1 + p_2 + p_3 = 0$$
as the equation of the line at infinity. Any other linear homogeneous equation
$$d_1 p_1 + d_2 p_2 + d_3 p_3 = 0$$
will represent a finite line.

The other discoverer of these coordinates was a much better known geometer, Alfred Möbius. His work is found in Möbius[2], repeated in Möbius[1]. His novel technique consists in considering discrete systems of weighted points and their centres of mass. Weights may be positive, negative, or zero. If in three dimensions we have the points $(x_1 y_1 z_1)$, $(x_2 y_2 z_2),..., (x_n y_n z_n)$ with the respective weights w_1, $w_2,..., w_n$, then the centre of mass or centre of gravity is

$$\bar{x} = \frac{\sum w_i x_i}{\sum w_i}, \qquad \bar{y} = \frac{\sum w_i y_i}{\sum w_i}, \qquad \bar{z} = \frac{\sum w_i z_i}{\sum w_i}.$$

Conversely, if $n > 3$ we have n points in three-space, not in a plane; we may attach to them weights w_1, $w_2,..., w_n$ in such a way that any

† Feuerbach[2], p. 5.

given finite point is their centre of mass, and when $n = 4$ this can be done in essentially only one way. As the unit of mass is immaterial, we may assume that
$$\sum w_i = 1.$$

Let us illustrate in the case of a plane, and pick three non-collinear points A, B, C and write the symbolic equation
$$P = pA + qB + rC.$$

This means that P is the centre of mass when we attach to them the weights p, q, r, and we may further assume
$$p + q + r = 1.$$

Owing to the equilibrium, the moment of P about BC must be the negative of the moment of A about that line, so that p is numerically the distance from P to a side of the triangle ABC divided by the corresponding altitude. We see that the Möbius barycentric coordinates are exactly the same as the coordinates of Feuerbach.

Suppose that
$$P = pA + qB + rC,$$
$$P_1 = p_1 A + q_1 B + r_1 C,$$
$$P_2 = p_2 A + q_2 B + r_2 C.$$

If P is on the line $P_1 P_2$ we can find two such weights l_1, l_2 that
$$P = l_1 P_1 + l_2 P_2$$
$$\begin{vmatrix} p & q & r \\ p_1 & q_1 & r_1 \\ p_2 & q_2 & r_2 \end{vmatrix} = 0.$$

Conversely, if
$$\alpha p + \beta q + \gamma r = 0,$$
all sets of solutions p, q, r are linearly dependent on two, or we have the points of a line. An exception occurs in the case of the equation
$$p + q + r = 0.$$

Every solution is a linear combination of $(1, -1, 0)$, $(1, 0, -1)$ and these are the infinite points of two sides of our triangle. We may take this as the equation of the line at infinity. Let us note in passing that the unit point, that is to say, the point whose three homogeneous coordinates are all equal, is the centre of gravity of the triangle, whose distances from the sides are one-third of the corresponding altitudes.

Möbius's principal application of his coordinates, at least in the plane, is to the study of curves
$$P = f(t)A + \phi(t)B + \psi(t)C.$$

Developing in power series,

$$P = [f(t_0)+(t-t_0)f'(t_0)+\ldots]A+[\phi(t_0)+(t-t_0)\phi'(t_0)+\ldots]B+$$
$$+[\psi(t_0)+(t-t_0)\psi'(t_0)+\ldots]C.$$

If we bring this to intersect the straight line

$$\begin{vmatrix} p & q & w \\ f(t_0) & \phi(t_0) & \psi(t_0) \\ f'(t_0) & \phi'(t_0) & \psi'(t_0) \end{vmatrix} = 0,$$

two intersections will fall on the point $t = t_0$ so that this is the tangent. When we have

$$f'(t_0) = \phi'(t_0) = \psi'(t_0) = 0,$$

the curve will have a cusp. The general equation of a conic will be

$$P = [a_0+a_1t+a_2t^2]A+[b_0+b_1t+b_2t^2]B+[c_0+c_1t+c_2t^2]C. \tag{5}$$

Möbius prefers to use a simpler form, where the conic is circumscribed to the triangle ABC.

$$P = a(t-\beta)(t-\gamma)A+b(t-\gamma)(t-\alpha)B+c(t-\alpha)(t-\beta)C.$$

An inscribed conic can be written

$$P = a(t-\alpha)^2A+b(t-\beta)^2B+c(t-\gamma)^2C.$$

Möbius uses such forms to determine the equations of conics given by a certain number of points and tangents.

The conics were first introduced by Menaechmus as projections of a circle. Such a projection can be expressed analytically as a linear transformation. This procedure was characteristic in the work of Poncelet. Chasles generalized slightly by introducing his favourite transformation, 'homology', a linear transformation where all points of a certain line were fixed. Möbius was the first geometer to face the problem of linear transformations in bold fashion, but his method was highly original. Our usual way is to assume a fixed coordinate system and compare the positions of two points whose coordinates are linearly related. In homogeneous Möbius coordinates we express the coordinates of one point as linear homogeneous functions of those of another. Möbius reverses this. He takes two points with identical coordinates with regard to two triangles. He carefully distinguishes four cases. (1) The triangles are equal. (2) The triangles are similar. (3) The triangles are dissimilar, but the infinite line is unaltered. (4) The general case.

The points A, B, C, D, where $D = q_1A+q_2B+q_3C$, correspond to A', B', C', D', where $D' = q_1'A'+q_2'B'+q_3'C'$.

Then the point $\qquad p_1A+p_2B+p_3C$

shall correspond to $p_1' A' + p_2' B' + p_2' C'$

where $$\frac{p_i}{q_i} = \frac{p'}{q'}.$$

In a previous section Möbius had given an elaborate discussion of the
six cross ratios of four collinear points, like that given ten years later
by Chasles, which I mentioned on p. 55. He does not, however, give
the cross ratios of lines, but does prove Pappus' theorem that cross
ratios are unaltered by projection. He uses for cross ratio the extended
word 'Doppelschnittverhältniss' for the more usual 'Doppelverhältniss',
which would seem sufficiently long to most of us. Such cross ratios are
easily expressed in Möbius coordinates, and so it is easy to show that
they are unaltered by the form of linear transformation which I have
just described. And this leads to an idea which Möbius did not expand,
but which was subsequently developed by Pasch. This Möbius calls
'Der abgekürzte barycentrische Calcul' where we attach to points,
instead of weights, certain numbers which are expressed in terms of
cross ratios, and so invariant under linear transformation.†

I think that Möbius's greatest contribution in the *Barycentrische
Calcul* is right here in the study of the general linear transformation,
which he understood more broadly than his predecessors. Moreover,
the coordinates invented by himself and Feuerbach mark a real advance.
On the other hand, the method of expressing points parametrically in
terms of others is inconvenient when it comes to studying curves which
are not rational. I feel a certain sympathy with the severe judgement
of Cauchy, quoted by Baltzer:‡ 'Il faut être bien sûr qu'on fait faire à
la science un grand pas, pour la surcharger de tant de termes nouveaux,
et d'exiger qu'ils vous suivent dans des recherches qui s'offrent à eux
avec tant d'étrangeté.'

The most marked step towards introducing these more general coordinates was taken by Plücker, in Plücker[4] and Plücker[5]. He states that
the most general coordinates which will give to a straight line a linear
equation will be of the form

$$\eta - \frac{\chi(y+a'x+b')}{\rho(y+a''x+b'')}, \qquad \zeta - \frac{\pi(y+ax+b)}{\rho(y+a''x+b'')}. \tag{6}$$

I shall turn aside to extend this theorem. Suppose that we have a set
of linear homogeneous coordinates $x_1,\ x_2,\ x_3$ where a straight line has a
linear homogeneous equation

$$(ux) \equiv \sum w_i x_i = 0.$$

What are the most general homogeneous coordinates $X_1,\ X_2,\ X_3$ such
that a straight line shall have a homogeneous linear equation? If a

† Möbius[1], pp. 333 ff.   ‡ Möbius[1], vol. i, p. xi.

straight line have a linear homogeneous equation, it can be expressed parametrically by showing the coordinates of a general point as a linear combination of those of two points of the line. Thus the point $x_i + t y_i$ will be expressed also in the form $X_i + T Y_i$

$$X_i(x_1+ty_1, x_2+ty_2, x_3+ty_3) = X_i(x_1, x_2, x_3) + t \sum_j y_j \frac{\partial X_i}{\partial x_j} + \frac{t^2}{2} \cdots$$

$$= X_i(x_1, x_2, x_3) + T(t) X_i(y_1, y_2, y_3).$$

But $T(t) X_i(y_1, y_2, y_3)$ is independent of x_1, x_2, x_3.

Hence $\dfrac{\partial X_i}{\partial x_j} = \text{constant}, \qquad X_i = \sum_j c_{ij} x_j.$

I return to Plücker's coordinates first announced in Plücker[4]. It is clear that the coordinates of a point, as we have written them, are quotients of constant multiples of its distances from three given lines. Plücker finds meanings for the multipliers ρ, χ, π and acknowledges his indebtedness to Möbius.† He also, like Möbius, sees the advantage of using the homogeneous coordinates

$$r = \rho(y+a''x+b''), \qquad q = \chi(y+a'x+b'), \qquad p = \pi(y+ax+b).$$

A straight line is given by a linear homogeneous equation. In the next section he takes up line coordinates, first in non-homogeneous, then in homogeneous form. These are proportional to constant multiples of a point's distances from the vertices of a triangle. A homogeneous linear equation gives a point. The general linear transformation in point and line coordinates appears next, and then something really new, the general linear transformation from point to line coordinates. This he calls a reciprocity: we should call it a correlation. Polar reciprocation in a conic is a very special case. The point and line treatments of conics go hand in hand, the canonical form for the equation being

$$pq + \mu r^2 = 0.$$

After this come pole and polar theory developed simultaneously for the two coordinate systems.

Plücker's contributions to this subject, in spite of their limitations of notation, are of very real importance. It is especially noticeable that he makes no use of determinants; the next step in advance comes with their introduction. The mathematicians of the British Isles seized on them with avidity. We find an early example, dated 1846, in Cayley's paper on the tangential equation of a plane cubic, to be found on p. 230 of Cayley (q.v.) vol. i.

Let the equation of the cubic be

$$f(x_1, x_2, x_3) = 0.$$

† Plücker[5], p. 7, note.

That of a straight line

$$u_1 x_1 + u_2 x_2 + u_3 x_3 = 0.$$

The line polar of (y) with regard to the curve is

$$\sum_i \frac{\partial f}{\partial y_i} x_i = 0.$$

These represent the same line, and (y) lies on it, if that line be a tangent. Euler's formula for differentiating a homogeneous polynomial gives

$$\sum_j \frac{\partial^2 f}{\partial y_i \partial y_j} y_j + \rho u_i = 0, \qquad \sum_i u_i y_i = 0.$$

Here we have four apparently linear homogeneous equations in y_1, y_2, y_3, ρ. Eliminating we get

$$\begin{vmatrix} \dfrac{\partial^2 f}{\partial y_1^2} & \dfrac{\partial^2 f}{\partial y_1 \partial y_2} & \dfrac{\partial^2 f}{\partial y_1 \partial y_3} & u_1 \\[2mm] \dfrac{\partial^2 f}{\partial y_2 \partial y_1} & \dfrac{\partial^2 f}{\partial y_2^2} & \dfrac{\partial^2 f}{\partial y_2 \partial y_3} & u_2 \\[2mm] \dfrac{\partial^2 f}{\partial y_3 \partial y_1} & \dfrac{\partial^2 f}{\partial y_3 \partial y_2} & \dfrac{\partial^2 f}{\partial y_3^2} & u_3 \\[2mm] u_1 & u_2 & u_3 & 0 \end{vmatrix} = 0.$$

I incline to think that this sort of bordered equation must have been familiar at the time, or soon after, for we find on p. 19 of Spottiswode[1] (q.v.), which appeared in 1851: 'As another example, the equation of a cone with its reciprocal will be seen to be

$$Ax^2 + By^2 + Cz^2 + 2(Fyz + Gzx + Hxy) = 0;$$

$$\begin{vmatrix} A & H & G & \xi \\ H & B & F & \eta \\ G & F & C & \zeta \\ \xi & \eta & \zeta & 0 \end{vmatrix} = 0.'$$

By 1861 we find in Hesse[1] abridged notation, homogeneous point and line coordinates, determinants, linear transformations, and quadric surfaces about as we should express them to-day, the only essential difference being that Hesse does not make the distinction between subscripts and superscripts which has become common since the rise of the theory of tensors. In Hesse's notation the standard form for the equation of a conic is

$$\sum_{ij} a_{ij} x_i x_j = 0 \qquad (a_{ij} = a_{ji}). \tag{7}$$

The tangential equation for the same curve is

$$\sum_{ij} A_{ij} u_i u_j = 0, \qquad A_{ij} = \frac{\partial |a_{pq}|}{\partial a_{ij}}. \tag{8}$$

Since the introduction of the absolute differential geometry, where there is little use for exponents greater than 2, there has come in the habit of using superscripts for point coordinates and subscripts for line coordinates. When the same symbol is repeated above and below, that means a summation, eliminating the Greek Σ. Thus the quadratic form above is written

$$a_{ij} x^i x^j = 0 \quad (a_{ij} = a_{ji}). \tag{9}$$

Instead of the cofactor A_{ij}, we write the cofactor divided by the determinant

$$\alpha^{ij} = \frac{\partial \log |a_{pq}|}{\partial a_{ij}}.$$

$$a_{ij} \alpha^{jk} = \delta_i^k; \qquad \delta_i^k = 0 \quad (i \neq k); \qquad \delta_i^k = 1 \quad (i = k).$$

The tangential equation of the same locus will be

$$\alpha^{ij} u_i u_j = 0.$$

When the coordinate triangle is self-conjugate, the equation of the conic takes the simpler form

$$a_i (x^i)^2 = 0.$$

If two conics have four common points, and so a common self-conjugate triangle, their equations can be written

$$b_i (x^i)^2 = 0; \qquad c_i (x^i)^2 = 0.$$

I should mention that until recently the English have been averse to the use of indices, preferring x, y, z as homogeneous point coordinates. There is one more notation, associated with the names of Clebsch and Aronhold, which I shall explain in the next section.

In the further development of linear coordinates there have been two tendencies. The first and most prominent is metrical. Two slightly different types of coordinates finally dominated the field. The first is the isobaric type of Feuerbach and Möbius, in homogeneous form. The coordinates of a point are proportional to its algebraic distances from the sides of a triangle, each divided by the corresponding altitude. The unit point is the centre of gravity. The other kind, which are sometimes called 'trilinear', are the three algebraic distances themselves, or numbers proportional to them. The unit point is the centre of the inscribed circle. The interest in such refinements would probably have died early had there not appeared a new body of doctrine called 'the geometry of the triangle'. Most of the material is best treated synthetically, but when algebraic treatment is necessary Cartesian coordinates fit extremely ill, whereas trilinear ones give pretty results. I will give an illustration.

Let a point have coordinates x^1, x^2, x^3 with regard to a triangle, the lengths of whose sides are a_1, a_2, a_3, while the magnitudes of the angles are A_1, A_2, A_3. If the coordinates are the actual lengths we have the identity

$$a_i x^i = 2\Delta.$$

Usually we take numbers proportional to the lengths. The line at infinity has the equation

$$a_i x^i = 0.$$

Suppose that we have two points with the coordinates

$$x^1 : x^2 : x^3; \qquad \frac{1}{x^1} : \frac{1}{x^2} : \frac{1}{x^3}.$$

They are said to be 'isogonally conjugate'. We pass from the one to the other by reflecting the lines to the vertices of the triangle in the bisectors of the corresponding angles. They are also two foci of the same conic tangent to the sides of the triangle. It is easy to show geometrically that if a point lie on the circumcircle of the triangle, its isogonal conjugate is at infinity, and conversely. Hence the equation of the circumcircle is

$$\sum a_i x^j x^k = 0.$$

A general circle is a conic which meets the circumscribed circle on the line at infinity. Hence the equation of a general circle is

$$\lambda \sum a_i x^j x^k + (a_i x^i)(u_i x^i) = 0.$$

The other line of development for linear coordinates is the projective one. I mentioned on p. 66, in connexion with von Staudt, that the concept of cross ratio can be built up on a purely descriptive basis, independent of all ideas of measurement.[†] If we have a triangle whose vertices are A_1, A_2, A_3, and a fixed unit point R not on any side of the triangle, and lastly a general point P, we have three cross ratios $A_i(A_j A_k, RP)$. It is not hard to show that the product of these is unity. We may call them $\frac{x^2}{x^3}$, $\frac{x^3}{x^1}$, $\frac{x^1}{x^2}$ and take $x^1 : x^2 : x^3$ as homogeneous coordinates of the point P. In the same way if a_1, a_2, a_3 be the labels of the sides and r a fixed unit line while l is a general line, we have three cross ratios $a_i(a_j a_k, rl)$ whose product is unity. We call these $\frac{u_2}{u_3}$, $\frac{u_3}{u_1}$, $\frac{u_1}{u_2}$ and take $u_1 : u_2 : u_3$ as homogeneous line coordinates. Lastly, let us suppose that the point R and the line r are so related that if B_i be the intersection of $A_i R$ with $A_j A_k$, then r is the line containing the intersections of the corresponding sides of the Desargues triangles $A_1 A_2 A_3$, $B_1 B_2 B_3$. Under these circumstances the necessary and sufficient condition that the point P should lie on the line l is

$$u_i x^i = 0.$$

[†] The germ of this idea is found in Möbius[1], as mentioned on p. 95. It is further developed in Pasch (q.v.). A good recent account is in Ch. X of Graustein (q.v.).

§ 3. The invariants.

It is decidedly surprising that although most of the writers who first studied the conic sections expressed in Cartesian form paid great attention to changes of rectangular axes, they did not seem to notice that certain expressions remained unchanged under these alterations. If we write the conic

$$Ax^2+2Bxy+Cy^2+2Dx+2Ey+F = 0, \tag{10}$$

it is quite easy to show that for every change of rectangular coordinates, these three expressions remain constant:

$$A+C, \qquad B^2-AC, \qquad \begin{vmatrix} A & B & D \\ B & C & E \\ D & E & F \end{vmatrix} \equiv \Delta.$$

It might happen, however, that during our operations we might wish to multiply the equation through by some constant. Then these three would be multiplied by the first, second, and third power of that constant respectively. But the following

$$\frac{B^2-AC}{(A+C)^2}; \qquad \frac{\Delta}{(A+C)^3} \tag{11}$$

are absolutely unchanged by any change of rectangular axes, or by multiplication of the equation by any number other than zero. They have geometrical meaning. If we start with a parabola, and change it to

$$y^2 = 2mx,$$

then
$$m = \sqrt{\left(\frac{-\Delta}{(A+C)^3}\right)}.$$

On the other hand, a central conic can be reduced to

$$\frac{x^2}{a^2}+\frac{y^2}{\pm b^2} = 1.$$

Then $1/a^2$ and $1/\pm b^2$ are roots of the quadratic equation

$$p^2-\frac{(B^2-AC)(A+C)}{\Delta}p+\frac{(B^2-AC)^3}{\Delta^2} = 0.$$

I am sorry to say that I do not know who first proved the invariance of these expressions; that of the first two is found on p. 158 of Salmon[1]. Far more attention has been paid to the projective invariants of conics. We find the essentials in that paper which may be taken as marking the beginning of the whole projective invariant theory, Boole (q.v.).

Suppose we have n homogeneous variables x_1, x_2,..., x_n and carry them into other variables y_1, y_2,..., y_n by a linear transformation

$$x_1 = \lambda_1 y_1 + \mu_1 y_2 + ...,$$
$$x_2 = \lambda_2 y_1 + \mu_2 y_2 + ..., \text{ etc.}$$

Suppose
$$f(x_1, x_2, ..., x_n) \equiv \phi(y_1, y_2, ..., y_2),$$

$$\frac{\partial f}{\partial y_1} = \lambda_1 \frac{\partial f}{\partial x_1} + \lambda_2 \frac{\partial f}{\partial x_2} + ... \equiv \frac{\partial \phi}{\partial y_1},$$

$$\frac{\partial f}{\partial y_2} = \mu_1 \frac{\partial f}{\partial x_1} + \mu_2 \frac{\partial f}{\partial x_2} + ... \equiv \frac{\partial \phi}{\partial y_2}, \text{ etc.}$$

If all of the expressions $\partial f/\partial x_i$ vanish, so do all of the expressions $\partial \phi/\partial y_j$, and conversely, provided that we have a non-degenerate transformation, i.e.

$$\frac{\partial(f_1, ..., f_n)}{\partial(x_1, ..., x_n)} \equiv |\lambda_1 \; \mu_2 \; ... | \neq 0.$$

Now usually a form does not possess the property that all of the partial derivatives may vanish at once when the variables are not all zero. The condition which allows this to happen must be the vanishing of some polynomial in the coordinates, and the corresponding polynomial made from ϕ must vanish at the same time, so that one polynomial must be equal to the other except for some factor depending merely on the coefficients of the transformation. This is Boole's rather bold reasoning. When it comes to giving examples, he reverts to more usual British notation. We write a conic

$$Ax^2 + 2Bxy + Cy^2 + 2Dxz + 2Eyz + Fz^2 = 0.$$

The three partial derivatives, divided by 2 and equated to zero, are

$$Ax + By + Dz = 0,$$
$$Bx + Cy + Ez = 0,$$
$$Bx + Ey + Fz = 0.$$

The compatibility condition is

$$\begin{vmatrix} A & B & D \\ B & C & E \\ D & E & F \end{vmatrix} \equiv \Delta = 0.$$

Boole remarks that when we have two forms f_1, f_2 which are carried into ϕ_1, ϕ_2, then $f_1 + \lambda f_2$ is carried into $\phi_1 + \lambda \phi_2$. The invariants will be polynomials in λ, and the different coefficients are simultaneous invariants of f_1 and f_2.

This is about the basis on which Boole builds his whole invariant theory. This grew into a vast edifice, developed on somewhat different lines in Great Britain and Germany. What I have just said about Boole is about all that we need to develop the theory as applied to the conics. The most complete account of the whole doctrine is found in Mayer (q.v.). The case for the conics is worked out in Salmon. The treatment is ingenious, but the notation clumsy. Salmon was a close collaborator with Cayley and Sylvester, who founded the English school of algebraists.

Suppose that we have a homogeneous quadratic equation in n variables

$$a_{ij}x^ix^j = 0.$$

The locus will have a double point (x) if

$$a_{ij}x^j = 0 \quad (i = 1, 2, ..., n).$$

The compatibility condition for these equations is

$$|a_{ij}| \equiv \Delta = 0. \tag{12}$$

When we are dealing with conics there will be three variables. A conic will have a double point when it is a pair of lines, or a line counted twice, in which case the three linear equations amount to but one, or the rank of the matrix $\|a_{ij}\|$ is unity.

Consider, next, the transformation

$$x^i = c^i_j \bar{x}^j, \qquad y^i = c^i_j \bar{y}^j, \qquad |c^p_q| \neq 0$$

$$\lambda x^i + \mu y^i = c^i_j (\lambda \bar{x}^j + \mu \bar{y}^j).$$

Suppose that
$$a_{ij}x^ix^j \equiv \bar{a}_{ij} \bar{x}^i \bar{x}^j$$

$$a_{ij}(\lambda x^i + \mu y^i)(\lambda x^j + \mu y^j) \equiv \bar{a}_{ij}(\lambda \bar{x}^i + \mu \bar{y}^i)(\lambda \bar{x}^j + \mu \bar{y}^j)$$

$$a_{ij}x^iy^j \equiv \bar{a}_{ij} \bar{x}^i \bar{y}^j$$

$$\equiv a'_{pj} \bar{x}^p y^j; \qquad a'_{pj} = a_{ij}c^i_p$$

$$|a'_{ij}| = |a_{ij}| . |c^p_q|.$$

Transforming (y) to $(\bar{y})$ in the same way.

$$|\bar{a}_{ij}| = |a_{ij}| . |c^p_q|^2. \tag{13}$$

It is a fundamental fact in invariant theory that the factor depending on the coefficients of the transformation is always a power of the determinant of the transformation. The exponent of this power is called the 'weight' of the invariant. We obtain the tangential equation of our quadratic locus by expressing the fact that a linear locus contains its pole. The hyperplane
$$u_i x^i = 0$$

will be tangent if we have compatibility for the equations

$$a_{11}y^1 + a_{12}y^2 + \ldots = -\rho u_1$$
$$a_{21}y^1 + a_{22}y^2 + \ldots = -\rho u_2$$
$$\cdot \quad \cdot \quad \cdot \quad \cdot \quad \cdot$$
$$a_{n1}y^1 + a_{n2}y^2 + \ldots = -\rho u_n$$
$$u_1 y^1 + u_2 y^2 + \ldots = 0.$$

$$\begin{vmatrix} a_{11} & a_{12} & \cdot & \cdot & a_{1n} & u_1 \\ a_{21} & a_{22} & \cdot & \cdot & a_{2n} & u_2 \\ \cdot & \cdot & \cdot & \cdot & \cdot & \cdot \\ \cdot & \cdot & \cdot & \cdot & \cdot & \cdot \\ a_{n1} & a_{n2} & \cdot & \cdot & a_{nn} & u_n \\ u_1 & u_2 & \cdot & \cdot & u_n & 0 \end{vmatrix} = 0. \qquad (14)$$

Dividing through by Δ,

$$\alpha^{ij} u_i u_j = 0.$$

We find simultaneous invariants by Boole's method. Restricting ourselves to conics

$$|\bar{a}_{ij}| + \lambda|\bar{a}_{ij}|\bar{\alpha}^{pq}\bar{b}_{pq} + \lambda^2|\bar{b}_{pq}|\bar{a}^{pq}\bar{\beta}^{pq} + \lambda^3|\bar{b}_{pq}|$$
$$\equiv |c_q^p|[|a_{ij}| + \lambda|a_{ij}|\alpha^{pq}b_{pq} + \lambda^2|b_{ij}|a_{pq}\beta^{pq} + \lambda^2|b_{pq}|].$$

Let us find the meaning of

$$a_{pq}\beta^{pq} = 0.$$

This is an invariant equation. We may take as coordinate triangle one which is self-conjugate with regard to the a conic, and has two sides tangent to the β conic. The equations of the two will then be

$$a_{11}(x^1)^2 + a_{22}(x^2)^2 + a_{33}(x^3)^2 = 0$$
$$2(\beta^{12}u_1 u_2 + \beta^{23}u_2 u_3 + \beta^{31}u_3 u_1) + \beta^{33}u_3^2 = 0,$$

but if $a_{pq}\beta^{pq} = 0$, then $\beta^{33} = 0$, and the second conic is inscribed in the triangle. This is the relation of a polarity which we discussed at such length in Chapter IV. The condition that two conics should touch is the easiest of a number of invariant conditions which call for special mention. We start with two general quadratic forms

$$a_{ij}x^i x^j = 0, \qquad b_{ij}x^i x^j = 0,$$

and the invariant equation

$$|d_{ij}| \equiv |a_{ij} + \lambda b_{ij}| \equiv |a_{ij}| + \lambda b_{pq}\frac{\partial|a_{ij}|}{\partial a_{pq}} + \ldots + \lambda^n|b_{ij}| = 0.$$

Let the roots be $\lambda_1, \lambda_2, \ldots, \lambda_n$. Consider in particular the root λ_p. Suppose that it has the multiplicity m_{p0}, while it makes each minor of $|d_{ij}|$ vanish with the multiplicity m_{p1}, each second minor with the multiplicity m_{p2}, etc.

Let
$$l_{p1} = m_{p0} - m_{p1}, \qquad l_{p2} = m_{p1} - m_{p2}, \qquad \dots.$$
$$m_{p0} = l_{p1} + l_{p2} + \dots, \qquad m_{p1} = l_{p2} + l_{p3} + \dots.$$

The factor $(\lambda - \lambda_p)^{l_{pi}}$ is called an 'elementary' divisor of $|d_{ij}|$. Weierstrass proved that the necessary and sufficient condition that two bilinear forms $a_{ij} x^i y^j$, $b_{ij} x^i y^j$ can be carried into the two forms $\bar{a}_{ij} \bar{x}^i \bar{y}^j$, $\bar{b}_{ij} \bar{x}^i \bar{y}^j$ by the same linear transformation is that the two polynomials $|a_{ij} + \lambda b_{ij}|$, $|\bar{a}_{ij} + \lambda \bar{b}_{ij}|$ shall have the same elementary divisors.[†]

The general theory of elementary divisors does not seem to me to merit the adjective in its name. The most elaborate discussion is in Muth (q.v.). When we have nothing worse to deal with than two conics, the matter is simple enough. We begin with

$$|d_{ij}| \equiv |a_{ij}| + \alpha^{pq} b_{pq} \lambda + \alpha^{pq} \beta_{pq} \lambda^2 + |b_{ij}| \lambda^3 = 0. \tag{15}$$

It is easy to show that the rank of $|d_{ij}|$ will not sink below 2 except for a multiple root. Then here is the situation:

(1) Three distinct roots; the conics meet in four points.
(2) Single root, and double which leaves the rank 2; simple tangency.
(3) Single root and double which reduces the rank to unity; double contact.
(4) Triple root leaving the rank 2; simple osculation.
(5) Triple root reducing the rank to unity; four-point contact.
(6) Triple root reducing the rank to 0. Conics are identical.

I mentioned on p. 98 that there was another notation much used in the algebra of invariants, especially by mathematicians of the German school. This first appeared in Clebsch[1] and Aronhold (q.v.) and is called after these two men. I shall only treat the ternary case here, and the quaternary later, but the general principles are the same for any number of variables. We note first of all that a linear transformation will carry a linear form

$$a_i x^i \equiv (ax)$$

into a linear form $(\bar{a}\bar{x})$ and the determinant $|a\ b\ c|$ of three linear forms (ax), (bx), (cx) will be an invariant, as will be that of three linear forms in the 'contragredient' variables $(u\alpha)$, $(u\beta)$, $(u\gamma)$. The trick consists in transforming the given forms into such a shape that these invariants are available. I first compare two ternary forms

$$\frac{n!}{p!\,q!\,r!} a_{pqr} (x^1)^p (x^2)^q (x^3)^r \quad (p+q+r = n), \qquad (a_i x^i)^n \equiv (ax)^n.$$

They are identical if
$$a_{pqr} \equiv a_1^p a_2^q a_3^r.$$

Now
$$a_1^p a_2^q a_3^r . a_1^k a_2^l a_3^m \equiv a_1^s a_2^t a_3^v a_1^{p+k-s} a_2^{q+l-t} a_3^{r+m-v}.$$

† Weierstrass (q.v.), vol. ii, p. 38.

Hence they are identical if

$$a_{pqr}\, a_{klm} \equiv a_{stv}\, a_{\lambda\mu\nu}$$
$$p+k = s+\lambda; \qquad q+l = t+\mu; \qquad r+m = v+\nu.$$

These equations are quadratic and irreducible in the coefficients. If we have an identity which holds when the forms involved are powers of linear forms, and if this identity involve the coefficients of any one form only to the first degree, this identity holds in every case. Now in most invariants and covariants the coefficients appear in higher degrees than the first, but we can reduce them to the first degree by an ingenious trick, akin to Boole's for grinding several invariants out of one. Suppose that we have

$$x^i = c_j^i\, \bar{x}^i, \qquad I(\bar{a}_{pqr}, \bar{b}_{lst}, \dots, \bar{x}^i, \bar{y}^j \dots) \equiv |c_q^p|^w\, I(a_{pqr}, \bar{b}_{lst}, \dots, x^i, y^j \dots);$$
$$I(\bar{a}_{pqr} + \lambda \bar{a}'_{pqr}, \bar{b}_{lst} + \lambda \bar{b}'_{lst}, \dots, \bar{x}^i, \bar{y}^j, \dots)$$
$$\equiv |c_q^p|^w\, I(a_{pqr} + \lambda a'_{pqr}, b_{lst} + \lambda b'_{lst}, x^i, y^j, \dots).$$

Comparing the coefficients of like powers of λ we get new invariants, if x^i, y^j, etc. are not present, otherwise covariants; this process may be repeated until we have

$$I(\bar{a}_{pqr}, \bar{a}'_{pqr}, \bar{a}''_{pqr}, \dots, \bar{b}_{lst}, \bar{b}'_{lst}, \bar{b}''_{lst}, \dots, \bar{x}^i, \bar{y}^j, \dots)$$
$$\equiv |c_q^p|^w\, I(a_{pqr}, a'_{pqr}, a''_{pqr}, \dots, b_{lst}, b'_{lst}, b''_{lst}, \dots, x^i, y^j, \dots), \quad (16)$$

a covariant where no individual coefficient appears above the first degree. The invariance will hold just as well when a_{pqr} and a'_{pqr} *mean the same thing.* Hence any system of invariants or covariants can be expressed in a form where no coefficients appear except linearly, yet when equivalent symbols are replaced by a single symbol, higher terms come in. I think the idea is clearer if we take a particular example. We start with a conic

$$f \equiv (ax)^2 \equiv (a'x)^2 \equiv (a''x)^2 = 0. \qquad (17)$$

The polar of (y) is $\quad \dfrac{1}{2} \sum y^i \dfrac{\partial f}{\partial x^i} \equiv (ay)(ax) = 0. \qquad (18)$

The conic will be two lines, distinct or coincident, if (y) can take such a value that (x) can be anywhere. We must then have

$$a_1(ay) = a'_2(a'y) = a'_3(a''y) = 0.$$

This involves $\qquad a_1 a'_2 a''_3 |a\ a'\ a''| = 0.$

Permuting equivalent symbols a, a', and adding,

$$|a\ a'\ a''|^2 = 0. \qquad (19)$$

It is to be noted that the symbols of each type appear to the second degree, which is necessary if they are to have a real meaning. When will the line

$$(ux) \equiv |y\ z\ x| = 0$$

be tangent to this conic?

$$u_i = y^j z^k - y^k z^j, \qquad x^i = \xi^1 y^i + \xi^2 z^i.$$
$$(ax)^2 \equiv [(ay)\xi^1 + (az)\xi^2]^2$$
$$\equiv (ay)^2(\xi^1)^2 + 2(ay)(az)\xi^1\xi^2 + (az)^2(\xi^2)^2$$
$$\equiv (a'y)^2(\xi^1)^2 + 2(a'y)(a'z)\xi^1\xi^2 + (a'z)^2(\xi^2)^2.$$

This will be a perfect square if

$$(ay)^2(a'z)^2 + (a'y)^2(az)^2 - 2(ay)(az)(a'y)(a'z) = 0$$
$$|a\ a'\ u|^2 \equiv (u\alpha)^2 = 0. \tag{20}$$

Suppose next that we have two conics

$$(ax)^2 \equiv (a'x)^2 = 0, \qquad (bx)^2 \equiv (b'x)^2 = 0.$$

We seek their intersections with the line from (y) to (z)

$$(ay)^2(\xi^1)^2 + 2(ay)(az)\xi^1\xi^2 + (az)^2(\xi^2)^2 = 0$$
$$(by)^2(\xi^1)^2 + 2(by)(bz)\xi^1\xi^2 + (bz)^2(\xi^2)^2 = 0.$$

Here we have two quadratic expressions in $\xi^1 : \xi^2$. The roots of one will divide those of the other harmonically if

$$(ay)^2(bz)^2 + (by)^2(az)^2 - 2(ay)(az)(by)(bz) = 0$$
$$|a\ b\ u|^2 = 0. \tag{21}$$

Similarly, if we have two line conics

$$(u\alpha)^2 = 0, \qquad (u\beta)^2 = 0,$$

the locus of points where the two pairs of tangents make a harmonic set is

$$|\alpha\ \beta\ x|^2 = 0. \tag{22}$$

This, I believe, is called Salmon's conic; in any case it is found, in very different notation, on p. 306 of Salmon. When one of the line conics is the circular points at infinity, this is the director circle, the locus of points whence tangents to a conic are mutually perpendicular. We saw on p. 44 that La Hire was familiar with this locus. Reverting to the general case of two conics, where will the Salmon conic meet either of them? At such a point two of the members of the harmonic set fall together, hence a third member falls in there, or we must be at a point of contact of a common tangent to the two curves. Here we find again a theorem which we mentioned on p. 66 in connexion with von Staudt,

the points of contact of two conics with their common tangents lie on
a conic. Suppose that we have a third conic $(cx)^2 = 0$ and the condition

$$|a\ b\ c| = 0. \tag{23}$$

This means that $|a\ b\ u|^2 = 0$ and $(cx)^2 = 0$ are apolar, or there are
an infinite number of triangles self-conjugate with regard to each conic
which cut the other two in a harmonic set.

Three pairs of points of a line form an involution if each pair be
divided harmonically by the roots of the Jacobian of the other two.
The conics $(ax)^2 = 0$, $(bx)^2 = 0$, $(cx)^2 = 0$ will meet the line from (y)
to (z) in the pairs of points given by the equations

$$(\alpha\rho)^2 \equiv [(ay)\rho_1 + (az)\rho_2]^2 = 0,$$
$$(\beta\rho)^2 \equiv [(by)\rho_2 + (bz)\rho)^2 = 0,$$
$$(\gamma\rho)^2 \equiv [(cy)\rho_1 + (cz)\rho_2]^2 = 0.$$

These will form an involution if

$$|\alpha\ \beta| \cdot |\beta\ \gamma| \cdot |\gamma\ \alpha| = 0$$
$$|a\ b\ u| \cdot |b\ c\ u| \cdot |c\ a\ u| = 0. \tag{24}$$

Suppose that we have three linearly independent point conics

$$f_1 = 0, \qquad f_2 = 0, \qquad f_3 = 0.$$

Their Jacobian
$$\frac{\partial(f_1, f_2, f_3)}{\partial(x^1, x^2, x^3)} = 0$$

is the locus of points whose polars with regard to the three are concurrent
and also the locus of such points of concurrence. If the three have a
common self-conjugate triangle, this cubic curve is nothing but the
three sides of the triangle. In this case we can express the two conics in
such a way that only the squared terms appear. But then if we calculate
the equation of Salmon's conic, we shall find only the squared terms
in the equation of that, so that the coordinate triangle is self-conjugate
with regard to the Salmon's conic; or the Jacobian of two conics and
their Salmon's conic is the sides of the common self-conjugate triangle,
or a limiting case of that locus. To find the equation of the sides of the
common self-conjugate triangle of $(ax)^2 = 0$, $(bx)^2 = 0$ we must equate
to zero the Jacobian of

$$(ax)^2 = 0, \qquad (bx)^2 = 0, \qquad |\alpha\ \beta\ x|^2 = 0,$$

which gives
$$\begin{vmatrix} (a\alpha) & (a\beta) \\ (b\alpha) & (b\beta) \end{vmatrix} (ax)(bx)|\alpha\ \beta\ x| = 0.$$

It can be shown with a little juggling that this can also be written

$$(a\beta)(b\alpha)(ax)(bx)|\alpha\ \beta\ x| = 0. \tag{25}$$

Let us finally find the equations of the common tangents to these two conics. This will involve a short excursion into the binary domain. If we have a polynomial $f(\xi^1, \xi^2, \eta^1, \eta^2)$ homogeneous in $\xi^1 : \xi^2$ and in $\eta^1 : \eta^2$, an immediate substitution shows that $\dfrac{\partial^2 f}{\partial \xi^1 \partial \eta^2} - \dfrac{\partial^2 f}{\partial \xi^2 \partial \eta^1}$ is invariant when the same linear substitution is performed simultaneously on both sets of binary variables. If we perform this twice on $(a\xi)^2(a'\eta)^2$, where a and a' mean the same thing, we get $4|a\,a'|^2$, and this vanishes when $(a\xi)^2$ is a perfect square.

Now suppose that we have two binary quadratic equations

$$(a\xi)^2 \equiv (a'\xi)^2 = 0; \qquad (b\xi)^2 \equiv (b'\xi)^2 = 0.$$

They have a common root if their Jacobian is a perfect square

$$|a\,b|\,.\,|a'\,b'|[\,|b\,b'|\,.\,|a\,a'|+|b\,a'|\,.\,|a\,b'|\,] = 0. \qquad (26)$$

Next take two line conics

$$(u\alpha)^2 = 0, \qquad (u\beta)^2 = 0.$$

Let (u) pass through (x) the intersection of (v) and (w)

$$u_i = \xi^1 v_i + \xi^2 w_i.$$

The tangents thence to the two conics are given by

$$[(\alpha v)\xi^1 + (\alpha w)\xi^2]^2 = 0, \qquad [(\beta v)\xi^1 + (\beta w)\xi^2]^2 = 0.$$

If (x) be on a common tangent, these two quadratic equations have a common root. Comparing this with the condition (26) a few lines back,

$$|a\,b| = (\alpha v)(\beta w) - (\beta v)(\alpha w) = |\alpha\,\beta\,x|,$$

with similar values for $|a\,a'|$. We get the final equation of the tangents

$$|\alpha\,\beta\,x|\,.\,|\alpha'\,\beta'\,x|[\,|\alpha\,\alpha'\,x|\,.\,|\beta\,\beta'\,x|+|\alpha\,\beta'\,x|\,.\,|\beta\,\alpha'\,x|\,] = 0. \qquad (27)$$

CHAPTER VII

MISCELLANEOUS METRICAL THEOREMS

§ 1. Maxima and minima.

In the preceding chapters I have traced the historical development of the various mathematical methods which have been found useful in studying the conic sections. In the present chapter I shall treat a number of disconnected topics which seem to offer some interest, showing thereby the application of some of the methods already sketched. I found much of this material mentioned in Dingeldey (q.v.) which contains a vast amount more.

An obscure French writer, professor in Cahors, set up and solved a number of rather pretty problems connected with the ellipse and ellipsoid.† The underlying idea is to reach the ellipse by a parallel projection of the circle. Now in such an affine collineation all areas are changed in the same ratio, the line at infinity goes into itself, parallel lines go into parallel lines, and the mid-point of a segment goes into the mid-point of a segment. Conjugate diameters of the circle will go into conjugate diameters of an ellipse.

Suppose, then, that we have a parallelogram inscribed in a circle. Since opposite angles are both equal and supplementary, they are right angles, so that the figure is a rectangle, and the diagonals are diameters. The area of a parallelogram is one-half of the product of the diagonals multiplied by the sine of the angle between, so that the largest of these parallelograms is a square, whose diagonals are mutually perpendicular, i.e. are conjugate diameters. This gives:

Theorem 1] *The largest parallelogram that can be inscribed in an ellipse is one whose diagonals are conjugate diameters. All such parallelograms have the same area.*

Suppose, secondly, that the parallelogram is circumscribed to the circle. Since the area is the product of the altitudes divided by the sine of the angle between the sides, the smallest parallelogram is one where the sides are mutually perpendicular, and so a square.

Theorem 2] *The smallest parallelogram circumscribed to an ellipse is one whose diagonals lie on conjugate diameters; all such parallelograms have the same area.*

Let us turn things about, starting with the parallelogram. Let c_1^2 be the circumscribed ellipse whose diagonals are conjugate diameters;

---

† For this whole section cf. Durande (q.v.).

let c_2^2 be any other circumscribed ellipse. This parallelogram is not the largest we can inscribe in c_2^2; we can inscribe a larger one with its diagonals on a pair of conjugate diameters. Now the area of this new parallelogram is to the area of c_2^2 as the area of the first parallelogram is to that of c_1^2. Hence the area of the ellipse c_1^2 must be less than that of c_2^2.

Theorem 3] *The smallest ellipse that can be circumscribed to a given parallelogram has the diagonals as conjugate diameters.*

Theorem 4] *The largest ellipse that can be inscribed in a given parallelogram has the conjugate diameters along the diagonals.*

What is the largest triangle that can be inscribed in a given circle? Clearly the tangent at each vertex must be parallel to the opposite side, or the triangle is equilateral, and the centre of gravity is the centre of the circle. All such triangles have the same area. In a parallel projection, the medians of a triangle go into the medians of a triangle, and the centre of gravity to the centre of gravity.

Theorem 5] *One vertex of a triangle of maximum area inscribed in an ellipse can be taken at pleasure. The centre of the ellipse will be the centre of gravity of the triangle. All such triangles have the same area.*

If we seek the smallest triangle which can be circumscribed to a circle, we see that this is also the triangle of minimum perimeter. A somewhat longer calculation shows that this also is equilateral.

Theorem 6] *The smallest triangle that can be circumscribed to an ellipse has the centre of the curve as its centre of gravity.*

Theorem 7] *The smallest ellipse that can be circumscribed to a given triangle has its centre at the centre of gravity of the triangle.*

Theorem 8] *The largest ellipse that can be inscribed in a given triangle has its centre at the centre of gravity of the triangle.*

§ 2. Closure problems.

I should have mentioned in discussing the work of Poncelet, that he paid a good deal of attention to polygons, inscribed in one conic, circumscribed to another. I will return to this subject presently, even though it is not metrical.

We mean by the cross ratios of four points of a conic those of the four lines connecting them with any fifth point of the curve. This shows what we mean by projective ranges on a conic, and involutions on a conic.

Suppose that we have an involution on a given conic, with H, K as the double points, while P, P' are a pair of points. The lines HH, HK,

HP, HP' are harmonic. Hence the tangent HH passes through the pole of HK, as does KK. Since

$$H(HPKP') \barwedge K(HPKP') \barwedge K(KPHP'),$$

we have two projective pencils with a corresponding line, and PP' passes through the pole of HK.

Theorem 9] *If an involution of points be given on a conic, the lines connecting the various pairs pass through the pole of the line connecting the double points.*

Theorem 10] *If an involution be established among the tangents to a given conic, the intersections of corresponding lines lie on the polar of the intersection of the self-corresponding ones.*

I am ashamed to say that I do not know who first discovered these two theorems, very likely either Steiner or Chasles.

If two conics have double contact they may be projected simultaneously into concentric circles. The tangents to one circle will cut projective ranges on the other, and these ranges are non-involutory.

Theorem 11] *If two conics have double or four-point contact, the tangent to one will cut non-involutory projective ranges on the other. The projectivity will be parabolic with a single self-corresponding point in case of four-point contact.*

Suppose conversely we have two projective ranges on a conic, and the relation is not involutory. We can find a conic having double contact with the given conic at the self-corresponding points, and tangent to a line connecting a corresponding pair, or having four-point contact in the parabolic case, and the tangents to this conic will set up the required projective relation.

Theorem 12] *If a non-involutory projective relation be set up among the points of a conic, the lines connecting corresponding points will touch a conic having double contact with the given conic at the self-corresponding points, or four-point contact in the parabolic case.*

Theorem 13] *If a non-involutory projective correspondence be established among the tangents to a conic, the locus of the intersections of corresponding pairs will be a conic having double or four-point contact with the given conic.*

Next, let us suppose that we have a polygon with n vertices $P_1, P_2, ..., P_n$ variable upon a conic c_1^2 and that the successive sides $P_1P_2, P_2P_3, ..., P_{n-1}P_n$ are all tangent to other conics $c_2^2, c_3^2, ..., c_{n-1}^2$ through four points of c_1^2; what can be said of the remaining side P_nP_1?

Poncelet handles this question by means of a long series of geometrical theorems, which I will not repeat, as we can proceed much more expeditiously with the aid of a little algebra. Let the equation of the conic be

$$-(x^1)^2+(x^2)^2+(x^3)^2 = 0.$$

We can express this parametrically in the form

$$x^1 = t^2+1, \qquad x^2 = t^2-1, \qquad x^3 = 2t.$$

The point P_i shall correspond to the parameter value t_i. When P_1 is given there correspond two values for P_2; when P_2 is given there are two values for P_3, but one of these is identical with P_1 and may be discarded, and so on up to P_n. We have thus, finally, a two-to-two symmetrical algebraic relation between t_1 and t_n which we may write

$$q_1(t_1 t_n)^2+q_2 t_1 t_n(t_1+t_n)+q_3(t_1+t_n)^2+h_1 t_1 t_n+h_2(t_1+t_n)+h_3 = 0.$$

This can also be written

$$a_0(t_1 t_n+1)^2+a_1(t_1 t_n-1)^2+2a_2(t_1 t_n+1)(t_1 t_n-1)+2b_0(t_1+t_n)^2-$$
$$-2b_1(t_1+t_n)(t_1 t_n+1)-2b_2(t_1+t_n)(t_1 t_n-1) = 0. \qquad (1)$$
$$x^1 = t_1^2+1, \qquad x^2 = t_1^2-1, \qquad x^3 = 2t_1,$$
$$z^1 = t_n^2+1, \qquad z^2 = t_n^2-1, \qquad z^3 = 2t_n.$$

The coordinates of the connecting line are

$$\rho u_1 = (t_1 t_n+1), \qquad \rho u_2 = (1-t_1 t_n), \qquad \rho u_3 = -(t_1+t_n);$$
$$a_0 u_1^2+a_1 u_2^2-2a_2 u_1 u_2+b_0 u_3^2+2b_1 u_1 u_3-2b_2 u_2 u_3 = 0.$$

It appears in this way that this line envelops a conic. If P_1 be very close to an intersection of the conics c_1^2, c_2^2, the two points P_2 are very close together, as are the two points $P_3,..., P_n$. Hence the two tangents $P_n P_1$ are close, or P_1 must be close to an intersection of c_1^2 and the new conic.

Theorem 14] *If all of the vertices of a variable polygon lie on a conic, and all of the successive sides but one touch conics through four points of the first, the remaining side will touch a conic through these intersections.*[†]

It is worth noting in passing that all of the diagonals will touch conics through these intersections.

In equation (1) if we put $t_1 = t_n$ we get an equation which is of the fourth degree in t_1. This degree is, however, deceptive. When P_1 is near a root, one tangent from P_1 to c_2^2 is near to one tangent from P_n to c_2^2. But as P_1, P_n lie on c_1^2 which does not touch these tangents, the other tangent from P_1 to c_2^2 lies near the other tangent from P_n, or the roots of this quartic count doubly, so that there could not be more than two distinct points where two fall together. If, then, we know there are more than two, there must be an infinite number.

Theorem 15] *If two polygons be so related that there is a polygon inscribed in the one whose sides touch the other, there are an infinite number of such polygons, one vertex being arbitrary.*†

We saw in Chapter III, p. 68, that when two conics are apolar, there is an infinite number of triangles inscribed in the one which are self-conjugate with regard to the other, a closely related situation. Suppose that we have two conics so situated that there is a polygon of an odd number of sides whose vertices are on the one, each vertex being the pole of the opposite side with regard to the other conic. We may set up just such a two-to-two relation as before, and reason as in that case.

Theorem 16] *If two conics be so related that there is a polygon of an odd number of sides either inscribed or circumscribed to the one, whose sides are polars with regard to the other of the opposite vertices, there are an infinite number of such polygons, one side being arbitrary.*

Let us return to the inscribed and circumscribed polygons; this time we suppose that the number of sides is even. We see by the remark following Theorem 14 that a diagonal connecting a pair of opposite vertices, say P_j, $P_{j+n/2}$, will envelop a conic through the intersections of c_1^2, c_2^2. Assuming that at least two of these are distinct, we may project them into the circular points at infinity, so that c_1^2, c_2^2 become two circles. If we take P_1 at one end of a common diameter, $P_{1+n/2}$ will be at the other end, and the lines $P_j P_{j+n/2}$ will meet in pairs on this line. But at such a point of meeting there would be three tangents to the enveloped conic, which must be a point-pair or single point counted twice

Theorem 17] *If two conics be so situated that there is a polygon of an even number of sides inscribed in the one and circumscribed to the other, the diagonals connecting opposite vertices will pass through a fixed point, and the intersections of opposite sides will be on a fixed line.*

The simplest case of Theorem 15 is that where there is a triangle inscribed in the one which is circumscribed to the other. Let us write this invariant condition algebraically. We take this triangle as coordinate triangle and write

$$(ax)^2 \equiv (a'x)^2 \equiv A_1 x^2 x^3 + A_2 x^3 x^1 + A_3 x^1 x^2 = 0; \quad (u\alpha)^2 = 0$$
$$(u\beta)^2 \equiv (u\beta')^2 \equiv B_1 u_2 u_3 + B_2 u_3 u_1 + B_3 u_1 u_2 = 0; \quad (bx)^2 = 0. \tag{2}$$

We find by a perfectly straight substitution

$$(b\alpha)^2 = 2(a\beta)^2. \tag{3}$$

† Poncelet (q.v.), vol. i, p. 349. This proof is from Hurwitz (q.v.).

If we have two circles with respective radii r and R while the distance of their centres is a, the conditions for a series of triangles, or a series of quadrilaterals, inscribed in the one and circumscribed to the other are†

$$\frac{1}{R+a}+\frac{1}{R-a}=\frac{1}{r}, \tag{4}$$

$$\frac{1}{(R+a)^2}+\frac{1}{(R-a)^2}=\frac{1}{r^2}. \tag{5}$$

It would seem as if we were fairly started towards a formula which

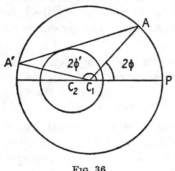

FIG. 36

will work in every case. Such, unfortunately, is not the fact. The formulae for polygons of five, six, or eight sides are given, without proof by Steiner.‡

The following general formula was worked out in Jacobi[1], p. 286. Suppose (Fig. 36) that the centres of the two circles are C_1, C_2; the line connecting them meets the outer circle in P, while AA' is a side of the polygon.

$$\angle PC_1 A = 2\phi; \qquad \angle PC_1 A' = 2\phi'.$$

The distance from C_1 to AA' is $R\cos(\phi'-\phi)$ and the distance from C_2 to this line is r. The difference between these distances is $\pm a\cos(\phi+\phi')$.

$$R\cos(\phi'-\phi)+a\cos(\phi'+\phi)=r,$$

$$(R+a)\cos\phi'\cos\phi+(R-a)\sin\phi'\sin\phi=r.$$

If we have a circumscribed polygon of n sides, the corresponding angles being $2\phi_1, 2\phi_2,..., 2\phi_n$,

$$(R+a)\cos\phi_2\cos\phi_1+(R-a)\sin\phi_2\sin\phi_1=r,$$

$$(R+a)\cos\phi_3\cos\phi_2+(R-a)\sin\phi_3\sin\phi_2=r,$$

$$\cdot \quad \cdot \quad \cdot \quad \cdot \quad \cdot \quad \cdot \quad \cdot \quad \cdot \quad \cdot$$

$$(R+a)\cos\phi_1\cos\phi_n+(R-a)\sin\phi_1\sin\phi_n=r.$$

$$\frac{(R+a)\cos\phi_i[\cos\phi_{i+1}-\cos\phi_{i-1}]}{(R-a)\sin\phi_i[\sin\phi_{i+1}-\sin\phi_{i-1}]}=-1,$$

$$\frac{R-a}{R+a}\tan\phi_i=\tan\frac{\phi_{i+1}+\phi_{i-1}}{2}. \tag{6}$$

† Coolidge[4], pp. 44-6.   ‡ Werke, vol. i, p. 284.

And now Jacobi, the great student of elliptic functions, introduces his classical formulae

$$\int_0^\phi \frac{d\phi}{\sqrt{(1-k^2\sin^2\phi)}} = u,$$

$$\phi = \operatorname{am} u, \qquad \sqrt{(1-k^2\sin^2\phi)} = \Delta \operatorname{am} u,$$

$$\phi' = \operatorname{am}(u+t), \qquad \phi'' = \operatorname{am}(u+2t).$$

Then, by the elementary theory of elliptic functions

$$\tan\frac{\phi+\phi''}{2} = (\Delta \operatorname{am} t)\tan\phi'.$$

We determine t so that

$$\frac{R-a}{R+a} = \Delta \operatorname{am} t. \tag{7}$$

$$\phi_{i-1} = \operatorname{am} u, \quad \phi_i = \operatorname{am}(u+t), \quad \phi_{i+1} = \Delta \operatorname{am}(u+2t). \tag{8}$$

§ 3. Curvature.

The problem of finding the curvature of a curve was completely solved by Newton. In his notation, if ρ be the radius of curvature,

$$z = \frac{\dot{y}}{\dot{x}}, \qquad \frac{1}{\rho} = \frac{\dot{x}^2\dot{z}}{(\dot{x}^2+\dot{y}^2)^{\frac{3}{2}}}. \tag{9}$$

If we indicate partial differentiation by a subscript, and write the equation of the curve

$$f(x,y) = 0,$$

$$\frac{1}{\rho} = \pm\frac{2f_{xy}f_xf_y-(f_x)^2f_{yy}-(f_y)^2f_{xx}}{[(f_x)^2+(f_y)^2]^{\frac{3}{2}}}. \tag{10}$$

For the ellipse

$$b^2x^2+a^2y^2-a^2b^2 = 0$$

we shall have

$$\frac{1}{\rho} = \pm\frac{a^4b^4}{(b^4x^2+a^4y^2)^{\frac{3}{2}}} = \frac{ab}{[a^2-e^2x^2]^{\frac{3}{2}}}. \tag{11}$$

The focal radii are

$$d_1 = a+ex, \qquad d_2 = a-ex,$$

$$\rho = \frac{(d_1 d_2)^{\frac{3}{2}}}{ab}.$$

The distance from the focus $(-ae, 0)$ to the tangent at (x, y) is

$$\frac{ab^2(a+ex)}{\sqrt{(b^4x^2+a^4y^2)}}.$$

The cosine of the angle between the focal radius and the normal is

$$\frac{ab^2}{\sqrt{(b^4x^2+a^4y^2)}} = \frac{b}{(d_1 d_2)^{\frac{1}{2}}} = \cos\theta.$$

Hence the projection of the radius of curvature on either focal radius is

$$\frac{d_1 d_2}{a}.$$

L'Hospital's Theorem 18] *The major axis of an ellipse is the fourth proportional to the radius of curvature and the two focal radii*†.

If we erect a perpendicular to a focal radius at the corresponding focus it will meet the normal at a point whose distance from the point of the curve is given by the formula

$$e_1 = d_1\sec\theta = \frac{d_1}{b}[d_1 d_2]^{\frac{1}{2}}; \quad d_1+d_2 = 2a.$$

$$2\rho = \frac{e_1 e_2}{e_1+e_2}.$$

This gives a theorem first published as far as I can find in Mack (q.v.), but ascribed by him to Gugler.

Theorem 19] *The centre of curvature corresponding to a point P of an ellipse is the harmonic conjugate of P with regard to the intersections of the normal with the perpendiculars to the focal radii at the corresponding foci.*

Let $(\bar{x}, \bar{y})$ a point on the normal at (x_1, y_1) and distant therefrom by the quantity r;

$$\bar{x} = x_1 + \frac{rb^2x_1}{\sqrt{(b^4x_1^2+a^4y_1^2)}}, \qquad \bar{y} = y_1 + \frac{ra^2y_1}{\sqrt{(b^4x_1^2+a^4y_1^2)}}.$$

If the circle whose centre is $(\bar{x}, \bar{y})$ and radius r is orthogonal to the major auxiliary circle whose equation is

$$x^2+y^2 = a^2+b^2,$$

then

$$\bar{x}^2+\bar{y}^2 = a^2+b^2+r^2,$$

$$2r = \rho.$$

Theorem 20] *If a circle be drawn tangent to an ellipse which is orthogonal to the major auxiliary circle, its diameter is equal to the radius of curvature at the point of contact.*‡

---

† L'Hospital², p. 109. The proof is very long.　　‡ Steiner², without proof.

Steiner was fond of giving such unproved theorems. Here is another.

Theorem 21] *Through a general point of a conic will pass three circles osculating elsewhere. Their points of contact are concyclic with the given point.*

One does not need to be a prophet, or the son of a prophet, to see how Steiner probably reached this theorem. We know that he was familiar with the transformation which we call inversion in a circle. If the centre of inversion be on a conic, the inverse curve will be a rational cubic, and this has three inflexions which lie on a line. These will invert back into the points of contact of osculating circles through the given point. Here is a somewhat similar theorem from the same source:

Theorem 22] *Through three non-collinear points of a cubic curve which has no singular point will pass nine conics which osculate the curve. The points of contact are so arranged that a conic through the three given points and two contact points will contain a third contact point.*

The explanation here is equally simple. We saw on p. 59 that Steiner invented a quadratic transformation called a skew projection, which carries a straight line into a conic through three given points. A cubic through the given points will be carried into another cubic. A conic through the three points which osculates the cubic will go into a line which osculates the new cubic. Now it is well known that a line which connects two inflexions of a cubic passes through a third inflexion. I do not think that Steiner was very well inspired in giving this theorem. He prefers to limit himself to real figures, but it is well known that only three of the inflexions of a cubic can be real.

§ 4. Parametric representation.

Conics are rational curves and there are occasions when the best way to study such a curve is to express the Cartesian coordinates rationally in terms of a parameter. We used this method once in the present chapter, p. 112. In some cases it is better to lead up to this indirectly. When we are dealing with an ellipse we can use the 'eccentric angle' or 'eccentric anomaly' as Kepler called it. Archimedes knew well that if all chords of a circle which are parallel to one another be shrunk in the same ratio, the resulting locus will be an ellipse, of which the given circle is the major auxiliary. We write

$$x' = a \cos u, \qquad y' = a \sin u, \qquad x^2 + y^2 = a^2,$$

$$x = x', \qquad y = \frac{by'}{a},$$

$$x = a \cos u, \qquad y = b \sin u, \qquad \frac{x^2}{a^2} + \frac{y^2}{b^2} = 1. \tag{12}$$

I regret that I do not know who first made use of this simple device. If we prefer an algebraic form, we can use the tangent of the half angle

$$t = \tan\frac{u}{2}, \qquad x = \frac{a(t^2-1)}{t^2+1}, \qquad y = \frac{2bt}{t^2+1}. \tag{13}$$

This is particularly convenient in certain problems dealing with normals. The equation of the normal will be

$$\frac{y-b\sin u}{x-a\cos u} = \frac{a\sin u}{b\cos u},$$

$$a\sin u\, x - b\cos u\, y - (a^2+b^2)\sin u\cos u = 0.$$

Suppose that the normals at the three points u_1, u_2, u_3 are concurrent

$$\begin{vmatrix} \sin u_1 & \cos u_1 & \sin u_1\cos u_1 \\ \sin u_2 & \cos u_2 & \sin u_2\cos u_2 \\ \sin u_3 & \cos u_3 & \sin u_3\cos u_3 \end{vmatrix} = 0,$$

$$\begin{vmatrix} t_1^3 & t_1^4-1 & t_1 \\ t_2^3 & t_2^4-1 & t_2 \\ t_3^3 & t_3^4-1 & t_3 \end{vmatrix} = 0,$$

$$(t_2-t_3)(t_3-t_1)(t_1-t_2)[t_1 t_2 t_3(t_2 t_3+t_3 t_1+t_1 t_2)-(t_1+t_2+t_3)] = 0. \tag{14}$$

We discard the first factor, divide through by $(t_1^2+1)(t_2^2+1)(t_3^2+1)$, and multiply by 2.

$$\sin(u_2+u_3)+\sin(u_3+u_1)+\sin(u_1+u_2) = 0. \tag{15}$$

This formula is attributed to Burnside.[†]

From a general point, as the Greeks knew well, we may drop four normals to our ellipse. We have four equations of the type (14)

$$t_j t_k t_l(t_k t_l+t_l t_j+t_j t_k) = t_j+t_k+t_l$$

$$1+t_1 t_2 t_3 t_4 = \frac{t_i t_j+t_i t_k+t_i t_l+t_k t_l+t_l t_j+t_j t_k}{t_k t_l+t_l t_j+t_j t_k}.$$

Permuting and adding,

$$(t_1 t_2 t_3 t_4-1)\sum t_i t_j = 0.$$

We could not have the general solution $t_1 t_2 t_3 t_4 = 1$, as that fails in the case of the axes.

Hence

$$\sum t_i t_j = 0, \qquad 1+t_1 t_2 t_3 t_4 = 0; \qquad 1+t_1 t_2 t_3 t_4 - \sum t_i t_j = 0.$$

Then $\tan\dfrac{u_1+u_2+u_3+u_4}{2} = \infty; \qquad u_1+u_2+u_3+u_4 = \pi. \tag{16}$

Theorem 23] *The sum of the eccentric angles of four points of an ellipse are congruent to π (mod 2π) when the normals at those points are concurrent.*[‡]

† Lauermann (q.v.), p. 388.   ‡ Lauermann (q.v.).

This theorem suggests another. What about the eccentric angles of four concyclic points?

$$A[a^2\cos^2u+b^2\sin^2u]+Ba\cos u+Cb\sin u+D=0,$$

$$\begin{vmatrix} \cos^2u_1 & \cos u_1 & \sin u_1 & \sin^2u_1 \\ \cdot & \cdot & \cdot & \cdot \\ \cdot & \cdot & \cdot & \cdot \\ \cos^2u_4 & \cos u_4 & \sin u_4 & \sin^2u_4 \end{vmatrix}=0.$$

$$\begin{vmatrix} t_1^4 & t_1^2 & (t_1^3+t_1) & 1 \\ \cdot & \cdot & \cdot & \cdot \\ \cdot & \cdot & \cdot & \cdot \\ t_4^4 & t_4^2 & (t_4^3+t_4) & 1 \end{vmatrix}=0.$$

Dividing out the non-vanishing factor

$$(t_2-t_3)(t_3-t_1)(t_1-t_2)(t_1-t_4)(t_2-t_4)(t_3-t_4)$$

$$=t_1t_2t_3t_4\sum\frac{1}{t_i}-\sum t_i.$$

$$\tan\left[\frac{u_1+u_2+u_3+u_4}{2}\right]=0. \tag{17}$$

Theorem 24] *The sum of the eccentric angles of four concyclic points of an ellipse is congruent to* 0 (mod 2π).

§ 5. Areas and lengths.

The formula for the area of an ellipse was familiar to Archimedes, and appears in the fourth theorem of his book on conoids and spheroids. He also developed a formula for the area of a parabolic segment. His proof, which is too long to reproduce, is based upon a careful use of the principle of exhaustion. As for the hyperbola, we saw on p. 37 that St. Vincent went far towards finding the formula for the area between an arc of the curve and the asymptote.

When it comes to studying the lengths of arcs of conics, the story is very different. We run into elliptic integrals, a very large topic which we cannot enter into here. There is, however, one theorem which I shall prove in detail, as it seems to me really interesting; it is an extension of the theorem which says that an ellipse is the locus of a point which draws tight a loop of fixed length that spans two fixed points. There are various proofs, the first is based on that found on pp. 33 ff. of Klein (q.v.), the most stimulating book ever written on geometry, to my way of thinking.

I start with a set of confocal conics

$$\frac{x^2}{a^2-\lambda}+\frac{y^2}{b^2-\lambda}=1. \tag{18}$$

When x and y are given we have a quadratic equation, with two roots, λ_1 corresponding to an ellipse, and λ_2 a hyperbola, through the given point. We take these as a new system of coordinates for the point. They were invented by Lamé, and called 'elliptic' coordinates'.†

$$x^2 = \frac{(a^2-\lambda_1)(a^2-\lambda_2)}{a^2-b^2}, \qquad y^2 = -\frac{(b^2-\lambda_1)(b^2-\lambda_2)}{a^2-b^2}. \qquad (19)$$

$$dx^2 = \frac{1}{4}\frac{[d(x^2)]^2}{x^2} = \frac{1}{4}\frac{[(a^2-\lambda_2)d\lambda_1+(a^2-\lambda_1)d\lambda_2]^2}{(a^2-\lambda_1)(a^2-\lambda_2)(a^2-b^2)};$$

$$dy^2 = -\frac{1}{4}\frac{[(b^2-\lambda_2)d\lambda_1+(b^2-\lambda_1)d\lambda_2]^2}{(b^2-\lambda_1)(b^2-\lambda_2)(a^2-b^2)};$$

$$ds^2 = \frac{1}{4}\left[\frac{\lambda_2-\lambda_1}{(a^2-\lambda_1)(b^2-\lambda_1)}d\lambda_1^2 + \frac{\lambda_1-\lambda_2}{(a^2-\lambda_2)(b^2-\lambda_2)}d\lambda_2^2\right]. \qquad (20)$$

The equation of the tangents from (x,y) to the ellipse $\lambda_1 = \lambda_1'$ is

$$\left[\frac{x^2}{a^2-\lambda_1'}+\frac{y^2}{b^2-\lambda_1'}-1\right]\left[\frac{\xi^2}{a^2-\lambda_1'}+\frac{\eta^2}{b^2-\lambda_1'}-1\right]-\left[\frac{x\xi}{a^2-\lambda_1'}+\frac{y\eta}{b^2-\lambda_1'}-1\right]^2 = 0.$$

Putting $\xi = x+dx$, $\eta = y+dy$, we get for the differential equation of such a tangent after higher infinitesimals have been dropped,

$$\frac{dx^2}{a^2-\lambda_1'}+\frac{dy^2}{b^2-\lambda_1'}-\frac{(x\,dy-y\,dx)^2}{(a^2-\lambda_1')(b^2-\lambda_1')} = 0.$$

It is rather a tedious business to write this out at length in the other variables. What is interesting is to find the square of the differential of arc along such a line. This will reduce to $\dfrac{1}{4}\dfrac{(\lambda_1'-\lambda_1)}{(a^2-\lambda_2)(b^2-\lambda_1)}d\lambda_1^2$ when $\lambda_2 = \lambda_1'$ and to $\dfrac{1}{4}\dfrac{\lambda_1'-\lambda_2}{(a^2-\lambda_2)(b^2-\lambda_2)}d\lambda_2^2$ when $\lambda_1 = \lambda_1'$. In fact the formula is

$$ds = \frac{\sqrt{(\lambda_1'-\lambda_1)}}{2\sqrt{(a^2-\lambda_1)}\sqrt{(b^2-\lambda_1)}}d\lambda_1 \pm \frac{\sqrt{(\lambda_1'-\lambda_2)}}{2\sqrt{(a^2-\lambda_2)}\sqrt{(b^2-\lambda_2)}}d\lambda_2.$$

We now find the length of a path made up as follows:

(A) From $\bar{\lambda}_1, \bar{\lambda}_2$ along the tangent to the curve $\lambda_1 = \lambda_1'$.
(B) Around the curve $\lambda_1 = \lambda_1'$ to the point of contact of the other tangent from $\bar{\lambda}_1, \bar{\lambda}_2$.
(C) Back to $\bar{\lambda}_1, \bar{\lambda}_2$ along that tangent.

This will be L the perimeter of the ellipse plus the sum of the lengths

† See Lamé[2], p. 137.

of the two tangents from $\bar{\lambda}_1, \bar{\lambda}_2$ less the length of the shorter arc between the two points of contact. We have, then,

$$L + \frac{1}{2} \int_{\bar{\lambda}_1}^{\bar{\lambda}_1'} \frac{\sqrt{(\lambda_1' - \lambda_1)}}{\sqrt{(a^2 - \lambda_1)}\sqrt{(b^2 - \lambda_1)}}\, d\lambda_1 + \frac{1}{2} \int_{\bar{\lambda}_2}^{\bar{\bar{\lambda}}_2} \frac{\sqrt{(\lambda_1' - \lambda_2)}}{\sqrt{(a^2 - \lambda_2)}\sqrt{(b^2 - \lambda_2)}}\, d\lambda_2 - $$

$$- \frac{1}{2} \int_{\bar{\bar{\lambda}}_2}^{\bar{\bar{\bar{\lambda}}}_2} \frac{\sqrt{(\lambda_1' - \lambda_2)}}{\sqrt{(a^2 - \lambda_2)}\sqrt{(b^2 - \lambda_2)}}\, d\lambda_2 - \frac{1}{2} \int_{\bar{\lambda}_1'}^{\bar{\lambda}_1} \frac{\sqrt{(\lambda_1' - \lambda_1)}}{\sqrt{(a^2 - \lambda_1)}\sqrt{(b^2 - \lambda_1)}}\, d\lambda_1 + $$

$$+ \frac{1}{2} \int_{\bar{\lambda}_2}^{\bar{\bar{\lambda}}_2} \frac{\sqrt{(\lambda_1' - \lambda_2)}}{\sqrt{(a^2 - \lambda_2)}\sqrt{(b^2 - \lambda_2)}}\, d\lambda_2.$$

With regard to algebraic signs, when we enter or leave the ellipse, as we reverse direction, we must reverse the sign of the coefficient of $d\lambda_2$. On the other hand, as we leave and re-enter $\bar{\lambda}_1, \bar{\lambda}_2$ along different tangents to λ_1' we must have different signs for the coefficient of $d\lambda_1$ as we have the same sign for that of $d\lambda_2$.

The sum is, then

$$L + \int_{\bar{\lambda}_1}^{\lambda_1} \frac{\sqrt{(\lambda_1' - \lambda_1)}}{\sqrt{(a^2 - \lambda_1)}\sqrt{(b^2 - \lambda_1)}}\, d\lambda_1.$$

This is a function of $\bar{\lambda}_1$ and independent of $\bar{\lambda}_2$.

Graves's Theorem 25] *If a loop of inextensible thread be drawn tight about a material ellipse, the locus of the point of strain is a confocal ellipse.*

The original of this is in Graves (q.v.), p. 77, but the paper deals with sphero-conics. This I have not seen. There is a proof by infinitesimal geometry on p. 377 of Salmon, q.v., which seems to me, frankly, bad. The following seems to be simple and satisfactory (Fig. 37).

We make two statements of the total length of the thread, and subtract from each the common arc $\overset{\frown}{ST}{}'$ measured below

$$\overset{\frown}{SS'} + S'P' + P'T' = SP + PT + \overset{\frown}{TT'}.$$

Disregarding higher infinitesimals

$$\overset{\frown}{SS'} = SS'' + S''S', \qquad \overset{\frown}{TT'} = TT'' + T''T',$$

$$SS'' + S''P' + P'T'' + T''T' = SS'' + S''P + PT'' + T''T',$$

$$S''P' + P'T'' = S''P + PT''.$$

This puts P, P' on an ellipse whose foci are S'' and T''. Passing to the limit, this means that the tangent to the locus at P makes equal angles

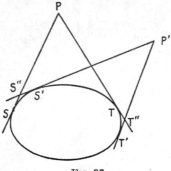

FIG. 37

with the tangents thence to the given ellipse. But this is characteristic of the tangent to the confocal ellipse through P. A great many proofs will be found mentioned on pp. 120, 121 of Dingeldey (q.v.) notes.

CHAPTER VIII

SYSTEMS OF CONICS

§ 1. Linear systems.

By far the greater part of our work till now has been concerned with the properties of individual conics, the only exception being the last section of Chapter IV. There is, nevertheless, a large mass of literature dealing with systems of conics; it is time to pay it more attention. But first it is well to draw a sharper distinction than we have done so far between point and line conics.

Definition] A point conic is either a projection of a circle, or a pair of lines, or a line counted twice. In dealing with these we shall use the two notations explained on pp. 98, 105, namely the tensor notation

$$a_{ij} x^i x^j = 0, \qquad a_{ij} = a_{ji}, \tag{1}$$

or the Clebsch-Aronhold notation

$$(ax)^2 \equiv (a'x)^2 \equiv (a''x)^2 = 0. \tag{1'}$$

The curve will be non-degenerate, i.e. not a line or two lines, if

$$|a_{ij}| = k |a \ a' \ a''|^2 \neq 0. \tag{2}$$

It will be a pair of lines if the rank of the matrix $|a_{ij}|$ be two, a single line if it be unity.

A line conic is a one-parameter system of lines which either (a) are tangents to a non-degenerate point conic, or (b) pass through either of two given points, or (c) pass through a given point. Algebraically we have

$$A^{ij} u_i u_j = 0, \qquad A^{ij} = A^{ji}, \tag{3}$$

or else

$$(ua)^2 \equiv (ua')^2 \equiv (ua'')^2 = 0. \tag{3'}$$

The distinction between the different kinds depends, as before, on the rank of the matrix. The line conic (3) is composed of tangents to the point conic (1) when, and only when,

$$A^{ij} = \rho \frac{\partial |a_{pq}|}{\partial a_{ij}}. \tag{4}$$

A system of conics is said to be 'linear' when the actual coefficients are subjected to a number of linear homogeneous equations, or are linearly dependent, with constant multipliers, on a certain number of given conics. Such were the systems studied in § 6 of Chapter IV. The present algebraic treatment will be found more satisfactory.

Definition] A pencil of point conics is the system linearly dependent on two given conics. Analytically

$$a_{ij} \equiv \lambda_1 b_{ij} + \lambda_2 c_{ij}, \tag{5}$$

$$(ax)^2 \equiv \lambda_1 (bx)^2 + \lambda_2 (cx)^2. \tag{5'}$$

Theorem 1] *The intersections of two point conics are common to all conics of the pencil which they determine.*

This may be put succinctly, if not too accurately, in the words: The conics of a pencil have in common the four points, distinct or adjacent, common to any two of them. Since the determinant $|a_{ij}|$ is cubic in λ_1, λ_2, we have

Theorem 2] *The determination of the degenerate conics of a pencil depends on an equation of the third order.*

We saw on p. 104 that when this equation has distinct roots, the conics pass through four points, and the degenerate conics of the pencil are the pairs of opposite sides of the resulting complete quadrangle. The diagonal triangle of this quadrangle is self-conjugate with regard to all of the conics of the pencil. When it is used as coordinate triangle, the equation of each conic of the pencil will involve only the squared terms.

Theorem 3] *If the point conics of a pencil have four common points, their equations may be all expressed simultaneously in a form involving only squared terms.*

If the conic (3) touch the line v

$$A^{ij} v_i v_j = 0, \qquad A^{ij} = \frac{\partial |a_{pq}|}{\partial a_{ij}}.$$

This will be quadratic in λ_1, λ_2

Theorem 4] *Two conics of a pencil will touch any line which does not pass through a point common to all of them, or a point which has the same polar with regard to all of them.*

This comes, of course, also from Desargues's involution theorem.

Theorem 5] *The polars of a point with regard to the conics of a pencil generate pencil of lines unless two of them are identical, in which case all are.*

Let us seek the locus of the poles of a given line with regard to the conics of a pencil. Here the Clebsch-Aronhold notation is the best. The polar of a point (y) with regard to the conic (3') is

$$(ay)(ax) = 0.$$

Let the line (u) be the polar of (x) with regard to the conic $(3')$

$$\lambda_1(bx)b_i + \lambda_2(cx)c_i = \rho u_i$$

$$|b \ c \ u|(bx)(cx) = 0. \tag{6}$$

This is Poncelet's eleven-point conic which we ran across in Chapter IV, Theorem 6.

Dual to the pencil of point conics is the linear series of line conics

$$A^{ij}u_i u_j = \lambda_1 B^{ij}u_i u_j + \lambda_2 C^{ij}u_i u_j \tag{7}$$

$$(u\alpha)^2 \equiv \lambda_1(u\beta)^2 + \lambda_2(u\gamma)^2 \tag{7'}$$

The properties of these conics correspond exactly to those of the pencil which we have just given. The polar of a point with regard to the conics of such a series will envelop an eleven-line conic, dual to the eleven point:

$$|\beta \ \gamma \ x|(u\beta)(u\gamma) = 0. \tag{8}$$

The conics of such a series are tangent to four lines, distinct or adjacent.

Theorem 6] *The only cases where the non-degenerate conics of a pencil are also the non-degenerate conics of a linear series is where all have double contact or four-point contact.*

The most interesting linear series are the sets of confocal conics. One line conic of such a series is the circular points at infinity. When a conic of the series is non-parabolic, the other degenerate conics are its real and its imaginary foci. Analytically, if we start with a standard ellipse

$$\frac{x^2}{a^2} + \frac{y^2}{b^2} - 1 = 0,$$

its tangential equation will be

$$a^2 u_1^2 + b^2 u_2^2 - u_3^2 = 0.$$

That of the circular points at infinity is

$$u_1^2 + u_2^2 = 0.$$

A conic of the confocal system is

$$(a^2 - \lambda)u_1^2 + (b^2 - \lambda)u_2^2 - u_3^2 = 0$$

$$\frac{x^2}{a^2 - \lambda} + \frac{y^2}{b^2 - \lambda} = 1. \tag{9}$$

If the parameters for the two conics through x_1, y_1 be λ_1, λ_2

$$\frac{x_1^2}{a^2 - \lambda_1} + \frac{y_1^2}{b^2 - \lambda_1} = 1, \qquad \frac{x_1^2}{a^2 - \lambda_2} + \frac{y_1^2}{b^2 - \lambda_2} = 1,$$

$$\frac{x_1^2}{(a^2 - \lambda_1)(a^2 - \lambda_2)} + \frac{y_1^2}{(b^2 - \lambda_1)(b^2 - \lambda_2)} = 0.$$

Theorem 7] *Confocal conics intersect at right angles.*

This comes also from the theorem, known to the Greeks, which says that the tangent and normal to a conic bisect the angles formed by the focal radii. We are here in touch with the elliptic coordinates mentioned in the last chapter in connexion with Graves's theorem.

The totality of conics linearly independent on three independent ones are in one-to-one correspondence with the points of a projective plane. Conics linearly dependent on two will correspond to points of a line. Now if *ABC* be three non-collinear points, and *A'* be collinear with *B* and *C*, while *B'* is collinear with *C* and *A*, there is a point *C'* which is collinear with *A* and *B* and also with *A'* and *B'*.

Theorem 8] *If A, B, C be three linearly independent point or line conics, and if A' be a conic linearly dependent on B and C, while B' is a conic linearly dependent on C and A, there is a conic C' which is linearly dependent on A and B, and also on A' and B'.*

This very easy theorem opens the door to a large number of theorems, and was first given, though for sphero-conics, in Chasles[4]. We are dealing with line conics, one being, in each case, the circular points at infinity.

Theorem 9] *If A and A' confocal conics, and B a conic not confocal with them, and if C touch all the common tangents to A and B, and C''' touch all the common tangents to A' and B, there is a conic confocal with A and A' which touches all the common tangents to C and C'', and another confocal with B which touches these tangents.*

Theorem 10] *If A and B are two conics which are not confocal, C' a conic touching their common tangents, B' a conic confocal with B, then the common tangents to B' and C' will touch a conic which is confocal with A.*

Suppose, in particular, that *B* is the pole, counted twice, of the line connecting *H* and *K*, two points of *A*, while *C'* is these two points looked on as a line conic. A conic confocal to a point counted twice is a circle, so that *B'* is a circle. Then the tangents to *B'* from *H* and *K* touch a conic confocal with *A*. The reasoning is reversible, which gives

Theorem 11] *If from two points of a conic tangents be drawn to a confocal conic, the four will touch a circle.*

This theorem seems to me rather striking. A proof of Graves's theorem may be based on it.

The system of point conics linearly dependent on three independent ones is called a 'linear net'. The system dual to this is the 'linear web'. We express the net analytically

$$d_{ij} \equiv \lambda_1 a_{ij} + \lambda_2 b_{ij} + \lambda_3 c_{ij}. \tag{10}$$

$$(dx)^2 \equiv \lambda_1 (ax)^2 + \lambda_2 (bx)^2 + \lambda_3 (cx)^2. \tag{10'}$$

The conics of a net apolar to a given line conic will be linearly dependent on two and so form a pencil. In particular, those through a given point form a pencil. If we take an arbitrary line (u), that will usually be the polar of a chosen point with regard to one conic of the net, for we may usually solve the three equations in $\lambda_1 : \lambda_2 : \lambda_3$

$$\lambda_1 (ay)a_i + \lambda_2 (by)b_i + \lambda_3 (cy)c_i = \rho u_i.$$

If, however, $$|a\ b\ c|(ay)(by)(cy) \equiv k\, \frac{\partial(f_1, f_2, f_3)}{\partial(y^1, y^2, y^3)} = 0, \tag{11}$$

this will not be the case. (y) lies on the Jacobian curve of the net; its polars with regard to all the curves form a pencil, converging at (z) which is conjugate to (y) with regard to all the conics of the net, and also a point of the Jacobian curve. When (11) is satisfied, the three equations

$$\lambda_1 (ay)a_i + \lambda_2 (by)b_i + \lambda_3 (cy)c_i = 0 \tag{12}$$

are compatible, and (y) is a double point for one conic of the net. The polars of all the curves of the net through (y) pass through that point and also through (z), so that all of these curves but the one with the double point have the same tangent.

Theorem 12] *The Jacobian curve of the conics of a linear net is of the third order. It is the locus of all points whose polars with regard to the conics of the net are concurrent, the point of concurrence being also a point of the Jacobian. It is also the locus of the double points of all conics of the net. All conics of the net through a point of the Jacobian, except that with the double point, have the same tangent there.*

A linear net will not usually include a line counted twice. Let (y) and (z) be conjugate with regard to all conics of the net. Let us study the line which joins them

$$x^i = \mu_1 y^i + \mu_2 z^i, \qquad \rho u_i = y_j z_k - y_k z_j.$$

The intersections with the three curves will be given by

$$(A\mu)^2 \equiv [(ay)\mu_1 + (az)\mu_2]^2 = 0$$

$$(B\mu)^2 \equiv [(by)\mu_1 + (bz)\mu_2]^2 = 0$$

$$(C\mu)^2 \equiv [(cy)\mu_1 + (cz)\mu_2]^2 = 0.$$

If (y) and (z) are conjugate, these three point-pairs belong to an involution. The condition for that is easily found to be

$$|B\ C|.\,|C\ A|.\,|A\ B| = 0,$$

where

$$|B\ C| \equiv \begin{vmatrix} (by) & (bz) \\ (cy) & (cz) \end{vmatrix} \equiv |b\ c\ u|,$$

i.e.

$$|b\ c\ u|.\,|c\ a\ u|.\,|a\ b\ u| = 0. \tag{13}$$

This cubic envelope is called the 'Cayleyan' of the net. Dual to the linear net we have the linear web

$$D^{ij} = \lambda_1 A^{ij} + \lambda_2 B^{ij} + \lambda_3 C^{ij}, \tag{14}$$

$$(u\delta)^2 \equiv \lambda_1(u\alpha)^2 + \lambda_2(u\beta)^2 + \lambda_3(u\gamma)^2. \tag{14'}$$

Corresponding to the Jacobian is the 'Hermitian envelope'

$$|\alpha\ \beta\ \gamma|.\,(u\alpha)(u\beta)(u\gamma) = 0, \tag{15}$$

also the Cayleyan

$$|\beta\ \gamma\ x|.\,|\gamma\ \alpha\ x|.\,|\alpha\ \beta\ x| = 0. \tag{16}$$

What is more interesting is to establish relations between these two two-parameter linear systems. We recall some results found in Chapter IV. If a point and line conic be so related that there is a conic inscribed in the former which is self-conjugate with regard to the latter, there are an infinite number of such, also an infinite number circumscribed to the latter which are self-conjugate with regard to the former. We saw on p. 103 that this condition could be expressed in the form $a_{ij} B^{ij} = 0$; $(a\beta)^2 = 0$.

As this condition is linear and homogeneous, we have

Theorem 13] *The conics apolar to those of a linear net will form a linear web, and vice versa.*

Let us find the linear net apolar to that given by (10) or (10'). The answer here does not come in the compact form we should expect. A general conic of the net will be determined by two arbitrary tangents, say (v) and (w)

$$a_{ij} D^{ij} = b_{ij} D^{ij} = c_{ij} D^{ij} = v_i v_j D^{ij} = w_i w_j D^{ij} = u_i u_j D^{ij} = 0$$

$$\begin{vmatrix} a_{11} & a_{12} & a_{13} & a_{22} & a_{23} & a_{33} \\ b_{11} & b_{12} & b_{13} & b_{22} & b_{23} & b_{33} \\ c_{11} & c_{12} & c_{13} & c_{22} & c_{23} & c_{33} \\ v_1^2 & v_1 v_2 & v_1 v_3 & v_2^2 & v_2 v_3 & v_3^2 \\ w_1^2 & w_1 w_2 & w_1 w_3 & w_2^2 & w_2 w_3 & w_3^2 \\ u_1^2 & u_1 u_2 & u_1 u_3 & u_2^2 & u_2 u_3 & u_3^2 \end{vmatrix} = 0.$$

If we have a point and a line conic which are apolar, in case the point conic is a pair of lines, they will be conjugate with regard to the line conic. If a line pair is apolar with regard to all the conics of a web, its lines are tangent to the Hermitian envelope. Now consider a pencil of conics through four points, and belonging to the net. The pairs of opposite sides of the complete quadrangle are pairs of tangents to the Hermitian envelope. Next, start with a general point (y). There are three tangents thence to the Hermitian envelope. Each of these has a mate. The three pairs of mates will be pairs of opposite sides of a complete quadrangle, every conic through the vertices will be apolar to the conics of the web. Every conic through (y) which is apolar to the conics of the web goes through the four vertices of the quadrangle. This gives a pretty theorem, due apparently to Rosanes, although he disclaims authorship.†

Theorem 14] *If the pairs of opposite sides of two complete quadrangles be conjugate with regard to the conics of a web, the eight vertices lie on a conic.*

Suppose that we have a general cubic curve

$$f(x^1, x^2, x^3) \equiv (dx)^3 = 0. \tag{17}$$

The conic polar of (y) is

$$\sum y^i \frac{\partial f}{\partial x^i} \equiv 3(dy)(dx)^2 = 0.$$

As (y) varies, these conics generate a linear net. The question arises, Does the general linear net consist of conic polars with regard to some cubic curve? Such is the case. The earliest proof is in Hermite (q.v.), by means of invariants. He uses the clumsy Cayleyan notation. Here is a very simple proof. We wish to find a cubic form such that the net of its conic polars will be the net (10)

$$\frac{\partial f}{\partial x^1} = \lambda_1 a_{ij} x^i x^j + \lambda_2 b_{ij} x^i x^j + \lambda_3 c_{ij} x^i x^j,$$

$$\frac{\partial f}{\partial x^2} = \mu_1 a_{ij} x^i x^j + \mu_2 b_{ij} x^i x^j + \mu_3 c_{ij} x^i x^j,$$

$$\frac{\partial f}{\partial x^3} = \nu_1 a_{ij} x^i x^j + \nu_2 b_{ij} x^i x^j + \nu_3 c_{ij} x^i x^j.$$

If we compare the coefficients of $x^i x^j$ we have eighteen linear homogeneous equations in the ten coefficients of f and the nine variables λ_p, μ_q, ν_r. When it comes to actually determining the cubic we become pretty deeply involved. A symbolic solution will be found in Rosanes (q.v.), p. 280. The most direct way would seem to be to start with the

† Rosanes (q.v.), p. 278.

apolar web, and write the conditions that the conics given by setting the partial derivatives of f equal to 0 are all apolar to three conics of the web

$$f \equiv (dx)^3 \qquad d_i(d\alpha)^2 = d_i(d\beta)^2 = d_i(d\gamma)^2 = 0.$$

The three-parameter system of conics linearly dependent on four has been extensively studied in Rosanes (q.v.), and elsewhere. It consists in the conics apolar to those of a linear series, and so is, in general, the set of conics with regard to which the pairs of opposite vertices of a complete quadrilateral are mutually conjugate. There are ∞^2 line pairs in the system; one line can be taken at random, the other line then contains the three points on the diagonals separated by a pair of vertices from the intersection with the given line. The fact that these three points are collinear is a projective generalization of the theorem which places the middle points of the diagonals of a complete quadrilateral on a straight line, the first part of the Gauss-Bodenmiller theorem of p. 90. Four conics consist in a line counted twice, the four sides of the quadrilateral. The four-parameter system of conics linearly dependent on five is the system of all conics apolar to a given line conic. The totality of rectangular hyperbolas is an example. There are a large number of problems of construction connected with linear systems; an account of them will be found in Smith (q.v).

§ 2. Chasles's theory of characteristics.

There is a type of problem which arises often, and which is very difficult of solution by direct attack, but yields to indirect methods. 'How many figures of a specified sort, depending on n parameters, will satisfy n independent conditions?' When it is a question of how many lines in the projective plane fulfil two algebraic conditions, the question usually boils down to finding the number of solutions of two algebraic equations in the coordinates of the lines, or the number of common tangents to two envelopes. When we deal with conics, not with lines, the matter is more complicated and has involved quite a bit of research.

At the beginning of the present chapter we defined carefully what we meant by a point and what by a line conic. In the non-degenerate cases the two are essentially the same, the line conic consists in the tangents to a point conic. When a point conic is two lines, it still produces a line conic, the intersection counted twice; and two points, a good line conic, produces a good point conic, the line twice counted. But a line counted twice does not produce a line conic, nor a point counted twice a point conic. If the equation of the point conic be

$$a_{ij}x^ix^j = 0, \tag{18}$$

the tangential equation of the line conic will be

$$A^{ij}u_i u_j = 0, \qquad A^{ij} = \rho \begin{vmatrix} a_{ij} & a_{ik} \\ a_{jk} & a_{kk} \end{vmatrix}; \qquad (19)$$

but when the rank of the matrix $||a_{ij}||$ is unity, the coefficients A^{ij} vanish.

But the matter does not end there. We are often concerned with continuous systems of conics. We may have a continuous system of point conics ending in a line counted twice. They will correspond to a continuous system of line conics, what will be their limiting envelope? For instance, suppose that we have a pencil of conics, including $(x^1)^2 = 0$,

$$a_{11} = 1 + \rho b_{11}, \qquad a_{ij} = \rho b_{ij}.$$

The equation of the corresponding line conic is

$$\begin{vmatrix} 1 + \rho b_{11} & \rho b_{12} & \rho b_{13} & u_1 \\ \rho b_{12} & \rho b_{22} & \rho b_{23} & u_2 \\ \rho b_{13} & \rho b_{23} & \rho b_{33} & u_3 \\ u_1 & u_2 & u_3 & 0 \end{vmatrix} = 0. \qquad (20)$$

We may divide ρ out of this. Then set $\rho = 0$. We get

$$b_{33} u_2^2 - 2 b_{23} u_2 u_3 + b_{22} u_3^2 = 0. \qquad (21)$$

This will represent a pair of points on $x^1 = 0$ or a single point when

$$b_{22} b_{33} - b_{23}^2 = 0. \qquad (22)$$

We have, in fact, three limiting cases:

  (1) The limiting point conic is a line counted twice, and the limiting line conic two distinct points thereon.
  (2) The limiting line conic is a point counted twice, and the limiting point conic two distinct lines through it.
  (3) The limiting point conic is a line counted twice, and the limiting line conic a point thereon counted twice.

The first systematic study of how many conics of a one-parameter system fulfil a given condition was made by Chasles. As the totality of conics fulfilling one condition are a four-parameter system, this amounts to asking how many conics are common to a one-parameter and a four-parameter system. He assigns to his one-parameter system two numbers, called 'characteristics': μ the number through a general point, and ν the number tangent to a general line:

Chasles's Assumption] *If a one-parameter system of conics have the characteristics μ and ν, the number of conics of the system which fulfil some condition independent of the system is*

$$\alpha\mu + \beta\nu,$$

where α, β are positive integers or 0, but independent of the system.

As a matter of fact these integers are easily determined. The characteristics of a system which consists in pairs of an involution of concurrent lines are $(1, 0)$; the characteristics of a system which consists in pairs of a collinear point involution are $(0, 1)$. Hence α is the number of line pairs of a general involution which satisfy the given condition, and β the number of point pairs.

These ideas are developed at length in Chasles[6]. He develops also many properties of the general (μ, ν) system. For instance, the pole of an arbitrary line will trace a curve of order ν, for it will meet that line in the points of contact with the conics tangent. Or, what will be the locus of the feet of the normals from a point P on the curves of the system? Take a line l through P. Let Q be a point on it. Through this point will pass μ conics of the system, and each will have two tangents perpendicular to l meeting it in two points Q'. To Q will correspond 2μ points Q'. On the other hand, when Q' is given on l, ν conics of the system will touch a line through it perpendicular to l, and each of these will cut l twice. There will thus be a 2μ to 2ν correspondence between Q and Q', giving $2\mu + 2\nu$ coincidences, which are points of the curve. But there are μ conics through P, hence the curve is of order $3\mu + 2\nu$. Chasles erroneously gives the number $2\mu + \nu$.

Suppose that we know the numbers α_1, β_1 for a system of conics satisfying a condition C. The numbers are:

(i) passing through four points $\alpha_1 + 2\beta_1$;

(ii) passing through three points and touching a line $2\alpha_1 + 4\beta_1$;

(iii) passing through two points and touching two lines $4\alpha_1 + 2\beta$;

(iv) passing through one point and touching three lines $2\alpha_1 + \beta_1$.

These figures will enable us to calculate the number of conics of a second four-parameter system (α_2, β_2) which satisfy C, and three point or line conditions, and so on. The number of conics common to five four-parameter systems with numbers (α_1, β_1), (α_2, β_2), (α_3, β_3), (α_4, β_4), (α_5, β_5) will be

$$\alpha_1 \alpha_2 \alpha_3 \alpha_4 \alpha_5 + 2(\alpha_1 \alpha_2 \alpha_3 \alpha_4 \beta_5 + \alpha_1 \beta_2 \beta_3 \beta_4 \beta_5) +$$
$$+ 4[\alpha_1 \alpha_2 \alpha_3 \beta_4 \beta_5 + \alpha_1 \alpha_2 \beta_3 \beta_4 \beta_5] + \beta_1 \beta_2 \beta_3 \beta_4 \beta_5.$$

But is all this true? Chasles gives no semblance of a real proof. Are limiting cases always to be counted as solutions? A very serious wrench was thrown into the whole works by Halphen (q.v.). He asks this question: The totality of conics touching two lines at two given points, and the totality of conics having four-point contact with a given conic at a given point, are each a system with the characteristics $(1, 1)$. How many conics of the system have the property that the length of the segment cut on a given line bears a given ratio to the sine of the angle between the tangents from a fixed point? In one case the answer is four, in the other three. We can simplify this ingenious arrangement by taking the fixed point at an infinite distance, and asking how many conics have the property that the segment cut on a fixed line bears a fixed ratio to that cut on that or on some other line by tangents having a given direction. Now conics of this sort will, by Desargues's involution theorem, cut a given line in pairs of an involution, and the pairs of tangents in a given direction will be pairs of an involution, and so cut an involution on any transversal. So the question is, How many pairs of one involution bear a given ratio to corresponding pairs in the other? We may write these involutions

$$(ax^2+2bx+c)+\rho(a'x^2+2b'x+c') = 0,$$

$$(\alpha\bar{x}^2+2\beta\bar{x}+\gamma)+\rho(\alpha'\bar{x}^2+2\beta'\bar{x}+\gamma') = 0;$$

$$\frac{\sqrt{\{(b+\rho b')^2-(a+\rho a')(c+\rho c')\}}}{\sqrt{\{(\beta+\rho\beta')^2-(\alpha+\rho\alpha')(\gamma+\rho\gamma')\}}} = k\frac{a+\rho a'}{\alpha+\rho\alpha'}. \tag{23}$$

This leads us to an equation of the fourth order in ρ. But in the case of conics having four-point contact, the common tangent is a limiting case of a point conic, and the point of contact a limiting case of a line conic, so that one double point in one involution corresponds to one double point in the other. We may assume that this comes when $\rho = 0$ and that a double point $x = 0$ in one involution corresponds to a double point $\bar{x} = \omega$ in the other

$$b = c = \alpha = \beta = 0.$$

The equation is now of the third degree. We have a limiting conic of the third kind, the ratio of the segments is $\frac{0}{0}$.

A vigorous attempt to put the whole business on a sounder foundation appears in Clebsch[2]. We express our one-parameter (algebraic) family of conics

$$a_{ij}x^ix^j = 0, \qquad a_{ij} = a_{ij}(X_1, X_2, X_3), \qquad F(X_1, X_2, X_3) = 0.$$

Here all of the functional symbols indicate homogeneous polynomials. How many of these conics will satisfy some algebraic condition independent of the system itself? Clebsch assumes that this is expressed by the vanishing of some invariant of the general conic. He stresses the difference between this and the identical vanishing of a covariant, which is what happens when the condition depends on the system. He gives no proof of this, but gives an example by requiring the conics to touch in a second point some curve which, by hypothesis, they touch already.

Suppose that the invariant condition is written

$$\pi(a_{ij}) = 0.$$

I assume that a_{ij} is of degree ρ in X and F of degree σ. Then when (x) is given, our curves in the (X) plane have $\rho\sigma$ intersections. Not all of these will necessarily depend on (x); let the number which do so be μ, Chasles's first characteristic. Then $\rho\sigma - \mu$ will not depend on (X), and are called exceptional points of the first sort.

Now consider the corresponding system of line conics. The equation $A^{ij}u_i u_j = 0$ will be of order $2\rho\sigma$ in (X). When (u) is given, suppose that we have ν intersections which depend on (X). Then $2\rho\sigma - \nu$ do not. They will include all of the exceptional points of the first sort, for at such a point a_{ij} will be independent of (X), or the tangent to the curve is indeterminate, $A^{ij} = 0$. But there may be exceptional values where the values in A^{ij} are independent of (u), as previously they were independent of (x). And lastly there might be points on $F = 0$ which are exceptional for both reasons.

Clebsch next studies at length the invariants of quadratic forms, using different symbolic expressions which I will not reproduce. He assumes that $\pi = 0$ involves not only the coefficients a_{ij} but the coordinates of certain auxiliary points. Such a situation would arise if we require the conics of a Chasles (μ, ν) system to separate two given points harmonically. He simplifies his conditions as far as possible by using the invariant operator $\sum_i \dfrac{\partial^2 f}{\partial x^i \partial u_i}$ and shows by that means that the only troublesome points on $F = 0$ are those of the last kind. He then works through to what is essentially Chasles's form.

I confess to finding a good many obscure passages in Clebsch, and subsequent writers have criticized his treatment of the difficult case. The simplest approach to the whole problem is in Zeuthen[2]. Here I find his reasoning far from rigorous. To my way of thinking much the best way of handling the whole thing is that given in Study (q.v.), which I shall now explain in some detail.

A general point conic is represented by a point a_{ij} in a projective five space S_5. A line conic will be represented by a hyperplane B^{ij} in the same space.† If the point and line conic be apolar we have

$$B^{ij}a_{ij} = 0,$$

or the corresponding point and hyperplane are incident. The degenerate point conics will be represented by the points of a hypersurface

$$V_4^3 \equiv |a_{pq}| = 0;$$

† Study turns point and line conic about; the change is immaterial.

the degenerate line conics by the three parameters set of hyperplanes

$$W_4^3 \equiv |B^{pq}| = 0.$$

The point conics which consist in single lines counted twice will correspond to the singular points of V_4^3, for in that case

$$\frac{\partial |a_{pq}|}{\partial a_{ij}} = 0.$$

The order of a surface or two-spread in S_5, as that of the singular points, is the number of intersections with a general S_3, say that corresponding to point conics apolar to two given line conics. Four of these are single lines counted twice, namely the four common tangents. Hence the surface in S_5 corresponding to such conics is of the fourth order. We call it F_2^4. Similarly, there is ϕ_2^4 corresponding to single points twice counted.

We have a fundamental birational point to hyperplane transformation

$$\Lambda^{ij} = \rho \, \frac{\partial |a_{pq}|}{\partial a_{ij}}; \qquad b_{ij} = \sigma \frac{\partial |B^{pq}|}{\partial B^{ij}}. \tag{24}$$

This is, of course, what corresponds to the relation of point to line conic when not singular of the third sort. In S_5 this is the relation of a point to its polar hyperplane with regard to V_4^3. It is illusory only for the points of F_2^4, the singular points of V_4^2, or the hyperplanes of ϕ_2^4.

A straight line in S_5 will correspond to a pencil of point conics. When the line cuts V_4^3 in three distinct points, the conics pass through four points. When the line is simply tangent to V_4^3 and also cuts it, the conics are tangent and cut in two points. When the line has three-point contact with V_4^3 the conics osculate, and cut in one point. All of this applies to lines which do not meet F_2^4. When the line meets F_2^4 and cuts V_4^3 elsewhere, the conics have double contact. When the line meets F_2^4 and also touches V_4^3 there, the conics have four-point contact.

There are also certain lines imbedded in V_4^3. When a line is imbedded but does not meet F_2^4, we have a quadratic involution of line pairs. Lastly there is the possibility of a line being imbedded, and meeting F_2^4 say in the point $(1, 0, 0, 0, 0, 0)$.

$$b_{11} = \rho + a_{11}; \qquad b_{ij} = a_{ij}; \qquad |a_{pq}| = 0.$$

If this is to vanish for all values of ϕ,

$$|b_{pq}| = 0, \qquad b_{22} b_{33} - b_{23}^2 = 0.$$

The limiting conic is of the third sort, and we have line pairs consisting of a given line and others through a given point of it.

There are also certain planes imbedded in V_4^3. First of all there are the tangent planes to F_2^4 which correspond to sets of all line pairs which include a given line, and secondly those which correspond to all line pairs through a given point. The former planes meet F_2^4 in a single point, the latter in a line.

It is time to return to Chasles. How many conics of a given one-parameter family will fulfil a given algebraic condition? We suppose that all conditions are given in rational form, so that this amounts to asking how many intersections does a curve in S_5 have with a certain hypersurface. Bézout's theorem tells us that this is the product of their orders. The order of a curve is the number of its intersections with a hyperplane, and so we have the number of conics apolar to a given line conic. The order of a hypersurface is the number of intersections with a line, and so the number of conics in an arbitrary pencil.

This answer is, however, too rough and ready, for the curve and hypersurface may have intersections on F_2^4 and these throw the count out badly. Suppose that a curve of order μ meets F_2^4 in m points, and suppose that it is carried by the transformation (24) into a set of hyperplanes of which ν pass through an arbitrary point, and n of them touch ϕ_2^4. Our birational transformation (24) carries a linear system of points into a quadratic system of hyperplanes, and a linear system of hyperplanes into a quadratic system of points. A curve of order μ will go into a one-parameter system of hyperplanes of order 2μ, but that does not mean that always there will be 2μ variable hyperplanes through an arbitrary point. The m intersections with F_2^4 will give hyperplanes with indeterminate coordinates $(0, 0,..., 0)$ and these must be deducted from the hyperplanes.

$$\nu = 2\mu - m, \qquad \mu = 2\nu - n. \tag{25}$$

Again, suppose that we have a hypersurface of order b in S_5 which contains F_2^4 with the multiplicity β, and that this corresponds to a set of hyperplanes of order a which contains those of ϕ_2^4 with a multiplicity α. The number a gives the number of variable hyperplanes in a general pencil. Such a pencil of hyperplanes will be transformed into the points of a conic of S_5, not a general conic, but one that meets F_2^4 three times, for the pencil of hyperplanes will correspond to the line conics touching the sides of a complete quadrilateral, and each diagonal counted twice will be a limiting case of the corresponding point conic.

$$a = 2b - 3\beta, \qquad b = 2a - 3\alpha. \tag{26}$$

We must now seek the number of conics common to the one-parameter and the four-parameter systems. A curve of order μ will meet a hypersurface of order b in μb points. Of these, however, $m\beta$ must be rejected, as they are on F_2^4. We have remaining

$$\mu b - m\beta = \mu \alpha + \nu \beta.$$

And what are the meanings of these numbers? μ is, as before, the number of conics through a general point, and ν the number of line conics tangent to a general line. The meanings of α and β we find as before, p. 132.

Chasles's Characteristic Theorem 15] *If a one-parameter system of conics be such that μ pass through an arbitrary point, and ν touch an arbitrary line, the number which fulfil such a condition that α pairs of a general line involution do so, and β point pairs of an arbitrary point involution do so, is $\mu\alpha+\nu\beta$.*

In practice the difficulties arise in the case of limiting conics of the third sort, as we saw in discussing Halphen's example. Moreover, we must be very careful to state clearly whether we consider such limiting conics as fulfilling this condition or not. A line counted twice will meet a curve in two superimposed points; the same is true of a tangent conic. Shall we include it among the tangent conics? Various attempts have been made to specify the conditions under which some solutions should be rejected. Study makes a distinction between movable and immovable solutions. He defines as immovable a solution which does not change its position in the one-parameter family when the four-parameter family is subjected to a linear transformation of the plane, and finds that immovable solutions only occur when we have limiting conics of the third sort. Personally I cannot find that this helps a great deal. This interesting formula must surely be handled with gloves, and we must specify very clearly which solutions we shall accept and which we shall reject.

CHAPTER IX

CONICS IN SPACE

§ 1. Algebraic systems.

PRACTICALLY everything which we have done so far in connexion with
the conic sections, whether as individual curves or systems of curves,
has been confined to conics in a single plane. In one way this is curious,
for the Greeks first reached the conics as projections of circles, although
they quickly dropped this to study them through their equations. It is
fair to say that the same thing is true of the circle. The greater part of
the vast material we have dealing with circles considers only those
which are in one plane. However, there is a certain amount of doctrine
of circles in different planes, and it is the purpose of the present chapter
to show what has been done to study conics which are not coplanar.

The fundamental problem in studying conics in different planes is to
set up some system of coordinates for a space conic, or the best system
of equations to handle it. The first writer to tackle this seems to have
been Spottiswoode[2], and a singularly clumsy bit of geometry was the
result. A space conic depends on eight parameters, but Spottiswoode
endows it with no less than eighteen coordinates connected, naturally,
by a large number of relations. Of course it is not always best to have
the exact number of coordinates that fit the number of degrees of
freedom. In projective geometry we usually have one extra coordinate,
as we use homogeneous variables. In studying algebraic systems of
circles in space it is well to give each circle, which depends on only six
parameters, ten homogeneous coordinates, like the Plücker line coordinates, but connected by five equations, which amount to three
independent ones; but eighteen coordinates seem a bit excessive.

Spottiswoode uses the clumsy Cayley notation. He starts with a
quadric surface and a plane, which he writes

$$(a, b, c, d, f, g, h, l, m, n)(x, y, z, t)^2 = 0, \tag{1}$$

$$\alpha x + \beta y + \gamma z + \delta t = 0. \tag{2}$$

One way to get the Plücker coordinates of a line is to write the
equations of two planes through it, then eliminate each homogeneous
variable in turn. Spottiswoode does something similar here, thus
getting the equations of four cones through the conic, whose vertices are
those of the coordinate tetrahedron, four equations of the general type

$$(C, B, F, L, L', A')(y, z, t)^2 = 0.$$

We thus get eighteen coordinates. But the same result can be reached in another way. Let the plane of equation (2) be brought to intersect the line common to the two planes

$$ux+vy+wz+\omega t = 0$$
$$u'x+v'y+w'z+\omega't = 0.$$

The coordinates of the common point will involve linearly the coordinates α, β, γ, δ and also the Plücker coordinates of the line common to the last two planes. Then substitute the coordinates of this point in the equation (1) of the quadric. We shall have a quadratic equation in the Plücker line coordinates, so that the lines meeting a conic in space generate a quadratic line complex. The coefficients in this equation are Spottiswoode's coordinates for the conic. It is not, by any means, a general quadratic line complex. Such complexes are characterized by the elementary divisors of the determinant built from the equation of the given complex and the identical relation which connects Plücker line coordinates. In the present case the complex has the characteristic symbol†

$$(2, 2, 2).$$

The determination of the equation of such a complex is vastly simplified if we use a better notation, say the tensor notation.

Let us write equations (1) and (2)

$$a_{ij}x^ix^j = 0, \qquad b_ix^i = 0.$$

A line from (y) to (z) will meet this plane in (x)

$$x^i = [(b_jy^j)]z^i - [(b_jz^j)]y^i,$$
$$a_{ij}b_kb_lp^{ik}p^{jl} = 0. \tag{3}$$

The next attempts to find conic coordinates seem to have been those in Godeaux[2]. He makes three suggestions. His third, and most obvious, is this. I use the Clebsch-Aronhold symbolic notation, and write the equation of the plane

$$(vx) = 0. \tag{4}$$

Now it imposes five conditions on a quadric surface to require it to pass through a given conic. Hence, as these conditions are linear, there is usually just one such conic linearly dependent on six given quadrics, which are, naturally, supposed linearly independent. We write, in consequence

$$(lx)^2 \equiv \mu_1(ax)^2+\mu_2(bx)^2+\mu_3(cx)^2+\mu_4(dx)^2+\mu_5(ex)^2+\mu_6(fx)^2 = 0. \tag{5}$$

Godeaux takes the four ν_i's and the six μ_j's as separately homogeneous coordinates for the conic. There are ten of them, but as they are separately homogeneous they only amount to eight independent ones,

† Jessop (q.v.), p. 232.

the right number. The condition that the conic should be degenerate, consist of two lines or a line counted twice, is the condition that the plane touch the quadric $|l\ l'\ l''\ v|^2 = 0.$

Godeaux's first system consists in expressing the conic in matrix form:

$$\left\|\begin{array}{ccc} (ax)^2 & (a'x) & a'' \\ (bx)^2 & (b'x) & b'' \end{array}\right\| = 0. \tag{6}$$

This means, when written at length:

$$(a'x)b'' - (b'x)a'' = 0,$$
$$(ax)^2 b'' - (bx)^2 a'' = 0,$$
$$(ax)^2(b'x) - (bx)^2(a'x) = 0.$$

The residual intersection of the cubic and plane is the line

$$(a'x) = (b'x) = 0.$$

This ingenious method of handling space curves apparently originated in Stuyvaert (q.v.). It is not necessary to use symbolic notation. The conic will degenerate if the plane touches the quadric. It will touch a given plane if the intersection of them with the plane of the conic touches the quadric.

Godeaux's second method comes similarly from the matrix equation

$$\left\|\begin{array}{ccc} (ax)^2 & (a'x) & (a''x) \\ (bx) & b' & b'' \end{array}\right\| = 0. \tag{7}$$

The great utility of such notations comes in when we are studying two- and three-parameter systems of conics. It is so used in Godeaux[1]. On the other hand, we have an elaborate purely geometrical study of such systems in Montessano[1] and Montessano[2]. This writer is especially interested in linear congruences, that is to say, two-parameter systems of conics of which but one passes through an arbitrary point. Such a system of curves will cut an arbitrary plane in pairs of points connected by an involutory Cremona transformation, and such transformations are well known.† We find in Montessano[1], pp. 589 ff., essentially the following reasoning. In a plane (u) consider a homoloidal net of curves, that is to say, such a net that all are linearly dependent on three, and two members have but one variable intersection. The conics which meet each curve of the net will generate a surface. We thus get a net of surfaces, linearly dependent on three. The conics of our system will be common to pencils of surfaces of the net. The remainder of the base of such a pencil will be such a curve, or set of curves, that through each point will pass an infinite number of our conics. Montessano assumes that as there are ∞^3 conics, in space, and only ∞^2 in a congruence, each

† Coolidge[3], pp. 478 ff.

must have six intersections with fixed curves—quite an unwarranted assumption as it seems to me.

A very much more satisfactory way of handling the whole matter is found in James (q.v.). He uses the technique which Stuyvaert used for cubic curves. We get the linear congruence from equation (6)

$$\left\| \begin{array}{ccc} \alpha_1(ax)^2+\alpha_2(bx)^2+\alpha_3(cx)^2 & \alpha_1(a'x)+\alpha_2(b'x)+\alpha_3(c'x) & \alpha_1 a''+\alpha_2 b''+\alpha_3 c'' \\ (dx)^2 & (d'x) & d'' \end{array} \right\| = 0. \quad (8)$$

Here we have a bundle of planes through the point

$$d''(a'x) - a''(d'x) = 0; \quad d''(b'x) - b''(d'x) = 0; \quad d''(c'x) - c''(d'x) = 0,$$

projectively related to a net of quadrics. When (x) is given, we have two linear homogeneous equations in $\alpha_1 : \alpha_2 : \alpha_3$, so that this is a linear congruence in the sense of Montessano. To find the parameters for the curve through (y) we write (y) for (x) and write the condition that the terms of the first row should be $-\omega$ times the corresponding terms of the second:

$$\alpha_1 : \alpha_2 : \alpha_3 : \omega = |(by)^2 \; (c'y) \; d''| : - |(ay)^2 \; (c'y) \; d''| :$$
$$|(ay)^2 \; (b'y) \; d''| : - |(ay)^2 \; (b'y) \; c''|. \quad (9)$$

This will be indeterminate when

$$\left\| \begin{array}{cccc} (ay)^2 & (by)^2 & (cy)^2 & (dy)^2 \\ (a'y) & (b'y) & (c'y) & (d'y \\ a'' & b'' & c'' & d'' \end{array} \right\| = 0. \quad (10)$$

Here we have two cubic surfaces

$$\left| \begin{array}{ccc} (ay^2) & (by)^2 & (cy)^2 \\ (a'y) & (b'y) & (c'y) \\ a'' & b'' & c'' \end{array} \right| = 0, \qquad \left| \begin{array}{ccc} (ay)^2 & (by)^2 & (dy)^2 \\ (a'y) & (b'y) & (dy') \\ a'' & b'' & d'' \end{array} \right| = 0.$$

Part of their intersection is the conic

$$\left\| \begin{array}{ccc} (ay)^2 & (a'y) & (a'') \\ (by)^2 & (b'y) & (b'') \end{array} \right\| = 0.$$

The residual intersection is a space curve of the seventh order. In a general plane there will thus be seven points through which pass an infinite number of conics. These are singular points of a Geiser involution, where corresponding points lie on the same cubic through seven given points.†

If we take the values $\alpha_1 : \alpha_2 : \alpha_3$ from (9) and substitute, we have the equation of the plane through (y)

$$|(a'x) \; (by)^2 \; (c'y) \; d''| = 0. \quad (11)$$

† Cf. Coolidge[3], p. 478.

If we hold (x) in place, and allow (y) to vary, we have a surface of the third order generated by the conics through a given point (x). If (x) lie on the conic through (y), then (y) will lie on the conic through (x)

$$|(a'x)\ (by)^2\ (c'y)\ d''| = 0, \qquad |(a'y)\ (bx)^2\ (c'x)\ d''| = 0,$$
$$|(ax)^2\ (by)^2\ (c'y)\ d''| = 0.$$

If we put $x^i = r^i + ls^i$ in this equation we get an equation which is quadratic in l but cubic in (y), whereas if we make the same substitution in the second from the last we get an equation which is linear in (l) and cubic in (y). If we eliminate (l) we get an equation of the ninth degree in (y) which gives the surface generated by the conics which meet a straight line. James treats a number of other systems of conics in much the same way, but I have given enough to explain his technique.

A number of years before the publication of James's paper, the study of conics in space was taken up in Johnson (q.v.). The original point here is that the conic is studied, not as a locus of points, but as the envelope of its tangent planes and a degenerate plane quadric surface. We write

$$A^{ij} u_i u_j = 0, \qquad A^{ij} = A^{ji}, \qquad |A^{pq}| = 0. \qquad (12)$$

These ten homogeneous coefficients, connected by this cubic identity, are the coordinates of the conic. The totality of such conics correspond to the points of an eight-dimensional hypersurface of the fourth order in nine space, a V_8 in S_9. We connect with the point equations by noticing that if we express a point conic parametrically

$$x^i = t_1^2 \alpha^i + 2t_1 t_2 \beta^i + t_2^2 \gamma^i \equiv (r^i t)^2 \equiv (r^{i'} t)^2,$$

and express the condition of tangency with the plane (u) will be

$$A^{ij} = \tfrac{1}{2} |r^i\ r^{j'}|^2.$$

These are line conics, not point conics. The degenerate conics are point pairs which appear when the rank of $||A^{pq}||$ is 2, and points doubly counted when it is 1. The conic (12) will contain the point (x) if

$$\begin{vmatrix} A^{11} & A^{12} & A^{13} & A^{14} & x^1 \\ A^{21} & A^{22} & A^{23} & A^{24} & x^2 \\ A^{31} & A^{32} & A^{33} & A^{34} & x^3 \\ A^{41} & A^{42} & A^{43} & A^{44} & x^4 \\ x^1 & x^2 & x^3 & x^4 & 0 \end{vmatrix} = 0. \qquad (13)$$

If a line conic meet a line in space, the two tangent planes through that line coincide. The line being given by

$$(vx) = 0, \qquad (xw) = 0$$

the condition is

$$A^{ij}v_i v_j . A^{ij}w_i w_j - (A^{ij}v_i w_j)^2 = 0.$$

This takes a neater form in Clebsch-Aronhold symbolism, and the Plücker line coordinates

$$p^{kl} \equiv v_i w_j - v_j w_i; \qquad A^{ij}u_i u_j \equiv (au)^2 \equiv (a'u)^2.$$

$$\begin{vmatrix} (av) & (aw) \\ (a'v) & (a'w) \end{vmatrix}^2 = 0, \qquad \left[\sum \begin{vmatrix} a_i & a_j \\ a'_i & a'_j \end{vmatrix} p^{kl} \right]^2 = 0.$$

If our coordinates be connected by a linear relation

$$b_{ij} A^{ij} = 0, \tag{14}$$

the conic is apolar to the quadric

$$b_{ij} x^i x^j = 0.$$

It is easy enough to show that, in general, this means that our line-conic is apolar to the point conic which the quadric cuts in its plane. Let us next consider the simplest relations of two conics. We find these from the characteristic equation, the equation of the conic envelopes linearly dependent on them:

$$\begin{vmatrix} \lambda A^{11} + \mu B^{11} & . & . & . & \lambda A^{14} + \mu B^{14} \\ . & . & . & . & . & . & . & . \\ . & . & . & . & . & . & . & . \\ \lambda A^{41} + \mu B^{41} & . & . & . & \lambda A^{44} + \mu B^{44} \end{vmatrix} = 0,$$

$$\lambda^3 \Theta(A, B) + 2\lambda\mu \Phi(A, B) + \mu^2 \Theta(B, A) = 0. \tag{15}$$

Here Θ, Φ are the fundamental simultaneous invariants. Assuming for the moment that the plane of the A conic is $x^4 = 0$,

$$\Theta(A, B) = \begin{vmatrix} A^{11} & . & A^{13} \\ . & . & . \\ A^{31} & . & A^{33} \end{vmatrix} B^{44}. \tag{16}$$

When the first factor vanishes, the A conic is two points, or a point twice counted; when the second factor vanishes, the second conic touches the plane of the first. Suppose now, that

$$\Phi(A, B) = 0. \tag{17}$$

If the two conics lie in the same plane, the condition is automatically fulfilled. If they do not, and if neither is a point pair or single point, let the plane of the A conic be $x^4 = 0$ and that of the B conic $x^3 = 0$. It is then easy to write the point equation of the cone from $(0, 0, 0, 1)$ to the first conic, and that of the cone from $(0, 0, 1, 0)$ to the second, and bring them to intersect the line $x^3 = x^4 = 0$:

$$p_{11}(x^1)^2 + 2p_{12} x^1 x^2 + p_{22}(x^2)^2 = 0, \qquad q_{11}(x^1)^2 + 2q_{12} x^1 x^2 + q_{22}(x^2)^2 = 0.$$

Now we find after a little calculation that when $\Phi(A, B) = 0$, the roots of these two equations separate one another harmonically. When they have a common root the conics intersect, and we shall have

$$\Theta(A, B)\Theta(B, A)-[\Phi(A, B)]^2 = 0,$$

so that (15) has a double root. When they have two common roots, the conics intersect twice; the Jacobian of the two quadratic forms vanishes identically, and equation (15) has a double root which makes the rank of the characteristic matrix equal to 2. It is curious that Johnson failed to mention this last case.

§ 2. Differential systems.

Besides the algebraic theory of conics in space there is a small amount of differential theory which seems worth some notice. The earliest article I have seen dealing with this is by Kawaguchi[2]. His approach is like this.

Suppose that we have a one-parameter system of conics in the planes

$$l_i y^i = 0; \qquad l_i = l_i(t).$$

We take (x) as point coordinates in the planes of the conics, the coordinate triangle shall be the diagonal triangle of the complete quadrilateral which the plane cuts from the coordinate tetrahedron— a peculiarly neat way of connecting projective coordinates *in plano* and *in spatio*. The vertices of the complete quadrilateral are

$$\rho y^i = -l_j, \qquad \rho y^j = l_i, \qquad y^p = y^q = 0.$$

The vertices of the coordinate triangle are linear combinations of these.

We find eventually:

$$\begin{aligned}
\rho l_1 y^1 &= x^1-x^2-x^3, & \sigma x^1 &= l_1 y^1+l_4 y^4, \\
\rho l_2 y^2 &= -x^1+x^2-x^3, & \sigma x^2 &= l_2 y^2+l_4 y^4, \\
\rho l_3 y^3 &= -x^1-x^2+x^3, & \sigma x^3 &= l_3 y^3+l_4 y^4. \\
\rho l_4 y^4 &= x^1+x^2+x^3,
\end{aligned} \qquad (18)$$

Now let the equation of the conic be

$$a_{ij} x^i x^j = 0, \qquad a_{ij} = a_{ij}(t) = a_{ji}.$$

We take the four quantities l_i and the six a_{ij} as separate homogeneous coordinates for the conic. The whole point of the article is to find projective invariants for these. Let us begin with the l_i's. We can always find such multipliers that

$$P l_i^{\text{iv}}+Q l_i'''+R l_i''+S l_i'+T l_i = 0.$$

There is no harm in assuming that the quantities l have absorbed such a factor that

$$|l\ l'\ l''\ l'''| = 1, \qquad |l\ l'\ l''\ l^{\text{iv}}| = 0,$$
$$l_i^{\text{iv}}+6 p l_i''+4 q l_i'+r l_i = 0.$$

The coefficients are projectively invariant for a change of coordinate triangle, but will usually be altered by a change of parameter. We may show, with a little patience, that the quantities

$$\tfrac{3}{5}p, \qquad q - \frac{3}{2}\frac{dp}{dt}, \qquad r - 2\frac{dq}{dt} + \frac{6}{5}\frac{d^2p}{dt^2} - \frac{81}{25}p^2,$$

are invariant, except for a multiplier, for a change of triangle, and also for a change of parameter.[†] Now for the other coordinates. Their invariants had been previously studied in Kawaguchi[1], an article which I should perhaps have mentioned when studying systems of conics *in plano*. He uses a very compact notation

$$\sum \begin{vmatrix} a_{11}^i & a_{12}^j & a_{13}^k \\ a_{21}^i & a_{22}^j & a_{23}^k \\ a_{31}^i & a_{32}^j & a_{33}^k \end{vmatrix} = (i,j,k). \tag{19}$$

The superscripts here indicate differentiation, the summation sign that we add all of the permutations of i, j, k, with proper algebraic signs prefixed.

$$6|a_{pq}| = (0,0,0) = 1$$
$$\frac{d}{dt}(0,0,0) = 3(1,0,0) = 0$$
$$(1,1,0) = -\tfrac{1}{2}(2,0,0).$$

Kawaguchi uses as independent variable

$$\sigma = i \int (1,1,0)\, dt.$$

The expressions (i,j,k) are clearly invariants for linear transformations. When it comes to dealing with two-parameter systems Kawaguchi starts with a fundamental quadratic differential form,

$$(1_i 1_j 0)\, du_i\, du_j,$$

and uses this as a basis for covariant differentiation. The rest of his work follows classical tensor methods; it would, however, take us too far afield to pursue him farther.

These methods are probably the best ones when we are looking for projective differential properties of conics. When it comes to metrical questions there is something to be said for using a totally different approach. The following is taken direct from Coolidge[5], the only paper I have seen dealing with these general questions, except Blutel (q.v.). The basic technique is that of the moving trihedral, developed in the first pages of Darboux[2]. The coordinates of a point with regard to a fixed right trihedral shall be X^1, X^2, X^3, while with regard to a moving one they are x^1, x^2, x^3. The coordinates of the moving origin shall be X_0^i. The direction cosines of the moving axes with regard to the

---

† Sannia (q.v.). I judge that Kawaguchi drew heavily from this source.

fixed ones shall be a_{ij}. We assume that these various parameters are analytic functions of an independent variable v.

$$X^i = X_0^i + a_{ik} x^k, \qquad |a_{pq}| = 1, \qquad a_{ij} = A^{ij}. \tag{20}$$

Differentiating with respect to v,

$$\frac{\partial X^i}{\partial v} = \frac{\partial X_0^i}{\partial v} + \frac{\partial a_{ik}}{\partial v} x^k + a_{ik} \frac{\delta x^k}{\delta v}.$$

The left side is the component with regard to the fixed axes of the total velocity of the point. The expression $\dfrac{\delta x^j}{\delta v}$ means the velocity with regard to the moving axes. We are interested in the components of this total velocity with regard to the moving axes.

$$a_{ji} \frac{\partial X^j}{\partial v} = \frac{\partial x^i}{\partial v} = \xi^i + \frac{\partial x^i}{\partial v} + q_{ij} x^j, \tag{21}$$

$$q_{ij} = -q_{ji} = a_{ik} \frac{\partial a_{kj}}{\partial v} \qquad \xi^i = a_{ki} \frac{\partial X_0^k}{\partial v}. \tag{22}$$

Suppose now that we have a central conic whose axes are the x^1 and x^2 axes in the moving plane, while the x^3 axis is normal to the plane. Write also $q_{ij} = -p_k$.

$$x^1 = a \cos u, \qquad x^2 = b \sin u, \qquad x^3 = 0$$

$$\frac{\partial x^1}{\partial u} = -a \sin u \qquad \frac{\partial x^1}{\partial v} = \xi^1 + \frac{\partial a}{\partial v} \cos u - p_3 b \sin u$$

$$\frac{\partial x^2}{\partial u} = b \cos u \qquad \frac{\partial x^2}{\partial v} = \xi^2 + \frac{\partial b}{\partial v} \sin u + p_3 \cos u$$

$$\frac{\partial x^3}{\partial u} = 0 \qquad \frac{\partial x^3}{\partial v} = \xi^3 + p_2 b \sin u - p_2 a \cos u.$$

$$E = a^2 \sin^2 u + b^2 \cos^2 u$$

$$F = b \xi^2 \cos u - a \xi^1 \sin u + \frac{1}{2} \frac{\partial (b^2 - a^2)}{\partial v} \cos u \sin u + p_3 \cos u$$

$$\frac{\partial (x^1, x^2)}{\partial (u, v)} = -\left[a \xi^2 \sin u + b \xi^1 \cos u + b \frac{\partial a}{\partial v} \cos^2 u - \right.$$
$$\left. - p_3 (b^2 - a^2) \sin u \cos u + a \frac{\partial b}{\partial v} \sin^2 u \right] \tag{23}$$

$$[EG - F^2]^{\frac{1}{2}} D = -ab \frac{\partial x^3}{\partial v}$$

$$[EG - F^2]^{\frac{1}{2}} D' = \frac{\partial^2 x^3}{\partial u \partial v} \frac{\partial (x^1, x^2)}{\partial (u, v)} - \frac{\partial x^3}{\partial u} \left[\left(b \frac{\partial a}{\partial v} - a \frac{\partial b}{\partial v} \right) \cos u \sin u + \right.$$
$$\left. + p_3 (b^2 \cos^2 u + a^2 \sin^2 u) \right].$$

Suppose, next, that we have, as here, a one-parameter family of conics. There are four possibilities:

(i) Adjacent conics do not intersect.
(ii) They intersect once.
(iii) They intersect twice.
(iv) They touch.

I exclude the case where they are in a fixed plane. These poetic statements may be translated into mathematical language:

(i) The conics are not all tangent to one curve.
(ii) They are tangent to one curve.
(iii) They touch two curves, or one curve twice.
(iv) They touch a curve and lie in the corresponding osculating planes.

The most interesting cases are (iii) and (iv), or rather the former, for the latter can be treated as a limiting case thereof. The guiding idea is that if two conics intersect twice or touch, they lie on two quadric cones. When they are infinitely close, one of these is 'squashed out' but the other is there in full force, and its generators set up a projective correspondence between them. The intersections of the adjacent conics lie in the characteristic lines of their respective planes, and are points of the developable surface generated by those planes. The equation of this line is

$$\frac{\partial x^3}{\partial v} = \xi^3 + p_1 b \sin u - p_2 a \cos u = 0.$$

At such a point the directions of advance $\frac{\partial x^i}{\partial u}, \frac{\partial x^i}{\partial v}$ are identical:

$$\frac{\partial(x^1, x^2)}{\partial(u, v)} = \rho \frac{\partial x^3}{\partial v} (\alpha \cos u + \beta \sin u + \gamma). \tag{24}$$

The equation of the tangent plane to the surface generated is

$$(X^1 - x^1)\frac{\partial(x^2, x^3)}{\partial(u, v)} + (X^2 - x^2)\frac{\partial(x^2, x^1)}{\partial(u, v)} + (X^3 - x^3)\frac{\partial(x^1, x^2)}{\partial(u, v)} = 0,$$

which becomes in the present case

$$X^1 b \cos u + X^2 a \sin u + X^3[\alpha \cos u + \beta \sin u + \gamma] - ab = 0.$$

The point $\left(-\frac{a\alpha}{\gamma}, -\frac{b\beta}{\gamma}, \frac{ab}{\gamma} \right)$ lies in the plane for every value of u, so that all of these tangent planes pass through this point, thus generating a quadric cone through the conic. If we develop (24) and compare with (23)

$$-p_2 a\alpha + \gamma\xi^3 = -b\frac{\partial a}{\partial v}; \qquad p_1 b\beta + \gamma\xi^3 = -a\frac{\partial b}{\partial v}; \tag{25}$$

$$p_1 b\alpha - p_2 a\beta = p_3(a^2 - b^2);$$
$$a\xi^3 - \gamma a p_2 = -b\xi^1; \qquad \beta\xi^3 + \gamma b p_1 = -a\xi^2.$$

The differential equation of curves conjugate to the conics on the surface generated is

$$D\,du + D'\,dv = 0.$$

Substituting, and using equations (25), we get an equation

$$du + [L(v) + M(v)\cos u + N(v)\sin u]\,dv = 0.$$

By changing to the tangent of the half angle this becomes a Riccati equation and the cross ratio of four solutions is constant. This gives

Blutel's Theorem] *If the central conics of a series be not coplanar, but touch two curves, the curves conjugate to them on the surface generated will establish a projective relation between them.*†

The theorem is still true when the adjacent conics touch. We may find similarly the condition that their orthogonal trajectories establish a projective relation among them.

When we are interested in two-parameter systems, we take two variables v_1, v_2 and set up equations like (23). To find the focal points where a conic touches one of the surfaces enveloped, or a curve which meets all, we must make u such a function of v_1 and v_2 that

$$\frac{\partial x^i}{\partial v_1}dv_1 + \frac{\partial x^i}{\partial v_2}dv_2 + \lambda\frac{\partial x^i}{\partial u}du = 0.$$

Setting the determinant of these three homogeneous equations equal to 0, we get an equation which is cubic in $\sin u$ and $\cos u$ or sextic in the tangent of half u. There are, thus, usually six focal points on each conic. This is a classical result.

Let us see under what circumstances our congruence will be a normal one. Here u must be such a function of v_1 and v_2 that

$$E\frac{\partial u}{\partial v_1} + F_1 = E\frac{\partial u}{\partial v_2} + F_2 = 0.$$

The integrability condition gives

$$E\left(\frac{\partial F_1}{\partial v_2} - \frac{\partial F_2}{\partial v_1}\right) + F_1\left(\frac{\partial F_2}{\partial u} - \frac{\partial E}{\partial v_2}\right) + F_2\left(\frac{\partial E}{\partial v_1} - \frac{\partial F_1}{\partial u}\right) = 0.$$

This is developed at length in Coolidge[5], p. 369, and is rather formidable. It is cubic in $\cos u$ and $\sin u$, so that, if the conics of a congruence be normal to more than six surfaces, the congruence is a normal one. It turns out that the identical vanishing of this expression involves seven conditions, one of which is

$$\frac{\partial(a, b)}{\partial(v_1, v_2)} = 0.$$

If then the congruence is a normal one, there is a functional relation between the lengths of the axes. It would lead us too far afield to pursue these matters farther.

† Blutel (q.v.).

CHAPTER X

THE MECHANICAL CONSTRUCTION OF CONICS

THE problem of devising mechanical means for drawing the different conics has, not unnaturally, received a good deal of attention. An historical account by von Braunmühl will be found in Dyck (q.v.). Such a problem was not naturally attractive to the Greek geometers, who held that anything connected with mechanical construction was a degradation to geometry. They had to allow the use of ruler and compass: farther they ordinarily would not go. Mathematicians of other races have held less rigorous views; for them it added to the interest of a curve if a neat and simple way of constructing it could be found.

We may divide the problem of drawing a conic mechanically into two parts:

(1) To construct a non-circular section of a cone of revolution.
(2) To utilize some familiar property of the conics to make a machine for constructing it.

The earliest discussion of the first of these problems, at least the first available, is by Abu Sahl Wijan al-Kuhi and was published about A.D. 1000. Some two hundred years later Muhamad ibn al-Husein wrote what he believed to be a reconstruction of this work, which was not available to him. The former remarked that he did not know whether the ancients were familiar with his instrument or not. Both articles are available, with French translation, in Woepcke[2]. The instrument in question is called the 'perfect compass' and consists essentially in four members:

(i) A straight heavy narrow metal base, lying on the plane of the paper.
(ii) An axis fastened to the base, the angle between them being variable.
(iii) A sleeve attached at the other end of the axis, turning freely about it, and making therewith an angle variable at pleasure.
(iv) A rod sliding freely up and down this sleeve, whose lower end is on the paper, and makes the design.

The sleeve in turning around the axis, which is the axis of a cone of revolution, permits the rod to generate this cone. When the axis is upright we shall have a circle, otherwise one of the other conics. All of the machines which I have seen described for solving problem (1) amount to this.

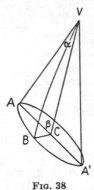

FIG. 38

The question which al-Kuhi, and al-Husein undertook to answer is the following. The length of the axis being determined by the machine, how shall the variable angles be set to describe a conic with given data? In a fourteen-page introduction to Woepcke[2] the translator undertakes to do this algebraically. His work seems to me so clumsy that I venture to put it into different form. Suppose that we are interested in constructing the conic whose equation, in Greek form, is

$$y^2 = \frac{b^2}{a^2}[x(2a-x)].$$

In Fig. 38 let C be the point where the axis VC meets the plane of the paper, β the variable angle which the axis makes with that plane, and α the variable angle between the axis and the rod. Let $AA' = 2a$ be the major axis of the ellipse, and B the end of the ordinate through C.

$$CB^2 = y^2 = \frac{b^2}{a^2}x(2a-x) = \frac{b^2}{a^2}.AC.CA',$$

$$CB^2 = CV^2\tan^2\alpha,$$

$$AC = x = CV.\frac{\sin\alpha}{\sin(\beta+\alpha)}\,; \qquad CA' = (2a-x) = CV\frac{\sin\alpha}{\sin(\beta-\alpha)}.$$

$$\tan^2\alpha = \frac{\sin^2\alpha}{\sin(\beta+\alpha)\sin(\beta-\alpha)}.\frac{b^2}{a^2},$$

$$\frac{\sin^2\beta\cos^2\alpha-\cos^2\beta\sin^2\alpha}{\cos^2\alpha} = \frac{\cos^2\alpha-\cos^2\beta}{\cos^2\alpha} = \frac{b^2}{a^2},$$

$$AC+CA' = 2a = \frac{2CV\sin\beta\sin\alpha\cos\alpha}{\cos^2\alpha-\cos^2\beta},$$

$$\frac{b^2}{a} = CV\sin\beta\tan\alpha.$$

From these formulae we may easily calculate the angles in terms of a, b, CV.

Various modifications of the perfect compass have been made, but they are merely modification of detail. An account of some of the forms used will be found in von Braunmühl[2].

I turn to problem (2) to construct a conic by some machine whose design depends on some property of the curve. Here the three conics require different sorts of machines, if we make an exception of the fact that it is easy to make an arrangement of a string and three pins which will construct either the ellipse or the hyperbola. The Greeks must have perceived that if the two ends of a piece of string be made fast, at two points whose distance apart is less than the length of the string, the locus of a point which pulls the string taut is an ellipse, whose foci are the given points. A better plan, when we only want one curve, is to throw a loop of string over the two pins, as then we can get the whole curve without resetting. Here is a further modification. We have three pins placed at the centre and foci of the curve. The ends are knotted together and held in one hand. From here the string passes around the centre pin on the left and right under the two foci, and is drawn tight by a pencil point above. If the hand holding the two ends remain fixed, the pencil point will move along an arc of an ellipse. By changing the position of the fixed hand this may be altered at pleasure, except that the foci are fixed. But if a small loop be made around the pencil point so that it cannot slip along the string, and the hand holding the ends be pulled down, then the pencil point will trace an arc of a hyperbola, for the difference in the lengths of the two paths from the hand to the point is constant, and so is the difference of the distances to the two foci. I first heard of this simple modification many years ago from Professor W. R. Ransome of Tufts College. The reputed first discoverer of the construction of the ellipse by means of a string, or at least the first to write about it, was Abud ben Muhamad, who wrote in the middle of the ninth century; there is a brief account in Woepcke[1].

Another device for constructing the ellipse is based on the fact that if all chords of a circle having a certain direction be shrunk or stretched in a constant ratio, the resulting curve is a circle. A description and drawing of a machine of an instrument, based on this principle, will be found in Dyck (q.v.), p. 228. But the neatest basis for an ellipsograph is

La Hire's Theorem] *If a circle roll, without slipping, so that it is constantly tangent internally to a fixed circle of twice its radius, the locus of a point on its circumference is a diameter of the fixed circle, while the locus of a point rigidly attached to it elsewhere is an ellipse.*†

La Hire's proof of this is based on the theory of rolling curves, which is the subject of the paper in question. But a much easier proof can be constructed from the writings of earlier geometers.

We find in Proclus (q.v.), p. 130, the following:

'Nor yet if you suppose a right line moving in a right angle, and by bisection to describe a circle, is the circular line, on this account, produced with mixture ? For the extremities of that which is moved, after this manner, since they are equally moved, will describe a straight line, and the

---

† La Hire[5], p. 351.

centre, since it is equally developed, will describe a circle, but other points will describe an ellipse.'

The proof is evident to anyone familiar with the modern equation for the ellipse; it is less clear if we try to get it from the ellipse with an equation in the Greek form. It is a moment's work to show that the lines do not need to be mutually perpendicular, they need not even be coplanar; but of course they must not be parallel. I pass now to Nasir Edin:[†]

'Deux cercles sont donnés dans le même plan, le diamètre de l'un est la moitié du diamètre de l'autre et on donne un point sur le plus petit: puis on fait mouvoir ces deux cercles de mouvements réguliers, en sens opposés, tel que le mouvement du plus petit soit double du mouvement du plus grand, le petit accomplit deux tours pendant que le grand accomplit un. On démontre que le point donné se meut sur le diamètre du grand cercle.'

This theorem has been rediscovered many times, but the priority seems to go to Nasir Edin, or such is the judgement of Dingeldey, op. cit., p. 86. It is obvious that it is not necessary to move both circles. If there is no slipping, we see in Fig. 39

$$OR = 2CR; \qquad \angle PCR = 2\angle POQ,$$

$$\text{arc } PR = \text{arc } QR,$$

so that P is the point originally at Q. Now if we have a point rigidly attached to the small circle, the line from there to C will meet the small circle in two points which subtend a right angle at O. These will trace two mutually perpendicular diameters; we then apply Proclus. A proof similar to this will be found in Suardi (q.v.), pp. 106–7; a very handsome book.

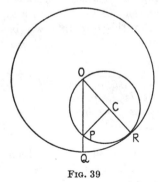

FIG. 39

The fact that C traces a circle suggests a mechanical improvement in such an ellipsograph. Suppose that we have a thin rod of fixed length, one of whose ends moves on a fixed line, while its other end traces a circle whose centre is on the line while its radius is equal to the length of the rod, a point rigidly attached to the rod will trace an ellipse. It is very easy to realize this mechanically. A long account will be found in van Schooten (q.v.). We have a metal triangle. One vertex moves along a straight line, a second traces a circle whose

† Tannery (q.v.), p. 348. A translation by Carra de Vaux.

centre lies on the line. The third vertex traces an ellipse. His proof of the correctness of the construction is much longer than ours.

The construction of the parabola is naturally less satisfactory. At best we can only draw a section of the curve. Dingeldey, op. cit., p. 87, and von Braunmühl[2], p. 58, ascribe to Isidore of Miletus the invention of an instrument for constructing parabolas, basing their statements on a passage in Eutocius which I have been unable to see. Dingeldey thinks that the scheme was the familiar one of attaching one end of the string to a pin at the focus of the curve while the other end is attached to a vertex of a right triangle at the point where the hypotenuse meets a leg whose length is that of the string. The other leg slides along the directrix, while the string is drawn tight at a point of the first leg, which traces the curve.

A string construction is always less satisfactory than a kinematical one, and a machine to draw parabolas is described on p. 359 of van Schooten

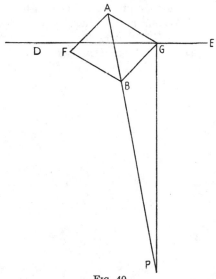

Fig. 40

(q.v.). $FAGB$ is a jointed rhombus (Fig. 40), F is the fixed focus, G slides along the directrix DE. Every point on AB is equidistant from F and G. A grooved rod runs along AB. A second passes through G making a right angle with DE, P is the intersection of the two and is clearly equidistant from F and from DE. I cannot believe this to be a very satisfactory machine, the motion of P must certainly be very jerky.

When it comes to drawing a hyperbola the same difficulties remain.

The earliest rigid ones I have seen described are in van Schooten, Ch. VI. Suppose we are concerned with the hyperbola (Fig. 41). O is the centre, A a vertex. QP is parallel to the asymptote OB, OC is the other

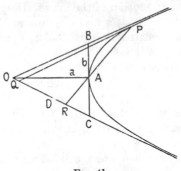

FIG. 41

asymptote. It is then easy to prove, either synthetically or algebraically that QR is a fixed length. Mechanically we have a bar QR of length $\frac{1}{2}OC$ sliding along OC. Through Q passes a grooved rod which remains parallel to the asymptote OB. Another grooved rod RAP rotates about A.

CHAPTER XI

QUADRIC SURFACES, SYNTHETIC TREATMENT†

§ 1. The informal period.

THE earliest writer to pay any attention to those surfaces whose Cartesian equation is of the second order, quadric surfaces as we shall call them henceforward, apart from spheres and cones, was Archimedes. He concerned himself solely with surfaces of revolution, and not even with all of them, for he did not look upon the two branches of a hyperbola as being part of the same curve, and so did not consider one-sheeted hyperboloids of revolution. In Archimedes (q.v.), we find ellipsoids, paraboloids, and two-sheeted hyperboloids of revolution studied under the general heading of conoids and spheroids. It will be remembered that in the earliest discussions of the conics the cutting plane was supposed to be perpendicular to one generator of the cone, and so the division was into the sections of the right-angled, the acute-angled, and the obtuse-angled cone. So the paraboloid of revolution was called the right-angled conoid, the non-rule hyperboloid of revolution was the obtuse-angled conoid, the ellipsoids of revolution were the oblong and the flat spheroids respectively, or such are Heath's translations of their names.

What sort of properties of these surfaces does Archimedes discover? First he discusses the sections in planes through the axis of rotation, or parallel to that axis, or perpendicular thereto. In some cases proofs are omitted. A tangent plane is the plane through the tangent to the generating curve, perpendicular to the plane of that curve; or rather he shows that such a plane will meet the surface in one point only. I have the impression that his main interest in such surfaces was to show his skill in calculating volume by the method of exhaustion, comparing the volume of a segment with that of a cone standing on the same base, whose vertex is the extremity of the conjugate diameter.

Nearly two thousand years elapsed between the death of Archimedes and the appearance of the next discussion of quadric surfaces, and this did not amount to much. The writer was Fermat: I give the translation of Paul Tannery in vol. iii of Fermat (q.v.), pp. 102 ff.

Introduction aux lieux en surface.

'Pour couronner l'*Introduction aux lieux plans et solides* il reste à traiter des *lieux en surface*. Les anciens n'ont fait qu'indiquer ce sujet, mais

---

† In the remaining chapters I have drawn heavily on Staude (q.v.).

n'ont pas enseigné des règles générales, ni même donné quelque exemple célèbre; . . .

'Cette théorie est, cependant, susceptible d'une méthode générale, comme le montrera cette courte dissertation.'

Fermat then proceeds to lay down certain general principles which he calls lemmas:

(i) If all sections of a surface are straight lines, the surface is a plane.

(ii) If all sections are circles, it is a sphere.

(iii) If all sections are circles or ellipses it is spheroid.

And here I must pause to note that if he means by 'spheroid' what Archimedes did, the theorem is manifestly false, unless 'surface' means surface of revolution. But if he does not mean this, we either have a theorem about a surface called a spheroid, whose definition is not given, or else this lemma is merely a definition of the surface. Similar obscurities occur in connexion with paraboloids and hyperbolic conoids. His most important result appears in

Theorem 1] *If a point move in such a way that the sum of the squares in given directions from some given planes bears a fixed ratio to the sum of the squares of its distances in given directions from certain other given planes, its locus is a spheroid or conoid.*

The proof comes from studying the sections in an arbitrary plane.

It is certainly surprising that the synthetic geometers of the seventeenth and eighteenth centuries who were so much interested in the conic sections should have shown no particular interest in the quadric surfaces. The reason, I should imagine, was that there was no immediate definition of these comparable to the definition of a conic as the projection of a circle. It was only after the algebraic geometers had made some progress that the synthetic brethren began to look up and deduce theorems about 'surfaces du second ordre' or 'second degré', without defining what these things might be. The earliest writing I have found was Brianchon[3]. He begins by noting the properties of the polar plane of a point with regard to a quadric. These enable him to prove that if a quadric cone meet a quadric surface in a conic, the residual intersection is another conic. This gives, incidentally, the theorem that, if tangents be drawn to a quadric from an external point, the points of contact lie on a conic. Brianchon finally shows that the polar reciprocal of a quadric, with regard to a quadric, is also a quadric.

A nearly contemporaneous, and much more original, discussion of the quadrics is found in Dupin. This piece of research is somewhat out of the natural line of advance of our subject, but is worth study. We saw in the last chapter how machines for constructing the ellipse are based on the theorem that if a rod of fixed length move with its ends on two lines, a point thereon will trace an ellipse. Dupin's idea is to study the locus of a point fixed on a rod, three of whose points move on three mutually perpendicular planes.

Suppose that a rod of fixed length move with its ends on two skew lines. A point fixed on the rod will move in a plane parallel to the skew lines. The rod will make a fixed angle with this plane; hence its projection thereon will have a fixed length. The locus of the chosen point is an ellipse whose centre is the intersection of the plane with the common perpendicular to the two lines.

Let us next suppose that the rod moves in such a way that three points on it move in three mutually perpendicular planes which I shall call the YZ, ZX, and XY planes; their intersection I call the axes, and their common point the origin. Assume the rod to be in a possible position. Let the point in the YZ plane move parallel to the Y-axis, and the point in the ZX plane move parallel to the X-axis. The third point will remain in the XY plane and trace an ellipse whose centre is where the XY plane meets the common perpendicular to the two lines parallel to the XY plane, that is to say, the intersection of their projections on this plane. These are two lines parallel to the Y-axis and X-axis, whose distances from these axes are proportional to the ratio in which the part of the rod between the YZ and ZX planes is divided by the point in the XY plane. The distance from the centre of this ellipse to the origin, and its scale of measurements is proportional to the cosine of the angle which the moving rod makes with the XY plane. This plane is thus covered with a set of similar and similarly placed ellipses, the origin being the centre of similitude.

Now consider another fixed point on the rod. While the point in the XY plane is tracing an ellipse, this new point is tracing a new ellipse in a parallel plane. Our surface is generated by a system of similar and similarly placed ellipses in parallel planes.

Dupin next has the ingenious idea of showing that the same surface could be generated by taking a different rod and different axes. There is one position where the rod will be perpendicular to the XY plane. This is the farthest position that the moving point can take away from the XY plane. The plane through it parallel to the XY plane will be tangent to the surface. The centres of the generating ellipses will be on the line from here to the origin. Now we may tilt the ZX and ZY planes about the Y and X axes, one tipping being arbitrary, to produce the same surface as before. We can thus change the direction of the axes in many ways. It is also possible to change the length of the rod.

Dupin states that we can do this in such a way that the trihedral shrinks to a plane and a line, and this shows that the surface has circular sections. Dupin's methods are certainly open to a good deal of question from the point of view of rigour, but they are highly imaginative and interesting.

Dupin had no followers in such discussion of the metric properties of the surfaces; the succeeding writers follow orthodox methods and projective properties. The next article is a rather slight one, Chasles[6]. He begins by proving Monge's theorem about the curve of contact of tangents from an external point, and the Brianchon's theorem of a cone cutting a quadric in two conics. From this he deduces the apparently original theorem that if two conics lie on a quadric surface and a quadric cone they lie on a second such cone. His proof is based on the doubtful assumption that two tangent planes to the surface may be passed through the line of intersection of the planes of the two conics; we are pretty well mixed up between real and imaginary at this point. He then makes the erroneous statement that the intersection of two cones circumscribed to the same quadric is a conic. It is two conics, as he states on p. 339 without apology. He generalizes to two quadrics, each of which cuts a third in two conics.

The next writer of this school was Poncelet. We must turn to that supplement of Poncelet (q.v.), which deals with projective properties of space figures. The starting-point is his own favourite transformation of homology, a linear transformation where corresponding points are collinear with a fixed point, while corresponding planes are coaxal with a fixed plane. He states without proof the fairly obvious fact that the homologue of a quadric is a quadric. The two are inscribed in the same quadric cone and meet in two conics. The same is true of two quadrics that have conical contact with a third.

Suppose we take a plane which meets our surface in a hyperbola. If there be a real tangent plane parallel to this, every line in this plane through the point of contact but not parallel to the asymptotes of the hyperbola will have two coincident intersections with the surface right there. A line parallel to one of the asymptotes would seem to have three intersections with the surface, i.e. it would be completely imbedded. This gives the rectilinear generators of the surface, previously discovered analytically as we shall see. Previous writers had also found the circular sections, but Poncelet gives them in the simplest possible form by means of his principle of continuity. It amounts to this: Whatever is true when the elements of a figure are real is true when they become imaginary by continuous change.† A quadric will cut the plane at infinity in a conic which has four intersections with the circle at infinity, conjugate imaginary in pairs when the quadric is real. A

† Coolidge[2], p. 94.

plane through such a pair will cut the quadric in a real circle. A real quadric, not a surface of revolution, has thus two real sets of circular sections in parallel planes. He points out truly that if we take the polar planes with regard to the quadric of the common self-conjugate triangle of the infinite section and the circle at infinity, we get three mutually perpendicular conjugate planes through the centre; their intersections are the principal axes, previously found by Euler.

A sphere through a circular section will meet the surface in another circle. The two surfaces, meeting in two conics, may be transformed into one another by homology. It is rather curious that Poncelet did not take this as the starting-point for his discussion of the quadric surfaces.

Poncelet tackles the intersection of two quadrics in heroic, if not foolhardy, fashion. It is intuitively evident that when this curve is real it will sometimes fall into two parts, and through a tangent to one we may pass two planes tangent to the other. Since this is sometimes possible he concludes by his principle of continuity, that it is always possible: we shall however sometimes have imaginary points and lines. Let a plane touch the total curve in two points A and B. It will cut the two quadrics in two conics having double contact at these two points. Another such plane near by will cut in two conics having double contact at A' and B'. The conics cut from the first quadric intersect in two points on the line of intersection of their planes, and the same is true of the conics cut from the second quadric.

I now turn back for a moment to the plane. If a circle have double contact with a hyperbola, the secant of contact is parallel to a bisector of the angle between the asymptotes, i.e. it will pass through one of the points which divide harmonically the intersection of the line at infinity with the two conics. Generalizing this projectively, let c_1^2 and c_2^2 intersect in P and Q while k_1^2 and k_2^2 intersect in two points H, K on PQ. I assume further that c_1^2 and k_1^2 have double contact and that c_2^2 and k_2^2 have double contact. Then the secants of contact either intersect on PQ or pass through the two points which are harmonically separated by P, Q and by H, K. This will remain the case even when the plane of c_1^2, k_1^2 is different from that of c_2^2, k_2^2. Returning to three dimensions, as the lines AB, $A'B'$ are close they actually meet say in V. This point will have the same polar with regard to the two conics which touch in A and B, as well as with regard to the two conics which touch in A' and B'. These two polar lines will intersect. It appears, then, that V has the same polar plane with regard to the two quadrics. In this plane we can, in general, find a triangle which is self-conjugate with regard to the conics cut from the two quadrics, and this triangle with V gives a tetrahedron self-conjugate with regard to the two quadric surfaces. We have here a very optimistic proof that two quadrics have, in general, a common self-conjugate tetrahedron.

I return to Chasles, especially Chasles[7], which is devoted to quadrics of revolution. His interest in these was quite different from that of Archimedes and his approach radically different. If we take the polar reciprocal of a circle with regard to a circle, we get a conic with one focus at the centre of the circle of reciprocation; if we take the polar reciprocal of a sphere with regard to another sphere, we get a quadric of revolution, one of whose foci is at the centre of reciprocation, the other at a symmetrical point on the line connecting the centres of the two spheres. Conversely, any quadric of revolution can be reciprocated into a sphere if we take one focus as centre of the reciprocating sphere.

I pass to consider a general quadric cone. This will, in general, have four tangent planes which touch the circle at infinity. These planes, in the case of a cone with real equation, will be conjugate imaginary in pairs, intersecting in two real lines, called 'focal lines' of the cone. They have the simple property that planes through them, conjugate with regard to the cone, are mutually perpendicular. They were first found algebraically in Magnus[1]. A plane section of a cone in a plane perpendicular to a focal line will have one focus at the intersection with that line. Taking this point as the centre of a sphere of reciprocation, the reciprocal of the cone will be a circle, for it will be a conic where conjugate diameters are mutually perpendicular. Through this circle we may pass a sphere. Hence in any quadric cone we may inscribe a quadric of revolution, whose foci will be on the focal lines of the cone.

A circle in a plane through the centre of the sphere of reciprocation will be polarized into a cylinder circumscribed to the quadric of revolution; it stands perpendicularly on a conic whose foci are the foci of the surface of revolution. Consider next a tangent plane to a quadric of revolution. This plane will touch a circumscribed cylinder whose base conic is the section in a plane through the axis of revolution, perpendicular to the tangent plane. Hence it will make equal angles with the two planes through the generator of contact and the two foci to the conic. And lastly we come back to the quadric cone. We inscribe therein a quadric of revolution. A tangent plane to the cone will touch the quadric, the generator of contact will be a generator of the circumscribed cylinder, the foci of the quadric are on the focal lines of the cone, and we have Chasles's pretty proof of

Magnus's first Theorem 2] *A tangent plane to a quadric cone makes equal angles with the planes through the generator of contact and the focal lines.*†

† Magnus[1].

The reader will find it quite easy to prove this from Laguerre's definition of the magnitude of an angle, and the dual to Desargues's involution theorem. Chasles next proceeds to prove by what he called 'La méthode de Roberval' the very beautiful

Magnus's second Theorem 3] *The sum of the angles which a generator of a quadric cone makes with the focal lines is constant.*

I must confess that I do not find the method of Roberval very convincing. Chasles probably sought an easy synthetic proof and failed to find one. Magnus's analytic proof is very simple. I note that he speaks of the focal lines of a quadric, meaning thereby the focal lines of the asymptotic cone, and shows that the theorem is true when we replace the generators of the cone by those of the hyperboloid, which are parallel to them. It is extremely easy to prove Theorem 2 from Theorem 3, just as we prove in our first study of the ellipse that a tangent makes equal angles with the focal radii.

Chasles[7] is a long paper. I have given only a few of the most interesting results. An equally long paper is Chasles[8], where that prolific writer returns to the cones in great style. The planes through the vertex of a cone perpendicular to the generators envelop a second cone. Each cone is the polar reciprocal of the other with regard to the cone of minimal lines through the vertex. Pole and polar go over into polar and pole. A focal line of a cone is distinguished by the property that pairs of conjugate planes through it are mutually perpendicular. Such a line will correspond to a plane through the vertex where conjugate lines through the vertex are mutually perpendicular. The section of the cone in such a plane is a null circle; the section in a parallel plane will be a not null circle. The two planes through the vertex are called by Chasles 'cyclic planes'. We have here a simple way to find new theorems about cones. Cut the cone by a plane perpendicular to a focal line. The section will be a conic whose focus is on that line. A theorem about a conic and its focus will give a theorem about a cone and a focal line, and a dual theorem about a cone and a cyclic section. Or we may start with a familiar theorem about a circle, obtain from this a theorem about a cone and cyclic section, and so a theorem about a cone and focal line.

For instance, the locus of the foot of the perpendicular from a focus on a moving tangent to a central conic is a circle having double contact with the conic at the ends of the axis through the foci.

Theorem 4] *If planes be drawn through a focal line of a quadric cone perpendicular to the tangent planes, the lines of intersection will generate a cone of revolution having double contact with the given cone along the generators in the plane through the focal lines.*

Theorem 4'] *If each generator of a quadric cone be connected by a plane with the line perpendicular thereto in a cyclic plane, these planes will envelop a cone of revolution, having double contact with the given cone, the lines of contact lying in a plane perpendicular to the two cyclic planes.*

If we connect the ends of the diameter of a circle with an arbitrary point on the circumference we have two mutually perpendicular lines.

Theorem 5] *If we connect the two generators of a quadric cone in a plane through the line of centres of a set of circular sections with any other generator, these planes will meet the corresponding cyclic plane in two mutually perpendicular lines.*

Let us call the polar plane of a focal line a 'directrix plane'. We have

Theorem 5'] *The tangent planes to a quadric cone from a line through the vertex in a directrix plane will meet any other tangent plane in lines which determine with the corresponding focal line mutually perpendicular planes.*

Chasles[8] has here a method for finding an astounding number of theorems, simple and pretty. But somehow one has the impression that it is not great mathematics.

§ 2. The formal period.

Chasles, as we saw in an earlier chapter, was the last of the school of projective geometers in France. After his time we must turn to Germany and Austria and Italy for important contributions to projective geometry. One would naturally expect to find that Steiner had added greatly to our knowledge of quadrics. Such, however, is not the case. His whole interest in these surfaces is centred in the rectilinear generators; his whole discussion is based on two fundamental propositions:

Theorem 6] *The lines of intersection of pairs of corresponding planes in two projectively related axial pencils, whose axes do not intersect, will generate a quadric surface. This surface will have two sets of rectilinear generators, all generators of one set determining two projectively related pencils of planes about any two of the other.*

Theorem 6'] *The lines connecting corresponding points on two projectively related ranges, whose bases have no common point, will generate a quadric surface. This surface will have two sets of rectilinear generators; all generators of one set will cut projective ranges on any two of the other.*

All of this is very easy and interesting, but it does not lead us very far into the theory of the quadric surfaces. We find a much more significant approach to the whole theory in von Staudt[1]. He was the first to start from his own definition of these surfaces, and not merely to pick up something which the algebraic geometers had left lying around. We saw in Chapter V how von Staudt based the whole theory of the conics on the relation of pole and polar, a transformation where to each point of the plane will correspond a single line, and to the points of a line will correspond lines through that point which correspond to it as above. If a single point lie on the corresponding line (we are in the real domain), an infinite number of points will do so; the curve which they generate is called a conic. In space we define a real polar system as a correspondence where each point P corresponds to a plane π and the points of each plane π will correspond to planes through the corresponding point P. If each point lie in the corresponding plane, the correspondence is called a 'null system'. There is nothing corresponding to this in the plane or in any projective space of an even number of dimensions. A line will correspond to a line; each is called the 'polar' of the other. If any line intersect its polar, the polar system is a null system.

Suppose, then, that we have a polar system which is not a null system, and that some point P lies in the corresponding plane π. In any other plane through P we have exactly the situation which we encountered on p. 64 when exhibiting von Staudt's approach to the conics, so that every such plane will contain a conic of points lying in their polar planes. The surface generated by all of these conics is defined as a quadric surface. If we take the plane π itself, we shall have an involution of pairs of mutually polar lines through P. If this involution be hyperbolic we shall have two self-polar lines which are completely imbedded in the surface. The plane π is in any case the tangent plane at P. The harmonic properties of poles and polars are deduced from the corresponding properties *in plano*. von Staudt closes his discussion with a number of problems of construction.

Problem 1] *To construct a quadric surface which touches a given quadric cone along a conic cut from that cone, and which also passes through a given point.*

The given conic is given by a polar system in its plane. We may build this into a space polar system where the vertex of the given cone corresponds to the plane of the given conic. This polar system will be completely determined if we also require the additional given point to correspond to that plane which connects it to the line in the plane of the conic which is polar to the intersection of the conic's plane with the line from the additional point to the vertex of the cone.

Problem 2] *To pass a quadric through a given conic, and through the vertices of a given tetrahedron.*

This is done by a projective generalization of the usual way of passing a sphere through the vertices of a tetrahedron, and then using Problem 1.

Problem 3] *To construct a quadric which has conical contact with a given quadric, and which passes then through four given points A, B, C, D, no one of which is on the quadric, and no two separated by it.*

This is the projective generalization of the problem of passing a sphere through four given points in a space of non-Euclidean measurement. On the line AB are two points P, P' harmonically separated by A and B and by the intersections with the given quadric, even when these are conjugate imaginary. We find corresponding points Q, Q' on AC and R, R' on AD. Let us assume that the plane PQR cuts the given quadric in a real curve, a real conic. We construct a quadric which touches the given quadric along the conic cut in the plane PQR and which passes through A. Every point in this plane PQR has the same polar plane with regard to the two quadrics; the polar of P goes through P', so that the quadric through A also goes through B. In like fashion we show it goes through C and D.

von Staudt gives the duals of these problems, which are easily stated. I have a strong feeling that this is essentially the right approach to a purely synthetic study of the quadrics, and regret that this author did not write more fully on the subject.

A totally different approach to the quadrics was outlined in the same year in Seydewitz (q.v.). Suppose that we have two points in space V_1 and V_2. We may establish a correlation between the bundles of which these are centres in such a way that the lines in one will correspond to the planes through the other, much as in a plane polar system points correspond to lines. Consider the points where the lines through V_1 meet the corresponding planes through V_2. If a line through V_1 trace a plane, the corresponding plane through V_2 will rotate about a line through V_2. If P be a point where a line through V_1 meets the corresponding plane through V_2, then the line $V_2 P$ will correspond to a plane through V_1, so that we get the same surface by taking lines through either point and planes through the other. This surface will clearly pass through V_1 and V_2 and cut any plane through these two points in a conic as we see from the Chasles-Steiner theorem. In any other plane we have a correlation of point to line, line to point. Seydewitz proves earlier in the same article that in such a correlation the points which lie on the corresponding lines generate a conic. His proof is algebraic and much simpler than a synthetic one, but it seems unsportsmanlike to use it in such an article. Seydewitz then proves that if a surface have the property that it meets the general plane in a conic, it can be generated in this way by two correlative bundles. Let V_1, V_2, E be three points on such a surface, not in the same straight line. Let two planes through $V_2 E$ meet the surface in two conics c_1^2, c_2^2, while a plane through V_1 meets these two curves again in B_1 and B_2. It is easy to show that we may establish such a correlation between the planes through V_1 and the lines through V_2 that $V_1 B_2 B_3$ corresponds to $V_2 E$, and the planes through $V_1 B_1$ and $V_1 B_2$ correspond to projective pencils of lines through V_2 meeting them on the two conics c_1^2, c_2^2. This correlation will generate a quadric through V_1 and the two conics which must be identical with the given surface, since an arbitrary plane cuts the two in two conics with five common points, i.e. two identical conics. This theorem enables Seydewitz to go ahead fast. We may take any two points of the surface as V_1 and V_2. Also the pole and polar theory comes quickly.

It is clear at this point that the von Staudt and Seydewitz lines of approach are coming together and will presently coalesce. Seydewitz's methods are developed in detail in Schroeter[1] and Reye[1]. Five years before the appearance of either Reye or Schroeter there appeared in Hesse[3] this very interesting problem: to construct a quadric surface through nine given points. He starts with a theorem of which a special case appeared on p. 37 of Lamé[1]. The polar planes of a point with regard to the quadrics through seven general points pass through a common point. The truth of this is immediately evident when we remember that the quadrics through seven given points are linearly dependent on seven of their number, and the same is true of the polars of any point with regard to them. Connect two of our given points by a line, and two others by another line. We assume these two skew to one another. Through each of three remaining points will pass a line meeting these two. We find in this way five lines on a quadric through seven of our points. As a matter of fact, we can find 105 quadrics through the seven points in this way if we wish to, but three will do if they are not linearly dependent. With their aid we may find a point on the polar plane of P with regard to every quadric through the seven points. But when we start with nine points, not seven, we may find 36 sets of 7, and so 36 points in the polar plane of P with regard to the quadric through all nine points. Three will do. If we know the polar plane of P with regard to a quadric through nine given points, we may find nine others by connecting P with the nine and finding a harmonic conjugate. In this way we may find as many points of the surface as we please. Another purely geometric construction will be found on pp. 464–75 of Schroeter[1], but it is decidedly difficult.

A pretty application of geometric methods to the study of the quadrics is found in the second volume of Reye[1], though much of the material is older. I define as an 'axis' of a central quadric any line which is perpendicular to its polar. The polar is, consequently, an axis also.

Theorem 7] *All normals to a central quadric, all lines in a plane of symmetry, and all lines perpendicular to these planes are axes.*

An axis is distinguished by the fact that its polar meets that line in the plane at infinity which is the polar with regard to the circle at infinity of the infinite point of the given line. This is true of any line through the centre. Hence we may, *by definition*, call such lines axes also. We shall also say, *by definition*, that a line at infinity is an axis.

Consider a plane cutting a central quadric in a central conic, that is to say, a plane not tangent to its infinite curve. The tangent planes to the surface at the extremities of each principal axis intersect in a line parallel to the other axis, and this is the polar of the given principal axis. On the other hand, consider an enveloping cone. Planes through the vertex which are conjugate with regard to the cone are also conjugate with regard to the surface. Each principal axis of this cone has its polar in the plane of the other two.

Theorem 8] *The principal axes of a plane section or of an enveloping cone of a central quadric are axes of the quadric.*

I postpone to a subsequent chapter a general discussion of confocal quadrics, but must touch on them slightly at this point. The common tangent planes to a quadric and the circle at infinity will envelop a developable surface. The quadrics inscribed in this developable are said to be confocal. The enveloping cones to them at any point are confocal cones, having the same focal lines. Since an axis and its polar are mutually perpendicular, there will pass a plane through each perpendicular to the other. The pole of this plane lies on the axis to which it is perpendicular; it is therefore perpendicular and conjugate to each plane through the axis to which it is perpendicular. Conversely, if we have two lines so situated that there is a plane through each perpendicular to the other and conjugate to every plane through the other, they are mutually polar lines, and also mutually perpendicular; they are an axis and its polar.

I next point out that we learnt from Desargues's involution theorem that, if two points be conjugate with regard to two conics, they are conjugate with regard to all conics through their intersections, and the same is true for quadrics. Dually, if two planes be conjugate with regard to two quadrics, they are conjugate with regard to all quadrics inscribed in their common enveloping developable. If two planes be mutually prependicular and conjugate with regard to a quadric, they are conjugate with regard to all confocal quadrics. Drawing all this together we have

Theorem 9] *Confocal quadrics have the same system of axes.*

Theorem 10] *The system of axes of a quadric is the system of normals of all confocal quadrics, and also the system of principal axes of nonparabolic sections of these quadrics.*

Consider a point P and its polar plane π. Pass a plane through P and the perpendicular on π; this shall be the rotating plane π'. In π there will be a pencil of parallel lines perpendicular to π'. Their polars will be a pencil of lines through P in a plane π'' which passes through the centre of the quadric. The intersection of π and π'' will be a line whose polar is in the parallel pencil and perpendicular to the line, that is, an axis. As π rotates about the perpendicular, π'' rotates projectively therewith.

Theorem 11] *The axes of a general quadric through a general point in space will generate a quadric cone through the centre of the surface. It has three generators parallel to the principal axes of the surface.*

Theorem 11'] *The axes of a central quadric in a general plane envelop a parabola which touches the three planes of symmetry.*

Let l_1 and l_2 be any two axes, l_3 any axis meeting them. By theorem 11, the cross ratio of four planes through l_1 and the centre and ends of the axes is equal to the cross ratio of four planes through l_3 and these four points, and so the cross ratio of planes through l_2 and them.

Theorem 12] *The axes of a central quadric generate a tetrahedral complex, the faces of the tetrahedron being the planes of symmetry and the plane at infinity.*

The study of the general tetrahedral complex is not part of our present business. If we have a general collineation in space, the lines connecting corresponding points will generate such a complex, the four fixed points being the vertices of the tetrahedron. As for the complex of axes, if we have the central quadric

$$\frac{x^2}{a^2}+\frac{y^2}{b^2}+\frac{z^2}{c^2}=1,$$

its axes will be generated by the collineation

$$x'=\left(\frac{\rho}{a^2}+1\right)x; \quad y'=\left(\frac{\rho}{b^2}+1\right)y; \quad z'=\left(\frac{\rho}{c^2}+1\right)z.$$

Many geometers besides Reye have studied one aspect or another of the complex of axes. A bibliography will be found in Staude (q.v.), § 44.

CHAPTER XII

QUADRIC SURFACES, ALGEBRAIC TREATMENT

§ 1. The earlier methods.

THE first writer to make a systematic algebraic study of the general quadric was Euler. He did not uncover many facts, but he forged a tool for probing into such surfaces in detail. His essential technique was the change of rectangular axes. We begin with the general equation

$$\alpha z^2+\beta yz+\gamma xz+\delta y^2+\epsilon xy+\zeta x^2+\eta x+\theta y+\iota z+\kappa = 0. \tag{1}$$

Let us look at the distant parts of the surface. Unless it lies entirely in the finite domain, it must be possible for at least one of the variables to take infinite values; let that variable be z. In comparison we may leave aside the constant and linear terms, so that at infinity the surface acts like the cone

$$\alpha z^2+\beta yz+\gamma xz+\delta y^2+\epsilon xy+\zeta x^2 = 0.$$

This cone conceivably has no real points at all except the origin. For that it is necessary that

$$4\alpha\delta-\beta^2 > 0; \qquad 4\alpha\zeta-\gamma^2 > 0; \qquad 4\delta\zeta-\epsilon^2 > 0.$$

These necessary conditions are not sufficient. It must be that for all values of x and y

$$4\alpha(\delta y^2+\epsilon xy+\zeta x^2) > (\beta y+\gamma x)^2,$$
$$(4\alpha\delta-\beta^2)y^2+2(2\alpha\epsilon-\beta\gamma)xy+(4\alpha\zeta-\gamma^2)x^2 > 0.$$

We have seen already that the first and last coefficients must be positive. For this expression never to change sign we must have in addition

$$\alpha > 0, \qquad 4\alpha\delta\zeta+\beta\gamma\epsilon-\beta^2\zeta-\gamma^2\delta-\epsilon^2\alpha > 0.$$

This is not really a very satisfactory way to handle the problem; we shall see later in the present chapter how it can be treated better.

Euler's next task is to simplify the quadratic terms. Here he states without adequate proof that by a rotation of the axes we may eliminate the three terms in xy, yz, zx. The resulting equation is

$$Ap^2+Bq^2+Cr^2+Gp+Hq+Ir+K = 0.$$

When $ABC \neq 0$ we may move to parallel axes so that

$$Ap^2+Bq^2+Cr^2+L = 0.$$

He adds:† 'Ce point sera, par cette raison, le centre de la surface, quoiqu'il-y-ait quelque cas où ce centre soit à une distance infinie.'

† Euler², vol. ii, p. 385.

Reverting to the possibility that one squared term, say z^2, should be lacking, he writes

$$Ap^2 + Bq^2 + Cp + Hq + Ir + L = 0.$$

He then switches to parallel axes, getting

$$Ap^2 + Bq^2 = ar.$$

So much for Euler. The earliest treatment where substantial further progress is found is Monge-Hachette (q.v.). I find myself unable to make a proper distribution of praise between these two writers. Monge was one of the world's great teachers, and we learn in the preface that a good deal of the contents of the book was in his lectures in the École Polytechnique. The standard equation is written

$$At^2 + A'u^2 + A''v^2 + 2Buv + 2B'vt + 2B''ut + 2Ct + 2C'u + 2C''v = K. \quad (2)$$

A line through (t', u', v') is written

$$t - t' = l(v - v') \qquad u - u' = m(v - v').$$

Assuming that (t', u', v') is on the surface, we substitute for t and u, and we have an equation which in linear in v. If we require this to have the root $v = v'$ and substitute for l and have m, we have the tangent plane

$$t(At' + B''u' + B'v' + C) + u(B''t' + A'u' + Bv' + C') +$$
$$+ v(B't' + Bu' + A''v' + C'') + Ct' + C'u' + C''v' - K = 0.$$

The authors now go in search of the centre. They substitute in (2)

$$t = x + \alpha, \qquad u = y + \beta, \qquad v = z + \gamma.$$

The coefficients of $2x$, $2y$, $2z$ are

$$A\alpha + B''\beta + B'\gamma + C, \quad B''\alpha + A'\beta + B\gamma + C', \quad B'\alpha + B\beta + A''\gamma + C''.$$

The first class of surfaces, which are the central ones, are those where these three expressions may be made to vanish at once. In our notation

$$\begin{vmatrix} A & B'' & B' \\ B'' & A' & B \\ B' & B & A'' \end{vmatrix} \neq 0.$$

We shall then have the reduced form

$$Ax^2 + A'y^2 + A''z^2 + 2Byz + 2B'zx + 2B''xy = H. \quad (3)$$

The next problem is the more difficult one of giving the axes such a twist that the product terms shall disappear. The equation of the tangent plane is

$$[Ax' + B''y' + B'z']x + [B''x' + A'y' + Bz']y + [B'x' + By' + A''z']z = H.$$

This can also be written

$$L(x-x')+M(y-y')+N(z-z') = 0.$$

If the normal go through the centre

$$\frac{L}{x'} = \frac{M}{y'} = \frac{N}{z'}.$$

The authors then go through a long series of manipulations which I shall not repeat, finally showing that the determination of these normals depends on the cubic equation

$$s^3(AB^2+A'B'^2+A''B''^2-2AA'A''-2BB'B'')+$$
$$+s^2(A'A''+A''A+AA'-B^2-B'^2-B'^2)+s(A+A'+A'')+1 = 0. \quad (4)$$

We can see, what the authors could not, that the coefficients here are invariants for a change of rectangular axes. Leaving this equation for a moment, I revert to (2), which I solve for t, u, v in turn

$$\tfrac{1}{2}t = -\frac{B'v+B''u+C}{A}+\sqrt{T}; \qquad \tfrac{1}{2}u = -\frac{B''t+Bv+C'}{A'}+\sqrt{U};$$

$$\tfrac{1}{2}v = -\frac{Bu+B'v+C''}{A''}+\sqrt{V}.$$

The middle points of the chords perpendicular to the u, v will lie in

$$At+B'v+B''u+C = 0.$$

This plane clearly goes through the centre. We see then that the middle points of any set of parallel chords lie in a plane through the centre. Furthermore, we see from the properties of parallel chords of central conics that we have ∞^3 sets of three diameters where the plane of each two bisects all chords parallel to the third, and is parallel to the plane at either extremity of the third.

Returning to our equation (4) which is cubic and real, we see it must have one real solution, giving one plane perpendicular to the chords which it bisects. The principal axes in this plane give two other diameters which do the same thing. Taking these principal axes as axes of coordinates, we have the canonical form for the equation of a central conic

$$\frac{x^2}{a^2}\pm\frac{y^2}{b^2}\pm\frac{z^2}{c^2} = 1. \quad (5)$$

I have somewhat abbreviated the authors' methods, trying to retain their spirit. They give as the typical equation of a paraboloid

$$px^2+p'y^2-4pp'x = 0.$$

They are at some pains to determine when a quadric shall be a surface of revolution.

The simple equation (5) enables us to determine new properties of the central quadric. These are developed in Monge-Hachette, pp. 194 ff. If we have two conics in a plane of such nature that the coefficients of the quadratic terms are proportional, we can write them

$$Ax^2+2Bxy+Cy^2+2Dx+2Ey+F = 0,$$
$$Ax^2+2Bxy+Cy^2+2D'x+2E'y+F' = 0.$$

But the first of these could be changed by a translation of the axes into
$$Ax^2+2Bxy+Cy^2+F_1 = 0,$$

while a similar translation of the axes might change the other to
$$Ax^2+2Bxy+Cy^2+F_2 = 0,$$

and this shows that the curves are similar, and similarly placed. Start next with equation (3) and cut the surface by

$$z = Lx+My+N$$
$$x^2(A+A''L^2+2B'L)+2xy(B''+BL+B'M+A''LM)+$$
$$+y^2(A'+A''M^2+2BM)+Px+Qy+R = 0.$$

The first three coefficients are independent of N. This gives

Theorem 1] *Parallel sections of a quadric are similar conics, and similarly placed.*

Consider in particular the ellipsoid

$$\frac{x^2}{a^2}+\frac{y^2}{b^2}+\frac{z^2}{c^2} = 1 \quad (a > b > c),$$

and cut it by the sphere
$$x^2+y^2+z^2 = b^2.$$
$$\left(\frac{x\sqrt{(a^2-b^2)}}{a} + \frac{z\sqrt{(b^2-c^2)}}{c}\right)\left(\frac{x\sqrt{(a^2-b^2)}}{a} - \frac{z\sqrt{(b^2-c^2)}}{c}\right) = 0.$$

The section of the ellipsoid and sphere is two circles. A similar treatment may be applied to the other central quadrics.

Theorem 2] *A central quadric which is not a surface of revolution has two sets of circular sections in parallel planes. The centres of the circles of either set will lie on a diameter.*

The first edition of Monge-Hachette appeared in 1802 and contained what seems to be the earliest mention of the circular sections of a quadric of which we said so much in the last chapter. It is fair to say, however, that on p. 163 of D'Alembert (q.v.) is the unproved statement that the ellipsoid, which he calls a spheroid, has circular section.

I write the equation of the one-sheeted hyperboloid in the form
$$Px^2+P'y^2-P''z^2 = 1,$$
and cut it by the plane $y = \alpha x+\beta.$

The projection of the intersection on the x, z plane is

$$(P+\alpha^2 P')x^2-P''z^2+2P'\alpha\beta x+P'\beta^2-1 = 0.$$

I chose α and β so that

$$\beta^2 P-\alpha^2 = \frac{P}{P'}, \qquad \beta = \sqrt{\left(\frac{\alpha^2}{P}+\frac{1}{P'}\right)};$$

then the projection is

$$\left(x\sqrt{(P+\alpha^2 P')}+\alpha\sqrt{\frac{P'}{P}}\right)^2 - (z\sqrt{P''})^2 = 0.$$

This is a pair of straight lines. The hyperbolic paraboloid can be treated in the same way

Theorem 3] *The one-sheeted hyperboloid and the hyperbolic paraboloid can be generated in two different ways by a line which moves so as always to intersect three mutually skew lines.*

The earliest statement of this theorem seems to be in Monge[2], p. 5, with no proof. Curiously enough, the theorem was proved much earlier for the hyperboloid of revolution, in Wren (q.v.), p. 333. Suppose

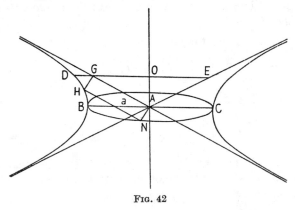

FIG. 42

(Fig. 42), that the hyperbola in the plane of the paper is rotated about the axis OA. Let AN be perpendicular to the plane of the paper. From G, any point on the asymptote, draw a line parallel to AN which shall meet the surface in H.

$$HG^2 = OH^2-OG^2 = OD^2-OG^2,$$

$$\frac{OD^2}{a^2}-\frac{OA^2}{b^2} = 1; \qquad \frac{OG^2}{OA^2} = \frac{a^2}{b^2}; \qquad \frac{OG^2}{a^2} = \frac{OA^2}{b^2}.$$

$$OD^2-OG^2 = a^2 = AN^2,$$

$$GH = AN.$$

Then NH is parallel to AG, or a line through N parallel to the asymptote is completely imbedded in the surface.

Wren's Theorem 4] *The section of a one-sheeted hyperboloid of revolution in a plane through the asymptote of a generating hyperbola perpendicular to the plane of this curve is two lines parallel to this asymptote.*

Here are two other theorems to be found in Monge-Hachette. Suppose that we cut an ellipse from an ellipsoid and take this as guiding curve of a cone, whose vertex is the end of a diameter which contains the centres of a lot of circles cut from the surface. Let us see how this cone will cut the ellipsoid. Part of the section is the ellipse. The rest must be a conic, through the vertex of the cone, and so two generators (imaginary ones). But as the tangent plane meets the surface in a null circle, the two lines are minimal lines, and a parallel plane will cut the cone in a circle.

Theorem 5] *If the vertex of a cone be a point on an ellipsoid which is the end of a diameter containing the centres of a set of circular sections, and the generators be guided by an ellipse cut from the ellipsoid, then those planes which cut circles from the ellipsoid will also cut circles from the cone.*

The Monge-Hachette proof is a good deal longer. Here is another of their theorems:

Theorem 6] *If three mutually perpendicular planes be tangent to an ellipsoid, the locus of their point of intersection is a sphere with the same centre as the ellipsoid.*

I copy their proof and their notation. Let the surface be

$$Px^2 + P'y^2 + P''z^2 = 1.$$

Let the points of contact be $(x', y', z'), (x'', y'', z''), (x''', y''', z''')$. We have:

Three equations of the type $Px'^2 + P'y'^2 + P''z'^2 = 1$.

Three tangent planes as $Px'x + P'y'y + P''z'z = 1$.

Three perpendicularity conditions $P^2x'x'' + P'^2y'y'' + P''^2z'z'' = 0$.

I now introduce nine new variables

$$Px' = a, \qquad Px'' = a', \qquad Px''' = a'',$$
$$P'y' = b, \qquad P'y'' = b', \qquad P'y''' = b'',$$
$$P''z' = c, \qquad P''z'' = c', \qquad P''z''' = c''.$$
$$\sum a^2 = R^2, \qquad \sum a'^2 = R'^2, \qquad \sum a''^2 = R''^2.$$

We have, then,

Three equations $\dfrac{a^2}{P}+\dfrac{b^2}{P'}+\dfrac{c^2}{P''} = 1.$

Three equations $ax+by+cz = 1.$

Three equations $aa'+bb'+cc' = 0.$

It then appears that the matrix

$$\left\lVert \begin{matrix} \dfrac{a}{R} & \dfrac{b}{R} & \dfrac{c}{R} \\[2mm] \dfrac{a'}{R'} & \dfrac{b'}{R'} & \dfrac{c'}{R'} \\[2mm] \dfrac{a''}{R''} & \dfrac{b''}{R''} & \dfrac{c''}{R''} \end{matrix} \right\rVert$$

is an orthogonal one;

$$x = \begin{vmatrix} \dfrac{1}{R} & \dfrac{b}{R} & \dfrac{c}{R} \\[2mm] \dfrac{1}{R'} & \dfrac{b}{R'} & \dfrac{c}{R'} \\[2mm] \dfrac{1}{R''} & \dfrac{b}{R''} & \dfrac{c}{R''} \end{vmatrix}, \quad y = \begin{vmatrix} \dfrac{a}{R} & \dfrac{1}{R} & \dfrac{c}{R} \\[2mm] \dfrac{a}{R'} & \dfrac{1}{R'} & \dfrac{c}{R'} \\[2mm] \dfrac{a}{R''} & \dfrac{1}{R''} & \dfrac{c}{R''} \end{vmatrix}, \quad z = \begin{vmatrix} \dfrac{a}{R} & \dfrac{b}{R} & \dfrac{1}{R} \\[2mm] \dfrac{a}{R'} & \dfrac{b}{R'} & \dfrac{1}{R'} \\[2mm] \dfrac{a}{R''} & \dfrac{b}{R''} & \dfrac{1}{R''} \end{vmatrix}$$

$$x^2+y^2+z^2 = \dfrac{1}{R^2}+\dfrac{1}{R'^2}+\dfrac{1}{R''^2}.$$

We find in exactly the same way

$$\dfrac{1}{P}+\dfrac{1}{P'}+\dfrac{1}{P''} = \dfrac{1}{R^2}+\dfrac{1}{R'^2}+\dfrac{1}{R''^2};$$

$$x^2+y^2+z^2 = \dfrac{1}{P}+\dfrac{1}{P'}+\dfrac{1}{P''}. \tag{6}$$

§ 2. The more modern techniques.

The machinery set up in such a work as Monge-Hachette is adequate for a good part of the study of the quadric surfaces. The modern improvements consist mostly in

(A) A more suggestive notation.
(B) The use of determinants.
(C) The theory of invariants and covariants.

As a means of illustrating the advantages which come from these means, I begin with certain affine and metrical properties, following

Salmon[2] rather loosely, with a modernized notation. Let the rectangular coordinates of a point be (x^1, x^2, x^3). We write a quadric

$$a_{ij}x^ix^j + 2b_ix^i + c = 0 \qquad (a_{ij} = a_{ji}, \; i,j = 1, 2, 3.)$$

The discriminant is

$$D = \begin{vmatrix} a_{11} & a_{12} & a_{13} & b_1 \\ a_{21} & a_{22} & a_{23} & b_2 \\ a_{31} & a_{32} & a_{33} & b_2 \\ b_1 & b_2 & b_3 & c \end{vmatrix}$$

and is a relative invariant for every change of linear coordinates. It is an absolute invariant for a change of rectangular axes. A translation

$$x^j = x^{j'} + \alpha^j$$

will leave the quadratic terms unaltered. The new linear coefficients are

$$b'_i = a_{ji}\alpha^j + b_i.$$

If then $|a_{ij}| \neq 0$ we may pass to such a new origin that $b'_i = 0$. I now give the rectangular axes a twist so that

$$a_{ij}x^ix^j = \bar{a}_{ij}\bar{x}^i\bar{x}^j; \qquad (x^1)^2 + (x^2)^2 + (x^3)^2 \equiv (\bar{x}^1)^2 + (\bar{x}^2)^2 + (\bar{x}^3)^2.$$

$$\begin{vmatrix} a_{11}-\rho & a_{12} & a_{13} \\ a_{21} & a_{22}-\rho & a_{23} \\ a_{31} & a_{32} & a_{33}-\rho \end{vmatrix} = \begin{vmatrix} \bar{a}_{11}-\rho & \bar{a}_{12} & \bar{a}_{13} \\ \bar{a}_{21} & \bar{a}_{22}-\rho & \bar{a}_{23} \\ \bar{a}_{31} & \bar{a}_{32} & \bar{a}_{33}-\rho \end{vmatrix} \qquad (7)$$

The coefficients of ρ give metrical invariants

$$\Delta = |\bar{a}_{ij}|; \qquad \theta_1 = \bar{a}_{11} + \bar{a}_{22} + \bar{a}_{33};$$

$$\theta_2 = \bar{A}^{11} + \bar{A}^{22} + \bar{A}^{33}; \quad A^{pq} = \frac{\partial |a_{ij}|}{\partial a_{pq}}. \qquad (8)$$

These expressions are, of course, unaltered by a translation, since here none of the quadratic terms are changed.

We are now ready to return to the old problem of reducing our equation to the squared terms alone. In the plane at infinity we have two curves

$$a_{ij}x^ix^j = 0, \qquad \sum (x^i)^2 = 0.$$

If our original quadric have a real equation, the intersections are conjugate imaginary in pairs. There are, in the general case, three distinct line pairs passing through these. They are obtained by giving to ρ values which are roots of the 'characteristic equation'

$$\rho^3 - \theta_1\rho^2 + \theta_2\rho - \Delta = 0. \qquad (9)$$

The roots of this give the directions of the principal axes. Taking these as coordinate axes we have the canonical equation of our quadric

$$a_1(x^1)^2 + a_2(x^2)^2 + a_3(x^3)^2 + a_4 = 0. \qquad (10)$$

$$D = a_1a_2a_3a_4; \qquad \Delta = a_1a_2a_3;$$
$$\theta_1 = a_1 + a_2 + a_3; \qquad \theta_2 = a_2a_3 + a_3a_1 + a_1a_2. \qquad (11)$$

We are now able to settle the nature of our surface without changing the axes at all. I assume that it is not conical and does not touch the infinite plane, so that
$$D \neq 0, \qquad \Delta \neq 0.$$

Ellipsoid. The real roots of (9) have like signs. The ellipsoid is real if $D < 0$, imaginary with a real equation if $D > 0$.

Hyperboloid. The three real roots of (9) have not like signs. The hyperboloid has real rulings if $D > 0$, otherwise not.

We can handle the paraboloids and cones in the same way.

Before leaving this matter I should like to take up again Euler's question, mentioned on p. 168, which amounts to asking when a homogeneous quadratic form is definite, that is to say, when it will never vanish for real values of the variables other than all 0. This has been studied by different writers. The first complete answer was given in Sylvester (q.v.). I give a simplified one found in Williamson (q.v.). Let us begin with the binary case. This will be definite if
$$f = a_{11}(x^1)^2 + 2a_{12}x^1x^2 + a_{22}(x^2)^2; \qquad a_{11} > 0, \quad a_{11}a_{22} - a_{12}^2 > 0.$$
Next take three variables:
$$a_{ij}x^ix^j \equiv \frac{1}{a_{11}}[a_{11}x^1 + a_{12}x^2 + a_{13}x^3]^2 +$$
$$+ \frac{1}{a_{11}}[(a_{11}a_{22} - a_{12}^2)(x^2)^2 + 2(a_{11}a_{23} - a_{12}a_{13})x^2x^3 + (a_{11}a_{33} - a_{13}^2)(x^3)^2].$$
Here we must have
$$a_{11} > 0, \qquad a_{11}a_{22} - a_{12}^2 > 0, \qquad \begin{vmatrix} a_{11}a_{22} - a_{12}^2 & a_{11}a_{23} - a_{12}a_{13} \\ a_{11}a_{23} - a_{12}a_{13} & a_{11}a_{33} - a_{13}^2 \end{vmatrix} > 0.$$
Or, more compactly,
$$a_{11} > 0, \qquad a_{11}a_{22} - a_{12}^2 > 0, \qquad a_{11}|a_{ij}| > 0.$$
Assume, then, in the case of $n-1$ variables we must have
$$a_{11} > 0; \quad |a_{11}\, a_{22}| > 0; \quad |a_{11}\, a_{22}\, a_{33}| > 0; \quad ...; \quad |a_{11}\, a_{22}\, ...\, a_{n-1,\, n-1}| > 0.$$
For the case of n variables
$$a_{ij}x^ix^j \equiv \frac{1}{a_{11}}[a_{1i}x^i]^2 + \frac{1}{a_{11}}[(a_{11}a_{jk} - a_{ij}a_{ik})x^jx^k].$$
This will give one new condition
$$\begin{vmatrix} a_{11}a_{22} - a_{12}^2 & a_{11}a_{23} - a_{12}a_{13} & \cdot & \cdot & a_{11}a_{2n} - a_{12}a_{1n} \\ \cdot & \cdot & \cdot & \cdot & \cdot \\ \cdot & \cdot & \cdot & \cdot & \cdot \\ \cdot & \cdot & \cdot & \cdot & a_{11}a_{nn} - a_{1n}^2 \end{vmatrix} > 0;$$
$$a_{11}^{n-2}|a_{ij}| > 0.$$

The conditions are, then,

$$a_{11} > 0; \quad |a_{11}\, a_{22}| > 0; \quad |a_{11}\, a_{22}\, a_{33}| > 0, \quad ..., \quad |a_{11}\, a_{22} \, ... \, a_{nn}| > 0.$$

The paraboloids and cones, as I said before, are easily handled in the same fashion. The surface will be one of revolution when the conics

$$a_{ij}\, x^i x^j = 0, \qquad \sum (x^i)^2 = 0$$

have double contact, and the condition for that was given on p. 104.

The determination of the circular sections which we gave on p. 171 cannot be much improved on. But the Monge-Hachette treatment of linear generators is needlessly clumsy. If I write the one-sheeted hyperboloid

$$a_1(x^1)^2 - a_2(x^2)^2 + a_3(x^3)^2 - a_4(x^4)^2 = 0,$$

the line of intersection of the two planes

$$\lambda[\sqrt{a_1}\, x^1 + \sqrt{a_2}\, x^2] = \sqrt{a_3}\, x^3 + \sqrt{a_4}\, x^4; \quad \sqrt{a_1}\, x^1 - \sqrt{a_2}\, x^2 = \lambda[-\sqrt{a_3}\, x^3 + \sqrt{a_4}\, x^4]$$

will be entirely in the surface, regardless of the value of λ, as we see by multiplying the two equations together. Another set comes from

$$\mu[\sqrt{a_1}\, x^1 + \sqrt{a_2}\, x^2] = -\sqrt{a_3}\, x^3 + \sqrt{a_4}\, x^4; \quad \sqrt{a_1}\, x^1 - \sqrt{a_2}\, x^2 = \mu[\sqrt{a_3}\, x^3 + \sqrt{a_4}\, x^4].$$

I shall now prove Magnus's second theorem of p. 161. I write the equation of a cone in point and plane coordinates,

$$\frac{(x^1)^2}{\alpha^1} - \frac{(x^2)^2}{\alpha^2} + \frac{(x^3)^2}{\alpha^3} = 0, \qquad \alpha^1 u_1^2 - \alpha^2 u_2^2 + \alpha^3 u_3^2 = 0 \qquad (\alpha^1 > \alpha^3).$$

The minimal cone with the same vertex is

$$u_1^2 + u_2^2 + u_3^2 = 0.$$

The tangential equation of a confocal cone is

$$(\alpha^1 - \lambda)u_1^2 - (\alpha^2 + \lambda)u_2^2 + (\alpha^3 - \lambda)u_3^2 = 0.$$

One degenerate cone of the series is

$$(\alpha^1 - \alpha^3)u_1^2 - (\alpha^0 + \alpha^0)u_2^2 = 0.$$

Let (x) be on a generator

$$\frac{(x^1)^2}{\alpha^1} - \frac{(x^2)^2}{\alpha^2} + \frac{(x^3)^3}{\alpha^3} = 0, \qquad \sum (x^i)^2 = \frac{\alpha^1 - \alpha^3}{\alpha^1}(x^1)^2 + \frac{\alpha^2 + \alpha^3}{\alpha^2}(x^2)^2.$$

The degenerate cone is a pair of focal lines with direction cosines

$$\left(\frac{\sqrt{(\alpha^1 - \alpha^3)}}{\sqrt{(\alpha^1 + \alpha^2)}}, \; \frac{\sqrt{(\alpha^2 + \alpha^3)}}{\sqrt{(\alpha^1 + \alpha^2)}}, \; 0\right), \quad \left(\frac{\sqrt{(\alpha^1 - \alpha^3)}}{\sqrt{(\alpha^1 + \alpha^2)}}, \; \frac{-\sqrt{(\alpha^2 + \alpha^3)}}{\sqrt{(\alpha^1 + \alpha^2)}}, \; 0\right).$$

To find the angles they form with the generator through (x)

$$\cos\theta_1 = \frac{\sqrt{(\alpha^1-\alpha^3)}x^1+\sqrt{(\alpha^2+\alpha^3)}x^2}{\sqrt{(\alpha^1+\alpha^2)}\bigg/\sqrt{\left(\dfrac{\alpha^1-\alpha^3}{\alpha^1}(x^1)^2+\dfrac{\alpha^2+\alpha^3}{\alpha^2}(x^2)^2\right)}},$$

$$\cos\theta_2 = \frac{\sqrt{(\alpha^1-\alpha^3)}x^1-\sqrt{(\alpha^2+\alpha^3)}x^2}{\sqrt{(\alpha^1+\alpha^2)}\bigg/\sqrt{\left(\dfrac{\alpha^1-\alpha^3}{\alpha^1}(x^1)^2+\dfrac{\alpha^2+\alpha^3}{\alpha^2}(x^2)^2\right)}},$$

$$\sin\theta_1 = \frac{\sqrt{(\alpha^1-\alpha^3)}\alpha^2 x^1-\sqrt{(\alpha^2+\alpha^3)}\alpha^1 x^2}{\sqrt{(\alpha^1+\alpha^2)}\sqrt{\{(\alpha^1-\alpha^3)\alpha^2(x^1)^2+(\alpha^2+\alpha^3)\alpha^1(x^2)^2\}}},$$

$$\sin\theta_2 = \frac{\sqrt{(\alpha^1-\alpha^3)}\alpha^2 x^1+\sqrt{(\alpha^2+\alpha^3)}\alpha^1 x^2}{\sqrt{(\alpha^1+\alpha^2)}\sqrt{\{(\alpha^1-\alpha^3)\alpha^2(x^1)^2+(\alpha^2+\alpha^3)\alpha^1(x^2)^2\}}}.$$

$$\cos(\theta_1+\theta_2) = \frac{\alpha^1-\alpha^2}{\alpha^1+\alpha^2}.$$

It is rather curious that α_3 does not appear in this formula.

The advantages of modern notation and abridged expressions appear especially when we pass to the study of the projective properties of quadrics. I follow especially Hesse and Clebsch-Lindemann (q.v.), but I use the more modern tensor notation with superscripts

$$a_{ij}x^ix^j = 0, \qquad a_{ij} = a_{ji} \qquad (i,j = 1,2,3,4), \tag{12}$$

and, interchangeably, the Clebsch-Aronhold symbolic notation

$$(ax)^2 \equiv (a'x)^2 \equiv (a''x)^2 = 0; \qquad (u\alpha)^2 \equiv (u\alpha')^2 \equiv (u\alpha'')^2 = 0. \tag{12'}$$

The number of independent coefficients is 10, which gives

Theorem 7] *Through nine points in general position will pass a single quadric.*

The quadrics through eight points are linearly dependent on two of their number.

Theorem 8] *The quadrics through eight points have a common curve.*

The quadrics through seven points are linearly dependent on three.

Theorem 9] *The quadrics through seven points will contain an eighth.*

This leads to a very famous problem: Given seven points in space, to find, by means of a linear construction, the eighth point common to the quadrics through the seven. The earliest solution is in Hesse[3], a simpler one in Schroeter[2]. But the problem is much more difficult than one would naturally imagine. Here is an interesting preliminary:

Hesse's Theorem 10] *The vertices of two tetrahedra which are self-conjugate with regard to a quadric are common to three linearly independent quadrics.*

To prove this I anticipate a result which will be established in the next chapter, namely, if a point quadric and a quadric envelope be apolar, there is an infinite number of tetrahedra inscribed in the point quadric which are self-conjugate with regard to the quadric envelope, and an infinite number of tetrahedra circumscribed to the latter which are self-conjugate with regard to the former. Assuming this to be the case, we take as coordinate tetrahedron one that is self-conjugate with regard to the quadric envelope. We write

$$a_{ij}x^ix^j = 0, \qquad \sum_i \beta^{ii}u_i^2 = 0, \qquad \sum_i a_{ii}\beta^{ii} = 0.$$

We need, then, impose but three independent conditions on the point quadric to make it pass through all of the vertices of the coordinate tetrahedron; that is to say, seven conditions will make it pass through the vertices of two such tetrahedra. There will, therefore, be a doubly infinite set of quadrics through eight such points.

Let us see where the line from (y) to (z) meets our quadric

$$x^i = \rho_1 y^i + \rho_2 z^i,$$

$$\rho_1^2 a_{ij}y^iy^j + 2\rho_1\rho_2 a_{ij}y^iz^j + \rho_2^2 a_{ij}z^iz^j = 0, \qquad (13)$$

$$\rho_1^2(ay)^2 + 2\rho_1\rho_2(ay)(az) + \rho_2^2(az)^2 = 0. \qquad (13')$$

Assuming first that (y) is not on the quadric. If

$$a_{ij}y^iz^j = 0; \qquad (ay)(az) = 0,$$

the ratio of the roots is -1, or these two points with (y) and (z) make a harmonic set. The plane

$$a_{ij}y^ix^j = 0, \qquad (14)$$

$$(ay)(ax) = 0 \qquad (14')$$

is called the 'polar' plane of (y) with regard to the surface. If, on the other hand, (y) is on the surface, and (z) is in the polar plane, the line from (y) to (z) either meets the surface at (y) alone or is completely imbedded. The plane is then tangent.

Theorem 11] *If (z) is in the polar plane of (y), then (y) is in the polar plane of (z).*

Can there be a point whose polar plane is illusory? For this to happen it must be possible to solve simultaneously the four equations

$$a_{ij}y^i = 0. \qquad (15)$$

This requires that the discriminant $|a_{pq}|$ be 0. If we put such a point into equations (14), (14') we find the whole line is imbedded. We have, thus, four possibilities:

Rank $|a_{pq}|$ is 4. No singular point.

Rank $|a_{pq}|$ is 3. One singular point, a cone.

Rank $|a_{pq}|$ is 2. A line of singular points, two cones.

Rank $|a_{pq}|$ is 1. The surface is a plane counted twice.

Theorem 12] *The necessary and sufficient condition that a plane should touch a point quadric is that it should include its own pole.*

Here we have five equations

$$a_{ij}y^j + \rho u_i = 0, \qquad (uy) = 0.$$

The compatibility condition is

$$\begin{vmatrix} a_{11} & a_{12} & a_{13} & a_{14} & u_1 \\ a_{21} & a_{22} & a_{23} & a_{24} & u_2 \\ a_{31} & a_{32} & a_{33} & a_{34} & u_3 \\ a_{41} & a_{42} & a_{43} & a_{44} & u_4 \\ u_1 & u_2 & u_3 & u_4 & 0 \end{vmatrix} = 0, \qquad (16)$$

$$\alpha^{ij}u_i u_j = 0. \qquad (17)$$

Symbolically,

$$\Delta = |a_{pq}| = \begin{vmatrix} a_1 a_1 & a_1 a_2 & a_1 a_3 & a_1 a_4 \\ a_2' a_1' & a_2' a_2' & a_2' a_3' & a_2' a_4' \\ a_3'' a_1'' & a_3'' a_2'' & a_3'' a_3'' & a_3'' a_4'' \\ a_4''' a_1''' & a_4''' a_2''' & a_4''' a_3''' & a_4''' a_4''' \end{vmatrix} = a_1 a_2' a_3'' a_4''' |a\ a'\ a''\ a'''|,$$

$$24\Delta = |a\ a'\ a''\ a'''|. \qquad (18)$$

Since the left-hand side of (17) can be written

$$\frac{1}{\Delta}\frac{\partial \Delta}{\partial a_{ij}}u_i u_j = 0,$$

we may write from (18) the tangential equation in symbolic form

$$|a\ a'\ a''\ u|^2 = 0. \qquad (17')$$

The equation of the tangent cone whose vertex is (y) may be found by writing the condition that (13) should have equal roots

$$a_{ij}y^i y^j a_{ij}x^i x^j - (a_{ij}y^i x^j)^2 = 0 \qquad (19)$$

$$(ay)^2(a'x)^2 + (ax)^2(a'y)^2 - 2(ay)(ax)(a'y)(a'x) = 0$$

$$|a\ a'\ y\ x|^2 = 0. \qquad (19')$$

If we use the Plücker line coordinates

$$p^{ij} = \begin{vmatrix} x^i & x^j \\ y^i & y^j \end{vmatrix}, \qquad q_{ij} = \begin{vmatrix} a_i & a_j \\ a_i' & a_j' \end{vmatrix},$$

$$(q_{kl} p^{ij})^2 = 0. \qquad (20')$$

In non-symbolic form,

$$\sum \frac{\partial^2 \Delta}{\partial a_{ql} \partial a_{r\lambda}} p^{qr} p^{l\lambda} = 0. \qquad (20)$$

This is the condition of tangency for the line

$$p^{ij} = \rho \begin{vmatrix} u_k & u_l \\ v_k & v_l \end{vmatrix},$$

where (u) and (v) are two planes through it. (20) gives

$$\begin{vmatrix} a_{11} & a_{12} & a_{13} & a_{14} & u_1 & v_1 \\ a_{21} & a_{22} & a_{23} & a_{24} & u_2 & v_2 \\ a_{31} & a_{32} & a_{33} & a_{34} & u_3 & v_3 \\ a_{41} & a_{42} & a_{43} & a_{44} & u_4 & v_4 \\ u_1 & u_2 & u_3 & u_4 & 0 & 0 \\ v_1 & v_2 & v_3 & v_4 & 0 & 0 \end{vmatrix} = 0. \qquad (21)$$

CHAPTER XIII

QUADRIC SURFACES, HIGHER ALGEBRAIC TREATMENT

§ 1. Pairs of quadrics.

THE best method for studying the possible intersections of two quadrics is the method of misnamed elementary divisors, which was explained in Chapter VI. We begin with the equations

$$a_{ij}x^ix^j = 0; \qquad b_{ij}x^ix^j = 0 \qquad (i,j = 1, 2, 3, 4). \tag{1}$$

$$(ax)^2 \equiv (a'x)^2 \equiv (a''x)^2 = 0; \qquad (bx)^2 \equiv (b'x)^2 \equiv (b''x)^2 = 0. \tag{1'}$$

We next write the 'characteristic' equation

$$|a_{pq}+\lambda b_{pq}| = 0$$

$$|a_{pq}|+\lambda b_{pq} A^{pq}+\lambda^2 a_{pq} a_{rq}\frac{\partial^2|B_{ij}|}{\partial b_{pq}\,\partial b_{rq}}+\lambda^3 a_{pq} B^{pq}+\lambda^4|b_{ij}| = 0. \tag{2}$$

$$|a\ a'\ a''\ a'''|^2+\lambda|a\ a'\ a''\ b|^2+\lambda^2|a\ a'\ b\ b'|^2+\lambda^3|a\ b\ b'\ b''|^2+\lambda^4|b\ b'\ b''\ b'''|^2 = 0. \tag{2'}$$

Let us enumerate the various possible types:

A) *Equations* (2) *or* (2') *have four distinct roots.*

There will pass four distinct quadric cones through the intersection. The vertices of two will be conjugate with regard to both cones, and so with regard to all the quadrics. Hence all of the quadrics have a common self-conjugate tetrahedron. Their equations may be thrown simultaneously into the forms

$$a_i(x^i)^2 = 0, \qquad b_i(x^i)^2 = 0. \tag{3}$$

One quadric of the set will pass through any point in space not on the common curve. Hence through a general point will pass two lines meeting the curve twice. Its projection on a plane will be a curve of the fourth order with two double points, as the space curve has no singular point. Hence by Plücker's equations the plane curve is of genus one, with eight double tangents. Hence the space curve is of the fourth order and genus one, with eight doubly tangent planes through a general point. They touch the four cones through the point.

B) *One double and two single roots.*

1) The double root does not give a quadric whose discriminant has the rank 2. The surfaces meet in a rational quartic curve with one double point.

2) The double root gives a quadric with discriminant of rank 2. The quadrics intersect in two conics meeting twice.

C) *Two double roots.*

1) Neither gives a quadric with discriminant of rank 2. The surfaces intersect in a cubic space curve and a line meeting it twice.
2) One gives a discriminant of rank 3 and one of rank 2. The surfaces intersect in a conic and two lines not meeting on it.
3) Both give discriminants of rank 2. The surfaces intersect in two pairs of opposite edges of a tetrahedron.

D) *A triple root and a single root.*

1) Triple root gives a discriminant of rank 3. The surfaces intersect in a rational quartic with a cusp.
2) Triple root gives a quadric with discriminant of rank 2. Two mutually tangent conics.
3) Triple root gives a discriminant of rank 1. The surfaces touch all along a conic.

E) *Quadruple root.*

1) Discriminant of rank 3. This is a limiting case of C) 1). The surfaces meet in a cubic and a tangent line thereto.
2) Discriminant of rank 2. This is a limiting case of C) 3). The surfaces intersect in a conic and two lines meeting on it.
3) Discriminant of rank 1. The surfaces touch along two intersecting lines.

F) *Equations* (2) *and* (2') *disappear.* Every surface of the system is conical.

1) Two of the cones have a common vertex. Then this is the vertex of all. The problem is the same as that for a pair of conics.
2) Two cones have different vertices. If they had no common ray, they would intersect in a quartic, through which would pass only four cones. If they had a common ray they could not also intersect in a space cubic, as here again there would be only a finite number of cones. Hence they must intersect in a line counted twice and a conic.†

The coefficients in equations (2) and (2') are projective simultaneous invariants of the two quadrics. It is worth while asking what happens

---

† For an elaborate discussion on somewhat different lines see Clebsch-Lindemann, vol. ii, pp. 215 ff.

when they vanish. If one of the end terms vanish in these equations, one or both quadrics is conical or planar. Suppose then

$$b_{pq}\alpha^{pq} = 0.$$

The quadrics are apolar. That means that there are an infinite number of tetrahedra which are self-conjugate with regard to the (α) quadric, and inscribed in the (b) quadric, as well as an infinite number of tetrahedra which are self-conjugate with regard to the (b) quadric, and circumscribed to the (α) quadric.

Suppose, now, $\qquad |a\ a'\ b\ b'|^2 = 0.$

The situation here is much more complicated. Suppose first that we can find a tetrahedron which is self-conjugate with regard to the (a) while its edges all touch the (b) quadric. Taking this as the coordinate tetrahedron, the quadrics have equations of the form

$$a_i(x^i)^2 = 0, \qquad b_{ij}x^i x^j = 0, \qquad b_{pp}b_{qq} - b_{pq}^2 = 0.$$

The invariant just written will vanish, so that its vanishing is a necessary condition for this situation. Is it also sufficient? The answer is 'yes'. It imposes one condition on a plane to require it to cut two quadrics in two apolar conics. There are ∞^1 triangles in the plane self-conjugate with regard to one quadric while their sides touch the other. Connecting them with the pole of the plane with regard to the first quadric, we have tetrahedra, self-conjugate with regard to the first quadric while three coplanar edges touch the second. We need therefore three more conditions to make all six edges touch. Two of these may be imposed on the first plane which still has two degrees of freedom. The vanishing of the invariant supplies the third condition. As a matter of fact, if two quadrics have this relation with regard to one tetrahedron, they have it with regard to an infinite number. There are ∞^3 planes in space, and in each ∞^3 triangles circumscribed to the second quadric. The tangent cones from the three vertices of such a triangle will meet in three points outside the plane. There are thus ∞^6 tetrahedra whose six edges touch the second quadric. There are ∞^3 quadrics with regard to which one of these tetrahedra is self-conjugate. If then two quadrics which have this relation with regard to one tetrahedron, only did so with regard to a finite number, there would be ∞^9 having this relation with regard to a given quadric, i.e. it would have this relation with regard to every quadric. But we have seen that the vanishing of the invariant is a necessary condition. The meaning of the vanishing of this invariant is given without proof in Salmon[2].

Let us write the equation of the cone which touches a given quadric along its intersection with a given plane (u). The pole of the plane will be

$$\rho y^i = \alpha^{ij}u_j.$$

The equation of the cone is

$$a_{ij} x^i x^j a_{ij} y^i y^j - (a_{ij} y^i x^j)^2 = 0.$$

$$a_{pq} x^p x^q a_{kl} \alpha^{kp} \alpha^{lq} u_p u_q - (a_{kl} \alpha^{kq} u_q x^l)^2 = 0$$

$$a_{kl} x^k x^l \alpha^{pq} u_p u_q - (u_p x^p)^2 = 0 \tag{4}$$

$$(ax)^2 |a' \ a'' \ a''' \ u|^2 - |a \ a' \ a'' \ a'''|^2 (ux)^2 = 0. \tag{4'}$$

The advantages of the modern notations stand out if we compare these formulae with those in Salmon[2], p. 185.

Let us find the condition that a line (p) should meet the curve of intersection of two quadrics. I use the Plücker notation.

$$\rho p^{ij} = y^i z^j - y^j z^i = u_k v_l - u_l v_k,$$

$$x^i = \rho_1 y^i + \rho_2 z^i,$$

$$\rho_1^2 (ay)^2 + 2\rho_1 \rho_2 (ay)(az) + \rho_2^2 (az)^2 \equiv (\bar{a}\rho)^2 = 0$$

$$\rho_1^2 (by)^2 + 2\rho_1 \rho_2 (by)(bz) + \rho_2^2 (bz)^2 \equiv (\bar{b}\rho)^2 = 0. \tag{5'}$$

The resultant must be 0. That means that the discriminant of the Jacobian vanishes.

$$|\bar{a} \ \bar{b}| \cdot |\bar{a}' \ \bar{b}'| \, [\,|\bar{a} \ \bar{a}'| \cdot |\bar{b} \ \bar{b}'| + |\bar{a} \ \bar{b}'| \cdot |\bar{b} \ \bar{a}'|\,] = 0.$$

Since

$$\begin{vmatrix} \bar{a}_1 & \bar{a}_2 & |a\bar{b}'| \\ \bar{b}_1 & \bar{b}_2 & |b\bar{b}'| \\ \bar{a}_1' & \bar{a}_2' & |\bar{a}'\bar{b}'| \end{vmatrix} = 0,$$

$$|\bar{a} \ \bar{b}'| \cdot |\bar{b} \ \bar{a}'| = |\bar{a} \ \bar{a}'| \cdot |\bar{b} \ \bar{b}'| - |\bar{a} \ \bar{b}| \cdot |\bar{a}' \ \bar{b}'|,$$

$$|\bar{a} \ \bar{b}|^2 |\bar{a}' \ \bar{b}'|^2 - 2|\bar{a} \ \bar{b}| \cdot |\bar{a}' \ \bar{b}'| \cdot |\bar{a} \ \bar{b}'| \cdot |\bar{a}' \ \bar{b}| = 0.$$

$$|\bar{a} \ \bar{b}|^2 = (ay)^2 (bz)^2 + (az)^2 (by)^2 - 2(ay)(az)(by)(bz) = |a \ b \ u \ v|$$

$$|\bar{a}' \ \bar{b}| \cdot |\bar{a} \ \bar{b}'| = |a' \ b \ u \ v| \cdot |a \ b' u \ v|$$

$$|a \ b \ u \ v|^2 |a' \ b' \ u \ v|^2 - 2|a \ b \ u \ v| \cdot |a' \ b' \ u \ v| \cdot |a' \ b \ u \ v| \cdot |a \ b' \ u \ v| = 0. \tag{6'}$$

We have a much simpler expression for the equation of the Battaglini complex of lines meeting two quadrics in harmonically separating pairs. In this case the simultaneous invariant of the two quadratic forms (5') must vanish

$$|a \ b \ u \ v|^2 = 0. \tag{7'}$$

Our equation (6') gives us a direct way to find the equation of the developable formed by the tangents to the curve of intersection. If (x) be on such a tangent, the point of contact lies on its polar with regard to both surfaces so that the intersection of these two planes must meet the curve. Conversely, if the line of intersection of two planes meets the curve, and these have a common pole, that pole lies in the tangent planes to the two surfaces at a point of the curve, and so on the tangent to the curve

$$(u\xi) \equiv (a''x)(a''\xi), \qquad (v\xi) \equiv (b''x)(b''\xi),$$
$$|a\ b\ u\ v| = |a\ b\ a''\ b''|(a''x)(b''x).$$

Substituting in (6') we get an equation of the eighth degree in (x). It requires six sets of equivalent symbols for (a) and (b), so that I forbear writing it.

I rewrite the equations of our two quadrics:

$$(ax)^2 \equiv (a'x)^2 = 0, \qquad (u\alpha)^2 \equiv (u\alpha')^2 = 0,$$
$$(bx)^2 \equiv (b'x)^2 = 0, \qquad (u\beta)^2 = (u\beta')^2 = 0.$$

Let (u) be tangent to the second quadric. If (x) be its pole with regard to the first

$$(ax)a_i = \rho u_i$$
$$(a\beta)(a'\beta)(ax)(a'x) = 0. \tag{8'}$$

This is the equation of the polar reciprocal of the second quadric with regard to the first. In the same way we have

$$(b\alpha)(b'\alpha)(bx)(b'x) = 0 \tag{9'}$$

is the polar reciprocal of the first with regard to the second. It appears that, if we reduce the original equation to the squared terms, by passing to the common self-conjugate tetrahedron, these quadrics show only the squared terms also. Hence all four have a common self-conjugate tetrahedron. Its faces are the Jacobian of the four surfaces, the locus of points whose polars with regard to them are concurrent. We have, then, for the equation of the faces of the common self-conjugate tetrahedron

$$(a'\beta)(a''\beta)(b'\alpha)(b''\alpha)\begin{vmatrix} (ax)a_1 & \cdot & \cdot & \cdot & \cdot & \cdot & \cdot \\ (bx)b_1 & \cdot & \cdot & \cdot & \cdot & \cdot & \cdot \\ (a'x)a_1''+(a''x)a_1' & \cdot & \cdot & \cdot & \cdot & \cdot \\ (b'x)b_1''+(b''x)b_1' & \cdot & \cdot & \cdot & \cdot & \cdot \end{vmatrix} = 0,$$

$$(a'\beta)(a''\beta)(b'\alpha)(b''\alpha)[\,|a\ b\ a''\ b''|(a'x)(b'x)+|a\ b\ a'\ b'|(a''x)(b''x)+$$
$$+|a\ b\ a'\ b''|(a''x)(b'x)+|a\ b\ a''\ b'|(a'x)(b''x)](ax)(bx) = 0.$$

Interchanging equivalent symbols and writing

$$(u\alpha) = |u\ a'''\ a^{iv}\ a^{v}|, \qquad (u\beta) = |u\ b''\ b^{iv}\ b^{v}|,$$
$$|a'\ b'''\ b^{iv}\ b^{v}|.|a''\ b''\ b^{iv}\ b^{v}|.|b'\ a'''\ a^{iv}\ a^{v}|.|b''\ a'''\ a^{iv}\ a^{v}|.$$
$$|a\ b\ a'\ b'|\ (ax)(bx)(a''x)(b''x) = 0. \tag{10'}$$

We may find further covariants and contravariants by a device due, I believe, to Hesse. A point in a plane may be written

$$x^i = \rho_1 y^i + \rho_2 z^i + \rho_3 t^i \tag{11}$$

$$(ax)^2 \equiv (\bar{a}\rho)^2; \qquad \bar{a}_1 = (ay) \quad \bar{a}_2 = (az) \quad \bar{a}_3 = (at).$$

If the plane be tangent to the quadric, the conic $(\bar{a}p)^2 = 0$ has a vanishing discriminant

$$|\bar{a}\ \bar{a}'\ \bar{a}''|^2 = 0$$

$$|\bar{a}\ \bar{a}'\ \bar{a}''| = \begin{vmatrix} (ay) & (az) & (at) \\ (a'y) & (a'z) & (a't) \\ (a''y) & (a''z) & (a''t) \end{vmatrix} = |a\ a'\ a''\ u|$$

$$|a\ a'\ a''\ u|^2 = 0. \tag{12'}$$

This is equation (17') of the last chapter. The conics cut from the two quadrics will be apolar if

$$|\bar{a}\ \bar{b}\ \bar{b}'| = 0$$

$$|a\ b\ b'\ u|^2 = 0. \tag{13'}$$

In the same way, if (x) be the vertex of two apolar cones, enveloping the two quadrics, we shall have

$$|\alpha\ \beta\ \beta'\ x|^2 = 0. \tag{14'}$$

Suppose that (β) is the circle at infinity. Then (x) is the vertex of an orthogonal tetrahedron circumscribed to

$$(u\alpha)^2 \equiv \sum \frac{u_i^2}{a_i} = 0, \qquad (u\beta)^2 \equiv u_1^2 + u_2^2 + u_3^2 = 0$$

$$\begin{vmatrix} \beta^2 & \beta^3 \\ \beta'^2 & \beta'^3 \end{vmatrix}^2 \cdot \begin{vmatrix} x^2 & x^3 \\ \alpha^2 & \alpha^3 \end{vmatrix}^2 + \begin{vmatrix} \beta^3 & \beta^1 \\ \beta'^3 & \beta'^1 \end{vmatrix}^2 \cdot \begin{vmatrix} x^3 & x^1 \\ \alpha^3 & \alpha^1 \end{vmatrix}^2 + \begin{vmatrix} \beta^1 & \beta^2 \\ \beta'^1 & \beta'^2 \end{vmatrix}^2 \begin{vmatrix} x^1 & x^2 \\ \alpha^1 & \alpha^2 \end{vmatrix}^2 = 0$$

$$(x^1)^2 + (x^2)^2 + (x^3)^2 + a_4\left[\sum \frac{1}{a_i}\right](x^4)^2 = 0. \tag{15}$$

This is equation (6) of Chapter XII. At a point where this sphere meets the given quadric the cone of tangent planes to the latter becomes two pencils of lines through the two generators, so that they must cut at right angles.

Theorem 1] *The locus of the vertices of right trihedrals whose faces touch a central quadric is a sphere which cuts the quadric at the points where the two generators are mutually perpendicular.*

This sphere is called the 'director sphere'. Returning to (14'), if (α) be the circle at infinity, we have the locus of vertices of right trihedrals whose edges touch a central quadric.

$$(u\alpha)^2 \equiv u_1^2 + u_2^2 + u_3^2, \qquad (u\beta)^2 = \sum \frac{u_i^2}{b_i}$$

$$\begin{vmatrix} x^2 & x^3 & x^4 \\ \beta^2 & \beta^3 & \beta^4 \\ \beta'^2 & \beta'^3 & \beta'^4 \end{vmatrix}^2 + \begin{vmatrix} x^3 & x^1 & x^4 \\ \beta^3 & \beta^1 & \beta^4 \\ \beta'^3 & \beta'^1 & \beta'^4 \end{vmatrix}^2 + \begin{vmatrix} x^1 & x^2 & x^4 \\ \beta^1 & \beta^2 & \beta^4 \\ \beta'^1 & \beta'^2 & \beta'^4 \end{vmatrix}^2 = 0$$

$$\left[\frac{1}{b_2} + \frac{1}{b_3}\right](x^1)^2 + \left[\frac{1}{b_3} + \frac{1}{b_1}\right](x^2)^2 + \left[\frac{1}{b_1} + \frac{1}{b_2}\right](x^3)^2 + \frac{b_4(b_1 + b_2 + b_3)}{b_1 b_2 b_3}(x^4)^2 = 0. \tag{16}$$

Given three quadrics
$$(ax)^2 = (bx)^2 = (cx)^2 = 0.$$

The quadric $\qquad\qquad |a\ b\ c\ u|^2 = 0 \qquad\qquad\qquad (17')$

is, by equation (22) of Chapter VI, the envelope of planes in which there are an infinite number of triangles, self-conjugate with regard to one quadric while their sides cut the other two in harmonic pairs. There is a dual meaning for the quadric

$$|\alpha\ \beta\ \gamma\ x|^2 = 0.$$

If we have a fourth quadric, and if

$$(dx)^2 = 0, \qquad |a\ b\ c\ d|^2 = 0. \qquad\qquad (18')$$

There are an infinite number of tetrahedra which are self-conjugate with regard to one of the four quadrics, while their faces bear to the other three the relation just described.

§ 2. Linear systems.

In the study of linear systems it is well to distinguish between point loci and envelopes of planes.

Theorem 2] *A general point quadric is apolar to a general quadric envelope when any two points of the former, which are conjugate with regard to the latter, are vertices of a tetrahedron self-conjugate with regard to the latter whose vertices lie on the former; and any two tangent planes to the latter which are conjugate with regard to the former are faces of a tetrahedron circumscribed to the latter which is self-conjugate with regard to the former.*

Theorem 3] *A general point quadric is apolar to a conic when the point conic of the former which is in the plane of the latter is apolar therewith.*

Theorem 4] *A general quadric envelope is apolar to a quadric cone when the enveloping cone whose vertex is the vertex of the given cone is apolar therewith.*

Theorem 5] *The totality of point quadrics linearly dependent on p linearly independent ones is apolar to all quadric envelopes linearly dependent on $10-p$ independent ones.*

The simplest linear system is the pencil, dependent on two,

$$r_1\,a_{ij}x^ix^j + r_2\,b_{ij}x^ix^j = 0 \qquad\qquad (19)$$

$$r_1(ax)^2 + r_2(bx)^2 = 0. \qquad\qquad (19')$$

The polars of a point with regard to these form an axial pencil. On the other hand, if we take three non-collinear points their polar planes generate three projective axial pencils.

Theorem 6] *The poles of a general plane with regard to the quadrics of a pencil generate a cubic space curve through the vertices of that tetrahedron which is self-conjugate with regard to all surfaces of the pencil.*

This theorem is due to Chasles, p. 405. This is merely an 'in general' statement, there are various limiting cases.

Theorem 7] *The polars of a general line with regard to the quadrics of a pencil generate a quadric surface through the vertices of the common self-conjugate tetrahedron.*

Let us work all of this out algebraically. Let (u) be the plane whose pole (x) we seek.

$$r_1(ax)a_i + r_2(bx)b_i + r_3 u_i = 0,$$

$$\begin{vmatrix} a_i & b_i & u_i \\ a_j & b_j & u_j \\ a_k & b_k & u_k \end{vmatrix} (ax)(bx) = 0. \tag{20'}$$

There are four such equations, giving four quadrics through the cubic curve. Suppose that (x) is in the polar planes of both (y) and (z).

$$r_1(ay)(ax) + r_2(by)(bx) = 0, \qquad r_1(az)(ax) + r_2(bz)(bx) = 0;$$

$$\begin{vmatrix} (ay)(ax) & (by)(bx) \\ (az)(ax) & (bz)(bx) \end{vmatrix} = 0.$$

$$\begin{vmatrix} y^k & y^l \\ z^k & z^l \end{vmatrix} \equiv p^{kl}, \qquad \sum \begin{vmatrix} a_i & a_j \\ b_i & b_j \end{vmatrix} p^{kl}(ax)(bx) = 0.$$

This is the quadric traced by the polar of the line (p). If (x) be on the conic where the polar plane of (y) meets one of these surfaces,

$$r_1(ay)(ax) + r_2(by)(bx) = 0, \qquad r_1(ax)^2 + r_2(bx)^2 = 0,$$

$$(ay)(ax)(bx)^2 - (by)(bx)(ax)^2 = 0.$$

The system of quadrics linearly dependent on three is called a bundle.

Theorem 8] *The system of all point quadrics through seven points, no six of which are coplanar, form a bundle, all of whose members will, in general, pass through an eighth point.*

A system of planes linearly dependent on three non-coaxal ones pass through a common point. There is, thus, usually, one point conjugate to a given point with regard to all quadrics of a bundle. We mentioned this fact in the last chapter, p. 178, in discussing the problem of finding the eighth point determined by seven. I will return presently to the meaning of the word 'usually' in this case. Let the bundle be given by

$$(ax)^2 = 0, \qquad (bx)^2 = 0, \qquad (cx)^2 = 0.$$

If (u) be a plane through the point (x) conjugate to the point (y) with regard to all of these quadrics,

$$(ay)(ax) = (by)(bx) = (cy)(cx) = 0, \qquad (ux) = 0;$$

$$|a\ b\ c\ u|(ay)(by)(cy) = 0. \tag{21'}$$

Conversely, when all of these equations are satisfied we may write

$$\rho_1(ay)a_i + \rho_2(by)b_i + \rho_3(cy)c_i + \rho_4 u_i = 0.$$

Theorem 9] *The poles of a given plane with regard to the quadrics of a bundle generate a surface of the third order through the vertices of the single infinite set of cones of the bundle. It meets the corresponding plane in the Jacobian cubic curve of the bundle of conics cut in it.*

The last part of this theorem comes from Theorem 12 of Chapter VII.

It might happen, however, that the polar planes of a point with regard to the quadrics of a bundle were coaxal, passed through a common line. Here we should have

$$\rho_1(ay)a_i + \rho_2(by)b_i + \rho_3(cy)c_i = 0.$$

(y) will trace a curve whose order we determine as follows; it was first discovered by Hesse[4]. An elaborate synthetic study is in Sturm (q.v.). I try to find how many intersections the curve has with the plane $x^4 = 0$. Our curve is the locus of the vertices of the cones of the bundle. We write in tensor notation

$$\rho_1 a_{ij}x^ix^j + \rho_2 b_{ij}x^ix^j + \rho_3 c_{ij}x^ix^j \equiv d_{ij}x^ix^j = 0.$$

This will be a cone with vertex in $x^4 = 0$, if

$$|d_{ij}| = 0; \qquad D^{44} = 0.$$

The first of the equations is quadratic in ρ_i; the second is cubic. It would seem that there would be twelve intersections. But

$$D^{ii}D^{44} - (D^{i4})^2 \equiv \begin{vmatrix} d_{ij} & d_{jk} \\ d_{jk} & d_{kl} \end{vmatrix} \cdot |d_{ij}|.$$

Hence the ρ_i curve $|d_{ij}| = 0$ will touch the curve $D^{44} = 0$ where it meets $D^{i4} = 0$, so that the twelve intersections fall together in pairs, giving but six sets of values of ρ_1, ρ_2, ρ_3.

Theorem 10] *The vertices of the cones of a bundle of quadrics generate a curve of the sixth order. It is the locus of points whose polar planes with regard to the quadrics of the bundle form axial pencils.*

The three-parameter linear system

$$\rho_1(ax)^2+\rho_2(bx)^2+\rho_3(cx)^2+\rho_4(dx)^2 = 0$$

has been considerably studied.[†] The first theorem comes at once.

Theorem 11] *The locus of points whose polar planes with regard to four linearly independent quadrics are concurrent is a surface of the fourth order. It is the locus of vertices of cones linearly dependent on the four.*

The equation of this locus is

$$|a\ b\ c\ d|(ax)(bx)(cx)(dx) = 0. \qquad (22')$$

We see that points of this locus appear in pairs, each lying in all the polar planes of the other. All quadrics through a point on a line connecting such a pair of points will meet again in the harmonic conjugate with regard to the pair, that is to say, the quadrics of the system meet such a line in pairs of an involution whose double points are on the Jacobian. Such a line is called a principal ray.

There are two other three-parameter systems which are interesting. One is the system of all quadrics through six given points, the other is that of all first polars with regard to a given cubic surface.

§ 3. Focal properties.[‡]

Dual to the pencil of point quadrics is the one-parameter linear system of quadric envelopes touching the common tangent planes to two of their number. In such a system at least one member must consist in the planes tangent to a conic.

Definition] A one-parameter linear system of quadric envelopes, one member of which is the circle at infinity, is called a confocal system.[§]

Suppose that we have a pencil of point quadrics, a general pencil where all pass through an elliptic space curve of the fourth order. They will meet a general plane in a pencil of conics through four distinct points. Three conics of the pencil are the pairs of opposite sides of the complete quadrangle formed by these points. Their intersections are the vertices of the diagonal triangle, each two are conjugate with regard to all conics of the pencil. Dual to this we have the very fundamental

Theorem 12] *Three quadrics of a confocal system pass through a general point in space, and intersect at right angles.*

The confocal quadrics including paraboloids form a system less

† Cf. Staude[1], pp. 250 ff.
‡ In the present section I have leaned heavily on Staude[1].
§ The earliest treatment of confocal quadrics from this definition is Chasles[1], pp 397 ff.

interesting than the central ones, so I shall limit myself to the latter. I also leave out the case of quadrics of revolution. The central confocal quadrics not of revolution are so interesting that I proceed to verify Theorem 12 algebraically. I use rectangular non-homogeneous Cartesian coordinates x^1, x^2, x^3 and start with an ellipsoid

$$\frac{(x^1)^2}{a_1^2}+\frac{(x^2)^2}{a_2^2}+\frac{(x^3)^2}{a_3^2}-1 = 0 \quad (a_1^2 > a_2^2 > a_3^2).$$

The tangential equation is

$$a_1^2 u_1^2 + a_2^2 u_2^2 + a_3^2 u_3^2 - u_4^2 = 0.$$

The circle at infinity is $\qquad u_1^2 + u_2^2 + u_3^2 = 0.$

The general confocal quadric is

$$(a_1^2-\lambda)u_1^2 + (a_2^2-\lambda)u_2^2 + (a_3^2-\lambda)u_4^2 - u_4^2 = 0$$

$$\frac{(x^1)^2}{a_1^2-\lambda}+\frac{(x^2)^2}{a_2^2-\lambda}+\frac{(x^3)^2}{a_3^2-\lambda}-1 = 0. \tag{23}$$

$$\phi(\lambda) \equiv (a_2^2-\lambda)(a_3^2-\lambda)(x^1)^2 + (a_3^2-\lambda)(a_1^2-\lambda)(x^2)^2 +$$
$$+ (a_1^2-\lambda)(a_2^2-\lambda)(x^3)^2 - (a_1^2-\lambda)(a_2^2-\lambda)(a_3^2-\lambda) = 0. \tag{24}$$

Assume, now, that (x) is given and that λ_1, λ_2 are two roots of (24) as an equation in λ.

$$f_1 \equiv \frac{(x^1)^2}{a_1^2-\lambda_1}+\frac{(x^2)^2}{a_2^2-\lambda_1}+\frac{(x^3)^2}{a_3^2-\lambda_1}-1 = 0,$$

$$f_2 \equiv \frac{(x^1)^2}{a_1^2-\lambda_2}+\frac{(x^2)^2}{a_2^2-\lambda_2}+\frac{(x^3)^2}{a_3^2-\lambda_2}-1 = 0;$$

$$\frac{(x^1)^2}{(a_1^2-\lambda_1)(a_1^2-\lambda_2)}+\frac{(x^2)^2}{(a_2^2-\lambda_1)(a_2^2-\lambda_2)}+\frac{(x^3)^2}{(a_3^2-\lambda_1)(a_3^2-\lambda_3)} = 0.$$

$$\frac{\partial f_1}{\partial x^1}\frac{\partial f_2}{\partial x^1}+\frac{\partial f_1}{\partial x^2}\frac{\partial f_2}{\partial x^2}+\frac{\partial f_1}{\partial x^3}\frac{\partial f_2}{\partial x^3} = 0,$$

and this gives the desired perpendicularity. Equation (24) is cubic, giving the three surfaces through the point (x). Let us now watch the algebraic signs of $\phi(\lambda)$

$$\lambda \geqslant a_1^2, \qquad \phi(\lambda) > 0.$$
$$\lambda = a_2^2, \qquad \phi(\lambda) < 0.$$
$$\lambda = a_3^2, \qquad \phi(\lambda) > 0.$$
$$\lambda = -\infty, \qquad \phi(\lambda) < 0.$$

It appears in this way that we shall have one root between a_1^2 and a_2^2 which will make (23) a two-sheeted hyperboloid, one between a_2^2 and

a_3^2 which will make a one-sheeted or ruled hyperboloid, and one root $< a_3^2$ giving an ellipsoid.

Theorem 13] *Three confocal central quadrics, not of revolution, will pass through a general point in space. One of these will be a two-sheeted hyperboloid, one a one-sheeted one, and one an ellipsoid.*

We must now study the limiting cases

$$\lambda = a_1^2: \qquad \frac{(x^2)^2}{a_2^2-a_1^2} + \frac{(x^3)^2}{a_3^2-a_1^2} - 1 = 0, \qquad x^1 = 0.$$

This is an imaginary conic.

$$\lambda = a_2^2: \qquad \frac{(x^1)^2}{a_1^2-a_2^2} - \frac{(x^3)^2}{a_2^2-a_3^2} - 1 = 0, \qquad x^2 = 0.$$

Hyperbola with vertices $\{\pm\sqrt{(a_1^2-a_2^2)}, 0, 0\}$, foci $\{\pm\sqrt{(a_1^2-a_3^2)}, 0, 0\}$.

$$\lambda = a_3^2: \qquad \frac{(x^1)^2}{a_1^2-a_3^2} + \frac{(x^2)^2}{a_2^2-a_3^2} - 1 = 0, \qquad x^3 = 0.$$

Ellipse with vertices $\{\pm\sqrt{(a_1^2-a_3^2)}\ 0, 0\}$, foci $\{\pm\sqrt{(a_1^2-a_2^2)}, 0, 0\}$.

These are called the 'focal conics' of the system. There is also, of course, the circle at infinity.

Theorem 14] *In a confocal system of real central quadrics not of revolution there are two real focal conics, an ellipse and a hyperbola. Their common centre is the centre of all the quadrics, they lie in two of the planes of symmetry, and the foci of each are the vertices of the other.*

A number of pretty theorems are obtained by approaching the subject from a totally different point of view first developed in Dupin,[3] pp. 200 ff. What can be said of a surface which has circles as one set of lines of curvature? The normals along such a circle generate a developable, and hence, by a theorem of Joachimsthal's they make a constant angle with the diameters of the circle. They therefore pass through a common point, and this point is the centre of a sphere which touches the envelope all along the circle. Our surface must, then, be the envelope of a one-parameter family of spheres. The converse is obviously true.

Now let us see if we can have a surface all of whose lines of curvature are circles. Such a surface can be generated in two different ways by a one-parameter family of spheres, and all of the spheres of one family are tangent to all of the other. Are there any such surfaces? An anchor ring is an obvious example, as is any surface into which an anchor ring can be converted by inversion.

Next take three non-coaxal spheres. If we take a centre of inversion whose power with regard to each sphere is proportional to the square

of the radius of that sphere, we shall invert into three equal spheres.†
If we rotate about their radical axis, they will generate an anchor ring,
all of the spheres into which they are rotated will be tangent to a set
of spheres whose centres lie on the radical axis.

Theorem 15] *Three non-coaxal spheres are members of a one-parameter system, all tangent to a second one-parameter system. The characteristic circles of the spheres of the two systems are lines of curvature of the
surface generated. The spheres of each system pass through two fixed
points which are singular for the surface. Such a surface, when not an
anchor ring, may be inverted into one.*

This surface is called a 'Dupin cyclide' and is very different from the
general cyclide. Dupin's development is somewhat longer; he was not
acquainted with the transformation of inversion in a sphere. Let us
seek the locus of the centres of the spheres when this is not a circle or
straight line.

The sum or difference of the distances of the centres of one system of
spheres from any two of the others will be constant, that is to say, will
depend merely on the choice of the two. If we take three spheres of one
system we see that the centres of those of the other system lie on two
quadrics of revolution, the foci of each being the centres of two of the
chosen spheres, and these two are not linearly dependent. We saw in
the first paragraph of Chapter XI, p. 160, that the polar reciprocal of
a sphere in another sphere is a quadric of revolution with one focus at
the centre of inversion, and the common tangent planes to two spheres
envelop two cones of revolution. Hence two quadrics of revolution
with a common focus intersect in two conics, and as our three quadrics
of revolution are not linearly dependent they share one conic, not two.
It appears thus that the centres of the spheres of one generation of a
Dupin cyclide generate a conic.

Let us next note that the cyclide is symmetrical in two mutually
perpendicular planes, and these are the planes of the conics. Furthermore, as the sum or difference of the distances of all points of one conic
from any two of the other depends merely on the choice of the latter,
each conic must pierce the plane of the other at the foci of that curve.
Lastly, let us note that the line connecting the centres of two infinitely
near spheres of one generation is the axis of the corresponding characteristic circle, and the lines from the centre of a sphere to a circle of
that sphere form a cone of revolution. We thus get, at long last, a very
beautiful theorem:

Theorem 16] *The focal conics of a confocal set of central quadrics are
the loci of the centres of generating spheres of a Dupin cyclide, and, con-*

† Cf. Coolidge⁴, p. 247.

*versely, when such a cyclide is not an anchor ring, the locus of the centres
of the generating spheres is the focal conics of a confocal quadric system.
Each conic is projected from any point of the other by a cone of revolution
whose axis is tangent to the first conic. The sum of the distances from
all points of the focal ellipse, and the difference of the distances of all
points of the focal hyperbola to any two points of the other curve, depends
merely on the choice of the latter.*

I return to the consideration of confocal quadrics. The minimal
planes, that is to say, the planes tangent to the circle at infinity which
touch a quadric, will touch also the quadrics confocal therewith, and
also touch the focal conics. Each point of a focal conic is vertex of a
minimal cone which has double contact with the quadric. If a cone
whose vertex is not on a quadric have double contact therewith, the
two will intersect in two conics. If (x_0) be a point of the focal conic,
the equation of the quadric can be written, in non-homogeneous rectangular coordinates,

$$\sum_i (x^i - x_0^i)^2 = (u_i x^i + u_4)(v_i x^i + v_4). \tag{25}$$

Amiot's Theorem 17] *The square of the distance of a point of a central
quadric from a point of a focal conic is a constant multiple of the product
of its distances from two planes whose position depends only on the point
of the conic.*†

The minimal planes tangent to a surface generate its focal developable. The curve of double points of this developable, as distinct from
its edge of regression, has a certain interest. In the case of a central
quadric the focal conics and circle at infinity are parts of this curve.
Is there any more of it? The intersection of two quadrics is, in general,
a space curve of order four and genus one. It will determine at a general
point a cone of the fourth order with two double generators. By
Plücker's equations this will have eight doubly tangent planes, two
touching each of the four quadric cones through the curve. Similarly
the double curve of the focal developable of a quadric is of the eighth
order.

Theorem 18] *The double curve of the focal developable of a central
quadric consists of the three focal conics and the circle at infinity.*

Theorem 19] *If a point bear such a relation to a central quadric that
the square of the distance therefrom of every point of the quadric bear a
constant ratio to the product of the point's distances from two planes, that
point is on a focal conic.*

† Amiot (q.v.), p. 162.

Theorem 20] *The polar reciprocal with regard to a central quadric of one of its focal conics is a cone whose vertex lies on the principal axis perpendicular to the conic. Each tangent plane to this cone cuts the quadric in a conic which determines a cone of revolution at the centre of the quadric.*

Let us bring our surface (25) to intersect the plane

$$u_i x^i + \omega_4 = 0$$

$$\sum (x^i - x_0^i)^2 + (\omega_4 - u_4)(v_i x^i + v_4) = 0.$$

Theorem 21] *The planes associated with a point of a focal conic in the manner described in Theorem 17 are planes of circular section.*

The line of intersection of the two planes associated with a point of the focal conic in this way has been called, unfortunately as it seems to me, a 'directrix'. Let the planes of circular section associated with the (u_1, u_2, u_3) direction meet the circle at infinity in P_1, P_2, while those associated with the (v_1, v_2, v_3) direction meet it in P_3, P_4. Let (w_1, w_2, w_3) be the direction components of normals to a plane through P_1, P_3.

$$\sum (u_j w_k - u_k w_j)^2 = 0, \qquad \sum (v_j w_k - v_k w_j)^2 = 0.$$

The equation of such a plane through (x) will be

$$w_i(\xi^i - x^i) = 0.$$

To find where this meets the directrix we write

$$u_i(\xi^i - x^i) = -u_i x^i - u_4$$

$$v_i(\xi^i - x^i) = -v_i x^i - v_4$$

$$\sum (\xi^i - x^i)^2 = (u_i x^i + u_4)(v_i x^i + v_4)[-2(\sum u_i v_i \sum w_i^2 - \sum u_i w_i \sum v_i w_i)].$$

Assuming that (x) is on the surface, and comparing with (25) we have

MacCullagh's Theorem 22] *The distance of a point on a central quadric from a point on a focal conic bears a constant ratio to the distance to that point on the corresponding directrix which lies with it on one of those planes of circular section not parallel to those through the directrix.*

MacCullagh (q.v.) approaches this from the other end. It is clear that if a point move in such a way that its distance from a fixed point bears a fixed ratio to the distance to the intersection with a fixed line of a plane through it of fixed aspect, the locus will be a quadric. He gives a good deal of attention to questions of real and imaginary. It is curious that MacCullagh's paper and Amiot's appeared in the same year.

Suppose that we have two points (ξ), (η) or P_1, P_2 of the same central quadric,

$$\sum_i \frac{(\xi^i)^2}{a_i^2} - 1 = 0, \qquad \sum_i \frac{(\eta^i)^2}{a_i^2} - 1 = 0.$$

We transform them into two points P_1', P_2' which lie on a confocal quadric as follows:

$$\xi^{i'} = \frac{b_i}{a_i}\xi^i; \qquad \eta^{i'} = \frac{b_i}{a_i}\eta^i; \qquad b_i^2 = a_i^2 - \lambda. \tag{26}$$

$$(P_1 P_2')^2 = \sum (\xi^i - \eta^{i'})^2 = \sum_i \left(\frac{a_i \xi^{i'}}{b_i} - \frac{b_i \eta^i}{a_i}\right)^2$$

$$= \sum_i \left[\frac{a_i^2 (\xi^{i'})^2}{a_i^2 - \lambda} + \frac{(a_i^2 - \lambda)\eta^{i2}}{a_i^2} - 2\xi^{i'}\eta^i\right]$$

$$= \sum_i [(\xi^{i'})^2 + (\eta^i)^2 - 2\xi^{i'}\eta^i] + 1 - 1$$

$$= (P_1' P_2)^2.$$

Theorem 23] *If a central quadric be carried into another confocal therewith by an affine collineation that leaves the planes of symmetry invariant, and, if $P_1 P_2$ be carried respectively into P_1', P_2',*

$$P_1 P_2' = P_1' P_2.$$

Let us assume that we have two homogeneous confocal ellipsoids, made of the same material, coordinates of points in the two being (ξ) and (ξ'). The total pull of the second on the first is

$$\rho \iiint d\xi^1\, d\xi^2\, d\xi^3 \iiint \frac{d\xi^{1'}\, d\xi^{2'}\, d\xi^{3'}}{(P_1 P_2')^2}$$

$$= \rho \iiint \frac{a_1 a_2 a_3}{b_1 b_2 b_3} d\xi^{1'}\, d\xi^{2'}\, d\xi^{3'} \iiint \frac{b_1 b_2 b_3}{a_1 a_2 a_3} \frac{d\xi^1\, d\xi^2\, d\xi^3}{(P_2 P_1')^2}$$

$$= \rho \iiint d\xi^{1'}\, d\xi^{2'}\, d\xi^{3'} \iiint \frac{d\xi^1\, d\xi^2\, d\xi^3}{(P_2 P_1')^2}.$$

Ivory's Theorem 24] *Two homogeneous confocal ellipsoids made of the same material exercise the same total pull each on the other.*†

Our transformation (26) being linear will carry the rectilinear generators of one quadric into those of the other.

$$\sum_i (d\xi^{i'})^2 = \sum_i (d\xi^i)^2 - \lambda \sum_i \left(\frac{d\xi^i}{a_i}\right)^2.$$

When the line of advance is along a rectilinear generator, the last term drops out.

† Ivory, q.v.

Theorem 25] *If a central quadric be carried into a confocal one by affine collineation which leaves the planes of symmetry invariant, corresponding lengths on corresponding generators are equal.*

We saw in Chapter VIII how a system of confocal conics will give us a system of elliptic coordinates. The same thing is true in space. The roots of (24) may be taken as elliptic space coordinates. The relation between them and Cartesian coordinates is entirely analogous to that worked out in equations (19) and (20) of that chapter. Here is the analogue of Graves's theorem given on p. 121.

Suppose that we have an ellipsoid and a one-sheeted confocal hyperboloid piercing through it in two curves. A loop of thread is slung around the two and pulled tight. The different sections of the loop are composed of arcs of the curve of intersection, arcs of curves on one surface whose tangents touch the other surface, which we shall later see are geodesic arcs, and straight pieces which are extensions of tangents to these arcs. The lengths of these can be computed as we did for Graves's theorem; it is merely necessary to watch very carefully the algebraic signs attached to certain radicals. We thus come to

Staude's Theorem 26] *If a loop of inextensible thread be drawn tight around an ellipsoid and a one-sheeted hyperboloid confocal therewith, the locus of the point of tension is a confocal ellipsoid.*

The proof is, as I said, quite analogous to that of Graves's theorem in Chapter VIII. An elaborate discussion of the whole subject will be found in Staude[2] with the description of a simple apparatus where the two surfaces are replaced by a pair of focal conics.

CHAPTER XIV

QUADRIC SURFACES, DIFFERENTIAL PROPERTIES

THERE is surprisingly little material dealing with the differential properties of the quadric surfaces. Perhaps this is because the answers to the most obvious questions are easy to find. It would, however, be a mistake to close the present work without some discussion of the subject.

There is nothing to be said about the asymptotic lines of the quadric surfaces, these are simply the rectilinear generators. There is more interest in the lines of curvature. Euler started by studying the curvature of different normal sections of a surface. This takes extremal values in two mutually perpendicular directions, the lines of curvature are curves whose tangents have these two directions. Monge[†] asked what curves on a surface have the property that the normals along them generate developable surfaces. He reasoned like this: the notation is Euler's.

$$z = f(x, y),$$

$$\frac{\partial z}{\partial x} = p, \qquad \frac{\partial z}{\partial y} = q,$$

$$\frac{\partial^2 z}{\partial x^2} = r; \qquad \frac{\partial^2 z}{\partial x \partial y} = s, \qquad \frac{\partial^2 z}{\partial y^2} = t.$$

A sphere with centre at (x', y', z') tangent to the surface has an equation

$$(x-x')^2 + (y-y')^2 + (z-z')^2 = R^2.$$

Since (x', y', z') is on the normal

$$(x-x') + (z-z')p = 0; \qquad (y-y') + (z-z')q = 0.$$

Now if we move in such a way that the first variation of (x', y', z') is 0,

$$dx + p^2\,dx + pq\,dy + (z-z')(r\,dx + s\,dy) = 0,$$

$$dy + pq\,dx + q^2\,dy + (z-z')(s\,dx + t\,dy) = 0,$$

$$\left(\frac{dy}{dx}\right)^2[(1+q^2)s - pqt] + \frac{dy}{dx}[(1+q^2)r - (1+p^2)t] - [(1+p^2)s - pqr] = 0. \quad (1)$$

But this is the differential equation for Euler's lines of curvature. If we place the axes so that the (x, y) plane is tangent, $p = q = 0$ and the product of the roots is -1. This shows that we have two mutually perpendicular directions. Monge goes on from here to study the case of the ellipsoid, but I pass over to the much simpler presentation that was presently discovered. The leader here was Charles Dupin, and he

† Monge[2], pp. 145 ff.

looked on the question both synthetically and analytically. I will first follow his geometric reasoning.†

What can be said about three systems of surfaces—let us call them the A system, the B system, and the C system—which cut orthogonally? We start at a point on an A surface, and erect a perpendicular. This will be in a normal plane tangent to the B surface. Move infinitesimally along the curve of intersection of the A and B surface. The tangent plane to the B surface will rotate about a line whose direction, on that surface, is conjugate to the direction of the curve of intersection. But it will also tend to rotate about a normal to the A surface. Hence the direction of the intersection of the A and B surface is perpendicular to its conjugate on the B surface, and so is a direction of curvature for that surface. As the three systems of surfaces appear symmetrically, it is clear that the curves of intersection are lines of curvature for all three surfaces.

This geometrical reasoning seems to me perfectly sound, which is more than can be said of some of his geometry. He backs it up with the following analysis. The direction cosines of the normals to the three surfaces are proportional to

$$(p',q',-1); \quad (p'',q'',-1); \quad (p''',q''',-1).$$

The orthogonality conditions are

$$1+p''p'''+q''q''' = 1+p'''p'+q'''q' = 1+p'p''+q'q'' = 0.$$

$$(p''p'''+q''q''')+(p'''p'+q'''q')(p'p''+q'q'') = 0.$$

Let us differentiate the next to the last equation moving along the third surface

$$p'(r''dx+s''dy)+q'(s''dx+t''dy)+p''(r'dx+s'dy)+q''(s'dx+t'dy) = 0.$$

But
$$\frac{dy}{dx} = \frac{q'''}{p'''}$$

$$[r'p''p'''+s'(q''p'''+p''q''')+t'q''q''']+[r''p'''p'+s''(q'''p'+p'''q')+t''q'''q'] = 0.$$

There are two other equations like this, but in each case we have the sum of two out of the same three square brackets equal to 0. Hence each square bracket is 0, so that we have three equations of the form

$$r'p''p'''+s'(q''p'''+p''q''')+t'q''q''' = 0.$$

Putting $\dfrac{q'''}{p'''} = \dfrac{dy}{dx}$ and eliminating $\dfrac{q''}{p''}$ between this and the equation following the three short ones we fall back on equation (1).

† Dupin², pp. 239, 324.

Dupin's Theorem 1] *A triply orthogonal system of surfaces intersect in their lines of curvature.*

Dupin had previously proved our Theorem 12 of the last chapter that confocal conics are an orthogonal system. The problem of finding the lines of curvature of a quadric is thus solved completely.

Here are two pretty theorems taken from the closing pages of Chasles[7]. Let two planes cut a quadric in two conics. Through these will pass two quadric cones whose vertices are harmonically separated by the two planes; each vertex lies in the polar plane of the other with regard to the quadric. The generators of the cones at a point of intersection of the conics have directions which are conjugate with regard to the surface.

Through a real finite point of a central quadric will pass a real pair of circular sections as well as two imaginary pairs, if the surface be not one of revolution. The tangents to such a pair of circles have directions which are conjugate with regard to the quadric, and also with regard to the sphere through the two circles, and so are mutually perpendicular.

Theorem 2] *The tangents to the lines of curvature of a central quadric not a surface of revolution through a finite point are generators of three pairs of cones through the three pairs of circular sections through that point.*

The curvature of a normal section through a given point of a surface was shown by Euler to depend in simple fashion on the square of the cosine of the angle which the plane of the section makes with the normal section through the tangent to a line of curvature.† As the planes of a pair of circular sections and the tangents to the lines of curvature are a harmonic set where one pair make a right angle, the former pair make equal angles with the latter. This gives

Theorem 3] *The normal sections of a quadric through a pair of circular sections have curvatures of the same absolute value.*

When it comes to a detailed study of the differential geometry of the central quadrics, according to the classical procedure of Gauss the best plan is to use elliptic coordinates

$$\frac{(x^1)^2}{a_1^2-\lambda}+\frac{(x^2)^2}{a_2^2-\lambda}+\frac{(x^3)^2}{a_3^2-\lambda}-1=0. \qquad (2)$$

† Cf. Coolidge[2], p. 326.

In particular, if we wish to study the ellipsoid, we take†

$$\lambda_1 = 0, \qquad \lambda_2 = u, \qquad \lambda_3 = v; \qquad (x^i)^2 = \frac{a_i^2(a_i^2-u)(a_i^2-v)}{(a_i^2-a_j^2)(a_i^2-a_k^2)}. \quad (3)$$

$$\frac{\partial \log x^i}{\partial u} = -\frac{1}{2(a_i^2-u)}; \qquad \frac{\partial \log x^i}{\partial v} = -\frac{1}{2(a_i^2-v)}.$$

$$E = \frac{u(u-v)}{4 \prod (a_i^2-u)}, \qquad F = 0, \qquad G = \frac{-v(u-v)}{4 \prod (a_i^2-v)}. \quad (4)$$

$$ds^2 = \frac{u-v}{4}\left[\frac{u\,du^2}{\prod(a_i^2-u)} - \frac{v\,dv^2}{\prod(a_i^2-v)}\right]. \quad (5)$$

We write

$$du' = \frac{1}{2}\sqrt{\left(\frac{u}{\prod(a_i^2-u)}\right)}\,du; \qquad dv' = \frac{1}{2}\sqrt{\left(\frac{-v}{\prod(a_i^2-u)}\right)}\,dv. \quad (6)$$

$$ds^2 = (u-v)(du'^2+dv'^2). \quad (7)$$

Theorem 4] *A central quadric is cut by confocal quadrics in an isothermal orthogonal system.*

From (7)
$$E' = G' = \sqrt{(E'G')} = u-v,$$

$$\frac{\partial \log G'}{\partial u'} = \frac{du/du'}{u-v}; \qquad \frac{\partial \log E'}{\partial v'} = \frac{-dv/dv'}{u-v}.$$

$$\frac{\partial}{\partial u'}\left(\frac{\partial \log G'}{\partial u'}\right) = \frac{(u-v)\dfrac{d^2u}{du'^2} - \left(\dfrac{du}{du'}\right)^2}{(u-v)^2};$$

$$\frac{\partial}{\partial v'}\left(\frac{\partial \log E'}{\partial v'}\right) = -\frac{(u-v)\dfrac{d^2v}{dv'^2} + \left(\dfrac{dv}{dv'}\right)^2}{(u-v)^2}.$$

$$\frac{d^2u}{du'^2} = \frac{1}{2}\frac{d}{du'}\left(\frac{du}{du'}\right)^2\bigg/\frac{du}{du'} = 2\frac{d}{du'}\left[\frac{\prod(a_i^2-u)}{u}\right]\bigg/\frac{du}{du'}$$

$$= \frac{-2\prod(a_i^2-u)}{u}\left[\sum\frac{1}{a_i^2-u} + \frac{1}{u}\right].$$

This gives the formula for the total curvature

$$K = \frac{1}{(u-v)^3}\left[\frac{\prod(a_i^2-u)}{u}\left((u-v)\sum\frac{1}{a_i^2-u} + \frac{3u-v}{u}\right) - \right.$$
$$\left. - \frac{\prod(a_i^2-v)}{v}\left((u-v)\sum\frac{1}{a_i^2-v} + \frac{u-3v}{v}\right)\right]. \quad (8)$$

† Cf. Knoblauch (q.v.), pp. 241.

One of the most satisfactory parts of the differential geometry of quadric surfaces is the treatment of geodesic curves. We must begin with a short discussion of differential line geometry. The lines of a two-parameter system or congruence may pass through a point, or meet a curve twice, or meet two curves, or meet a curve and touch a surface, but in general they touch two surfaces called the focal surfaces. The lines tangent to the asymptotic curves of a surface will touch no other surface, but the lines of a general congruence touch two surfaces. They may be assembled in two different ways as generators of a one-parameter family of developable surfaces. Such a developable will have its edge of regression on one of the focal surfaces and 'scratch' the other surface. On each surface the edges of regression and the curves 'scratched' form a conjugate system of curves. The osculating plane of the developable is, in each case, tangent to the surface at the point on which the edge of regression does not lie. The necessary and sufficient condition that a congruence should be a normal one is that the osculating planes through each line to the two developables to which it belongs should be mutually perpendicular. The osculating plane will, then, be perpendicular to that surface which it does not touch.

Let us take the case of a quadric. The cones of given vertex which envelop the quadrics of a confocal system are confocal cones, touch the same four minimal planes. Two, cutting orthogonally, pass through each line through the vertex of the cone. The lines which touch two confocal quadrics will thus form a normal congruence. The lines which they determine on either surface will have the property that their osculating planes are normal to the surface, and this is the characteristic property of geodesic lines.

Theorem 5] *The tangents to a geodesic on a quadric will all touch the same confocal quadric.*

This is the property of geodesics we mentioned on p. 198 in connexion with Staude's theorem. It leads us to the differential equation of a geodesic on a central quadric, say an ellipsoid

$$\frac{(x^1)^2}{a_1^2} + \frac{(x^2)^2}{a_2^2} + \frac{(x^3)^2}{a_3^2} - 1 = 0, \tag{9}$$

$$\sum \frac{x^i \, dx^i}{a_i^2} = 0. \tag{10}$$

Let us seek the differential equation of the geodesic whose tangents touch the quadric with equation (2).

Let $$\xi^i = x^i + r \, dx^i.$$

Substitute in (2) and write the condition that the resulting quadratic in r has equal roots:

$$\left(\sum \frac{(x^i)^2}{a_i^2 - \lambda} - 1\right)\left(\sum \frac{(dx^i)^2}{a_i^2 - \lambda}\right) - \left(\sum \frac{x^i \, dx^i}{a_i^2 - \lambda}\right)^2 = 0. \tag{11}$$

$$\sum \frac{(dx^i)^2}{a_i^2 - \lambda} - \sum \frac{(x^j \, dx^k - x^k \, dx^j)^2}{(a_j^2 - \lambda)(a_k^2 - \lambda)} = 0.$$

$$\sum (a_j^2 - \lambda)(a_k^2 - \lambda)(dx^i)^2 - \sum (a_i^2 - \lambda)(x^j \, dx^k - x^k \, dx^j)^2 = 0. \tag{12}$$

The term independent of λ is

$$a_1^2 a_2^2 a_3^2 \left[\sum \frac{(dx^i)^2}{a_i^2} - \sum \left(\frac{x^j}{a_j} \frac{dx^k}{a_k} - \frac{x^k}{a_k} \frac{dx^j}{a_j}\right)^2\right] = 0.$$

From (9) and (10),

$$\lambda \sum (dx^i)^2 + \sum (x^j \, dx^k - x^k \, dx^j)^2 - \sum (a_j^2 + a_k^2)(dx^i)^2 = 0,$$

$$[\lambda + \sum (x^i)^2 - \sum a_i^2] \sum (dx^i)^2 + \sum (a_i \, dx^i)^2 - \sum (x_i^2 \, dx^i)^2 = 0. \tag{13}$$

By (3),

$$\sum [(x^i)^2 - a_i^2] = \sum \frac{a_i^2[(a_i^2 - u)(a_i^2 - v) - (a_i^2 - a_j^2)(a_i^2 - a_k^2)]}{(a_i^2 - a_j^2)(a_i^2 - a_k^2)}.$$

Put

$$P = (a_1^2 - a_2^2)(a_2^2 - a_3^2)(a_3^2 - a_1^2) = -\sum a_i^4(a_j^2 - a_k^2).$$

$$\sum [(x^i)^2 - a_i^2] = -\frac{1}{P} \sum a_i^2(a_j^2 - a_k^2)[(a_i^2 - u)(a_i^2 - v) - (a_i^2 - a_j^2)(a_i^2 - a_k^2)]$$

$$= -(u + v).$$

$$\sum (x^i)^2 = -(u + v) + \sum a_i^2; \qquad \sum x^i \, dx^i = -\tfrac{1}{2}[du + dv].$$

$$dx^i = \frac{-i a_i \sqrt{(a_j^2 - a_k^2)}}{2\sqrt{P}} \left[\sqrt{\left(\frac{a_i^2 - v}{a_i^2 - u}\right)} du + \sqrt{\left(\frac{a_i^2 - u}{a_i^2 - v}\right)} dv\right]$$

$$\sum (a_i \, dx^i)^2 = \sum \frac{-a_i^4(a_j^2 - a_k^2)}{4P} \left[(du + dv)^2 + (u - v)\left(\frac{u \, du^2}{a_i^2 - u} - \frac{v \, dv^2}{a_i^2 - v}\right)\right]$$

$$= \frac{(du + dv)^2}{4} + (u - v)\left[\frac{u^2 \, du^2}{\prod (a_i^2 - u)} - \frac{v^2 \, dv^2}{\prod (a_i^2 - v)}\right].$$

Substituting in (13) and dividing by $(u - v)$

$$[\lambda - (u + v)]\left[\frac{u \, du^2}{\prod (a_i^2 - u)} - \frac{v \, dv^2}{\prod (a_i^2 - v)}\right] + \frac{u \, du^2}{\prod (a_i^2 - u)} - \frac{v \, dv^2}{\prod (a_i^2 - v)} = 0$$

$$\frac{u \, du^2}{\prod (a_i^2 - u)(\lambda - u)} = \frac{v \, dv^2}{\prod (a_i^2 - v)(\lambda - v)}. \tag{14}$$

Along a geodesic $\qquad ds = \dfrac{i(u - v)\sqrt{u} \, du}{\sqrt{\{\prod (a_i^2 - u)\}(\lambda - u)}}.$ $\qquad$ (15)

Theorem 6] *The differential equation of a geodesic on a central quadric expresses the identity of the absolute values of the same hyperelliptic integral in two different variables.*

This theorem is conceded to Jacobi; see p. 60 of Jacobi[2], vol. ii. What he actually writes is this, changing to our notation:

$$x^1 = \sqrt{\left(\frac{a_1^2}{a_3^2-a_1^2}\right)} \sin\phi \sqrt{(a_2^2\cos^2\psi+a_3^2\sin^2\psi-a_1^2)}; \quad x^2 = \sqrt{a_2^2}\cos\phi\sin\psi.$$

$$x^3 = \sqrt{\left(\frac{a_1^2}{a_3^2-a_1^2}\right)}\cos\psi\sqrt{(a_3^2-a_1^2\cos^2\phi-a_2^2\sin^2\phi)}.$$

The formula for the differential of length on a geodesic is

$$ds = \frac{\sqrt{(a_1^2\cos^2\phi+a_2^2\sin^2\phi)\,d\phi}}{\sqrt{(a_3^2-a_1^2\cos^2\phi-a_2^2\sin^2\phi)}\sqrt{\{(a_2^2-a_1^2)\cos^2\phi-B\}}} -$$
$$-\frac{\sqrt{(a_2^2\cos^2\psi+a_3^2\sin^2\psi)\,d\psi}}{\sqrt{(a_2^2\cos^2\psi+a_3^2\sin^2\psi-a_1^2)}\sqrt{\{(a_3^2-a_2^2)\sin^2\psi+B\}}}. \tag{16}$$

He appends this remark, p. 61: 'Die hier angewandte Art, die drei Coordinaten des Punktes eines Ellipsoids durch zwei Winkel ϕ und ψ auszudrucken, ist dieselbe auf welche man geführt wird, wenn man den Punkt des Ellipsoids als Intersection der beiden Krümmungslinien bestimmt.' Similarly, we read on p. 30 of Klein (q.v.), in discussing equation (14): 'Eben dieses sind Jacobis Formeln für die geodätische Linien auf dem Ellipsoid.' I confess that I have not had the courage to verify these interesting statements.

A simpler form for the differential equation can be found if we use geodesic polar coordinates, the geodesics originating at an umbilical point. Here we can reduce to the compact form

$$ds^2 = dp^2 + \frac{a_3^2(a_3^2-u)(a_3^2-v)}{(a_1^2-a_3^2)(a_2^2-a_3^2)}\cos^2\omega\,d\omega^2.$$

This formula is equivalent to that on p. 3 of Roberts (q.v.). Further detail will be found in Chapter VII of Eisenhart[2]. A study of those surfaces which can be developed on the quadrics appears in Chapter X of the same work.

INDEX OF AUTHORS QUOTED

Chasles[2], 'Sur une propriété générale des coniques', *Correspondance mathématique*, vol. iv, Brussels, 1828, 56.

Chasles[3], *Traité des sections coniques*, Paris, 1865.

Chasles[4], 'Résumé d'une théorie des coniques sphériques homofocales', *Liouville* (2), vol. v, 1860, 126.

Chasles[5], 'Construction des coniques qui satisfont à cinque conditions', *Comptes Rendus*, vols. lviii and lix, 1864, 131.

Chasles[6], 'Propositions rélatives aux courbes et aux surfaces du second ordre', *Correspondance de l'École Impériale Polytechnique*, vol. iii, 1814, 132, 158.

Charles[7], 'Recherches de géométrie pure sur les lignes et les surfaces du second ordre', *Nouveaux Mémoires de l'Académie Royale de Belgique*, vol. v, 1829, 160, 161.

Chasles[8], 'Mémoire de géometrie pure sur les propriétés générales des cones du second degré', ibid, vol. vi, 1830, 161, 162.

Clebsch, Alfred[1], 1833–1872, 'Ueber symbolische Darstellung algebraischer Formen', *Crelle*, vol. lix, 1861, 104.

Clebsch[2], 'Theorie der Charakteristiken', *Math. Annalen*, vol. vi, 1873, 133.

Clebsch and Lindemann, Ferdinand (1852–), *Vorlesungen über Geometrie*, Leipzig, 1876, 178, 183.

Coolidge, Julian Lowell[1], 1873– , *The Geometry of the Complex Domain*, Oxford, 1924, 51.

Coolidge[2], *A History of Geometrical Methods*, Oxford, 1940, 52, 53, 72, 158, 201.

Coolidge[3], *A Treatise on Algebraic Plane Curves*, Oxford, 1931, 83, 140, 141.

Coolidge[4], *A Treatise on the Circle and the Sphere*, Oxford, 1916, 114, 194.

Coolidge[5], 'Analytic systems of central conics in space', *Transactions American Math. Soc.*, vol. xlviii, 1940, 145.

D'Alembert, Jean Le Rond, 1717–1783, *Opuscules mathématiques*, vol. vii, Paris, 1780, 171.

Darboux, Gaston[1], 1842–1917, 'Sur le théorème fondamental de la géométrie projective', *Math. Annalen*, vol. xvii, 1880, 63.

Darboux[2], *Théorie générale des surfaces*, vol. i, Paris, 1887, 145.

Desargues, Girard, 1593–1661, *Œuvres de Desargues*, réunies et analysées, par M. Poudra, Paris, 1864, 28, 31, 32.

Descartes, Réné[1], 1596–1650, *La géométrie*, edition Hermann, 2nd ed., Paris, 1927, 74.

Descartes[2], *Geometria a Renato Des Cartes. Una cum notis Florimonde de Beaune*, 3rd ed., Amsterdam, 1683, 76.

de Witt, Jan, 1625–1672, *Elementa Curvarum*; see Descartes[2], 38, 40, 76.

Dingeldey, Friedrich, 1859– , 'Kegelschnitte und Kegelschnittsysteme', *Encyklopädie der Math. Wissenschaften*, iii, C. 1, 122, 151, 153.

Dupin, Charles[1], 1784–1873, 'Sur la description des lignes et des surfaces du second ordre', *Journal de l'École Polytechnique*, vol. vi, 1808, 156.

Dupin[2], *Développements de géométrie*, Paris, 1822, 206.

Dupin[3], *Application de géométrie*, Paris, 1822, 193.

Durrande, Jean Batiste, 'Démonstration géométrique de diverses propriétés de l'ellipsoïde', *Annales de Mathématiques*, vol. xii, 1822, 109, 110.

SUBJECT INDEX

CATALOGUE OF DOVER BOOKS

BOOKS EXPLAINING SCIENCE AND MATHEMATICS

General

WHAT IS SCIENCE?, Norman Campbell. This excellent introduction explains scientific method, rôle of mathematics, types of scientific laws. Contents: 2 aspects of science, science & nature, laws of science, discovery of laws, explanation of laws, measurement & numerical laws, applications of science. 192pp. 5⅜ x 8. S43 Paperbound **$1.25**

THE COMMON SENSE OF THE EXACT SCIENCES, W. K. Clifford. Introduction by James Newman, edited by Karl Pearson. For 70 years this has been a guide to classical scientific and mathematical thought. Explains with unusual clarity basic concepts, such as extension of meaning of symbols, characteristics of surface boundaries, properties of plane figures, vectors, Cartesian method of determining position, etc. Long preface by Bertrand Russell. Bibliography of Clifford. Corrected, 130 diagrams redrawn. 249pp. 5⅜ x 8.
T61 Paperbound **$1.60**

SCIENCE THEORY AND MAN, Erwin Schrödinger. This is a complete and unabridged reissue of SCIENCE AND THE HUMAN TEMPERAMENT plus an additional essay: "What is an Elementary Particle?" Nobel laureate Schrödinger discusses such topics as nature of scientific method, the nature of science, chance and determinism, science and society, conceptual models for physical entities, elementary particles and wave mechanics. Presentation is popular and may be followed by most people with little or no scientific training. "Fine practical preparation for a time when laws of nature, human institutions . . . are undergoing a critical examination without parallel," Waldemar Kaempffert, N. Y. TIMES. 192pp. 5⅜ x 8.
T428 Paperbound **$1.35**

FADS AND FALLACIES IN THE NAME OF SCIENCE, Martin Gardner. Examines various cults, quack systems, frauds, delusions which at various times have masqueraded as science. Accounts of hollow-earth fanatics like Symmes; Velikovsky and wandering planets; Hoerbiger; Bellamy and the theory of multiple moons; Charles Fort; dowsing, pseudoscientific methods for finding water, ores, oil. Sections on naturopathy, iridiagnosis, zone therapy, food fads, etc. Analytical accounts of Wilhelm Reich and orgone sex energy; L. Ron Hubbard and Dianetics; A. Korzybski and General Semantics; many others. Brought up to date to include Bridey Murphy, others. Not just a collection of anecdotes, but a fair, reasoned appraisal of eccentric theory. Formerly titled IN THE NAME OF SCIENCE. Preface. Index. x + 384pp. 5⅜ x 8. T394 Paperbound **$1.75**

A DOVER SCIENCE SAMPLER, edited by George Barkin. 64-page book, sturdily bound, containing excerpts from over 20 Dover books, explaining science. Edwin Hubble, George Sarton, Ernst Mach, A. d'Abro, Galileo, Newton, others, discussing island-universes, scientific truth, biological phenomena, stability in bridges, etc. Copies limited; no more than 1 to a customer,
FREE

POPULAR SCIENTIFIC LECTURES, Hermann von Helmholtz. Helmholtz was a superb expositor as well as a scientist of genius in many areas. The seven essays in this volume are models of clarity, and even today they rank among the best general descriptions of their subjects ever written. "The Physiological Causes of Harmony in Music" was the first significant physiological explanation of musical consonance and dissonance. Two essays, "On the Interaction of Natural Forces" and "On the Conservation of Force," were of great importance in the history of science, for they firmly established the principle of the conservation of energy. Other lectures include "On the Relation of Optics to Painting," "On Recent Progress in the Theory of Vision," "On Goethe's Scientific Researches," and "On the Origin and Significance of Geometrical Axioms." Selected and edited with an introduction by Professor Morris Kline. xii + 286pp. 5⅜ x 8½. T799 Paperbound **$1.45**

BOOKS EXPLAINING SCIENCE AND MATHEMATICS

Physics

CONCERNING THE NATURE OF THINGS, Sir William Bragg. Christmas lectures delivered at the Royal Society by Nobel laureate. Why a spinning ball travels in a curved track; how uranium is transmuted to lead, etc. Partial contents: atoms, gases, liquids, crystals, metals, etc. No scientific background needed; wonderful for intelligent child. 32pp. of photos, 57 figures. xii + 232pp. 5⅜ x 8. T31 Paperbound **$1.50**

THE RESTLESS UNIVERSE, Max Born. New enlarged version of this remarkably readable account by a Nobel laureate. Moving from sub-atomic particles to universe, the author explains in very simple terms the latest theories of wave mechanics. Partial contents: air and its relatives, electrons & ions, waves & particles, electronic structure of the atom, nuclear physics. Nearly 1000 illustrations, including 7 animated sequences. 325pp. 6 x 9.
T412 Paperbound **$2.00**

FROM EUCLID TO EDDINGTON: A STUDY OF THE CONCEPTIONS OF THE EXTERNAL WORLD, Sir Edmund Whittaker. A foremost British scientist traces the development of theories of natural philosophy from the western rediscovery of Euclid to Eddington, Einstein, Dirac, etc. The inadequacy of classical physics is contrasted with present day attempts to understand the physical world through relativity, non-Euclidean geometry, space curvature, wave mechanics, etc. 5 major divisions of examination: Space; Time and Movement; the Concepts of Classical Physics; the Concepts of Quantum Mechanics; the Eddington Universe. 212pp. 5⅜ x 8.   T491 Paperbound **$1.35**

PHYSICS, THE PIONEER SCIENCE, L. W. Taylor. First thorough text to place all important physical phenomena in cultural-historical framework; remains best work of its kind. Exposition of physical laws, theories- developed chronologically, with great historical, illustrative experiments diagrammed, described, worked out mathematically. Excellent physics text for self-study as well as class work. Vol. 1: Heat, Sound: motion, acceleration, gravitation, conservation of energy, heat engines, rotation, heat, mechanical energy, etc. 211 illus. 407pp. 5⅜ x 8. Vol. 2: Light, Electricity: images, lenses, prisms, magnetism, Ohm's law, dynamos, telegraph, quantum theory, decline of mechanical view of nature, etc. Bibliography. 13 table appendix. Index. 551 illus. 2 color plates. 508pp. 5⅜ x 8.

Vol. 1 S565 Paperbound **$2.25**
Vol. 2 S566 Paperbound **$2.25**
The set **$4.50**

A SURVEY OF PHYSICAL THEORY, Max Planck. One of the greatest scientists of all time, creator of the quantum revolution in physics, writes in non-technical terms of his own discoveries and those of other outstanding creators of modern physics. Planck wrote this book when science had just crossed the threshold of the new physics, and he communicates the excitement felt then as he discusses electromagnetic theories, statistical methods, evolution of the concept of light, a step-by-step description of how he developed his own momentous theory, and many more of the basic ideas behind modern physics. Formerly "A Survey of Physics." Bibliography. Index. 128pp. 5⅜ x 8.   S650 Paperbound **$1.15**

THE ATOMIC NUCLEUS, M. Korsunsky. The only non-technical comprehensive account of the atomic nucleus in English. For college physics students, etc. Chapters cover: Radioactivity, the Nuclear Model of the Atom, the Mass of Atomic Nuclei, the Disintegration of Atomic Nuclei, the Discovery of the Positron, the Artificial Transformation of Atomic Nuclei, Artificial Radioactivity, Mesons, the Neutrino, the Structure of Atomic Nuclei and Forces Acting Between Nuclear Particles, Nuclear Fission, Chain Reaction, Peaceful Uses, Thermonuclear Reactions. Slightly abridged edition. Translated by G. Yankovsky. 65 figures. Appendix includes 45 photographic illustrations. 413 pp. 5⅜ x 8.   S1052 Paperbound **$2.00**

PRINCIPLES OF MECHANICS SIMPLY EXPLAINED, Morton Mott-Smith. Excellent, highly readable introduction to the theories and discoveries of classical physics. Ideal for the layman who desires a foundation which will enable him to understand and appreciate contemporary developments in the physical sciences. Discusses: Density, The Law of Gravitation, Mass and Weight, Action and Reaction, Kinetic and Potential Energy, The Law of Inertia, Effects of Acceleration, The Independence of Motions, Galileo and the New Science of Dynamics, Newton and the New Cosmos, The Conservation of Momentum, and other topics. Revised edition of "This Mechanical World." Illustrated by E. Kosa, Jr. Bibliography and Chronology. Index. xiv + 171pp. 5⅜ x 8½.   T1067 Paperbound **$1.35**

THE CONCEPT OF ENERGY SIMPLY EXPLAINED, Morton Mott-Smith. Elementary, non-technical exposition which traces the story of man's conquest of energy, with particular emphasis on the developments during the nineteenth century and the first three decades of our own century. Discusses man's earlier efforts to harness energy, more recent experiments and discoveries relating to the steam engine, the engine indicator, the motive power of heat, the principle of excluded perpetual motion, the bases of the conservation of energy, the concept of entropy, the internal combustion engine, mechanical refrigeration, and many other related topics. Also much biographical material. Index. Bibliography. 33 illustrations. ix + 215pp. 5⅜ x 8½.   T1071 Paperbound **$1.25**

HEAT AND ITS WORKINGS, Morton Mott-Smith. One of the best elementary introductions to the theory and attributes of heat, covering such matters as the laws governing the effect of heat on solids, liquids and gases, the methods by which heat is measured, the conversion of a substance from one form to another through heating and cooling, evaporation, the effects of pressure on boiling and freezing points, and the three ways in which heat is transmitted (conduction, convection, radiation). Also brief notes on major experiments and discoveries. Concise, but complete, it presents all the essential facts about the subject in readable style. Will give the layman and beginning student a first-rate background in this major topic in physics. Index. Bibliography. 50 illustrations. x + 165pp. 5⅜ x 8½. T978 Paperbound **$1.15**

THE STORY OF ATOMIC THEORY AND ATOMIC ENERGY, J. G. Feinberg. Wider range of facts on physical theory, cultural implications, than any other similar source. Completely non-technical. Begins with first atomic theory, 600 B.C., goes through A-bomb, developments to 1959. Avogadro, Rutherford, Bohr, Einstein, radioactive decay, binding energy, radiation danger, future benefits of nuclear power, dozens of other topics, told in lively, related, informal manner. Particular stress on European atomic research. "Deserves special mention . . . authoritative," Saturday Review. Formerly "The Atom Story." New chapter to 1959. Index. 34 illustrations. 251pp. 5⅜ x 8.   T625 Paperbound **$1.60**

THE STRANGE STORY OF THE QUANTUM, AN ACCOUNT FOR THE GENERAL READER OF THE GROWTH OF IDEAS UNDERLYING OUR PRESENT ATOMIC KNOWLEDGE, B. Hoffmann. Presents lucidly and expertly, with barest amount of mathematics, the problems and theories which led to modern quantum physics. Dr. Hoffmann begins with the closing years of the 19th century, when certain trifling discrepancies were noticed, and with illuminating analogies and examples takes you through the brilliant concepts of Planck, Einstein, Pauli, de Broglie, Bohr, Schroedinger, Heisenberg, Dirac, Sommerfeld, Feynman, etc. This edition includes a new, long postscript carrying the story through 1958. "Of the books attempting an account of the history and contents of our modern atomic physics which have come to my attention, this is the best," H. Margenau, Yale University, in "American Journal of Physics." 32 tables and line illustrations. Index. 275pp. 5⅜ x 8.   T518 Paperbound **$1.75**

THE EVOLUTION OF SCIENTIFIC THOUGHT FROM NEWTON TO EINSTEIN, A. d'Abro. Einstein's special and general theories of relativity, with their historical implications, are analyzed in non-technical terms. Excellent accounts of the contributions of Newton, Riemann, Weyl, Planck, Eddington, Maxwell, Lorentz and others are treated in terms of space and time, equations of electromagnetics, finiteness of the universe, methodology of science. 21 diagrams. 482pp. 5⅜ x 8.   T2 Paperound **$2.25**

THE RISE OF THE NEW PHYSICS, A. d'Abro. A half-million word exposition, formerly titled THE DECLINE OF MECHANISM, for readers not versed in higher mathematics. The only thorough explanation, in everyday language, of the central core of modern mathematical physical theory, treating both classical and modern theoretical physics, and presenting jn terms almost anyone can understand the equivalent of 5 years of study of mathematical physics. Scientifically impeccable coverage of mathematical-physical thought from the Newtonian system up through the electronic theories of Dirac and Heisenberg and Fermi's statistics. Combines both history and exposition; provides a broad yet unified and detailed view, with constant comparison of classical and modern views on phenomena and theories. "A must for anyone doing serious study in the physical sciences," JOURNAL OF THE FRANKLIN INSTITUTE. "Extraordinary faculty . . . to explain ideas and theories of theoretical physics in the language of daily life," ISIS. First part of set covers philosophy of science, drawing upon the practice of Newton, Maxwell, Poincaré, Einstein, others, discussing modes of thought; experiment, interpretations of causality, etc. In the second part, 100 pages explain grammar and vocabulary of mathematics, with discussions of functions, groups, series, Fourier series, etc. The remainder is devoted to concrete, detailed coverage of both classical and quantum physics, explaining such topics as analytic mechanics, Hamilton's principle, wave theory of light, electromagnetic waves, groups of transformations, thermodynamics, phase rule, Brownian movement, kinetics, special relativity, Planck's original quantum theory, Bohr's atom, Zeeman effect, Broglie's wave mechanics, Heisenberg's uncertainty, Eigen-values, matrices, scores of other important topics. Discoveries and theories are covered for such men as Alembert, Born, Cantor, Debye, Euler, Foucault, Galois, Gauss, Hadamard, Kelvin, Kepler, Laplace, Maxwell, Pauli, Rayleigh, Volterra, Weyl, Young, more than 180 others. Indexed. 97 illustrations. ix + 982pp. 5⅜ x 8.   T3 Volume 1, Paperbound **$2.25**
T4 Volume 2, Paperbound **$2.25**

SPINNING TOPS AND GYROSCOPIC MOTION, John Perry. Well-known classic of science still unsurpassed for lucid, accurate, delightful exposition. How quasi-rigidity is induced in flexible and fluid bodies by rapid motions; why gyrostat falls, top rises; nature and effect on climatic conditions of earth's precessional movement; effect of internal fluidity on rotating bodies, etc. Appendixes describe practical uses to which gyroscopes have been put in ships, compasses, monorail transportation. 62 figures. 128pp. 5⅜ x 8.   T416 Paperbound **$1.25**

THE UNIVERSE OF LIGHT, Sir William Bragg. No scientific training needed to read Nobel Prize winner's expansion of his Royal Institute Christmas Lectures. Insight into nature of light, methods and philosophy of science. Explains lenses, reflection, color, resonance, polarization, x-rays, the spectrum, Newton's work with prisms, Huygens' with polarization, Crookes' with cathode ray, etc. Leads into clear statement of 2 major historical theories of light, corpuscle and wave. Dozens of experiments you can do. 199 illus., including 2 full-page color plates. 293pp. 5⅜ x 8.   S538 Paperbound **$1.85**

THE STORY OF X-RAYS FROM RÖNTGEN TO ISOTOPES, A. R. Bleich. Non-technical history of x-rays, their scientific explanation, their applications in medicine, industry, research, and art, and their effect on the individual and his descendants. Includes amusing early reactions to Röntgen's discovery, cancer therapy, detections of art and stamp forgeries, potential risks to patient and operator, etc. Illustrations show x-rays of flower structure, the gall bladder, gears with hidden defects, etc. Original Dover publication. Glossary. Bibliography. Index. 55 photos and figures. xiv + 186pp. 5⅜ x 8.   T662 Paperbound **$1.50**

ELECTRONS, ATOMS, METALS AND ALLOYS, Wm. Hume-Rothery. An introductory-level explanation of the application of the electronic theory to the structure and properties ot metals and alloys, taking into account the new theoretical work done by mathematical physicists. Material presented in dialogue-form between an "Old Metallurgist" and a "Young Scientist." Their discussion falls into 4 main parts: the nature of an atom, the nature of a metal, the nature of an alloy, and the structure of the nucleus. They cover such topics as the hydrogen atom, electron waves, wave mechanics, Brillouin zones, co-valent bonds, radioactivity and natural disintegration, fundamental particles, structure and fission of the nucleus, etc. Revised, enlarged edition. 177 illustrations. Subject and name indexes. 407pp. 5⅜ x 8½.   S1046 Paperbound **$2.25**

OUT OF THE SKY, H. H. Nininger. A non-technical but comprehensive introduction to "meteoritics", the young science concerned with all aspects of the arrival of matter from outer space. Written by one of the world's experts on meteorites, this work shows how, despite difficulties of observation and sparseness of data, a considerable body of knowledge has arisen. It defines meteors and meteorites; studies fireball clusters and processions, meteorite composition, size, distribution, showers, explosions, origins, craters, and much more. A true connecting link between astronomy and geology. More than 175 photos, 22 other illustrations. References. Bibliography of author's publications on meteorites. Index. viii + 336pp. 5⅜ x 8.   T519 Paperbound **$1.85**

SATELLITES AND SCIENTIFIC RESEARCH, D. King-Hele. Non-technical account of the manmade satellites and the discoveries they have yielded up to the autumn of 1961. Brings together information hitherto published only in hard-to-get scientific journals. Includes the life history of a typical satellite, methods of tracking, new information on the shape of the earth, zones of radiation, etc. Over 60 diagrams and 6 photographs. Mathematical appendix. Bibliography of over 100 items. Index. xii + 180pp. 5⅜ x 8½.   T703 Paperbound **$2.00**

BOOKS EXPLAINING SCIENCE AND MATHEMATICS

Mathematics

CHANCE, LUCK AND STATISTICS: THE SCIENCE OF CHANCE, Horace C. Levinson. Theory of probability and science of statistics in simple, non-technical language. Part I deals with theory of probability, covering odd superstitions in regard to "luck," the meaning of betting odds, the law of mathematical expectation, gambling, and applications in poker, roulette, lotteries, dice, bridge, and other games of chance. Part II discusses the misuse of statistics, the concept of statistical probabilities, normal and skew frequency distributions, and statistics applied to various fields—birth rates, stock speculation, insurance rates, advertising, etc. "Presented in an easy humorous style which I consider the best kind of expository writing," Prof. A. C. Cohen, Industry Quality Control. Enlarged revised edition. Formerly titled "The Science of Chance." Preface and two new appendices by the author. Index. xiv + 365pp. 5⅜ x 8.   T1007 Paperbound **$1.85**

PROBABILITIES AND LIFE, Emile Borel. Translated by M. Baudin. Non-technical, highly readable introduction to the results of probability as applied to everyday situations. Partial contents: Fallacies About Probabilities Concerning Life After Death; Negligible Probabilities and the Probabilities of Everyday Life; Events of Small Probability; Application of Probabilities to Certain Problems of Heredity; Probabilities of Deaths, Diseases, and Accidents; On Poisson's Formula. Index. 3 Appendices of statistical studies and tables. vi + 87pp. 5⅜ x 8½.   T121 Paperbound **$1.00**

GREAT IDEAS OF MODERN MATHEMATICS: THEIR NATURE AND USE, Jagjit Singh. Reader with only high school math will understand main mathematical ideas of modern physics, astronomy, genetics, psychology, evolution, etc., better than many who use them as tools, but comprehend little of their basic structure. Author uses his wide knowledge of non-mathematical fields in brilliant exposition of differential equations, matrices, group theory, logic, statistics, problems of mathematical foundations, imaginary numbers, vectors, etc. Original publication. 2 appendices. 2 indexes. 65 illustr. 322pp. 5⅜ x 8.   S587 Paperbound **$2.00**

MATHEMATICS IN ACTION, O. G. Sutton. Everyone with a command of high school algebra will find this book one of the finest possible introductions to the application of mathematics to physical theory. Ballistics, numerical analysis, waves and wavelike phenomena, Fourier series, group concepts, fluid flow and aerodynamics, statistical measures, and meteorology are discussed with unusual clarity. Some calculus and differential equations theory is developed by the author for the reader's help in the more difficult sections. 88 figures. Index. viii + 236pp. 5⅜ x 8.   T440 Clothbound **$3.50**

THE FOURTH DIMENSION SIMPLY EXPLAINED, edited by H. P. Manning. 22 essays, originally Scientific American contest entries, that use a minimum of mathematics to explain aspects of 4-dimensional geometry: analogues to 3-dimensional space, 4-dimensional absurdities and curiosities (such as removing the contents of an egg without puncturing its shell), possible measurements and forms, etc. Introduction by the editor. Only book of its sort on a truly elementary level, excellent introduction to advanced works. 82 figures. 251pp. 5⅜ x 8.   T711 Paperbound **$1.50**

MATHEMATICS—INTERMEDIATE TO ADVANCED

General

INTRODUCTION TO APPLIED MATHEMATICS, Francis D. Murnaghan. A practical and thoroughly sound introduction to a number of advanced branches of higher mathematics. Among the selected topics covered in detail are: vector and matrix analysis, partial and differential equations, integral equations, calculus of variations, Laplace transform theory, the vector triple product, linear vector functions, quadratic and bilinear forms, Fourier series, spherical harmonics, Bessel functions, the Heaviside expansion formula, and many others. Extremely useful book for graduate students in physics, engineering, chemistry, and mathematics. Index. 111 study exercises with answers. 41 illustrations. ix + 389pp. 5⅜ x 8½.
S1042 Paperbound **$2.25**

OPERATIONAL METHODS IN APPLIED MATHEMATICS, H. S. Carslaw and J. C. Jaeger. Explanation of the application of the Laplace Transformation to differential equations, a simple and effective substitute for more difficult and obscure operational methods. Of great practical value to engineers and to all workers in applied mathematics. Chapters on: Ordinary Linear Differential Equations with Constant Coefficients;; Electric Circuit Theory; Dynamical Applications; The Inversion Theorem for the Laplace Transformation; Conduction of Heat; Vibrations of Continuous Mechanical Systems; Hydrodynamics; Impulsive Functions; Chains of Differential Equations; and other related matters. 3 appendices. 153 problems, many with answers. 22 figures. xvi + 359pp. 5⅜ x 8½.
S1011 Paperbound **$2.25**

APPLIED MATHEMATICS FOR RADIO AND COMMUNICATIONS ENGINEERS, C. E. Smith. No extraneous material here!—only the theories, equations, and operations essential and immediately useful for radio work. Can be used as refresher, as handbook of applications and tables, or as full home-study course. Ranges from simplest arithmetic through calculus, series, and wave forms, hyperbolic trigonometry, simultaneous equations in mesh circuits, etc. Supplies applications right along with each math topic discussed. 22 useful tables of functions, formulas, logs, etc. Index. 166 exercises, 140 examples, all with answers. 95 diagrams. Bibliography. x + 336pp. 5⅜ x 8.
S141 Paperbound **$1.75**

Algebra, group theory, determinants, sets, matrix theory

ALGEBRAS AND THEIR ARITHMETICS, L. E. Dickson. Provides the foundation and background necessary to any advanced undergraduate or graduate student studying abstract algebra. Begins with elementary introduction to linear transformations, matrices, field of complex numbers; proceeds to order, basal units, modulus, quaternions, etc.; develops calculus of linears sets, describes various examples of algebras including invariant, difference, nilpotent, semi-simple. "Makes the reader marvel at his genius for clear and profound analysis," Amer. Mathematical Monthly. Index. xii + 241pp. 5⅜ x 8.
S616 Paperbound **$1.50**

THE THEORY OF EQUATIONS WITH AN INTRODUCTION TO THE THEORY OF BINARY ALGEBRAIC FORMS, W. S. Burnside and A. W. Panton. Extremely thorough and concrete discussion of the theory of equations, with extensive detailed treatment of many topics curtailed in later texts. Covers theory of algebraic equations, properties of polynomials, symmetric functions, derived functions, Horner's process, complex numbers and the complex variable, determinants and methods of elimination, invariant theory (nearly 100 pages), transformations, introduction to Galois theory, Abelian equations, and much more. Invaluable supplementary work for modern students and teachers. 759 examples and exercises. Index in each volume. Two volume set. Total of xxiv + 604pp. 5⅜ x 8.
S714 Vol I Paperbound **$1.85**
S715 Vol II Paperbound **$1.85**
The set **$3.70**

COMPUTATIONAL METHODS OF LINEAR ALGEBRA, V. N. Faddeeva, translated by **C. D. Benster.** First English translation of a unique and valuable work, the only work in English presenting a systematic exposition of the most important methods of linear algebra—classical and contemporary. Shows in detail how to derive numerical solutions of problems in mathematical physics which are frequently connected with those of linear algebra. Theory as well as individual practice. Part I surveys the mathematical background that is indispensable to what follows. Parts II and III, the conclusion, set forth the most important methods of solution, for both exact and iterative groups. One of the most outstanding and valuable features of this work is the 23 tables, double and triple checked for accuracy. These tables will not be found elsewhere. Author's preface. Translator's note. New bibliography and index. x + 252pp. 5⅜ x 8.
S424 Paperbound **$2.00**

ALGEBRAIC EQUATIONS, E. Dehn. Careful and complete presentation of Galois' theory of algebraic equations; theories of Lagrange and Galois developed in logical rather than historical form, with a more thorough exposition than in most modern books. Many concrete applications and fully-worked-out examples. Discusses basic theory (very clear exposition of the symmetric group); isomorphic, transitive, and Abelian groups; applications of Lagrange's and Galois' theories; and much more. Newly revised by the author. Index. List of Theorems. xi + 208pp. 5⅜ x 8.
S697 Paperbound **$1.45**

Differential equations, ordinary and partial; integral equations

INTRODUCTION TO THE DIFFERENTIAL EQUATIONS OF PHYSICS, L. Hopf. Especially valuable to the engineer with no math beyond elementary calculus. Emphasizing intuitive rather than formal aspects of concepts, the author covers an extensive territory. Partial contents: Law of causality, energy theorem, damped oscillations, coupling by friction, cylindrical and spherical coordinates, heat source, etc. Index. 48 figures. 160pp. 5⅜ x 8.
S120 Paperbound **$1.35**

INTRODUCTION TO THE THEORY OF LINEAR DIFFERENTIAL EQUATIONS, E. G. Poole. Authoritative discussions of important topics, with methods of solution more detailed than usual, for students with background of elementary course in differential equations. Studies existence theorems, linearly independent solutions; equations with constant coefficients; with uniform analytic coefficients; regular singularities; the hypergeometric equation; conformal representation; etc. Exercises. Index. 210pp. 5⅜ x 8.
S629 Paperbound **$1.65**

DIFFERENTIAL EQUATIONS FOR ENGINEERS, P. Franklin. Outgrowth of a course given 10 years at M. I. T. Makes most useful branch of pure math accessible for practical work. Theoretical basis of D.E.'s; solution of ordinary D.E.'s and partial derivatives arising from heat flow, steady-state temperature of a plate, wave equations; analytic functions; convergence of Fourier Series. 400 problems on electricity, vibratory systems, other topics. Formerly "Differential Equations for Electrical Engineers." Index 41 illus. 307pp. 5⅜ x 8.
S601 Paperbound **$2.00**

DIFFERENTIAL EQUATIONS, F. R. Moulton. A detailed, rigorous exposition of all the non-elementary processes of solving ordinary differential equations. Several chapters devoted to the treatment of practical problems, especially those of a physical nature, which are far more advanced than problems usually given as illustrations. Includes analytic differential equations; variations of a parameter; integrals of differential equations; analytic implicit functions; problems of elliptic motion; sine-amplitude functions; deviation of formal bodies; Cauchy-Lipschitz process; linear differential equations with periodic coefficients; differential equations in infinitely many variations; much more. Historical notes. 10 figures. 222 problems. Index. xv + 395pp. 5⅜ x 8.
S451 Paperbound **$2.00**

DIFFERENTIAL AND INTEGRAL EQUATIONS OF MECHANICS AND PHYSICS (DIE DIFFERENTIAL-UND ÎNTEGRALGLEICHUNGEN DER MECHANIK UND PHYSIK), edited by P. Frank and R. von Mises. Most comprehensive and authoritative work on the mathematics of mathematical physics available today in the United States: the standard, definitive reference for teachers, physicists, engineers, and mathematicians—now published (in the original German) at a relatively inexpensive price for the first time! Every chapter in this 2,000-page set is by an expert in his field: Carathéodory, Courant, Frank, Mises, and a dozen others. Vol I, on mathematics, gives concise but complete coverages of advanced calculus, differential equations, integral equations, and potential, and partial differential equations. Index. xxiii + 916pp. Vol. II (physics): classical mechanics, optics, continuous mechanics, heat conduction and diffusion, the stationary and quasi-stationary electromagnetic field, electromagnetic oscillations, and wave mechanics. Index. xxiv + 1106pp. Two volume set. Each volume available separately. 5⅝ x 8⅜.
S787 Vol I Clothbound **$7.50**
S788 Vol II Clothbound **$7.50**
The set **$15.00**

LECTURES ON CAUCHY'S PROBLEM, J. Hadamard. Based on lectures given at Columbia, Rome, this discusses work of Riemann, Kirchhoff, Volterra, and the author's own research on the hyperbolic case in linear partial differential equations. It extends spherical and cylindrical waves to apply to all (normal) hyperbolic equations. Partial contents: Cauchy's problem, fundamental formula, equations with odd number, with even number of independent variables; method of descent. 32 figures. Index. iii + 316pp. 5⅜ x 8.   S105 Paperbound **$1.75**

THEORY OF DIFFERENTIAL EQUATIONS, A. R. Forsyth. Out of print for over a decade, the complete 6 volumes (now bound as 3) of this monumental work represent the most comprehensive treatment of differential equations ever written. Historical presentation includes in 2500 pages every substantial development. Vol. 1, 2: EXACT EQUATIONS, PFAFF'S PROBLEM; ORDINARY EQUATIONS, NOT LINEAR: methods of Grassmann, Clebsch, Lie, Darboux; Cauchy's theorem; branch points; etc. Vol. 3, 4: ORDINARY EQUATIONS, NOT LINEAR; ORDINARY LINEAR EQUATIONS: Zeta Fuchsian functions, general theorems on algebraic integrals, Brun's theorem, equations with uniform periodic cofficients, etc. Vol. 4, 5: PARTIAL DIFFERENTIAL EQUATIONS: 2 existence-theorems, equations of theoretical dynamics, Laplace transformations, general transformation of equations of the 2nd order, much more. Indexes. Total of 2766pp. 5⅜ x 8.   S576-7-8 Clothbound: the set **$15.00**

PARTIAL DIFFERENTIAL EQUATIONS OF MATHEMATICAL PHYSICS, A. G. Webster. A keystone work in the library of every mature physicist, engineer, researcher. Valuable sections on elasticity, compression theory, potential theory, theory of sound, heat conduction, wave propagation, vibration theory. Contents include: deduction of differential equations, vibrations, normal functions, Fourier's series, Cauchy's method, boundary problems, method of Riemann-Volterra. Spherical, cylindrical, ellipsoidal harmonics, applications, etc. 97 figures. vii + 440pp. 5⅜ x 8.   S263 Paperbound **$2.25**

ELEMENTARY CONCEPTS OF TOPOLOGY, P. Alexandroff. First English translation of the famous brief introduction to topology for the beginner or for the mathematician not undertaking extensive study. This unusually useful intuitive approach deals primarily with the concepts of complex, cycle, and homology, and is wholly consistent with current investigations. Ranges from basic concepts of set-theoretic topology to the concept of Betti groups. "Glowing example of harmony between intuition and thought," David Hilbert. Translated by A. E. Farley. Introduction by D. Hilbert. Index. 25 figures. 73pp. 5⅜ x 8.   S747 Paperbound **$1.00**

Number theory

INTRODUCTION TO THE THEORY OF NUMBERS, L. E. Dickson. Thorough, comprehensive approach with adequate coverage of classical literature, an introductory volume beginners can follow. Chapters on divisibility, congruences, quadratic residues & reciprocity, Diophantine equations, etc. Full treatment of binary quadratic forms without usual restriction to integral coefficients. Covers infinitude of primes, least residues, Fermat's theorem, Euler's phi function, Legendre's symbol, Gauss's lemma, automorphs, reduced forms, recent theorems of Thue & Siegel, many more. Much material not readily available elsewhere. 239 problems. Index. I figure. viii + 183pp. 5⅜ x 8.   S342 Paperbound **$1.75**

ELEMENTS OF NUMBER THEORY, I. M. Vinogradov. Detailed 1st course for persons without advanced mathematics; 95% of this book can be understood by readers who have gone no farther than high school algebra. Partial contents: divisibility theory, important number theoretical functions, congruences, primitive roots and indices, etc. Solutions to both problems and exercises. Tables of primes, indices, etc. Covers almost every essential formula in elementary number theory! Translated from Russian. 233 problems, 104 exercises. viii + 227pp. 5⅜ x 8.   S259 Paperbound **$1.75**

THEORY OF NUMBERS and DIOPHANTINE ANALYSIS, R. D. Carmichael. These two complete works in one volume form one of the most lucid introductions to number theory, requiring only a firm foundation in high school mathematics. "Theory of Numbers," partial contents: Eratosthenes' sieve, Euclid's fundamental theorem, G.C.F. and L.C.M. of two or more integers, linear congruences, etc "Diophantine Analysis": rational triangles, Pythagorean triangles, equations of third, fourth, higher degrees, method of functional equations, much more. "Theory of Numbers": 76 problems. Index. 94pp. "Diophantine Analysis": 222 problems. Index. 118pp. 5⅜ x 8.   S529 Paperbound **$1.35**

Numerical analysis, tables

MATHEMATICAL TABLES AND FORMULAS, Compiled by Robert D. Carmichael and Edwin R. Smith. Valuable collection for students, etc. Contains all tables necessary in college algebra and trigonometry, such as five-place common logarithms, logarithmic sines and tangents of small angles, logarithmic trigonometric functions, natural trigonometric functions, four-place antilogarithms, tables for changing from sexagesimal to circular and from circular to sexagesimal measure of angles, etc. Also many tables and formulas not ordinarily accessible, including powers, roots, and reciprocals, exponential and hyperbolic functions, ten-place logarithms of prime numbers, and formulas and theorems from analytical and elementary geometry and from calculus. Explanatory introduction. viii + 269pp. 5⅜ x 8½.   S111 Paperbound **$1.25**

MATHEMATICAL TABLES, H. B. Dwight. Unique for its coverage in one volume of almost every function of importance in applied mathematics, engineering, and the physical sciences. Three extremely fine tables of the three trig functions and their inverse functions to thousandths of radians; natural and common logarithms; squares, cubes; hyperbolic functions and the inverse hyperbolic functions; $(a^2 + b^2)$ exp. $\frac{1}{2}a$; complete elliptic integrals of the 1st and 2nd kind; sine and cosine integrals; exponential integrals $Ei(x)$ and $Ei(-x)$; binomial coefficients; factorials to 250; surface zonal harmonics and first derivatives; Bernoulli and Euler numbers and their logs to base of 10; Gamma function; normal probability integral; over 60 pages of Bessel functions; the Riemann Zeta function. Each table with formulae generally used, sources of more extensive tables, interpolation data, etc. Over half have columns of differences, to facilitate interpolation. Introduction. Index. viii + 231pp. 5⅜ x 8.   S445 Paperbound **$2.00**

TABLES OF FUNCTIONS WITH FORMULAE AND CURVES, E. Jahnke & F. Emde. The world's most comprehensive 1-volume English-text collection of tables, formulae, curves of transcendent functions. 4th corrected edition, new 76-page section giving tables, formulae for elementary functions—not in other English editions. Partial contents: sine, cosine, logarithmic integral; factorial function; error function; theta functions; elliptic integrals, functions; Legendre, Bessel, Riemann, Mathieu, hypergeometric functions, etc. Supplementary books. Bibliography. Indexed. "Out of the way functions for which we know no other source," SCIENTIFIC COMPUTING SERVICE, Ltd. 212 figures. 400pp. 5⅜ x 8.   S133 Paperbound **$2.00**

CHEMISTRY AND PHYSICAL CHEMISTRY

ORGANIC CHEMISTRY, F. C. Whitmore. The entire subject of organic chemistry for the practicing chemist and the advanced student. Storehouse of facts, theories, processes found elsewhere only in specialized journals. Covers aliphatic compounds (500 pages on the properties and synthetic preparation of hydrocarbons, halides, proteins, ketones, etc.), alicyclic compounds, aromatic compounds, heterocyclic compounds, organophosphorus and organometallic compounds. Methods of synthetic preparation analyzed critically throughout. Includes much of biochemical interest. "The scope of this volume is astonishing," INDUSTRIAL AND ENGINEERING CHEMISTRY. 12,000-reference index. 2387-item bibliography. Total of x + 1005pp. 5⅜ x 8. Two volume set.

S700 Vol I Paperbound **$2.25**
S701 Vol II Paperbound **$2.25**
The set **$4.50**

THE MODERN THEORY OF MOLECULAR STRUCTURE, Bernard Pullman. A reasonably popular account of recent developments in atomic and molecular theory. Contents: The Wave Function and Wave Equations (history and bases of present theories of molecular structure); The Electronic Structure of Atoms (Description and classification of atomic wave functions, etc.); Diatomic Molecules; Non-Conjugated Polyatomic Molecules; Conjugated Polyatomic Molecules; The Structure of Complexes. Minimum of mathematical background needed. New translation by David Antin of "La Structure Moléculaire." Index. Bibliography. vii + 87pp. 5⅜ x 8½.

S987 Paperbound **$1.00**

CATALYSIS AND CATALYSTS, Marcel Prettre, Director, Research Institute on Catalysis. This brief book, translated into English for the first time, is the finest summary of the principal modern concepts, methods, and results of catalysis. Ideal introduction for beginning chemistry and physics students. Chapters: Basic Definitions of Catalysis (true catalysis and generalization of the concept of catalysis); The Scientific Bases of Catalysis (Catalysis and chemical thermodynamics, catalysis and chemical kinetics); Homogeneous Catalysis (acid-base catalysis, etc.); Chain Reactions; Contact Masses; Heterogeneous Catalysis (Mechanisms of contact catalyses, etc.); and Industrial Applications (acids and fertilizers, petroleum and petroleum chemistry, rubber, plastics, synthetic resins, and fibers). Translated by David Antin. Index. vi + 88pp. 5⅜ x 8½.

S998 Paperbound **$1.00**

POLAR MOLECULES, Pieter Debye. This work by Nobel laureate Debye offers a complete guide to fundamental electrostatic field relations, polarizability, molecular structure. Partial contents: electric intensity, displacement and force, polarization by orientation, molar polarization and molar refraction, halogen-hydrides, polar liquids, ionic saturation, dielectric constant, etc. Special chapter considers quantum theory. Indexed. 172pp. 5⅜ x 8.

S64 Paperbound **$1.65**

THE ELECTRONIC THEORY OF ACIDS AND BASES, W. F. Luder and Saverio Zuffanti. The first full systematic presentation of the electronic theory of acids and bases—treating the theory and its ramifications in an uncomplicated manner. Chapters: Historical Background; Atomic Orbitals and Valence; The Electronic Theory of Acids and Bases; Electrophilic and Electrodotic Reagents; Acidic and Basic Radicals; Neutralization; Titrations with Indicators; Displacement; Catalysis; Acid Catalysis; Base Catalysis; Alkoxides and Catalysts; Conclusion. Required reading for all chemists. Second revised (1961) eidtion, with additional examples and references. 3 figures. 9 tables. Index. Bibliography xii + 165pp. 5⅜ x 8.

S201 Paperbound **$1.50**

KINETIC THEORY OF LIQUIDS, J. Frenkel. Regarding the kinetic theory of liquids as a generalization and extension of the theory of solid bodies, this volume covers all types of arrangements of solids, thermal displacements of atoms, interstitial atoms and ions, orientational and rotational motion of molecules, and transition between states of matter. Mathematical theory is developed close to the physical subject matter. 216 bibliographical footnotes. 55 figures. xi + 485pp. 5⅜ x 8.

S95 Paperbound **$2.55**

THE PRINCIPLES OF ELECTROCHEMISTRY, D. A. MacInnes. Basic equations for almost every subfield of electrochemistry from first principles, referring at all times to the soundest and most recent theories and results; unusually useful as text or as reference. Covers coulometers and Faraday's Law, electrolytic conductance, the Debye-Hueckel method for the theoretical calculation of activity coefficients, concentration cells, standard electrode potentials, thermodynamic ionization constants, pH, potentiometric titrations, irreversible phenomena, Planck's equation, and much more. "Excellent treatise," AMERICAN CHEMICAL SOCIETY JOURNAL. "Highly recommended," CHEMICAL AND METALLURGICAL ENGINEERING. 2 Indices. Appendix. 585-item bibliography. 137 figures. 94 tables. ii + 478pp. 5⅝ x 8⅜.

S52 Paperbound **$2.75**

THE PHASE RULE AND ITS APPLICATION, Alexander Findlay. Covering chemical phenomena of 1, 2, 3, 4, and multiple component systems, this "standard work on the subject" (NATURE, London), has been completely revised and brought up to date by A. N. Campbell and N. O. Smith. Brand new material has been added on such matters as binary, tertiary liquid equilibria, solid solutions in ternary systems, quinary systems of salts and water. Completely revised to triangular coordinates in ternary systems, clarified graphic representation, solid models, etc. 9th revised edition. Author, subject indexes. 236 figures. 505 footnotes, mostly bibliographic. xii + 494pp. 5⅜ x 8.

S91 Paperbound **$2.50**

PHYSICS

General physics

FOUNDATIONS OF PHYSICS, R. B. Lindsay & H. Margenau. Excellent bridge between semi-popular works & technical treatises. A discussion of methods of physical description, construction of theory; valuable for physicist with elementary calculus who is interested in ideas that give meaning to data, tools of modern physics. Contents include symbolism, mathematical equations; space & time foundations of mechanics; probability; physics & continua; electron theory; special & general relativity; quantum mechanics; causality. "Thorough and yet not overdetailed. Unreservedly recommended," NATURE (London). Unabridged, corrected edition. List of recommended readings. 35 illustrations. xi + 537pp. 5⅜ x 8.
S377 Paperbound **$3.00**

FUNDAMENTAL FORMULAS OF PHYSICS, ed. by D. H. Menzel. Highly useful, fully inexpensive reference and study text, ranging from simple to highly sophisticated operations. Mathematics integrated into text—each chapter stands as short textbook of field represented. Vol. 1: Statistics, Physical Constants, Special Theory of Relativity, Hydrodynamics, Aerodynamics, Boundary Value Problems in Math. Physics; Viscosity, Electromagnetic Theory, etc. Vol. 2: Sound, Acoustics, Geometrical Optics, Electron Optics, High-Energy Phenomena, Magnetism, Biophysics, much more. Index. Total of 800pp. 5⅜ x 8.   Vol. 1 S595 Paperbound **$2.25**
Vol. 2 S596 Paperbound **$2.25**

MATHEMATICAL PHYSICS, D. H. Menzel. Thorough one-volume treatment of the mathematical techniques vital for classic mechanics, electromagnetic theory, quantum theory, and relativity. Written by the Harvard Professor of Astrophysics for junior, senior, and graduate courses, it gives clear explanations of all those aspects of function theory, vectors, matrices, dyadics, tensors, partial differential equations, etc., necessary for the understanding of the various physical theories. Electron theory, relativity, and other topics seldom presented appear here in considerable detail. Scores of definitions, conversion factors, dimensional constants, etc. "More detailed than normal for an advanced text . . . excellent set of sections on Dyadics, Matrices, and Tensors," JOURNAL OF THE FRANKLIN INSTITUTE. Index. 193 problems, with answers. x + 412pp. 5⅜ x 8.   S56 Paperbound **$2.50**

THE SCIENTIFIC PAPERS OF J. WILLARD GIBBS. All the published papers of America's outstanding theoretical scientist (except for "Statistical Mechanics" and "Vector Analysis"). Vol I (thermodynamics) contains one of the most brilliant of all 19th-century scientific papers—the 300-page "On the Equilibrium of Heterogeneous Substances," which founded the science of physical chemistry, and clearly stated a number of highly important natural laws for the first time; 8 other papers complete the first volume. Vol II includes 2 papers on dynamics, 8 on vector analysis and multiple algebra, 5 on the electromagnetic theory of light, and 6 miscellaneous papers. Biographical sketch by H. A. Bumstead. Total of xxxvi + 718pp. 5⅝ x 8⅜.
S721 Vol I Paperbound **$2.50**
S722 Vol II Paperbound **$2.25**
The set **$4.75**

BASIC THEORIES OF PHYSICS, Peter Gabriel Bergmann. Two-volume set which presents a critical examination of important topics in the major subdivisions of classical and modern physics. The first volume is concerned with classical mechanics and electrodynamics: mechanics of mass points, analytical mechanics, matter in bulk, electrostatics and magnetostatics, electromagnetic interaction, the field waves, special relativity, and waves. The second volume (Heat and Quanta) contains discussions of the kinetic hypothesis, physics and statistics, stationary ensembles, laws of thermodynamics, early quantum theories, atomic spectra, probability waves, quantization in wave mechanics, approximation methods, and abstract quantum theory. A valuable supplement to any thorough course or text.
Heat and Quanta: Index. 8 figures. x + 300pp. 5⅜ x 8½.   S968 Paperbound **$2.00**
Mechanics and Electrodynamics: Index. 14 figures. vii + 280pp. 5⅜ x 8½.
S969 Paperbound **$1.85**

THEORETICAL PHYSICS, A. S. Kompaneyets. One of the very few thorough studies of the subject in this price range. Provides advanced students with a comprehensive theoretical background. Especially strong on recent experimentation and developments in quantum theory. Contents: Mechanics (Generalized Coordinates, Lagrange's Equation, Collision of Particles, etc.), Electrodynamics (Vector Analysis, Maxwell's equations, Transmission of Signals, Theory of Relativity, etc.), Quantum Mechanics (the Inadequacy of Classical Mechanics, the Wave Equation, Motion in a Central Field, Quantum Theory of Radiation, Quantum Theories of Dispersion and Scattering, etc.), and Statistical Physics (Equilibrium Distribution of Molecules in an Ideal Gas, Boltzmann statistics, Bose and Fermi Distribution, Thermodynamic Quantities, etc.). Revised to 1961. Translated by George Yankovsky, authorized by Kompaneyets. 137 exercises. 56 figures. 529pp. 5⅜ x 8½. S972 Paperbound **$2.50**

ANALYTICAL AND CANONICAL FORMALISM IN PHYSICS, André Mercier. A survey, in one volume, of the variational principles (the key principles—in mathematical form—from which the basic laws of any one branch of physics can be derived) of the several branches of physical theory, together with an examination of the relationships among them. Contents: the Lagrangian Formalism, Lagrangian Densities, Canonical Formalism, Canonical Form of Electrodynamics, Hamiltonian Densities, Transformations, and Canonical Form with Vanishing Jacobian Determinant. Numerous examples and exercises. For advanced students, teachers, etc. 6 figures. Index. viii + 222pp. 5⅜ x 8½.   S1077 Paperbound **$1.75**

MATHEMATICAL PUZZLES AND RECREATIONS

AMUSEMENTS IN MATHEMATICS, Henry Ernest Dudeney. The foremost British originator of mathematical puzzles is always intriguing, witty, and paradoxical in this classic, one of the largest collections of mathematical amusements. More than 430 puzzles, problems, and paradoxes. Mazes and games, problems on number manipulation, unicursal and other route problems, puzzles on measuring, weighing, packing, age, kinship, chessboards, joining, crossing river, plane figure dissection, and many others. Solutions. More than 450 illustrations. vii + 258pp. 5⅜ x 8.   T473 Paperbound **$1.25**

SYMBOLIC LOGIC and THE GAME OF LOGIC, Lewis Carroll. "Symbolic Logic" is not concerned with modern symbolic logic, but is instead a collection of over 380 problems posed with charm and imagination, using the syllogism, and a fascinating diagrammatic method of drawing conclusions. In "The Game of Logic," Carroll's whimsical imagination devises a logical game played with 2 diagrams and counters (included) to manipulate hundreds of tricky syllogisms. The final section, "Hit or Miss" is a lagniappe of 101 additional puzzles in the delightful Carroll manner. Until this reprint edition, both of these books were rarities costing up to $15 each. Symbolic Logic: Index, xxxi + 199pp. The Game of Logic: 96pp. Two vols. bound as one. 5⅜ x 8.   T492 Paperbound **$1.75**

MAZES AND LABYRINTHS: A BOOK OF PUZZLES, W. Shepherd. Mazes, formerly associated with mystery and ritual, are still among the most intriguing of intellectual puzzles. This is a novel and different collection of 50 amusements that embody the principle of the maze: mazes in the classical tradition; 3-dimensional, ribbon, and Möbius-strip mazes; hidden messages; spatial arrangements; etc.—almost all built on amusing story situations. 84 illustrations. Essay on maze psychology. Solutions. xv + 122pp. 5⅜ x 8.   T731 Paperbound **$1.00**

MATHEMATICAL RECREATIONS, M. Kraitchik. Some 250 puzzles, problems, demonstrations of recreational mathematics for beginners & advanced mathematicians. Unusual historical problems from Greek, Medieval, Arabic, Hindu sources: modern problems based on "mathematics without numbers," geometry, topology, arithmetic, etc. Pastimes derived from figurative numbers, Mersenne numbers, Fermat numbers; fairy chess, latruncles, reversi, many topics. Full solutions. Excellent for insights into special fields of math. 181 illustrations. 330pp. 5⅜ x 8.   T163 Paperbound **$1.75**

MATHEMATICAL PUZZLES OF SAM LOYD, Vol. I, selected and edited by M. Gardner. Puzzles by the greatest puzzle creator and innovator. Selected from his famous "Cyclopedia of Puzzles," they retain the unique style and historical flavor of the originals. There are posers based on arithmetic, algebra, probability, game theory, route tracing, topology, counter, sliding block, operations research, geometrical dissection. Includes his famous "14-15" puzzle which was a national craze, and his "Horse of a Different Color" which sold millions of copies. 117 of his most ingenious puzzles in all, 120 line drawings and diagrams. Solutions. Selected references. xx + 167pp. 5⅜ x 8.   T498 Paperbound **$1.00**

MY BEST PUZZLES IN MATHEMATICS, Hubert Phillips ("Caliban"). Caliban is generally considered the best of the modern problemists. Here are 100 of his best and wittiest puzzles, selected by the author himself from such publications as the London Daily Telegraph, and each puzzle is guaranteed to put even the sharpest puzzle detective through his paces. Perfect for the development of clear thinking and a logical mind. Complete solutions are provided for every puzzle. x + 107pp. 5⅜ x 8½.   T91 Paperbound **$1.00**

MY BEST PUZZLES IN LOGIC AND REASONING, H. Phillips ("Caliban"). 100 choice, hitherto unavailable puzzles by England's best-known problemist. No special knowledge needed to solve these logical or inferential problems, just an unclouded mind, nerves of steel, and fast reflexes. Data presented are both necessary and just sufficient to allow one unambiguous answer. More than 30 different types of puzzles, all ingenious and varied, many one of a kind, that will challenge the expert, please the beginner. Original publication. 100 puzzles, full solutions. x + 107pp. 5⅜ x 8½.   T119 Paperbound **$1.00**

MATHEMATICAL PUZZLES FOR BEGINNERS AND ENTHUSIASTS, G. Mott-Smith. 188 mathematical puzzles to test mental agility. Inference, interpretation, algebra, dissection of plane figures, geometry, properties of numbers, decimation, permutations, probability, all enter these delightful problems. Puzzles like the Odic Force, How to Draw an Ellipse, Spider's Cousin, more than 180 others. Detailed solutions. Appendix with square roots, triangular numbers, primes, etc. 135 illustrations. 2nd revised edition. 248pp. 5⅜ x 8.   T198 Paperbound **$1.25**

MATHEMATICS, MAGIC AND MYSTERY, Martin Gardner. Card tricks, feats of mental mathematics, stage mind-reading, other "magic" explained as applications of probability, sets, theory of numbers, topology, various branches of mathematics. Creative examination of laws and their applications with scores of new tricks and insights. 115 sections discuss tricks wtih cards, dice, coins; geometrical vanishing tricks, dozens of others. No sleight of hand needed; mathematics guarantees success. 115 illustrations. xii + 174pp. 5⅜ x 8.
T335 Paperbound **$1.00**

RECREATIONS IN THE THEORY OF NUMBERS: THE QUEEN OF MATHEMATICS ENTERTAINS, Albert H. Beiler. The theory of numbers is often referred to as the "Queen of Mathematics." In this book Mr. Beiler has compiled the first English volume to deal exclusively with the recreational aspects of number theory, an inherently recreational branch of mathematics. The author's clear style makes for enjoyable reading as he deals with such topics as: perfect numbers, amicable numbers, Fermat's theorem, Wilson's theorem, interesting properties of digits, methods of factoring, primitive roots, Euler's function, polygonal and figurate numbers, Mersenne numbers, congruence, repeating decimals, etc. Countless puzzle problems, with full answers and explanations. For mathematicians and mathematically-inclined laymen, etc. New publication. 28 figures. 9 illustrations. 103 tables. Bibliography at chapter ends. vi + 247pp. 5⅜ x 8½.　　　　　　　　　　　　　　　　　　　　　T1096 Paperbound **$2.00**

PAPER FOLDING FOR BEGINNERS, W. D. Murray and F. J. Rigney. A delightful introduction to the varied and entertaining Japanese art of origami (paper folding), with a full crystal-clear text that anticipates every difficulty; over 275 clearly labeled diagrams of all important stages in creation. You get results at each stage, since complex figures are logically developed from simpler ones. 43 different pieces are explained: place mats, drinking cups, bonbon boxes, sailboats, frogs, roosters, etc. 6 photographic plates. 279 diagrams. 95pp. 5⅝ x 8⅜.　　　　　　　　　　　　　　　　　　　　　　　　　　　　T713 Paperbound **$1.00**

1800 RIDDLES, ENIGMAS AND CONUNDRUMS, Darwin A. Hindman. Entertaining collection ranging from hilarious gags to outrageous puns to sheer nonsense—a welcome respite from sophisticated humor. Children, toastmasters, and practically anyone with a funny bone will find these zany riddles tickling and eminently repeatable. Sample: "Why does Santa Claus always go down the chimney?" "Because it soots him." Some old, some new—covering a wide variety of subjects. New publication. iii + 154pp. 5⅜ x 8½. T1059 Paperbound **$1.00**

EASY-TO-DO ENTERTAINMENTS AND DIVERSIONS WITH CARDS, STRING, COINS, PAPER AND MATCHES, R. M. Abraham. Over 300 entertaining games, tricks, puzzles, and pastimes for children and adults. Invaluable to anyone in charge of groups of youngsters, for party givers, etc. Contains sections on card tricks and games, making things by paperfolding—toys, decorations, and the like; tricks with coins, matches, and pieces of string; descriptions of games; toys that can be made from common household objects; mathematical recreations; word games; and 50 miscellaneous entertainments. Formerly "Winter Nights Entertainments." Introduction by Lord Baden Powell. 329 illustrations. v + 186pp. 5⅜ x 8.　　　　　　　　　　　　　　　　　　　　　　　　　　　　　　T921 Paperbound **$1.00**

DIVERSIONS AND PASTIMES WITH CARDS, STRING, PAPER AND MATCHES, R. M. Abraham. Another collection of amusements and diversion for game and puzzle fans of all ages. Many new paperfolding ideas and tricks, an extensive section on amusements with knots and splices, two chapters of easy and not-so-easy problems, coin and match tricks, and lots of other parlor pastimes from the agile mind of the late British problemist and gamester. Corrected and revised version. Illustrations. 160pp. 5⅜ x 8½.　　T1127 Paperbound **$1.00**

STRING FIGURES AND HOW TO MAKE THEM: A STUDY OF CAT'S-CRADLE IN MANY LANDS, Caroline Furness Jayne. In a simple and easy-to-follow manner, this book describes how to make 107 different string figures. Not only is looping and crossing string between the fingers a common youthful diversion, but it is an ancient form of amusement practiced in all parts of the globe, especially popular among primitive tribes. These games are fun for all ages and offer an excellent means for developing manual dexterity and coordination. Much insight also for the anthropological observer on games and diversions in many different cultures. Index. Bibliography. Introduction by A. C. Haddon, Cambridge University. 17 full-page plates. 950 illustrations. xxiii + 407pp. 5⅜ x 8½.　　　　　T152 Paperbound **$2.00**

CRYPTANALYSIS, Helen F. Gaines. (Formerly ELEMENTARY CRYPTANALYSIS.) A standard elementary and intermediate text for serious students. It does not confine itself to old material, but contains much that is not generally known, except to experts. Concealment, Transposition, Substitution ciphers; Vigenere, Kasiski, Playfair, multafid, dozens of other techniques. Appendix with sequence charts, letter frequencies in English, 5 other languages, English word frequencies. Bibliography. 167 codes. New to this edition: solution to codes. vi + 230pp. 5⅜ x 8.　　　　　　　　　　　　　　　　　　　　　　　　　T97 Paperbound **$2.25**

MAGIC SQUARES AND CUBES, W. S. Andrews. Only book-length treatment in English, a thorough non-technical description and analysis. Here are nasik, overlapping, pandiagonal, serrated squares; magic circles, cubes, spheres, rhombuses. Try your hand at 4-dimensional magical figures! Much unusual folklore and tradition included. High school algebra is sufficient. 754 diagrams and illustrations. viii + 419pp. 5⅜ x 8.　　　T658 Paperbound **$1.85**

CALIBAN'S PROBLEM BOOK: MATHEMATICAL, INFERENTIAL, AND CRYPTOGRAPHIC PUZZLES, H. Phillips ("Caliban"), S. T. Shovelton, G. S. Marshall. 105 ingenious problems by the greatest living creator of puzzles based on logic and inference. Rigorous, modern, piquant, and reflecting their author's unusual personality, these intermediate and advanced puzzles all involve the ability to reason clearly through complex situations; some call for mathematical knowledge, ranging from algebra to number theory. Solutions. xi + 180pp. 5⅜ x 8.　　　　　　　　　　　　　　　　　　　　　　　　　　　　　　T736 Paperbound **$1.25**

FICTION

THE LAND THAT TIME FORGOT and THE MOON MAID, Edgar Rice Burrougns. In the opinion of many, Burroughs' best work. The first concerns a strange island where evolution is individual rather than phylogenetic. Speechless anthropoids develop into intelligent human beings within a single generation. The second projects the reader far into the future and describes the first voyage to the Moon (in the year 2025), the conquest of the Earth by the Moon, and years of violence and adventure as the enslaved Earthmen try to regain possession of their planet. "An imaginative tour de force that keeps the reader keyed up and expectant," NEW YORK TIMES. Complete, unabridged text of the original two novels (three parts in each). 5 illustrations by J. Allen St. John. vi + 552pp. 5⅜ x 8½.

T1020 Clothbound **$3.75**
T358 Paperbound **$2.00**

AT THE EARTH'S CORE, PELLUCIDAR, TANAR OF PELLUCIDAR: THREE SCIENCE FICTION NOVELS BY EDGAR RICE BURROUGHS. Complete, unabridged texts of the first three Pellucidar novels. Tales of derring-do by the famous master of science fiction. The locale for these three related stories is the inner surface of the hollow Earth where we discover the world of Pellucidar, complete with all types of bizarre, menacing creatures, strange peoples, and alluring maidens—guaranteed to delight all Burroughs fans and a wide circle of advenutre lovers. Illustrated by J. Allen St. John and P. F. Berdanier. vi + 433pp. 5⅜ x 8½.

T1051 Paperbound **$2.00**

THE PIRATES OF VENUS and LOST ON VENUS: TWO VENUS NOVELS BY EDGAR RICE BURROUGHS. Two related novels, complete and unabridged. Exciting adventure on the planet Venus with Earthman Carson Napier broken-field running through one dangerous episode after another. All lovers of swashbuckling science fiction will enjoy these two stories set in a world of fascinating societies, fierce beasts, 5000-ft. trees, lush vegetation, and wide seas. Illustrations by Fortunino Matania. Total of vi + 340pp. 5⅜ x 8½.   T1053 Paperbound **$1.75**

A PRINCESS OF MARS and A FIGHTING MAN OF MARS: TWO MARTIAN NOVELS BY EDGAR RICE BURROUGHS. "Princess of Mars" is the very first of the great Martian novels written by Burroughs, and it is probably the best of them all; it set the pattern for all of his later fantasy novels and contains a thrilling cast of strange peoples and creatures and the formula of Olympian heroism amidst ever-fluctuating fortunes which Burroughs carries off so successfully. "Fighting Man" returns to the same scenes and cities—many years later. A mad scientist, a degenerate dictator, and an indomitable defender of the right clash—with the fate of the Red Planet at stake! Complete, unabridged reprinting of original editions. Illustrations by F. E. Schoonover and Hugh Hutton. v + 356pp. 5⅜ x 8½.

T1140 Paperbound **$1.75**

THREE MARTIAN NOVELS, Edgar Rice Burroughs. Contains: Thuvia, Maid of Mars; The Chessmen of Mars; and The Master Mind of Mars. High adventure set in an imaginative and intricate conception of the Red Planet. Mars is peopled with an intelligent, heroic human race which lives in densely populated cities and with fierce barbarians who inhabit dead sea bottoms. Other exciting creatures abound amidst an inventive framework of Martian history and geography. Complete unabridged reprintings of the first edition. 16 illustrations by J. Allen St. John. vi + 499pp. 5⅜ x 8½.   T39 Paperbound **$1.85**

THREE PROPHETIC NOVELS BY H. G. WELLS, edited by E. F. Bleiler. Complete texts of "When the Sleeper Wakes" (1st book printing in 50 years), "A Story of the Days to Come," "The Time Machine" (1st complete printing in book form). Exciting adventures in the future are as enjoyable today as 50 years ago when first printed. Predict TV, movies, intercontinental airplanes, prefabricated houses, air-conditioned cities, etc. First important author to foresee problems of mind control, technological dictatorships. "Absolute best of imaginative fiction," N. Y. Times. Introduction. 335pp. 5⅜ x 8.   T605 Paperbound **$1.50**

28 SCIENCE FICTION STORIES OF H. G. WELLS. Two full unabridged novels, MEN LIKE GODS and STAR BEGOTTEN, plus 26 short stories by the master science-fiction writer of all time. Stories of space, time, invention, exploration, future adventure—an indispensable part of the library of everyone interested in science and adventure. PARTIAL CONTENTS: Men Like Gods, The Country of the Blind, In the Abyss, The Crystal Egg, The Man Who Could Work Miracles, A Story of the Days to Come, The Valley of Spiders, and 21 more! 928pp. 5⅜ x 8.

T265 Clothbound **$4.50**

THE WAR IN THE AIR, IN THE DAYS OF THE COMET, THE FOOD OF THE GODS: THREE SCIENCE FICTION NOVELS BY H. G. WELLS. Three exciting Wells offerings bearing on vital social and philosophical issues of his and our own day. Here are tales of air power, strategic bombing, East vs. West, the potential miracles of science, the potential disasters from outer space, the relationship between scientific advancement and moral progress, etc. First reprinting of "War in the Air" in almost 50 years. An excellent sampling of Wells at his storytelling best. Complete, unabridged reprintings. 16 illustrations. 645pp. 5⅜ x 8½.

T1135 Paperbound **$2.00**

SEVEN SCIENCE FICTION NOVELS, H. G. Wells. Full unabridged texts of 7 science-fiction novels of the master. Ranging from biology, physics, chemistry, astronomy to sociology and other studies, Mr. Wells extrapolates whole worlds of strange and intriguing character. "One will have to go far to match this for entertainment, excitement, and sheer pleasure . . . ," NEW YORK TIMES. Contents: The Time Machine, The Island of Dr. Moreau, First Men in the Moon, The Invisible Man, The War of the Worlds, The Food of the Gods, In the Days of the Comet. 1015pp. 5⅜ x 8.   T264 Clothbound **$4.50**

BEST GHOST STORIES OF J. S. LE FANU, Selected and introduced by E. F. Bleiler. LeFanu is deemed the greatest name in Victorian supernatural fiction. Here are 16 of his best horror stories, including 2 nouvelles: "Carmilla," a classic vampire tale couched in a perverse eroticism, and "The Haunted Baronet." Also: "Sir Toby's Will," "Green Tea," "Schalken the Painter," "Ultor de Lacy," "The Familiar," etc. The first American publication of about half of this material: a long-overdue opportunity to get a choice sampling of LeFanu's work. New selection (1964). 8 illustrations. 5⅜ x 8⅜.   T415 Paperbound **$1.85**

THE WONDERFUL WIZARD OF OZ, L. F. Baum. Only edition in print with all the original W. W. Denslow illustrations in full color—as much a part of "The Wizard" as Tenniel's drawings are for "Alice in Wonderland." "The Wizard" is still America's best-loved fairy tale, in which, as the author expresses it, "The wonderment and joy are retained and the heartaches and nightmares left out." Now today's young readers can enjoy every word and wonderful picture of the original book. New introduction by Martin Gardner. A Baum bibliography. 23 full-page color plates. viii + 268pp. 5⅜ x 8.   T691 Paperbound **$1.50**

GHOST AND HORROR STORIES OF AMBROSE BIERCE, Selected and introduced by E. F. Bleiler. 24 morbid, eerie tales—the cream of Bierce's fiction output. Contains such memorable pieces as "The Moonlit Road," "The Damned Thing," "An Inhabitant of Carcosa," "The Eyes of the Panther," "The Famous Gilson Bequest," "The Middle Toe of the Right Foot," and other chilling stories, plus the essay, "Visions of the Night" in which Bierce gives us a kind of rationale for his aesthetic of horror. New collection (1964). xxii + 199pp. 5⅜ x 8⅜.   T767 Paperbound **$1.00**

HUMOR

MR. DOOLEY ON IVRYTHING AND IVRYBODY, Finley Peter Dunne. Since the time of his appearance in 1893, "Mr. Dooley," the fictitious Chicago bartender, has been recognized as America's most humorous social and political commentator. Collected in this volume are 102 of the best Dooley pieces—all written around the turn of the century, the height of his popularity. Mr. Dooley's Irish brogue is employed wittily and penetratingly on subjects which are just as fresh and relevant today as they were then: corruption and hypocrisy of politicans, war preparations and chauvinism, automation, Latin American affairs, superbombs, etc. Other articles range from Rudyard Kipling to football. Selected with an introduction by Robert Hutchinson. xii + 244pp. 5⅜ x 8½.   T626 Paperbound **$1.00**

RUTHLESS RHYMES FOR HEARTLESS HOMES and MORE RUTHLESS RHYMES FOR HEARTLESS HOMES, Harry Graham ("Col. D. Streamer"). A collection of Little Willy and 48 other poetic "disasters." Graham's funniest and most disrespectful verse, accompanied by original illustrations. Nonsensical, wry humor which employs stern parents, careless nurses, uninhibited children, practical jokers, single-minded golfers, Scottish lairds, etc. in the leading roles. A precursor of the "sick joke" school of today. This volume contains, bound together for the first time, two of the most perennially popular books of humor in England and America. Index. vi + 69pp. 5⅜ x 8.   T930 Paperbound **75¢**

A WHIMSEY ANTHOLOGY, Collected by Carolyn Wells. 250 of the most amusing rhymes ever written. Acrostics, anagrams, palindromes, alphabetical jingles, tongue twisters, echo verses, alliterative verses, riddles, mnemonic rhymes, interior rhymes, over 40 limericks, etc. by Lewis Carroll, Edward Lear, Joseph Addison, W. S. Gilbert, Christina Rossetti, Chas. Lamb, James Boswell, Hood, Dickens, Swinburne, Leigh Hunt, Harry Graham, Poe, Eugene Field, and many others. xiv + 221pp. 5⅜ x 8½.   T195 Paperbound **$1.25**

MY PIOUS FRIENDS AND DRUNKEN COMPANIONS and MORE PIOUS FRIENDS AND DRUNKEN COMPANIONS, Songs and ballads of Conviviality Collected by Frank Shay. Magnificently illuminated by John Held, Jr. 132 ballads, blues, vaudeville numbers, drinking songs, cowboy songs, sea chanties, comedy songs, etc. of the Naughty Nineties and early 20th century. Over a third are reprinted with music. Many perennial favorites such as: The Band Played On, Frankie and Johnnie, The Old Grey Mare, The Face on the Bar-room Floor, etc. Many others unlocatable elsewhere: The Dog-Catcher's Child, The Cannibal Maiden, Don't Go in the Lion's Cage Tonight, Mother, etc. Complete verses and introductions to songs. Unabridged republication of first editions, 2 Indexes (song titles and first lines and choruses). Introduction by Frank Shay. 2 volumes bounds as 1. Total of xvi + 235pp. 5⅜ x 8½.   T946 Paperbound **$1.25**

MAX AND MORITZ, Wilhelm Busch. Edited and annotated by H. Arthur Klein. Translated by H. Arthur Klein, M. C. Klein, and others. The mischievous high jinks of Max and Moritz, Peter and Paul, Ker and Plunk, etc. are delightfully captured in sketch and rhyme. (Companion volume to "Hypocritical Helena.") In addition to the title piece, it contians: Ker and Plunk; Two Dogs and Two Boys; The Egghead and the Two Cut-ups of Corinth; Deceitful Henry; The Boys and the Pipe; Cat and Mouse; and others. (Original German text with accompanying English translations.) Afterword by H. A. Klein. vi + 216pp. 5⅜ x 8½.
T181 Paperbound **$1.15**

THROUGH THE ALIMENTARY CANAL WITH GUN AND CAMERA: A FASCINATING TRIP TO THE INTERIOR, Personally Conducted by George S. Chappell. In mock-travelogue style, the amusing account of an imaginative journey down the alimentary canal. The "explorers" enter the esophagus, round the Adam's Apple, narrowly escape from a fierce Amoeba, struggle through the impenetrable Nerve Forests of the Lumbar Region, etc. Illustrated by the famous cartoonist, Otto Soglow, the book is as much a brilliant satire of academic pomposity and professional travel literature as it is a clever use of the facts of physiology for supremely comic purposes. Preface by Robert Benchley. Author's Foreword. 1 Photograph. 17 illustrations by O. Soglow. xii + 114pp. 5⅜ x 8½.
T376 Paperbound **$1.00**

THE BAD CHILD'S BOOK OF BEASTS, MORE BEASTS FOR WORSE CHILDREN, and A MORAL ALPHABET, H. Belloc. Hardly an anthology of humorous verse has appeared in the last 50 years without at least a couple of these famous nonsense verses. But one must see the entire volumes—with all the delightful original illustrations by Sir Basil Blackwood—to appreciate fully Belloc's charming and witty verses that play so subacidly on the platitudes of life and morals that beset his day—and ours. A great humor classic. Three books in one. Total of 157pp. 5⅜ x 8.
T749 Paperbound **$1.00**

THE DEVIL'S DICTIONARY, Ambrose Bierce. Sardonic and irreverent barbs puncturing the pomposities and absurdities of American politics, business, religion, literature, and arts, by the country's greatest satirist in the classic tradition. Epigrammatic as Shaw, piercing as Swift, American as Mark Twain, Will Rogers, and Fred Allen. Bierce will always remain the favorite of a small coterie of enthusiasts, and of writers and speakers whom he supplies with "some of the most gorgeous witticisms of the English language." (H. L. Mencken) Over 1000 entries in alphabetical order. 144pp. 5⅜ x 8.
T487 Paperbound **$1.00**

THE COMPLETE NONSENSE OF EDWARD LEAR. This is the only complete edition of this master of gentle madness available at a popular price. A BOOK OF NONSENSE, NONSENSE SONGS, MORE NONSENSE SONGS AND STORIES in their entirety with all the old favorites that have delighted children and adults for years. The Dong With A Luminous Nose, The Jumblies, The Owl and the Pussycat, and hundreds of other bits of wonderful nonsense. 214 limericks, 3 sets of Nonsense Botany, 5 Nonsense Alphabets. 546 drawings by Lear himself, and much more. 320pp. 5⅜ x 8.
T167 Paperbound **$1.00**

SINGULAR TRAVELS, CAMPAIGNS, AND ADVENTURES OF BARON MUNCHAUSEN, R. E. Raspe, with 90 illustrations by Gustave Doré. The first edition in over 150 years to reestablish the deeds of the Prince of Liars exactly as Raspe first recorded them in 1785—the genuine Baron Munchausen, one of the most popular personalities in English literature. Included also are the best of the many sequels, written by other hands. Introduction on Raspe by J. Carswell. Bibliography of early editions. xliv + 192pp. 5⅜ x 8.   T698 Paperbound **$1.00**

HOW TO TELL THE BIRDS FROM THE FLOWERS, R. W. Wood. How not to confuse a carrot with a parrot, a grape with an ape, a puffin with nuffin. Delightful drawings, clever puns, absurd little poems point out farfetched resemblances in nature. The author was a leading physicist. Introduction by Margaret Wood White. 106 illus. 60pp. 5⅜ x 8.
T523 Paperbound **75¢**

JOE MILLER'S JESTS OR, THE WITS VADE-MECUM. The original Joe Miller jest book. Gives a keen and pungent impression of life in 18th-century England. Many are somewhat on the bawdy side and they are still capable of provoking amusement and good fun. This volume is a facsimile of the original "Joe Miller" first published in 1739. It remains the most popular and influential humor book of all time. New introduction by Robert Hutchinson. xxi + 70pp. 5⅜ x 8½.
T423 Paperbound **$1.00**

Prices subject to change without notice.

Dover publishes books on art, music, philosophy, literature, languages, history, social sciences, psychology, handcrafts, orientalia, puzzles and entertainments, chess, pets and gardens, books explaining science, intermediate and higher mathematics, mathematical physics, engineering, biological sciences, earth sciences, classics of science, etc. Write to:

Dept. catrr.
Dover Publications, Inc.
180 Varick Street, N.Y. 14, N.Y.